DISCOVERING
THE BODY

DISCOVERING
THE BODY

MARY HOWARD

WILLIAM MORROW
An Imprint of HarperCollins*Publishers*

HarperCollins books may be purchased for educational, business, or sales promotional use. For information please write: Special Markets Department, HarperCollins Publishers Inc., 10 East 53rd Street, New York, NY 10022.

FIRST EDITION

Printed on acid-free paper

Designed by Oksana Kushnir

Library of Congress Cataloging-in-Publication Data

Howard, Mary, 1942–
Discovering the body / Mary Howard.—1st ed.
p. cm.
ISBN 0-688-17156-7
I. Title.
PS3558.O88226 D57 2000
813'.54—dc21
99-048159

00 01 02 03 04 BP 10 9 8 7 6 5 4 3 2

For my sons,
Paul and David

ACKNOWLEDGMENTS

Thanks to Mary Richards, County Attorney, Story County, Iowa; Detective Captain Terry Bird, Ames Police Force; Public Safety Officer John Tinker, Coordinator, Story County Drug Task Force; entomologist Dr. Marlin Rice; and beekeeper Fred G.H. Freund for providing me with invaluable information as I was writing this novel. If I got a detail wrong, it's my error, not theirs.

I have been blessed by the good will and encouragement of many friends and colleagues in the Art and Design Department at Iowa State University, whose knowledge and insights helped me see the world through the eyes of a visual artist. I particularly want to thank Barbara Bruene, Barbara Caldwell, Paula Curran, Cindy Gould, Robin Kaneshiro, April Katz, Ingrid Lilligren, Nancy Polster, and Carol Prusa. Also thanks to Rebecca Burke, Joe Geha, Jamie Horwitz, Fern Kupfer, Deb Marquardt, and Susan Poague.

Thanks to my agent Elyse Cheney, who is savvy, smart, and fierce on my behalf; and to my editor Claire Wachtel, an inspiring, enthusiastic reader who has taught me a lot. I appreciate them both very much. And as always, a heartfelt thanks to my husband, Bob Bataille.

DISCOVERING
THE BODY

1 ◆ USUALLY CHARLIE AND I wake up together, but not this morning. When I open my eyes, I hear the shower and smell coffee. I find him standing at the kitchen sink, dark brown hair and beard, usually wild and bushy, still wet and close to his head. Two streaks mark the back of his shirt where he hurried drying himself. Parting the yellow curtains, he says, "I couldn't sleep. I dreamed the horses were back."

I join him to look where he's looking, toward the fence line and the weedy pasture beyond and the empty house next door. When I murmur something about how he doesn't often remember dreams, the curtain drops. "Sometimes I do," he says, turning to meet my good-morning kiss. My arms encircle him, a hand caressing the broad muscles of his back. "But I can't ever seem to tell you before they vanish. I'm jealous of yours. All that color and plot." He smiles, then grows sober again. "This was so real I woke up to the trumpeting sound horses make when they're spooked. I still think I heard something out there."

"Freud had a theory about horses in dreams."

"Not these horses," he says.

"We should call the realtor—"

"And certainly not today."

"—see if they can't mow the lawn over there." I insert two slices of bread into the toaster. The sign's gone again, but as far as I know, the place is still for sale. I open the refrigerator. As I reach over things for the marmalade, a bottle of tomato juice falls forward and strikes the floor at my feet, the bright liquid exploding outward. For a split second a gaudy Rorschach of red lies suspended across the gray-and-white grid of ceramic tile, then resumes its flow, thick as pigment. It drips down the front of the white refrigerator, down the table legs.

Miraculously unbroken, the container has spun out and come to rest against the wall, and I think I should pick it up. But I don't. I'm swallowing instead of breathing. Flecks of light dart across my vision as Charlie turns me gently away by the shoulders, toward the hallway. "Come on, Linda," he says. "Take a deep breath."

I cross the hall and the living room to pull open the front door, admitting a morning breeze full of dust and starch from the field across the road. This early a mist hangs above the corn, the mature plants streaked ivory in the muted light, the surface of the sky lightly scrubbed in, the color of smoke. I'm gasping for air. Dread mingles with relief and a vague third feeling I push away—the fear I've been fighting for months now, that there's someone out there, watching for me to make an appearance. This is the closest I've come to letting my panic show in front of Charlie.

"All done," he says from the doorway, a twisted, wrung-out rag in his hand. But the rapid thickening of his features, the look of repulsion with which he untwists the cloth, and the way he turns to fasten that same look of distaste upon me all give lie to his "Everything's good as new." There have been other moments lately when I've caught a flash of his anguish like this, as if there are two Charlies, one behind the scrim of the other. My mind slows, sees past him to the floor in front of the refrigerator. "Let it go," he says. I let the finality of his tone end the matter and do the easy thing, go back to buttering the toast, cold by now. And the day goes back to starting like one that can't end soon enough.

Charlie loves to speculate about weather, crops, and insects, but when it comes to people, he's so matter-of-fact that talking about feelings can make him anxious and secretive. The sign on the side of his van says CHARLIE CARPENTER, BEEKEEPER—THE HONEY BARN, LINDEN GROVE, IOWA. My appreciation of what he does for a living has been fairly romantic, like the way I'm apt to gloss over the dollar value of pollination to American agriculture while remembering how he marks the backs of queens with dabs of bright paint, to keep track of them. Work stories he keeps to himself, as a rule, along with his worries. Like many Midwesterners he's proud of his self-reliance, something we have in common. Then along comes something like a dream about horses, and the fact that he remembered it long enough to tell me.

Breakfast over, dishes in the sink, I catch him shifting his stare to the light pooled at the base of the refrigerator, where the tile's still streaked with water from the cleanup. Just for a moment he studies the floor, then returns his gaze to my face. His mouth is soft. A quick kiss. "About the horses," I say. "What do you think?"

"I haven't thought of her for a while. There's no way out today." He runs his open palm over his forehead, combs his fingers through his damp hair. "You okay?"

I nod. But I'm not.

Two years ago I was staying here with Luci Cole and Charlie until the kitchen plumbing was installed in the loft of the warehouse I'd bought in town, the space that's still my studio. Luci and I were old friends from art school. It was August 1, 1995. I'd been here three days, and I came home about five-fifteen that afternoon to help her start supper. It was Charlie's habit to arrive about six. It was a hot day, as this one promises to be, and I rushed into this room thinking only about my thirst.

This morning Charlie and I will proceed to the usual things we

do on a Friday in August, and not dwell too much on the circumstances of Luci's death. She had her problems, like all of us, and
neither of us knew her as well as we thought we did—a fact that
sometimes lies between Charlie and me. I envied Luci when she
was alive, and in a strange way, after everything I learned about
her when she died, I still do. Not a day passes without my thinking
about her.

For a while after Peter Garvey was convicted and sent to prison
for killing Luci, I thought I might succeed in putting the awful
experience behind me. But for months now, since late winter, I
have frequently *felt* someone watching to see if I'm finally beginning to show signs of nervousness, or fear. Often, at such times,
I'll turn to look over my shoulder, and there he'll be: a certain guy,
tall, dark-eyed, with long hair pulled back into a rubber band at
the nape of his neck. He always wears jeans and sandals. Though
he appears easygoing when he moves, I become most aware of him
when he stands motionless—aloof, but with the taut musculature
of intense awareness. A week or two will pass without him, and
then he'll show up in the neighborhood of my studio two or three
times in one day—crossing the street, checking out at Hy-Vee,
waiting in line at the Shazam machine. His sudden appearance on
the scene a few months ago is what made me start thinking about
Luci's murder all over again. Charlie thinks it's the other way
around, that I'm still fearful because of what happened and so I
imagine I'm being watched. He tells me to forget about my suspicions. Even in a small town like this, he'll point out, there are
quite a few people I don't know but whom I see every day, just in
passing. They're not all following me. This man isn't either.

But then I'll see him again—like now, this afternoon, waiting at
the intersection of Main Street and Third. He stands perfectly still.
His shoulders are broad for a man so slender, his shirt bright white
in the sun. I wait for the quick flash of his sunglasses as he turns
and sees me, and then without pause he faces away again as the

light changes to green. He doesn't cross the street. Instead he turns
and walks toward me, and past—like he doesn't see me, that's what
gives him away. As tall as I am, and the way I like to be noticed,
I'm hard to miss. I know that. I've cultivated it, arms to my sides,
head high.

I suppose I exhibit the inverse vanity of a woman who knows
she's not beautiful. Another woman might assume it was her appearance that attracted this man's attention, perhaps staring him
down to challenge his rude behavior, or at least asking around to
find out who he is. Judy Allard, who runs the bookshop down the
street, probably knows. I've seen him go in there. But I haven't
asked her. I've told no one except Charlie about this dilemma of
mine. What I haven't managed to tell him is that if I'm right, and
this man is observing me, I'm pretty sure I know why.

I get my hair cut at Le's Salon, a tiny basement establishment
under the Grubstake Café, just around the block from my studio,
where I do my printmaking and graphic-design work. I thought I
might have my hair cut short today, but descending the cement
stairs to Le's, I suffer doubts even about that. Charlie prefers it
long. Stopping at the top of the steep, cellarlike steps, I watch the
stranger's quickening stride as he continues down the street. He
moves as if he's sure of his destination, but then he slows, finally
pausing to consider something in the bookstore window. He hasn't
looked back since we passed on the sidewalk just now. It's always
like this: He slows down when he sees me, averting his gaze—or
hiding behind those mirrored sunglasses—then speeds up once his
back is to me. Then stops down the line and waits.

I tense, fingering the ends of my hair.

Doug Le greets me with his usual: "Ah, Garbo, let's try something new today." Sylvie, his only employee, looks up from painting her nails and smiles. In a few moments I'm lathered and rinsed
and in front of the mirror again, where Doug appraises my wet
hair. I'm staring into the glass, when in the reflection of the room

I see the longhaired guy cross behind me from the direction of the doorway, the sleeves of his shirt rolled up to his elbows, headed for the shelves of products, out of the mirror's range.

Doug bows my head so my long hair hides my face. "Great hair," he murmurs. He not only collects my prints—we trade art for haircuts—but also likes to praise what he calls my unconventional beauty. He doesn't see broad shoulders, shovel-like hips, arms that could move a piano. My pale lashes and square jaw are abstract, malleable elements of design to him. Now his comb moves slowly down through the curtain of hair. With my face hidden and my eyes closed, I concentrate on his flattery while back there in the corner of the room, that guy is watching me. As Doug lifts my chin, directing me to watch in the mirror as he lifts and loops my wet hair, he proposes a short, asymmetrical cut, but I barely listen. I flinch at the sudden sound of rushing water as plump, kohl-eyed Sylvie begins to wash the stranger's hair.

The sink is only a few feet away, in the corner of the room. Lying back for the shampoo, his long body stretches toward me close enough to touch—knees bent at right angles, neck cradled by the lip of the sink. He seems vulnerable. I've always seen him at a distance, his glance sliding over and past me with an expertness I've learned to practice on him, too. Now, horizontal, he can't see me. Turning to Doug, who lowers his face near mine, I whisper, "Who *is* that guy?"

"Russell Weber, from upstairs." Now at least he has a name. Over the blast of water, I can hear the man's voice—indistinct, but I hear the word "dreadlocks." I remember his long hair as lank and moth brown. Maybe I heard him wrong.

"Uncross your legs, Linda," Doug says. As I square my shoulders so he can cut the first layer of hair straight across my shoulder blades, Weber and Sylvie laugh. Not many guys come into Doug Le's salon, but judging by the easy conversation about his plans for the evening, Weber must be a regular here. Sylvie's kneading the towel around his head, and just as he sits up, I turn to face him, my heart beating hard. But when she lifts the towel from his hair, it's ropy, bleached bright as brass, and no more than four inches long.

For a moment I'm stunned, confused by the switch. This isn't the man who's been following me, the man I saw in the mirror. *This* man, Russell Weber, is the cook at the Grubstake upstairs. He's looking straight at me, missing a beat before he says, "I know you. Tabbouleh and cottage cheese, right?"

Nodding, I try to return his smile even as my hands contract into fists under the long plastic cape. It takes me a moment to recover from my mistake, to realize that Weber must have come into the room when my head was down. I look at Sylvie. "There was someone else who came in, after I did." In the mirror I search past myself into the space behind me. "White shirt, jeans, long hair. I thought he was someone I knew."

"No," says Sylvie, her inflection rising with uncertainty. She's touching up Weber's dark roots, separating clumps of hair with surgical-gloved fingers. "I don't think so." Stopping her hands, she pauses to reconsider. "I don't remember anybody." She shakes her head, satisfied.

Doug reaches for a bright-blue bottle, announcing some five-syllable ingredient beginning with "hydro," and rubs it into my wet hair. "Someone did come in and look at the products rack. I was watching him."

"Really?" says Sylvie.

"He didn't buy anything," says Doug, pulling long scissors out of his holster.

"I do sort of remember," says Sylvie.

"Did you know him?" I ask.

"Huh-uh," says Sylvie.

"Never saw him before," says Doug.

Not even Russell Weber knows who he was.

Later, climbing the narrow steps to the street, I look right and left, but he's nowhere to be seen. The shortest way to my studio is through the alley around to the right and across the parking lot, the way I came. Instead I walk to the far end of the block, around the Firstar Bank at the corner, and enter the parking lot from Hayward. It's hot. I'm beginning to sweat.

As I cross the parking lot, I tilt my head back, shake my hair. I'm glad I left it long. I like to feel it move. *See that?* I wonder. But if he's here, he's out of sight. Approaching the rear end of the alley I avoided before, my heart thumps. I've been so scared lately of letting fear affect my judgment. Right now I can't help heeding instincts this strong. Moving around the corner of the brick building, I see him, facing away from me. He's leaning sideways, his left shoulder against the brick wall. I want this over with.

It's cooler in the alley. From about ten feet behind him, I watch. My stature—I'm six-two—gives me a kind of routine confidence I often take for granted. But it's posture, not size, that conveys power, so I draw myself up, unclasping my hands and relaxing my arms at my sides, instantly more in command. Staring at the backside of that guy so innocently leaning against the wall, waiting for me to appear at the other end of the alley, I feel a flutter in my throat, and the urge to laugh. I cough instead.

He twists his body toward the sound, and I move closer. He's as tall as I am. He's put his sunglasses in his chest pocket. His eyes are very dark brown. Even sunburned he pinkens slightly.

"Waiting for someone?" I ask him. All he has in his hand is a cigarette. He bites his lower lip but doesn't speak. "There's a law against this, you know."

He looks perplexed, drops the cigarette in the dust, steps on it. He continues to stare at his right foot. "Look—" he begins finally, and after weeks of refusing to make eye contact, his gaze is so direct and unflinching my body feels the shock of it. He smiles a little, as if now that we have finally crossed some mysterious line, he's *relieved.*

"You have to stop this," I say calmly. He looks uncomfortable as I stare silently at his deep-set eyes, broad cheekbones, squared-off chin. "You've been following me for months."

"Why would I do that?"

"Who *are* you?"

He steps forward, so close I can smell the cigarette smoke on his clothes. "Bender," he says. "John." I stare at his hand, extended toward me as if I might actually want to shake it. The wristbones are prominent. His nails are short and clean. Finally he lowers his hand. "Look," he says gently. "Linda—"

The sound of my name makes my throat close, and I swallow with difficulty. "You draw attention to yourself by watching me the way you do. You're not very good at it."

"I started to speak to you one day on the street," he says slowly, "right after I moved to this neighborhood from the other side of town." He clears his throat. "I suppose I've avoided you since then for your own sake, since I knew you would associate me with a terrible experience." He looks over his shoulder at the cars moving across the opening of the alley behind him, like he's deciding something. "Of course, I never could have forgotten you, after spending all those hours watching your face. You were at the center of things. I was an observer." He turns back to stare at me for long moments before he says, "I'm a reporter. I covered the trial."

"I don't remember you."

"I wrote the original stories for *The Linden Times*." He pauses, probably hoping for a reaction. "Peter Garvey still says he wasn't working on Luci Cole's car that afternoon."

"He's had his appeals. No one else ever believed him. Are you telling me you do?"

"I went to see him recently. He still insists you lied."

"Do you think I did?"

"No."

I can't look at Bender another moment, can't listen to his off-hand tone—*I went to see him recently*—as if the killer were a casual, mutual friend. I know my mistake even as I turn away from him. The asphalt surface of the parking lot is so hot it gives under my sandals as I hurry through the blazing sunlight to the back door of my studio. I make a mental note: The next time any detail even remotely connected to Luci's death triggers this kind of take-flight reaction, I've got to stand and ask questions, not rush off like I'm the guilty one.

Inside my studio the phone is ringing, and I practically run the length of the long room to answer.

"You sound out of breath."

"*Ohhh* . . ." The relief I feel at hearing Charlie's voice escapes like a sigh as I sink into the desk chair. "I just came in."

"Can you pick me up about five-thirty? The van's in the shop until tomorrow."

"What happened?"

Charlie explains that a broken spring began banging against the underside of the wheel well on his way into town this morning. "*Whomp*," he says, "every time I went round a corner, or a curve." I want to interrupt and tell him, *I just talked to that man who's been watching me*, but my lips stick to my teeth and my heart still pounds. So I just listen, taking comfort from the timbre of Charlie's deep voice. While he complains about how much the bill will be for the new springs, I pick up a pencil and idly sketch the shape of John Bender's head, the frank gaze of those dark eyes, the strong jawline. I'm biting my lower lip with concentration.

Finally Charlie is silent, and I look up, focusing on the sign hanging inside my plate-glass window—lime-green neon script, LINDA GARBO DESIGNS, in an oval of pink and lavender. "Charlie?" My voice trembles.

"It's getting worse, isn't it, your anxiety." The way he says it, it's not a question. "What exactly happened this morning? You were in a bad state there for a few minutes, standing at the front door. I didn't like the way you were having trouble breathing. You didn't think you saw somebody out there, did you?"

"Of course not." All summer Charlie has been pressuring me to seek help. He's been stopping by my studio a couple of times a week to take me out for coffee at the Grubstake Café, or to walk around the neighborhood with me, but the man who has turned out to be John Bender never materialized for Charlie to see. "I'm beginning to confront my fears," I say quietly.

"I'm worried about you."

"I know you are. But I'm not losing my mental health, Charlie. You know better than that." A bitter note has sounded in my voice, and I go on quickly, using a gentler tone. "You think about her, too. I know you do. Do you realize this morning's the first time you've told me one of your dreams?"

"Dreams," Charlie says flatly, as if the word came out of nowhere and doesn't belong in this conversation.

"I remember that trumpeting sound, too, from the day Luci died. I'm sure I do. The sound of horses, spooked. I'm working hard to remember everything that happened that day."

"I didn't give that dream another thought, after I mentioned it to you," he says. "I've had other things on my mind." I wish I could see his face as silence falls here in my studio, and at his end, too, where I can imagine the cloying sweetness of slow, silent honey dripping into cylindrical ripening tanks. Finally he says, "It was a nightmare, Linda, a bad memory trying to come back. I'm not about to give it much of my conscious attention, and you shouldn't either. You only hurt yourself, going back to that time, over and over. Do you know how often, how *literally*, you look over your shoulder? There's a name for that."

"Paranoia is when you look over your shoulder and there's never anybody there, Charlie." I'm staring at my sketch of John Bender's face.

"Pick me up at five-thirty." I hear a door closing at Charlie's end, and voices. He says he has a customer.

But I can't let him go yet. "That man was in the alley across the parking lot again today. He was watching for me. I finally did what you've been urging me to do, Charlie. I talked to him. Turns out he moved into the neighborhood about the time I started noticing him. He says he's a reporter for the local paper."

"Well then, it will be easy enough to check him out. We'll talk about it at supper. And maybe you can manage to explain to me why it took you four or five months to walk up to this guy and ask him who he is. Can I assume you got his name?"

"Yes. Why are you so angry, Charlie? I thought you'd be pleased."

"I'm not angry. I have to get back to work."

I repeat that I'll pick him up at five-thirty. He suggests we go for pizza tonight, as we often do on Fridays, and I agree, all the while adding detail to the reporter's face. I sharpen the jawline, deepen the brow a little, while Charlie is saying, "It's a bad day to be without the van. I'm restless. Call before you come by. I might leave a little early and walk home."

Linden Grove is a small community. It takes only forty minutes to walk from The Honey Barn on the north side to our house, which is about a mile west of town along the county road. From my studio it's not that far. I used to walk it a lot, for the exercise, but I've gotten lazy. Driving out there that afternoon, two years ago today, I was sorry I wasn't on foot so it would take longer to get there. On the seat next to me was a bag of groceries from Hy-Vee— yogurt, Shredded Wheat, three chicken breasts—and the receipt, of course, printed with the date of purchase and the time—5:05 P.M. It was sprinkling. I turned on my windshield wipers.

I was really thirsty as I finally reached the crest of the hill at the town limits and started down the road's curving approach to the house. Descending the hill, I could see the house for a quarter of a mile, the valley before me rich with color. Staying with Luci and

Charlie had turned out to be very uncomfortable for me, and despite my thirst I stopped my car on the shoulder of the gravel road to delay my arrival. Luci and I had argued that morning, which had made me determined to move into the loft over my studio as soon as possible. So during the afternoon I had gone to see Ben Webb, the plumber, in his shop. I persuaded him to substitute some used kitchen cabinets we found in his cluttered warehouse for the ones I'd wanted, which were back-ordered. That way he would be able to install the sink the next day so I could arrange the final building inspection and move in. Luci was expecting me to stay with her for another week, at least. I was uneasy, thinking of what I'd say to explain my change in plans.

From my vantage point on the road I had a tree-framed view of the farmhouse, its wood-shingled roof pitched like a book turned onto its pages, and the neighbor's five horses immobile in the verdant shade of the hillside beyond. The very air was lit by that golden green that follows a storm, when the sun breaks through. The rain had turned the ditch along the road into a stream, a shiny wire of light.

I was in no hurry to get there. Peter Garvey, Luci and Charlie's only close neighbor and the caretaker of the horses, was probably in the house with her. Sure enough, a few minutes later I saw him walk out the front door as I was rounding the bend at the top of the hill. A row of honeysuckle bushes blocked my view for about a hundred feet. As I continued on and could see the house again, he had slid himself under Luci's old Chevy Nova. The front of the car was elevated, and Peter'd been working on it off and on for the three days I'd been staying there—giving the place a low-rent look for which I resented him.

When I arrived at the house, I said, "Hi, Peter," to be polite, as I walked around the car to the front door. His head and shoulders were underneath the car. He wagged his foot in response. Inside, the living room was dark because the shades were pulled against the heat, but I could see into the kitchen, and my thirst drew me forward. The light slanting through the window straight ahead made me squint. There was an odor, sort of like potatoes rotting.

Luci lay sprawled, her T-shirt pulled up to show the pale skin above her belly, her peach-colored shorts silky-looking, her legs bowed open doll-like at a vulgar angle. There was a smear of blood under one staring eye, but the long wound across her throat gaped where an awful blood vessel protruded—hollow and already bone-colored, bloodless, like a curved piece of macaroni.

I tilted away from the body and felt my left shoulder touch the wall, felt my stomach lift and settle, leaving a terrible pressure in my throat. My mind reeled. A roar in my ears made my eyes open wide. I had to be alert, had to look at Luci, get the bag of groceries out of my hands, crouch and touch her. The flesh was warm, but her tongue was fallen back into her open mouth. Blood has a familiar smell. My throat constricted so suddenly that I gasped, and I heard that roar again. The table legs and the pine floor were spattered with blood, and the knife lay over an odd, circular smear, blade still shiny. I reached, but then I stopped myself and left the knife where it was.

Listening intently, straining to hear, I found myself on my feet, the phone in my hand, my fingers finding 911, my mind fastening on the best words to start with—*I just found my friend, Luci Cole*—in a voice barely loud enough for the dispatcher to hear. As I answered her questions, I moved across the living room toward the front door until I came to the end of the phone cord's tether. Through the coarse canvas of the screen, Luci's faded Chevy came into view. The voice on the phone told me to stay inside until help arrived.

I went all the way to the front door, fingers fumbling to lock it, and looked out at the car. Peter's disembodied boots were on the far side, out of sight. Without thinking, I unhooked the door and stepped out into the open. "Peter?" I said, testing my voice, circling the car slowly. My left hand rested flat on the warmth of the car's hood. "Peter?" One more step and he'd be lying there.

He was gone, of course. I stood in the baking heat and surveyed the empty road, the stand of weeds along the fence separating Peter's property from Charlie's, the rise of green pasture beyond. The distant oak trees with touches of red among the leaves. I remembered the spots on the leg of his jeans.

Now, two years later, I still experience the same drop in body temperature I felt then when I contemplate the terrible fact of what that man did to her. Heart pounding, I felt fully alert, wildly memorizing particulars for all that I'd be called upon to do in the coming weeks: answer questions, testify against Peter Garvey. I can still see the precise array of rust spots across the car's hood, smell the heat rising from the gravel drive, hear the gasp that escaped me as something drew my attention to the house next door. All five horses in the pasture raised their heads in the shade. Two reared back, and all of them began to run in a loose circle. The taste in my mouth was sharp.

My life was divided forever by what I had seen and by what I was sure it meant—calm before, and now this curse of memory. Today the abundance of detail that assaulted me that afternoon as I approached the house and as I found her in the kitchen has been replaced by the list of observations I related to the police and recited perfectly every time I answered the lawyers' questions, every time I went over the events in the middle of the night when I couldn't sleep. Waiting outside the house, I wanted to run. But I had to stand my ground, guard her body until help arrived. For courage, I suppose, I bent forward to strike the roof of the car with my fists, many times, each time shouting *Charlie, Charlie*, the bold kettledrum booms punctuating both syllables of his name. *Why didn't you see what she was doing?* I yelled, staring at the road where it broke the horizon. *Right under your nose, Charlie.* When he appeared at last, jogging toward me in the heat—so innocent of what had happened—my heart lifted.

Now, since hanging up the phone with Charlie, that same urgency to see him has quickened my pulse. To stay calm, I have kept my pencil moving these past few minutes over the lines of John Bender's face. But my fingers tremble, and the lines waver, as I find in the shadows at the corners of his eyes and the curve of his brow bone the face I remember better and better as I reconstruct it on the page. *Pay attention.* I wonder why I never once remembered pounding the car and shouting Charlie's name like that—with a boldness strong enough to drive back fear—until now.

2 ◆ THE WAITRESS PLACES our pizza on the table just as Charlie glances up at her and says, "Why don't you make me a print?" He ignores her confusion as he pours me a second glass of beer from the pitcher between us. I struggle to keep my attention on Charlie even as the red line of Route 2 pushes east across the map in my mind toward the Mississippi, toward the Iowa State Penitentiary. Since my discovery this afternoon that John Bender has talked with the killer recently, I know I have to face Garvey myself. Charlie clears his throat. I hope that doesn't mean he's noticed my lapse of attention. "Why don't you do an etching for me?" he says. His thirty-sixth birthday is three weeks away. "It wouldn't cost you much."

"I'm not looking to get off cheap, Charlie." I silence my irritation with a mouthful of garlicky, double-cheese pizza. I often tease him about being tight with money. My prints hang in galleries in West Des Moines and on Canyon Road's Gypsy Alley in Sante Fe. Though most of my income comes from logos and illustrations for area business ads, printmaking is my real love, and I'm sensitive if I think it's being undervalued. "A copper plate is up to thirty-six dollars."

"That's not what I meant." He's reaching for a triangle of pizza. "The gift would be your time. Tell me that Italian word for the etching process again?" He answers his own question, "In-*tall*-yo," gesturing upward with his free left hand while prolonging the syllables, making them sound sexual, as if they were words for love. All I hear is *tagliare*. *To cut*. "And your talent," he insists. "Your *gift* would be the gift. The value of your work is not an issue. Am I off the hook?" I must look puzzled, because he covers my hand with his and adds, "About the value of the print you're planning to surprise me with?"

"I want to give you something you want, that's all."

"I have what I really want." He opens his mouth around another bite, his lower lip burnished by the olive oil. He crushes a paper napkin in his hand. He wipes his mouth. All with his right hand. I'm stroking his left arm with my fingertips. From the minute I picked him up at work earlier and told him the reporter's name—and promised I'd check Bender out, to satisfy myself he's who he says he is—Charlie's been acting as though we have reason to celebrate. "I have to visit three farmers tomorrow. If you don't have appointments, maybe you could come with me. We could—"

"Oh, I can't, Charlie, I'm sorry." I withdraw my hand. "I have a meeting planned for the afternoon."

"That's okay," he says. "We'll do it another time." His face moves closer to mine, and I feel a twinge of guilt for my lie of omission. Charlie's deeply tanned cheeks and nose are polished with red from too much sun. So are the backs of his hands. Even his short, dark beard has bleached, red highlights. He studied entomology at Iowa State, and he makes his living by contracting with growers all over the area to install hives at the edges of fields and orchards before the plants flower. After pollination, when Charlie reclaims the hives, he extracts and packages the honey at The Honey Barn, an "add-on" benefit of his work, he calls it. So he's outside a lot and seems to know everyone in this part of the state. This is the first time he's invited me to go along on his

Saturday rounds. My lips part. I should just cancel my plans to visit the prison and go with him.

"Umm," says Charlie, as if something has occurred to him. "How about a drawing of the house?" Confusion must show on my face. "For my print," he reminds me.

"Oh." *The house.* "I'll think about it." I sip my beer, hoping its dark, nutty taste will relax me. He couldn't know that every time I relive my surveillance of the house from the road that awful afternoon, I picture the view that would make the best composition. "You seem to have managed to disconnect Luci's death from the place where it happened. I'm not sure living there has been such a good idea for me."

"The first six months we were married, you seemed so relaxed and happy there, I forget it was still a new place to you when you found Luci." He straightens his shoulders. "That house has always been a part of my life. I guess you're right. I have disassociated Luci's murder from the place it happened. After all, I didn't—"

See her lying there is what he can't say, and in a flash I see the vivid splash of red across the floor this morning and remember Charlie's avoidance of any immediate discussion about the way it upset me. He draws his open hand down over his features, keeping his mouth covered for a moment to hide what he must be feeling. The house was his grandparents', where he visited each summer when he was a boy. About ten years ago, long after they had died and the house had passed out of the family, he returned to the area and bought it back. He moved it onto a new foundation, rewired it. It's his work-in-progress. Our decision to live there when we got married last September was one we made together, of course. I decided that since I couldn't escape walking around for the rest of my life inside the same nerves and skin that had endured everything associated with Luci's death, I could certainly try to live in the place where she died. "You thought I spilled that juice on purpose, didn't you?"

"Accidents can arise from unconscious motives." He looks across the restaurant. "It's almost as if you've come to feel responsible for what happened. You seem to want to put yourself through it all again. And to take me along with you. For both our sakes, I have to resist."

"Outside the house that day, after I'd found her," I say quickly, "while I was waiting for help to come, I yelled your name over and over, half blamed you for not being there to defend her. Pounded on the car—"

"You were frantic because you didn't want to be there alone. As soon as I got there, you were never alone with it again. You're still not alone. I'm here."

"But if I could suddenly recall yelling your name, Charlie, I might remember some other detail I didn't report at the time, because finding her was so traumatic."

He stares at me, fists side by side on the table, his patience palpable. As we gaze at each other, his eyes narrow with what he's thinking. "What happened to Luci was not your fault."

"The county attorney told me during the trial that often an eyewitness in a murder case feels guilty."

"You can't go back there and change things, Linda. You can't make things turn out differently, no matter how many new details you remember." At once his expression darkens. He draws his lips between his teeth and, for just a moment, squeezes his eyes shut. I think this is what anguish looks like. He tips his glass and stares into it.

"I wasn't a good witness, Charlie."

"Maybe next year on August first we'll be able to go the entire day without talking about Luci. That will be a better day than this one." He drains his glass.

Leaning away, shoulders meeting the back of the chair, I'm literally biting my tongue to keep from saying it again: *I wasn't a good witness.* As the conversation stalls, I begin reliving the afternoon earlier in the month when I tried, but failed, to face Peter Garvey. I drove all the way to Fort Madison, then up the hill to the penitentiary. I must have sat in the parking lot for ten minutes, staring at the immense limestone building with its windowless façade and square towers, intimidated by the very architecture of the prison. Finally I walked past the NO CAMERAS ALLOWED sign and through the front door. The uniformed guard behind the counter by the walk-through security equipment, the kind airports use, handed me a Request for Visiting Permit, but I didn't get very far in filling it out. Before I'd even written Peter Garvey's name on the "Inmate" line, I focused on the item below: "Business." What *was* my business with the man I had helped put in this place for life?

I drove to a Quick Trip at the edge of town to use the bathroom, then made it home in three hours, justifying my flight as I sped along. *What would have been the point? Peter isn't going to change his story, and I am certainly not prepared to tell him I might change mine. He's the last person I would tell, not the first.*

Charlie picks up his paper napkin and wipes his fingers with a twisting motion, signaling he's done with his meal. Under cover of his short beard, his jaw moves with tension. He looks away. "Tomorrow morning you can inquire about John Bender. Then maybe we can get back to living our lives in the present, regain our peace of mind."

Even as I let Charlie take my silence as agreement, I can't help but wonder what sort of conversation Peter Garvey and I will have tomorrow. My testimony wasn't the only evidence that convicted Peter of Luci's murder, of course. His fingerprints were all over the kitchen, including a thumbprint on the knife. Peter never did deny he was in Luci's yard that afternoon. He simply said he drank so much before the police found him passed out in the house next door that he couldn't recall anything past his argument with Luci that morning. What would happen if I pushed him to remember, as if I were on his side? The bite of pizza crust on my tongue has formed a doughy ball, and I'm not sure I can get it down without choking. The last inch of beer in my glass saves me.

Mona's is a small place. Most of their business is delivery, accomplished with a minivan graced with a line drawing of Mona Lisa and a scrawled MONA'S ITALIAN, my first design job when I moved here. Kids from the local community college come here a lot, but summer school ends about now, and the place is quiet tonight, only one other couple. Even the usual music has been turned down low. A ceiling fan turns lazily over our table, stirring the aromas of basil and garlic.

The other couple leaves Mona's just ahead of us. Outside, the parking lot is empty except for my red VW. It's a shock to leave the air-conditioning. At seven-thirty the temperature is still above eighty, and the humidity is high. We stand for a moment. Charlie squeezes my hand and then lets go and puts his arm around my shoulder. Maybe it's the couple of beers, or the way he's rubbing the cool skin of my upper arm with his fingers, or his unwavering skepticism about my fears, but the anxiety of the day slides a little, and I feel my head tilt back. Across the street is Kinko's with its blue-and-coral neon sign, and next to it a wide-windowed Laundromat. A flock of crows, lifting off from trees behind the buildings, caws and flaps across a luminous sky. I watch until the last speck has vanished. Layers of small, fleecy clouds, with flags of blue behind them, are shot through with streaks of silver. "A mackerel sky," says Charlie.

I study his profile. His was by far the greatest loss when Luci was murdered, and as I follow his gaze back up to the sky, it occurs to me that I'm struggling to remember a time he's still trying hard to forget. I can be at the prison by two o'clock tomorrow and be home by six. Maybe that will put an end to my doubts, and Charlie will forgive me for not telling him about the trip ahead of time. "Mackerel sky?" I ask him. I'm looking for the shape of a fish in the clouds.

"See the striped belly?" He's waving his hand broadly, side to side.

High-school kids in a passing car wave back, and Charlie laughs at their mistake and lowers his arm around my shoulders again. Before I get into the driver's seat, I stand for a moment beside the car, closing my eyes to concentrate on the caress of a slight breeze. If only Charlie could ease my fears the way he wishes to. When I open my eyes and focus my gaze above the line of storefronts across the street, it's there—his giant fish, scales shimmering with silver across the summer sky.

"I didn't get what you meant at first," I say, sliding behind the wheel and starting the car, "but now I see." A glance at his face tells me he's relieved he's brought me around to his way of thinking. For the sake of his peace of mind, I let him misunderstand.

Saturday morning about ten I drop Charlie off at Shuey's Garage to pick up his van, then drive downtown to the police station, an old brick building a block off Main Street, across from the post office. On either side of the wide entrance, a pillar supports a frosted-glass globe bearing the word POLICE. Inside, I discover Detective Kenneth Hansen has moved into a front, corner office. The door is open, and I take one step into the room. From down the hall I can hear indistinct voices and the sound of a phone answered mid-ring.

Actually I'm relieved he's not here. Old feelings of dread and longing for protection have returned, primed by the smells of pine oil and cigarette smoke. Though this office is bigger than his old one, the wall to my right is lined with the same padlocked, varnished cabinets. The tops of the cupboards are littered with confiscated drug paraphernalia. To me they always looked like a tangled lineup of Aladdin's lamps and Turkish water pipes. Detective Hansen interviewed me the day Luci was killed, and a few days later he had me return to read the typed statement. He instructed me to initial any changes I wanted to make before I signed the statement. Certain parts of the interview are cut into my memory forever:

DETECTIVE HANSEN: So you saw Peter Garvey walk out the front door of the house, and you continued driving. Did you wave at each other?

LINDA GARBO: No.

HANSEN: Would he have been able to recognize you at that distance?

GARBO: Well, I recognized him.

HANSEN: But it could have been someone else at that distance?

GARBO: It was Peter. When I got to the yard, he was lying under Luci's car, working on it. He was on his back. Only his feet and legs were showing. I said, "Hi, Peter," and went into the house.

HANSEN: He didn't speak to you?

GARBO: I tapped the sole of his shoe with my foot as I said hello to him. And he wobbled his foot, you know, from side to side and then slid out from under the car, and yes, he spoke to me, but I don't remember what he said. He had a dirty red bandanna tied around his forehead, and he had streaks of dirt under his eyes, I suppose from wiping sweat away with greasy hands.

HANSEN: Anything else?

GARBO: Before he stood up, I noticed dark drops of something staining the legs of his jeans. At the time I thought it was oil.

I feel cold, standing here, as the panic I've been fighting for months begins its inevitable rise. But this time, maybe because I'm in the police station, the dilemma I have tried to repress for so long asserts itself with full force, and I feel myself grow very still. *Did I actually see Peter's face outside the house that day?*

I was questioned by Ken Hansen a few hours after discovering Luci's body. The statement I signed, a transcription of that interview, became the truth for me. Standing here now, sick to my stomach all over again from shock at what the stains on the legs of those jeans really were, I remember how I hesitated, pen in hand. As I read my own words, I couldn't be sure if it had been *that day* Peter slid out from under the car and talked to me—his face streaked with grime—*or the day before.* It would have been ridiculous to think anyone but Peter Garvey would have been lying under Luci's car. Of course it was Peter. I had recognized him from the top of the hill. And he had been there both days before the murder, in the late afternoon, when the house casts its shadow over the front drive where the car was parked.

But reading my typed words, I realized it had been soon after Hansen asked *But it could have been someone else at that distance?* that I'd added that *I'd seen Peter face to face when I got to the house.* I knew what was at stake as I read the statement over, only a couple of days after I had made it. Despite my confusion, I didn't make any changes. I signed it the way it was: . . . *he had streaks of dirt under his eyes.*

Throughout the trial—with all the other evidence that backed me up—I never once doubted that my memory at the time of the interview had been the most accurate, and that I'd been right to stay with it. What I couldn't anticipate was the attention of a certain newspaper reporter who didn't miss a day of the trial—a man I wouldn't be able to keep my eyes off when he would move into my neighborhood months later.

At some level I must have recognized Bender.

Now a small sound behind me makes me turn around to find myself face to face with Detective Hansen for the first time since Peter's trial. Though I'm sure I look startled, he maintains the calm expression I remember, his eyes a steady gray behind wire-rimmed glasses, his dark hair military-short. His lips are chapped. Even his thick-bodied stance—hands on his belt, as if he has been standing there for a while—is familiar. He's wearing a gray shirt and a tie printed with bright yellow Woodstocks, the Peanuts cartoon bird, tumbling down it. When he gestures me farther into the room, I sit in the varnished oak armchair facing the desk. "What brings you by? I see Charlie around once in a while. But I haven't seen you since I don't know when."

"I just stopped in to say hello," I answer, realizing at once how phony that sounds. "And to ask you something. You have time?"

"You're saving me from paperwork." He inserts a finger under the collar of his shirt, tugging at it the way I remember. "What can I do for you?"

"I ran into John Bender. He says he's talked to Peter Garvey recently."

Hansen moves back and forth slightly in his swivel desk chair, his glasses reflecting coins of light. I remember how controlled his reactions always were, how well suited he always seemed to his task of questioning me without reacting to anything I said. His demeanor then was so wooden, so apparently passive, and now in a moment I'm seeing the more natural animation of the earlier part of this conversation vanish. After that one quick swivel, back, then forth, he's sitting perfectly still.

"Did it ever occur to you I might have killed Luci? Did you ever doubt any part of my statement?"

His laugh is a short, dismissive exhale. "For a time there was a theory you and Charlie were in it together. No one around here knew anything about you, you know." I refuse to blink, and he shrugs. "You had a grocery-store receipt in your car, as I recall, with the time of purchase printed on it. We checked Charlie's alibi, too, talked to his secretary. And we found three or four people who had driven by during the time period in question. One of them saw a man walking out of the backside of the woods behind your house—'average height, with dark hair, or he could have been wearing a cap.' But there were a couple of kids fishing that afternoon, and they didn't see anyone." He pauses. "Personally, I never doubted you." He frowns at the wall behind me. "I don't know that it was smart of John to mention Garvey to you at this point."

Smart?

"It was one of Hilda Clark's strongest cases," he goes on, "not that it was an easy one to prosecute. Garvey wasn't the fool he made himself out to be. He killed her, all right. Bender's upset you for no reason."

"I think he has a reason. I think you know what it is."

Hansen stands abruptly and leans forward, his broad hands gripping the edge of the desk. "He does still talk about the case. You have to remember that Bender is a reporter. I swear the guy's looking for a story even in his sleep. Or if he has a story he's not satisfied with, he's looking for a new angle. The more he thinks about your friend's murder, the more he's convinced that the whole story never came out. That doesn't mean he doubts Garvey did it." Hansen straightens up. "He just isn't convinced we ever understood *why*."

I stand, too, but if Hansen's trying to dismiss me, it isn't going to work. "If he were following me, observing me, would he be breaking any law?"

"Trust me, Linda, Bender's a nice guy. He's known Pete Garvey his whole life, is all—not well, but they're about the same age and went to high school here at the same time. Bender's fascinated by what he calls Garvey's lack of moral center. John's the kind of guy who wants to know what went wrong. I'd trust him with my life."

"When you questioned Garvey the next day, after he had sobered up, what was that like?"

Hansen gives me one of his noncommittal stares. "He was very emotional, even sentimental about her death. But when I told him you had placed him at the scene, he barely reacted. He didn't seem worried until we arrested him, after a preliminary match of his prints with those on the knife. After that he thought everyone was against him. You, me. He suffered delirium tremens and got pretty sick, even more paranoid. If you recall, we put him in the hospital for a few days." Hansen's mouth curves down. He looks at me intently without changing his expression. The detective is shorter than I am, and he rocks himself up on his toes for a split second. I'm sure he doesn't realize he's doing it. "Being part of a murder investigation," he says, "being the one who found Luci Cole, well, of course, it's bound to have affected you. The more shocking things I've seen in this job come back to me from time to time as fresh as when they first happened. It's nothing to be ashamed of, unless there's something you're not telling me. If you want me to say something to John, I will."

"No, please don't." Realizing that they are friends, and that he probably will repeat this entire conversation to Bender anyway, I feel my face heat up. "I'm not asking you to do that for me. I don't want you to. Thanks for listening."

It's a wonder I don't tell him to have a nice day.

My studio is near the center of town. After I bought the building, I renovated the loft over the back twenty feet of the space—an area that had previously been the office when this was a factory producing screen-printed sweatshirts—remodeling the bathroom and turning the rest of the space into one large bedroom/sitting room, with a small kitchen along the side wall.

All the businesses on the four sides of this block back onto a large central parking lot. Directly across from my studio are the green clapboard back of the Grubstake Café and the candy-apple red of The Little Read Book Shop, which Judy Allard runs. The rear wall of The Little Read is mostly taken up by a huge grid of windows. Through the glass you can see stacks of cardboard cartons. That space would have made a great studio. I keep telling Judy she should take out the inside wall that blocks all that light, but she just looks at me funny. To her, ripping out a wall is a bigger deal than it would be to me.

As I pull into the parking lot, Tess Allard, Judy's fifteen-year-old daughter, is coming out the back door of The Little Read. She's slender, with long, sand-colored hair, and she's wearing a tight yellow tank dress that shows off her legs. She's watching her feet, and I barely hit the horn to make her look up. Startled, she lifts her hand to wave but doesn't come any closer. "Hey, Tessie, you in a mood, or what?"

Her answer is an exaggerated frown followed by a shrug and a weak smile to remind me the dirty look wasn't for me. "Later," she sings out, stepping back inside the store.

I'm here to pick up my camera so I can take a picture of our house from the road on my way home tonight. I figure I'll take three or four shots over the weekend—at different hours, in different light—so next week I can do a sketch for Charlie's print, maybe even get the image onto the plate.

Inside my studio, a skylight illuminates the main work area. A wide counter all along one side of the narrow, fifty-foot-long room holds a shallow sink and running water and an acid bath. The litho and etching presses separate the main work area from the front desk, where I talk with clients. Up front I pull the sketch of John Bender off the wall by the phone and put it in the bottom file drawer where I keep my camera.

On the way out I stop at the back window that faces the parking lot and twist the camera lens as I scan the vivid lot full of red, blue, and white vehicles. Tess has come outside again and is standing behind the Grubstake, facing away from me. Her long legs are thin up to the hem of her short yellow dress. I find myself observing her patiently through the viewfinder, waiting for her to turn around.

Glancing over her shoulder, she has a sweet, relaxed profile. When she turns fully, her gaze moves from one side of the parking lot to the other as if she's looking both ways before crossing a street. Then something, perhaps some sound behind her, catches her attention, and her features sharpen. Something has pleased her. Peering past the camera, I see it's Russell Weber.

Curious, I adjust the lens again and snap a shot of the two of them as Tess takes one more sweeping glance across the lot. As the shutter whispers, Weber reaches high, throwing his head back in a stretch—that awful hair tied into a blue bandanna. Then he cups his hand around his cigarette as he lights it and exhales smoke. If I hadn't learned his name yesterday, it's unlikely I'd be noticing him now. He's probably taken breaks like this ever since he started working over there. I press the shutter two, three more times as Tess listens to him intently, a smile never quite forming on her lips. Whenever she glances up at Weber, he looks away, and her expression turns grave again. Moving the camera slightly to the right to find the edge of the building for the compositional boundary I'm trained to look for, I snap one last picture—of John Bender, standing in the very alley where I faced him yesterday. He's staring at Weber.

Even when I open my door to step outside, letting it slap shut behind me, Bender doesn't glance my way at all.

My camera heavy around my neck, I cross the parking lot before Weber can finish his cigarette. I remind him about yesterday, down in Le's Salon. "Yes, I know who you are," he says. "You married Charlie." His manner is hesitant, even wary, as he studies my reaction. When I ask him how he knows my husband, he says, "I stopped by to see him the other day. He wasn't very friendly. He owed me money. I don't think he counted on my ever turning up to collect it."

"He owed you money?" I lift the camera a fraction of an inch to relieve the weight against the cord on the back of my neck. Angela, the owner of the Grubstake, opens the door and orders Weber to get back inside, there are customers. He drops his cigarette, steps on it, and raises his eyes to meet mine. "I noticed you talking to Tess."

His lips part for an uncertain moment before he says, "She's a nice kid."

"I know that."

"She comes in a lot, has since she was a little girl, apparently. To see Angela."

"I suppose you know John Bender, too."

Weber shakes his head.

"Tall guy. Ponytail. Hangs around here sometimes like he has nothing better to do."

"Sounds like me," says Weber. He smiles. One of his front teeth is darker than the others. "Don't know the guy."

Weber hears his name again. He turns his head, and he's inside the restaurant before I can ask my next question. I look at my watch. I'd better get going if I'm going to make it to the prison by two.

3 ◈ PRISON HAS CHANGED Peter Garvey's appearance. Gone is the puffiness under the eyes, which are clear and green. Gone is the sag below the jaw, though he's gained weight. His blond hair is darker. And he's wearing oval, wire-rimmed glasses. That's something new.

When I pick up the phone on my side of the glass embedded with tiny hexagons of wire, he keeps his hands below the counter, in no hurry to hear what I have on my mind. I lick the dry corners of my mouth and recognize what's changed most about him. From the first moment I met him, in Luci's kitchen, he avoided looking me in the eye, as if he knew we were going to be adversaries. Now he considers me calmly. And picks up the phone.

"Bender's been to see you." I mean it as a question.

"For a reporter, he's slow to take a challenge." Peter's speech is deliberate. He has all the time in the world. "Still, if he got *you* here . . ."

I shake my head. "This visit was my idea, to see if my hunches about you are on the mark."

"Well, I hope it's working." The irony is all in his tone. There's no hint of a sneer around his mouth, not so much as a flare of the nostrils.

"The fact that you told Bender—"

"I thought you weren't here because of him."

I hold my gaze steady, as impassive as Peter's. "Would you like to call me a liar, the way you did in court?" My face moves closer to the glass.

"You and I are the only ones who know the truth," he says evenly. "What's the point of pretending with each other?"

"Exactly." I start to breathe again.

He leans back. "You're very good." His eyes tighten with the word "good." "We seem to have you scared."

I refuse to falter. "You wrote to Bender."

He nods. His eyes move to the side for a moment, his head staying still. I wonder if anyone is listening in on these phones. "You almost had *me* convinced of the dirt on my hands, the greasy smell of my own sweat. The blood on my jeans was a good trick, in full color yet." He looks past me. "You're an artist, all right."

"You want John Bender to prove I made it up."

"Whoever killed Luci is still out there. I think you know who it is."

"Bender's interested in your motives, not mine."

"He didn't waste any time talking to you about me."

"That was an accident." Before Peter can react, I ask him about the argument he had with Luci the morning of the day she died. As if on cue, he recites word for word what he said in court, that she didn't want him in the house anymore. Everything was over between them. "She'd felt guilty before, sent me away. Then she'd get over it. It's not a reason to kill a woman, because she turns you down. Every man in the world would kill, sooner or later." He smiles a grim smile.

"You grabbed her so hard you left ten clear prints on her skin."

He tightens the fist holding the phone, veins standing out on the back of his hand. "I took a hold of her, sure. But not to hurt her. She still wanted me to finish her car. Before the day was over."

"So you worked on the car to get back in her good graces."

"No one with any balls would have done that. Ask Bender." For a moment he has forgotten himself, anger rising in his voice, and he even holds up his left fist, the one without the phone, as if to show me how memory is affecting him. "I told her she should have gotten the car running before she kissed me off. She wanted to sell it. I told her that was *her* problem."

Peter testified in court that he had not returned to Luci's after their argument late in the morning, but he also insisted he had blacked out, so he remembered nothing of that afternoon. That contradiction between certainty he had not killed her and forget-fulness of the time period of her death bewildered him, causing him to doubt himself visibly, right on the witness stand. As if he knows he's led me back to that moment, he says, "There's not a lot to remember about drinking in front of the TV on a hot af-ternoon in August." He pauses. "I'd had blackouts before. But I know I could never have seen Luci the way you found her and then forgotten, no matter how much I drank that afternoon. I would never have hurt her. I've strained to remember if I saw anyone around her house. Things about that day come back sometimes." He pauses to swallow again, with an effort that causes his chin to bob forward. After a long silence, he rouses himself from thought. "I went back to see her," he says softly, "after we argued. Maybe an hour later. About noon." His lips nearly touch the phone. "We talked through the screen door."

I hold my breath. This is something new, not part of his trial testimony. I suppose I've asked to be lied to, coming here like this. But if he's invented a story, I have to hear all of it. "What did you talk about?"

"She wouldn't unlock the door." Peter narrows his eyes, con-centrating. "The crows were flying over, making that hoarse cawing racket, roosting in the trees, behind the house. She hated them."

It occurs to me how much Peter Garvey's manner has changed as we've been talking. He's lost the cool, confrontational authority with which he greeted me. But maybe he hasn't lost command of this conversation at all. He's prepared this story carefully. "She complained about the crows?"

"She wouldn't come outside. Her hair was wet. She had washed her hair. I had taken a shower, too, before I went back over there, and shaved, put on shorts and a clean shirt. It was very hot and humid. She was holding a book, a finger stuck into it to save her place, a pen in her other hand, hugging the book to her chest. She said she was writing to you, and she tapped on the book with her pen. She was quiet. She told me she was sorry she had hurt me. Then she turned and walked away, leaving me standing there. That time was different. I knew she meant it. I never saw her again."

"So it was the kind of book you write in? A notebook?"

"I asked her why she would be writing to you, when you were staying right there in the house. She didn't answer. She talked about you all the time."

"What did it look like, this book? Small as my hand? What color?"

"Some dull color. If she hadn't talked you into moving to town, she wouldn't have thrown me over like that. We understood each other." His expression has softened, but as he focuses fully on my face, his features sharpen again. "Then all of a sudden it was you she wanted to be with. She said writing in that book was like writing to you."

We stare at each other.

"She wouldn't unlock the door or come outside. She didn't like to be around me when I'd been drinking."

"I thought she wouldn't come out because of the crows." Even as I hear my cynical tone, I know it will end the conversation. He knows I don't believe him.

He frowns, but catches himself and says, "She had a diary," too determined to be convincing.

"Of course she did."

His expression stiffens again, and I see how he hates me for all I have done to him. With a slow lowering of my hand, I hang up the phone and turn away.

I arrive home from seeing Peter Garvey just in time to make supper. Charlie doesn't seem to notice he's doing most of the talking while we eat. It's his turn to clean up the kitchen. As the dishwasher begins to churn, I curl up on the living-room couch with the evening paper and open to the editorial page, which gives me a place to look as Charlie settles into his recliner across the room.

Every once in a while something of Luci's will appear in the house—a single earring caught at the back of a drawer, a knot of pantyhose on the floor behind the dryer in the basement, a grocery list in her handwriting curled at the bottom of the potato bin. Just last week I moved a jug of drain cleaner aside under the bathroom sink and found a Q-tip stained with green eye shadow. It's as if her lost things are rising to the surface one by one to remind me that she was here first. Maybe the next lost thing will be a diary.

I'm still puzzling over the way Peter tempted me to believe that Luci's diary might exist: *Then all of a sudden it was you she wanted to be with. She said writing in that book was like writing to you.*

Luci and I were not always close. When I first met her, we rented rooms down the hall from each other near campus one summer in Kansas City, where we were both studying art. Because she was small and pretty, I immediately attributed to her a natural advantage over me in all things. But she never talked much about herself, and the friendship didn't really develop until a certain Saturday morning in late July. I was sitting on my bed reading, a cup of coffee in my hand, when I became aware of muffled crying on the other side of the wall. I lowered my book. No one else was there that weekend besides Luci and me. She was talking softly. I realized she was on the phone in the hall.

I swung my legs over the side of the bed and stared at the open door. She was explaining to someone—she told me later it was a social worker—that she was pregnant. When she sobbed so hard she couldn't go on, I set my coffee cup silently on the drafting table by my bed and waited. The voice on the phone must have calmed her, because when Luci finally continued, her own voice was distinct, almost angry. She'd already given up a baby for adoption. She didn't want an abortion this time either. She was about to make a trip home to tell her mother. We had talked every day as we fixed meals together, walked to class—but all of this was shocking to me. *Who?* I was wondering. I didn't have a clue.

When she finally hung up and I stepped through the doorway, she was expecting me. "I didn't know any other way to tell you," she said. Sobbing, she pulled her nightgown over her head in one quick motion and asked me to come with her into into the bathroom, where she turned the water on full blast to fill the tub and lowered herself, lying back until the ends of her hair were wet. She told me how ashamed she was going to feel when she told her mother. I watched her slide her soapy hands over her slender body, her belly so softly curved, her navel a dimple full of water. "Anyone who ever sees me naked will *know*, will see that my aureoles are brown," she said, pressing the palms of her hands against her small breasts as tears started again. The first time she was pregnant, she explained, her nipples had darkened. "A stain." She moved her hands to show me. I'd never heard the birdlike word "aureole" before, or imagined the slippery feel of her nipples budding against the palms of her hands as I crouched down to reassure her. *Not a stain, Luci.* The steam from the tub made the room too warm.

I insisted that hating her body was hating herself, but she began sobbing noisily as she reached for a towel and headed for her room. I sat beside her on the bed and my arms were around her, fingers tracing the delicate spine beneath the smooth, damp skin. In a while the after-quakes of her crying stopped, and she relaxed quietly against me. And then she arched her back and took hold of my hand, moving it around to the front of her body. Her face was very close to mine, and I felt the heel of my hand press to resist. Abruptly she pushed my hand away, as if touching her had been my idea. "No," she said. *No*. She lay down, hugging herself. Her sudden change of mood made me unsure what had just happened. The front of my T-shirt was still damp from her hair, my hands still moist from her skin. I tried to think of what to say, but she was pretending to sleep.

We never talked about that morning again, but through her bus trip home to a small town in central Missouri, and through the miscarriage she suffered on the way back to school, I was the one she called twice a day, the one she told those few facts. A flulike illness kept her in bed for days after she returned. Gradually she recovered, and we went back to sharing an occasional supper, walks to class, conversations about our work. I asked her a couple of times if she needed to talk about that trip, but she said no. I don't remember her dating at all during that school year, and she seemed almost prudish in the way she talked about her body. It occurs to me now that seeing the color of her nipples as shameful marks, stigmata, revealed some kind of hysteria. But at the time I was as glad as she was to drop the whole subject. To speak of it at all would have meant wondering what she had wanted from me that morning, when she had become angry with me for pulling away. Now, looking back, I think she was inviting me to cross a line she was sure I wouldn't cross—to see if I would reject her altogether. I was her only friend. Once I woke up in a sweat from an unwelcome dream of stroking her there, where she was the color of an oak leaf in the fall, my tongue feeling the flesh gather and rise. A warm, golden brown muted to pinkish brown. Not a stain at all. She had planted a possibility in my mind that I didn't want.

I've never been sure I remembered it right.

That was ten years ago, when Luci and I were both in our mid-twenties. During the years after school we didn't see each other, but she called me six or seven times a year. I was in Minneapolis, and she was teaching art at the community college here in Linden Grove. She made a point of mentioning, whenever we talked, that she had no man in her life and that she still made time for her own art, as if the two pieces of information were connected. I was working for a graphic-design firm and living with Brad Tripple-horn—a tall, athletic dental surgeon I expected to spend the rest of my life with. He dared me to face all kinds of adventures: white-water rafting, technical climbing, spelunking. Brad insisted that if we lost the will to struggle against the calmness in our natures, we'd be doomed to dull, conventional lives. It was skydiving that finally did us in. Defying the fear of falling was supposed to save me from being ordinary. Next, I imagined, would come the Idi-tarod sled-dog marathon across Alaska—or whatever it took to find my limits *out there* somewhere, pitted against nature. I had begun to wonder about limits that were *in here*.

Standing in the open hatch of that plane with his hands on my shoulders, I finally realized I loved being unsafe, but I hated having to meet his requirements. Six months later he told me we needed some time apart. He needed a woman who could take risks with him. My first reaction was to be sorry I hadn't jumped.

I was lonely, of course, during the breakup, and one day I called Luci, just to talk. During that conversation our friendship seemed close all of a sudden, after years of having an edge of politeness to it. She was the first to suggest that I might move to Linden Grove. I made a number of weekend visits, staying with her and Charlie, before I decided I could be happy in such a small town. When I found an old warehouse for sale, the idea of living here more cheaply than I could in a city began to interest me. I could do just enough commercial work to make a living, and have time for fine-art printmaking, too. I had to make some changes in the building in order to live in it. When the work was nearly completed, I made the move. The plan was to stay with Luci and Charlie just until the city inspector signed the final permit.

For the first few hours I spent with her in this house she seemed happier and more self-possessed than I'd ever seen her. The kitchen was painted lime green then, and the first night we stayed up late talking at the kitchen table. She'd been thinking about finding a small gallery space in town—white walls, track lighting, low rent— supporting it by offering art lessons. She wanted to find kindred spirits in the area, other artists, because Charlie didn't think she was making friends.

The next morning, though I was anxious to get to my building and work on setting up the studio, she asked me to stick around after Charlie left. She was still in the T-shirt and underpants she slept in, her dark brown hair tangled in kinky spirals. Her heavy-lidded eyes were bruised with eye shadow, her mouth generous, with a slight overbite. When she teased, she'd try to smile with her lips closed, but she usually didn't succeed. Laughter came easily to Luci. "A person could dry up and vanish in a place like this," she said, but then she grew serious. She leaned forward to tuck my hair behind my ear. "I just hope this will be a good move for you. At first I thought this would be the best kind of place to do my work, laid-back, safe, no traffic jams. But if a mime suddenly appeared on Main Street—" Her head wobbled, mimelike. "Perched on a trash barrel, say, appealing to passersby to come close—" Her arms reached, fingers imploring. "Remember?"

"A mime, Luci?"

"Remember that photo of a mime, perched with his knees up like a frog, on an open-mesh barrel on the street in New York? In SoHo, I think it was. People stopping to stare? Well, in *this* town, people would keep on going, like they didn't notice anything, pretending no one was there. As if the novelty of seeing someone so out of place were reason not to look. I feel silent *and* invisible, you know?"

Although she seemed happy with Charlie, she apparently felt like an outsider in Linden Grove, but I sensed it wasn't time to pursue the idea. Maybe the next day. Or the day after that. She was nodding her head, the hoops in her ears bumping against her jaw.

I reached out to trace the gold circles. "You sleep in these?"

She touched her earrings with both hands to remind herself which ones she had on, her fingers touching mine. "Of course not, but I don't want to look completely let go when Charlie leaves the house, do I?"

Her body stiffened as she said his name. "All I want is to please him," she said. We studied each other for long moments. Her skin was clear and lightly freckled, without makeup, except for the pale eye shadow. She was the sort of woman you'd notice and remember as striking—and smaller than she really was at five-four and barely a hundred pounds. "There's not much excitement here. People don't argue and fight. Everyone's so nice. Like you." She accused me with a laugh. "You'll be right at home in no time. You'll see. Everyone's so polite."

"How terrible." I watched her consider the bitten nails of her right hand. "You don't seem to be suffering too much. You seem content. And Charlie—"

"Oh, *Char*lie," she said, her voice catching. She got out of her chair and yanked open the refrigerator, studying its contents, her back to me. She brought an orange to the table, where she proceeded to peel it with her short fingernails. I was surprised to see tears pool along a bright line inside her lower lids, then spill over. "He's the sort of man you can't find fault with," she said softly. "That's the trouble. He's *so* good." Somehow I knew what was coming. "And I'm not. You should know that better than anybody."

"Okay," I said when I could see she wanted me to press. "What is it you're trying to say?" She wiped her eyes with her fingers.

All at once the door opened, and in walked a tall, muscular man, oak blond. He smiled like a kid, though he looked thirty-five around the eyes and jawline. An oily smear curved over his right

temple and under the eye, apparently where he'd touched his face
with his fingers, which were soiled a glossy black. Luci recovered
herself, sniffing her tears. As she introduced me to him, it became
clear Peter Garvey was more at home than I was. He'd headed
right for the sink to wash his hands with some kind of tar-smelling
cleaner in a can by the faucet. Then he proceeded to get a glass
out of the cupboard, find a lemon in a plastic bag in the refrigerator, and cut a slice for his iced tea, using a knife he pulled from
a wooden holder on the counter by the sink. Before he sat down,
he got himself an orange, too, peeling the fruit in one continuous
ribbon. He gave the long curl of orange rind to Luci.

The three of us sat there for an hour, the two of them doing
most of the talking. A spot of color bloomed on each of Luci's
cheeks, and as she gestured and laughed, her pointy nipples poked
against her thin T-shirt. I was appalled by her careless behavior,
and embarrassed that she seemed so comfortable sitting there half
dressed. Her refusal to look at me made me feel even more con-
spicuous. His fingernails were dirty, and he scratched his chest a
lot. Every time he took a swig of iced tea, he'd celebrate with a
robust "*Ahhh.*" I hated the scent of oranges in the room.

As soon as he was out the door, I said, "I shouldn't be staying
here. I'm obviously cramping your style." I stood up and turned
my back on her. "What about Charlie? He'd be devastated if he
knew. Charlie loves you." I paused. "He doesn't know, does he?"

Her face crumpled. "I'm in such trouble. I'm not sure I can get
out of this." She looked up at me, wet under the eyes. "But you're
wrong if you think you shouldn't be here. I *wanted* you here. I
knew telling you would make it real. I *need* to feel ashamed."

I stared at her as if I'd never seen her before.

Now I look over at Charlie as he drops the newspaper onto the
floor beside his chair and closes his eyes. He works too hard. It's
a good thing tomorrow is Sunday. We both need a day of rest.

My gaze settles on the bookcase across the room. During the
murder investigation it came out that I was the only one who knew

about Luci and Peter. If not for my arrival on the scene, her affair with Peter might have run its natural course, Charlie might never have known about it, and Luci's books would still be on these shelves. Her possessions would be stashed and strewn everywhere in this small house, as they were before I packed them into boxes and carried them out to her studio room at the back of the garage, where they've been stored ever since. Charlie couldn't face the task, so I gathered up her clothes, her shoe collection, her earrings, her letters and newspaper clippings, her books. If there had been a diary, a journal, a sketchbook—any record of Luci's private thoughts—I would have found it. I spent a whole day alone here, getting Luci's possessions out of his sight.

4 ◈ SURPRISINGLY, GIVEN ALL I HAVE on my mind, I sleep until after ten the next morning and wake up refreshed. Charlie is in the kitchen, making pancakes. We spend what's left of the morning at the kitchen table drinking coffee and reading *The Des Moines Register*, which we have delivered every Sunday. Charlie works six days a week this time of year; I take Wednesday off and work Saturday. Sunday is our one day together, and we usually go somewhere, a tradition we have maintained—religiously, as Charlie says—since before we were married.

When I fold up the travel section, done with the paper, I realize the coffee is gone. I've had enough anyway. I'm feeling jumpy again. As I start to rinse off the dishes, I notice the pinecone that's been on the windowsill above the sink all summer and suggest we take a drive later, maybe go to The Ledges. The state park is a couple of hours from here, a beautiful place Charlie introduced me to one Sunday afternoon last spring. "We could take another walk on the wild chives," I say, trying my best to make it sound like "the wild side."

He gives me a blank look, and I start to remind him what I'm referring to. "Yes," he says, stopping me, "I remember," but he doesn't smile. His eyes are still puffy, like when he first gets out of bed. I've distracted him from the crossword puzzle he's working. He makes a mark on it with his pen and says it's going to be too hot and humid to spend the day outside—the mosquitoes are terrible this year—and anyway, he doesn't feel like going anywhere. He's tired from the week. But he'll go if I really want him to.

"No, that's okay."

He looks at me to be sure I mean it, and I smile at him.

The Sunday I'm remembering was in May, the first beautiful, sunny weekend after a spring that had been cloudy, cool, and rainy. Temperatures were predicted to reach eighty. As soon as we got to the park that afternoon, about three, we unloaded a red-plaid blanket and Styrofoam cooler from Charlie's van and claimed a picnic table near the shallow stream that meanders between high, butterscotch-colored cliffs. The rock walls of The Ledges rise up perpendicular to the floor on each side of a narrow valley. In some places the rock is browner, and wind erosion has rounded the rock formations into huge, organic shapes like elephants or hippos. I noticed signs warning NO CLIMBING OR RAPPELING ALLOWED ON FRAGILE SANDSTONE. Charlie pointed out ascending toeholds worn into the rock by climbers, and grooves here and there along the top edges of the cliffs where ropes had left their marks. There was graffiti, too, initials carved high on the cliffs. The park was filling up with families setting up volleyball nets, couples holding hands, children wading in the brook.

Charlie and I took off our shoes and socks, rolled up our jeans, and stepped into the shallow stream. Laughing with surprise at the shock of the icy water, we put our arms out for balance as we made our way over broad, slippery boulders in the gentle current. I was beginning to think that negotiating the treacherous rocks was more tedious than fun when Charlie, who was ahead of me, reached a sandbar. He held out his hand to pull me onto safe footing, and we stood there, ankle deep in the clear water, securely grounded, holding on to each other. The air smelled of charcoal fires and roasting meat. We waded back to our picnic site to start our own fire in the rusty iron grill by the table.

Charlie had packed the food: T-bone steaks, potato salad from the Hy-Vee deli, a tomato to slice, a package of chocolate-chip cookies, and four cans of root beer. While we waited for the charcoal to burn to powdery white, then red, we lay on our backs and closed our eyes and listened to the stream whispering, and birds singing, and people shouting to each other happily off in the distance.

After we ate, we took a walk. Charlie pointed out particular birds: cedar waxwings feeding on red berries in a chokecherry tree, a redheaded woodpecker tat-tatting away on a dead oak. He spotted a group of tiny, ruby-crowned kinglets and—high above the cliffs in the cloudless sky—a red-tailed hawk. "You're quite a nature guide," I teased him.

"Count yourself lucky I'm not identifying the insects." He proved his point with a Latin term, long as a sentence.

"It wasn't a complaint, Charlie. I *like* it. I was never good at remembering names. And you have a better eye than I do, for detailed markings." I thought I detected the faint scent of onions as a couple of teenagers approached. The girl, wearing a tight pink T-shirt, was in the lead. She was talking in a forceful, animated manner, gesturing broadly until she saw us. Then she dropped her arms to her sides, clamped her lips shut, and walked faster. The boy followed solemnly, a few paces behind. "Rosy-breasted warbler," I whispered to Charlie when they were safely past.

"And isn't that a gray titmouse?"

"*Tit*mouse?"

Charlie bumped into me as I turned to glance back at the retreating couple, and his arm went around me as we kept walking, but more slowly. "He's following her like a sleepwalker. The least he could do is puff himself up a little." Charlie paused, inhaling deeply to demonstrate. "You smell onions?"

"I thought I imagined it."

He hunkered down. "This area's been mowed recently, see?" He pulled a handful of bright green, grasslike plants, pinching the roots off with a thumbnail and offering me a whiff of delicate, oniony scent. "Wild chives. Mowing released the smell, and so did walking on them." At that moment the sun went behind a cloud, and we decided to head back. On the way I gave my version of a nature tour, spotting a "red-faced realtor" in plaid Bermuda shorts and, as we passed a group of giggling middle-school-aged girls, a "gaggle of guinea friends."

Along the path Charlie picked up four large pinecones, their surfaces closed tight and formal as the overlapping scales of a fish. To my surprise, he began tossing them into the air, first in a circle, then in a fountain pattern, higher and higher. "I was in the juggling club in college."

"And you're showing off to impress me."

"You bet." He changed the pattern of what he was doing, stooping to pick up another pinecone, then another, until he had seven going. Finally he launched them forward onto the grass, one by one—except for the last, which he handed to me with a bow. "For you," he said.

That's the pinecone on the windowsill. I'm looking at it now.

I leave him to his crossword puzzle. I guess I'll work in the yard for a while before taking my shower. I soon work up a sweat trimming the bushes across the front of the house. As I stand back to appraise my work, Charlie comes to the front door and asks me for a seven-letter word that starts with D, "a person who occupies a particular place regularly," but I can't help him. My mind is full of what Peter Garvey told me: *We talked through the screen door.... She was holding a book.... Some dull color.*

After I take a shower to wash off the salty perspiration and oily insect repellent, I close up the house and turn on the air-conditioner and bake a cherry pie while Charlie takes a nap. The day slows. The house is silent. I don't know what to do with myself. When I hear Charlie get up, I fire up the grill for steaks, but I cook them too long and they're not as pink in the center as we like them. We don't talk much while we eat. *If she hadn't talked you into moving to town, she wouldn't have thrown me over like that . . . Then all of a sudden it was you she wanted to be with.* "Did you hear me?" Charlie is saying.

"Oh, sorry. I guess I was thinking about something else."

"I said I'm going to watch a golf tournament."

He goes into the spare room, but when I go in there and curl next to him on the bed, he puts the TV on mute and pulls one of the pillows out from behind his back, so I can recline next to him. "I'm not exactly a bundle of energy today, am I?" he says. "I just didn't feel like going anywhere, but maybe I should have made the effort. You haven't been able to sit still." He's watching the silent screen of the TV, an instant replay of a ball circling the rim before dropping into the hole. When he notices me watching, he turns the TV off.

"I didn't want you to do that."

"Yes you did," he says gently, pulling me against him. "Now you have my full attention."

I rear back enough to smile at him. "Maybe I don't always know what I want."

"None of us does. Let's talk. Ask me anything."

"What's the secret of juggling?"

"Keeping the balls in the air."

"No, really, Charlie." I settle my head into the hollow of his neck.

"You might imagine the secret is to keep your eye on the ball," he says, "but that advice doesn't apply to juggling. You have to shift your attention from one ball—"

"Or pinecone . . ."

"—or pinecone to the next, so you see only part of each object's flight. You have to look at the highest point and throw the next object when the previous one reaches the top." He pauses. "Maybe that's what we need to do. As we recognize a high point, we can aim for another just as high. Knowing there will always be ups and downs. And that there won't be any more highs without effort."

I look at his face again and see that he's serious. "I wouldn't have guessed you were thinking about *us* today."

"I wasn't really, until you asked."

"I asked about juggling."

"Point well taken," he says. "You've unlocked the secrets of my mind." He kisses me on the nose. He seems content. "Now tell me what you've been thinking about today."

"Why would you owe Russell Weber money?"

"How do you know Weber?"

"He's the cook at the Grubstake."

"He helped me build the garage. But he walked off the job when he was half done staining the siding, and he never came back. Never collected his last few hours' pay. Why?"

"I just didn't know you knew him."

"He could be a hell of a good worker, when I was here to keep an eye on him. A fair carpenter, good at finishing cement. Could even do wiring. The kind of guy who knows how to do a hundred jobs but never sticks to one. Later, when I tried to send the check to him, I discovered he'd left town. I never saw him again, until the other day."

"What brought him back?"

"Apparently an uncle has some rental property where he can stay, so he can get his feet on the ground. Told me he's starting a band. I didn't realize he was a cook." Charlie shifts his body away from me, pulling a pillow up behind his shoulders so he can sit up straighter. "He wanted his money. He apologized for taking off, but it's no longer important. I was plenty mad at the time. Now it just makes me sick."

"Because he left before the garage was finished?"

"The work was pretty much done."

"That couldn't have been too long before Luci died."

"Two or three weeks." Charlie hunches his shoulders, then lowers them again, as if he's trying to shake something off. "I might have been wrong," he says quickly, "but it occurred to me that in coming after his pay, he wasn't at all sure I'd give it to him. He told me he was sorry about my loss, that sort of thing. And all the time he was watching me like I was a bomb about to go off. I've never seen a guy so jumpy. On the other hand, would he come back for a hundred bucks if he'd been—" Charlie raises the remote control and turns the TV back on. The camera is tight on the golfer as he sizes up his final shot on the green, the commentator so close he's whispering.

"If he'd been what, Charlie?"

"Weber was around here for weeks. I can't help wondering if Luci was messing around with him, too. I gave him his check the other day, but I told him I never wanted to see his face again." Charlie clicks off the TV and swings around to sit on the edge of the bed, his back to me. "He's not worth thinking about."

I put my hand on his shoulder. "You know," he says, "up until now, today has been one of those high points I was talking about, knowing I can restore myself at home with you, when I need to. Comfortable and quiet. We almost got through the whole day without mentioning Luci."

"I didn't know asking about Weber would bring up her name," I say gently. "Why don't you turn the TV back on? I'll lie here and watch it with you."

"I didn't know you liked golf."

"The whispering will relax me," I joke as he clicks the TV on and lies beside me. "I just want to be close."

A while later I rouse myself and a seven-letter word starting with D comes to me unbidden: "D-E-N-I-Z-E-N," I murmur, but Charlie's breathing is so regular I know he's asleep. *One who occupies a particular place.* The room is dark and quiet. I get up and put on my nightgown and crawl into our own bed, but now sleep is out of the question. My shoulder muscles tense as my conversation with Peter Garvey resumes its unrelenting replay in my brain.

As soon as Charlie leaves for work on Monday morning, I take a cup of coffee out to the garage and unlock the studio room.

The first thing I do is open the windows to admit a pleasant, loamy breeze. Luci's large worktable is shoved against the inside wall, stacked with boxes, and her loom stands in the middle of the big room, draped in a white sheet. She brought me here the day I arrived, pointing out the slanted, eighteen-inch louvers across the ceiling that diffuse the light from the skylights and naming the trees outside the back windows: oak and ash, maple and linden. "What a perfect place to work," I remember saying. "No one would know it's here, hidden away behind what looks for all the world like an ordinary garage."

"You always were this odd mix of artist and thief," she said, laughing. "Balancing your need to show off with a need to conceal. Very neurotic. I love you for it."

Recalling *artist and thief*, I miss her, angry we can't finish the arguments we started during the final days of her life. Before I could accuse her of contriving drama to avoid revealing herself directly, she evaded me. "You're right. You look great. Big and beautiful as ever."

Hearing only the "big," I looked down over the hill of my chest past curved belly and broad, tanned knees, all the way down to stretched-out cotton socks and size-twelve sandals, and then over at Luci, in tucked-in white T-shirt and frayed cutoffs, who by that time had slid sideways onto the bench of her loom. "I'd be hard to hide. Like a thief or otherwise." I was watching her bare feet shift the treadles of the loom.

She slipped a butterfly of yarn onto her fingers and began feeding it from behind through the weave of her tapestry, each movement effortless as a caress, while I admired the room, walking in

front of the floor-to-ceiling windows. Though the garage is on
solid ground, this room, supported by huge vertical timbers set in
concrete footings, juts out over the ravine. Looking out those windows into the treetops, I felt like I was in a tree house. The two
overhead fans weren't needed that day. When I turned back to her
again, she was beating the wool tight with a fork that looked like
an Afro pick.

Suddenly she stopped. The woods outside, stirred by a breeze,
burst into applause. "When I started this piece," she said, smiling,
"I was afraid I wouldn't be able to do it. But I had to prove something to you." She ran a fingertip along the last line of wool.
"Weaving is unnatural for me. I'm nearly defeated by the monot-
ony, and taming materials that want to twist and tangle is penance
for me. Did you know that?" She barely hesitated for an answer.
"I didn't dream you'd actually pull up stakes and *move* here, Linda."
She pulled the batten hard against the weave with a hearty *whomp*.
"Time will tell if you're my friend or if you couldn't resist coming
here to watch me disintegrate."

I was too appalled to speak.

"I slip, you see," she said. "Charlie's such a trusting soul, he
looks at me and figures he sees me for all time. I'm not even sure
what he should expect of me. Sometimes I can barely keep from
running for my life." The loom shifted again with the finality of a
door slamming shut.

The fact that I've remembered her words all this time reminds
me how mysterious they were at the time, how typically I listened
without asking a single question. *I slip.* What was that about? The
tapestry she had going involved many colors. While we talked, she
was constantly trading the shuttle loaded with the background blue
with loops of ivory, chamois, and citron yellow for what was left
of the pattern. By the end of our conversation she was working in
deep-blue yarn all the way across. "It's finished. One by one, I'm
bringing things to completion." She smiled sadly. "Charlie and I
might as well be married. What's the difference, if I'm never going

to leave this place? And why would I do that?" The loom shifted again, for the last time. "Would you?"

Now her once-rhetorical question haunts me as I walk over to the loom and lift the sheet so I can trace a line of the tapestry with my own finger. Was she testing the idea of leaving Charlie by denying she'd ever consider such a thing? It was only the next morning that she would sit at the kitchen table, complaining of being bored here. And what about her question? Would I leave? Will this place ever be as much mine as it was hers? Only now— as I begin to open every box and handle every silky undergarment, every soft T-shirt and gauzy skirt, every skein of brightly dyed wool, every letter and folded newspaper clipping I packed away all those months ago—do such thoughts occur to me.

Finally, with both hands, I yank open the four-square-tuck closure of the only box marked BOOKS—the word scrawled in my handwriting across the red, heraldic Seagram shield on the side. I packed this box neatly, out of respect for Luci, layering her paperbacks—the small size, with covers showing busty women bent backward in the arms of men with biceps like ninepins under titles promising PASSION, DESIRE, and LUST, the sort of romance novels I never knew her to read. There are a few others, pop-psych books about "the child within," or "deciding to heal."

I open the shoe boxes, lining up the dozen pairs of spiky heels on one of the open shelves, puzzled all over again by why she saved these gaudy, never-worn shoes with their rhinestone buckles, pleated bows, tiny straps to snake around the ankle. One pair is tomato and purple with bill-like toes, another gold lamé with Lucite heels in which threads of gold swim like excretions of tiny fish. The boxes are labeled UNITED STATES SHOE CORPORATION, the company her father was working for in Missouri when Luci and I were in school together. I never saw her wear anything other than flat brown-leather sandals. These shoes are not even her size.

When I've reached the end—opened every box, read every letter, unfolded every garment—I lock the room and walk to the back of the yard. Just a few feet into the trees the ground drops off sharply. It's at least fifteen feet to the bottom of the ravine. Birds whistle and chirp. Not a crow in sight.

Before I can think better of the impulse, I hurry inside the kitchen and find the phone listing for the newspaper. John Bender will hear Peter's version of our visit soon enough. He may as well hear mine first. As the phone whirs, I plan what I'll say: *You're going to get another letter from prison. I think you should help him.* But when Bender's machine picks up after four rings, my heart trips. I hit the switch hook with my finger. The dial tone drones.

This impulse to call Bender must have been like wanting to press the body where it hurts, to see if the pain is illusive. It's real all right. No matter what Hansen says, I still think Bender's been watching me.

I head for the basement, where I search along the tops of rafters, behind fruit jars, under a dried-up can of paint. Whether or not it's true that Peter saw Luci around noon with a diary in her hand, his story sent me home to look through her things all over again. Something I would do only if I were worried I had put the wrong man in prison. The phone rings overhead, but I let it ring as I search and search. And find nothing but dust.

I get to my studio later than usual and spend a couple hours fiddling with a brochure layout on the computer—a project I'm doing for BodyWorks, a local fitness center. By a quarter to twelve I'm starving, so I walk over to the Grubstake. The place is filling up already. I get the last table. As I order my food, a shadow falls across the menu. "I take it you had second thoughts about calling me this morning."

I stare at John Bender long enough to figure out that *The Linden Times* has Caller ID on its phones. My hanging up without leaving a message this morning has brought him here, looking for me. He didn't waste any time. I'm more sure than ever that I've been right all along: He has more than a casual interest in me. Steam rises from his mug of coffee as he proceeds to sit sideways on the chair across from mine, the temporary posture of the uninvited. I don't know how to send him on his way without showing my anger, so I get up from the table and head for the back of the restaurant. I pause at the coffee urn, staring dumbly at the shiny surface of the coffee in my cup, two-thirds full, as I slide it under the spigot and touch the handle lightly for effect.

Of course, Bender is watching, but when I return to my chair, his attention remains focused on something behind me. I turn to look. Beyond the pass-through to the kitchen, Russell Weber is reaching overhead for a long-handled pot, a red bandanna covering what I know are flattened ropes of yarnlike hair. "You know him?" I ask.

Bender ignores my question. "You walked back there with a full cup of coffee." He takes a sip of his own, then clears his throat. "To follow up on our conversation from the other day, I think Garvey may try and contact you directly. He wants you to come and see him."

"He told you that?"

"Yes."

"What else did he tell you?"

"Nothing new. Just that you lied about seeing him that afternoon."

Most days I eat lunch here at Angela's Grubstake Café, a neighborhood place offering a few vegetarian dishes and light curries alongside homemade pies, chicken-fried steaks, and pork tenderloins. The ten tables are covered with bright oilcloth in an abstract tropical print and surrounded by wooden chairs painted the same vivid colors—coral, cobalt blue, bright citron yellow, and the soft turquoise of copper oxide. Bender leans against the ancient pine paneling and fingers a package of Winstons in the pocket of his pale shirt. There's not an ashtray in sight. "I called you right back this morning, but you didn't answer." He smiles, but it does him no good.

I gaze at him, unblinking, until he shakes his head and considers the unlit cigarette in his hand. In a moment the waitress arrives with my Angela's Special, an odd but delicious arrangement of tabbouleh, cottage cheese, and tortilla chips.

Bender dumps a packet of sugar into his coffee and stirs, studying the empty envelope before dropping it on top of the other two beside his cup. "Prisons are full of innocent men, Linda. None of the younger ones are ready to give up the hope they can escape by their wits. Pete Garvey asked me to visit him, but it isn't really my attention he's after." Bender bites his lower lip as I refuse to respond. "When you accused me of following you last Friday, I was really caught off guard. Why would I do such a thing?"

"Maybe Garvey's convinced you I have something to hide."

Bender shakes his head, studying my face. I have to look away. He rubs the crystal of his watch, then runs the fingers of his right hand back and forth along a white line from wrist to the base of his little finger. It's a scar, and I think of asking, but to my dismay my face warms as his eyes meet mine again—a bonding look, that intense. He might actually be attractive, if he weren't such a threat. Turning my head, I can see my reflection in the plate-glass window of the café—the long streaks of light hair, the tilt of my oval face. Encouraged by the vaporous reflection, I smile at Bender. His eyes stop blinking, for three long seconds. "You actually interviewed me when Luci died?"

"Only once," he says, "out at the house, the day it happened. You were holding up better than I would have under the circumstances. But I remember the way you were breathing, forgetting to inhale. And then when you did, it was like someone coming up from a dive. We only spoke for a few minutes. I don't go for the kind of journalism that puts the victims of misfortune in the spotlight at the height of trauma."

"I wasn't the victim."

"So I didn't feel the need to interview you more than that once."

"Luci was the victim."

"A crime like that has many victims." We lift our heavy, ceramic mugs simultaneously, then lower them in silence, while Luci's body floats like the ghost of a flashbulb's afterburn. I want this conversation to be over.

I pick up the check and reach for my purse, but I hesitate, remembering something Peter said: *She still wanted me to finish her car. Before the day was over. . . . No one with any balls would have done that. Ask Bender.* I clear my throat. "I've always believed Garvey worked on Luci's car to be near her, but if he killed her, why on earth would he . . . ?"

"That was always the question, wasn't it? But don't try to think like a killer, Linda. A psychopath can commit murder, then resume watching television, mowing the lawn, fixing a car, as if nothing happened." If Bender noticed I said "if he killed her," he isn't letting on. He succeeds in looking sleepy, even bored. But he interrupted me just now a little too eagerly, which tells me he's repeating an explanation he has come to doubt. "If we know he was there, why do we have to know why?"

It occurs to me I have something I can give Bender, a piece of information to send him on his way. "Charlie gave Luci's car to the local high school," I say slowly, "so the auto-mechanics class could practice on it."

Bender nods thoughtfully. Then, as if I have given him an assignment, he places a few coins on the table, drains his coffee cup, and excuses himself. I smile at my reflection in the window glass as he walks away.

After finishing my lunch, I drive halfway home and park on the shoulder of the road at the exact spot where I saw Peter slide himself under Luci's car that day. My sandals scatter loose gravel as I slide down the steep embankment at the road's edge and find a footing where I can aim my camera through the break in the honeysuckle bushes.

On the other side of the cornfield below, the house casts a

shadow over the drive that circles past the front door and back to the road. By the nearest corner of the house, the drive Y's away from the circle and goes straight back to the double garage door, which is wide open most of the time, as it is now.

The camera shutter's *ch-ch* is answered by insects as the place moves closer through the viewfinder. I lower the camera. From the opposite side of the valley Charlie's putty-colored van is approaching the house, trailing a wake of dust. Even through the lens I can't see his features at this distance as he gets out of the van. He walks out to the road and opens the mailbox, then turns this way and looks up at the sky, which is cloudless and faded this afternoon. As I wonder what he's thinking, just standing there so long, he turns and walks into the garage.

I should snap another picture and hurry back to my studio. Develop the pictures. Start on a sketch of the house for Charlie's etching. But I'm unable to move. In the heat of August the underbrush—high and in flower—is abuzz with gnats and bees. Maybe my Calvinist ancestors have imprinted me with some genetic homing device drawing me to this hair shirt of a place. Above me on the road I hear a car slow to a stop, then the slam of a car door and the crunch of gravel under someone's foot. At once I'm flushed with panic. Inching up the eroded path, I stop when I've got the road at eye level. My lungs fill with heat. I can smell the dust that colors the air above the road behind the departing car. One I recognize.

I return to my station down here over the edge, to my surveillance of the house. Charlie's secretary, Rosemary, drives a silvery-green Toyota like the one I watch as it slows down for the house and turns into the driveway. I take a shallow breath and wait until the dust settles. Her white blouse is untucked over bright blue slacks, her bottle-blond hair big and loose. She stands at the back door, then gives up. For a moment she plants herself in the driveway, hands on hips, looking around. I can almost hear her calling out his name as she approaches the open garage door, then stops.

I can guess by the way her animated hand gestures stop and start that they're disagreeing about something. She doesn't go in. And he doesn't come out.

Finally Rosemary turns on her heels, gets into her car, and heads this way. Looking down at the house that in an odd way Luci and I still share, I lift the camera and take one last picture before I go back to work to develop the film. The shadows have shifted a little in the few minutes I've been standing here.

I spend the rest of the workday printing photographs and sketching versions of the house. When I arrive home at the end of the afternoon, Charlie is in the kitchen unloading a basketful of carrots, tomatoes, onions, and peppers, the vegetables still muddy from the garden. He's facing away from the door and doesn't turn to look when he hears me. So I know something is wrong. When I hug him from behind, he keeps his hands in the sink. "Were you rummaging around in the room behind the garage?" he wants to know. "Because if it wasn't you . . ."

"It was me."

His eyebrows draw together with displeasure, and the room is silent for a moment except for the plopping of the soup on the stove. Charlie glances in that direction, and I know he wants to turn down the heat under the kettle, but he's waiting for more.

"I thought there might have been something Luci wrote, something to help me understand her better. She wrote to me over the years, about her thoughts. I think she kept a diary. Lots of people do."

"Do they?" He glances at me just long enough to see my shrug, then returns to the mound of carrots and tomatoes. The bread dough I mixed this morning has risen too high and is spongy with gas bubbles. I punch it down a little harder than necessary, forming two loaves, until I notice that Charlie is standing still, watching me slap the dough into shape. "At first I thought someone had broken in, when I saw the mess. Then I noticed your coffee cup." He nods toward my favorite blue mug, back in its usual place in the dish rack by the sink. "I straightened things up out there. So you don't have to face it all again."

Cleaning up after me implies I can't be trusted to finish what I started, or that I'm careless, I want to tell him. Instead, I concentrate on placing the loaves into tins, coating my hands with shortening and sliding them gently over the top of the dough, which is warm and soft as flesh. "I took some pictures of the house today," I say, keeping my voice calm. "When the sun was high, early afternoon."

He doesn't look up.

"Charlie?"

Again he ignores me. After sliding a pile of diced potato off the cutting board into the soup pot, he returns to the counter, where he rocks his knife against the cutting board like an expert.

"What was Rosemary doing out here today? I saw her from the road, when I was photographing the house. Was anything wrong?"

He heads for the stove, cupping a two-handed measure of sliced carrots. "I'd missed an appointment with a customer, and when I didn't answer the phone all morning, she decided she'd drive out here. She said she was worried."

"About what?"

"Oh, she thinks I'm not taking care of business. It is *my* business. I told her that. She's getting tiresome. I'm afraid I said so when she came by here. I apologized later. She say something to you?" He studies my face for an answer.

"Of course not. I rarely even see her, Charlie. She doesn't tell me things."

That puts an end to conversation for now. Opening the baking cupboard next to the sink, I have to think of what I want to do next. I find the Karo corn syrup way in the back. When I tilt the sticky bottle in my hand, the quarter inch of syrup in the bottom barely moves, stiff with age. "Do honey and corn syrup—"

"Hmmm?" He doesn't look up, so I reach for the pint jar of

honey on the counter and pull it forward. It's basswood honey, from our own hives in the woods behind the house, and I don't see why I can't substitute it for Karo in my recipe. Charlie's knife against the cutting board continues its march.

I pour five ounces of honey into a Pyrex measuring cup and then hunker down to rummage in the counter under the sink for a quart Ball jar—pale water-blue glass with a heavy lid of dull, pewter-gray metal. I scrape the honey into it and then head for the laundry room to get the orange box of Tide off the top of the washing machine. Back in the kitchen I add a couple teaspoons of soap to the honey. As I glance through the window into the backyard, I comment that the rabbits are back. But the look of fear on Charlie's face stops me midsentence. "Luci was not the reflective person you say she was, Linda. She could barely manage to write a grocery list. She didn't keep a diary." He's visibly unnerved, watching the blue flecks of Tide dissolve into the honey. He doesn't ask, so he must assume I'm doing something crazy.

To answer the question he's so carefully avoiding, I tell him the formula for sugar-lift ground—the solution of honey, detergent, india ink, and gum arabic I'll use to paint an image of the house onto a copper etching plate tomorrow. My stomach tightens. "Did you pack her shoes away, too? When you cleaned up after me?" I am angry now, but it's a passive anger, the kind that holds things back.

"No one wants her possessions, Linda. It's time to get rid of them." He bows in front of the stove to peer under the iron kettle and adjust the ring of blue flames I know are there, out of sight, like all remembered things.

5 ◈ TUESDAY MORNING WHEN I dip my brush into the sugar solution, the bitter scent of ink, cut by the honey's sweetness, brings back the pain of Charlie's attitude that my behavior is sometimes irrational. With the first brushstroke across the copper plate I pull back and stare at the long, wet mark and wonder if I have set in motion a series of deceptions that will end with my losing him to Luci. I'm beginning to suspect he hasn't grieved for her fully. He's still very angry.

I work quickly, focused as ever. By eleven I've painted about half the image onto the copper plate, which is lying flat on a layer of newspapers. It's upside down because I'm doing the branches that overarch the roof, and I want that area closest to me for now. The sketch I'm working from is propped in front of me, also upside down. The photos of the house, along with the six of Tess and Russell Weber, are scattered along the table. I finish the curving branches of trees framing the composition and begin to apply horizontal strokes that drag the still-wet vertical lines, forming a net of Cézanne-like puzzle pieces. My right shoulder aches with the effort of holding wrist and elbow up so as not to touch the plate accidentally. Later, when I coat the plate and soak it in hot water to lift the image, I don't want fingerprints to appear on the plate along with the house and the trees.

The police found a lot of prints in that kitchen: mine on a coffee cup and on the frame of the aluminum screen door, Charlie's on a fresh apple in a bowl on the table and on the flat surface of the kitchen counter, Peter's on a glass by the sink as well as on the knife and on Luci's forearm. There were unidentified prints, from two different individuals. In hot, humid weather, prints can last for weeks. The touch of the hand is like that. Touch can leave a mark forever.

I lift the plate by the edges and rotate it right side up. All I have left to do is fill in the blank copper above the roof. I've taken liberties with the camera's view, pushing the trees back to open up the sky. I lift my shoulders, rolling the kinks out. I've been working for two hours straight.

Right after Luci's murder Charlie and I had the sense that our perceptions of each other would always be heightened by matters of life and death. The afternoon it happened, when he showed up drenched with sweat and thirsty from jogging, I put my hands on his shoulders and backed him away from the house, made him wait with me in the shade of an oak tree while the police finished taping off the crime scene. I didn't want him to see Luci there on the floor, that terrible wound and all the blood, and have to live with that sight for the rest of his life. He lifted his white T-shirt to wipe his forehead and kept his face covered for a few seconds. I thought he might be crying, but he was composing himself. The ambulance driver and paramedics questioned the police in the yard about what had happened; bystanders gathered to speculate among themselves as quietly as if they were already at a funeral. When Detective Hansen stepped out of the kitchen door, pulling surgical gloves off with two loud snaps, the abrupt, rubbery sounds made everyone in the yard fall silent. In that moment I knew we were in the hands of some terrible evil and that at all costs I must stay in control of myself. So much was going to be up to me.

Only when they brought her out on one of those gurneys and uncovered her face carefully down to the chin for him to see did Charlie have to look. He averted his eyes from the people gathered around as someone asked me questions, a reporter. I seem to remember that now. But I wouldn't let him talk to Charlie. I can almost, but not quite, remember that it was John Bender.

We closed ranks after that, Charlie and I, sitting there in the yard, turning to face each other. He took hold of both of my hands, stroking one knuckle after another with his thumbs—a series of tiny, quickening circles of touch that took my breath away. I knew he didn't realize he was doing it. Nor could he know that even under such terrible circumstances he was affecting me in a way that had nothing to do with terror, or death, and everything to do with being needed. He even lifted my hand to his mouth, pressing his lips firmly against my fingers as if to steady himself. Much later, when I asked him about that moment, he didn't remember touching me at all that afternoon.

Now the ring of the phone brings me back from such thoughts. It's Judy, calling from the bookstore. Her voice is tight, breathy. "Come over. Can you?"

"What's wrong?"

"It's Tess. Can you come *now*?"

The hot asphalt surface of the parking lot is a field of puddles dimpled by a sizzle of rain. Judy Allard is at the front of the bookstore, making change for an elderly man in a yellow mackintosh. Judy is plump, lively, about forty, her strawberry-blond hair a crown of curls. Her customer nods, actually bows a little, as she tells him good-bye in her husky, smoker's voice. She turns and smiles at me. If she hadn't hung up on me just now, to make me hurry, I'd never have guessed she's upset.

The farm report for today, August 5, is on the radio here in the back corner she refers to as her office. "Hogs are an eighth to two-eighths higher. Corn down an eighth." Last night at supper Charlie was explaining a jump in clover-seed yields, from one to sixteen bushels an acre, after he set one of his farmers up with maximum bee pollination. Crops are beginning to interest me.

Judy frowns as she approaches. *Soybeans steady*. Out of the small refrigerator on the end of the table, which doubles as her desk, she takes a wedge of cheese and a large can of V-8 pierced by crusty, triangular pour-holes. She dumps a box of Wheat Thins into a basket lined with a paper napkin. "Did you see Mr. Fredericks?" She points toward the front of the shop. "He wanted to know why I named the store Little Reed. 'Past tense,' I kept telling him, 'past tense. Like the color red.' He doesn't get it."

I turn the radio off. "What's this about Tess?"

Judy pulls her lips between her teeth and looks away. Finally she inhales deeply and blows air out through ballooned cheeks. "She's probably at a friend's house, hiding out." The little bell at the front door dings. "Honestly, before I called you, hardly a soul had darkened my door all morning." She escapes toward the sound, but I'm right behind her, and I stay at her elbow while she collects for a magazine. The customer is a clerk from Ace Hardware around the corner.

In contrast to her white blouse, Judy's skin is almost blue, like skim milk, a real achievement in Iowa, in August. She avoids the sun like a mole because of a tendency to freckle. I notice she's wearing a nicotine patch on her upper arm, something she's tried before. She's worrying the edges of the shiny patch with her pink fingernails as the customer finally leaves. "Stress makes me crave cigarettes all the more." She pauses, changes her mind about something. "Tess was helping me on Saturday."

"I know. I saw her. I even took her picture."

When we get back to the rear of the store, Judy puts her hand on the phone. "She rode her bike over wearing a really short dress, and I was mad at her. I don't like my daughter showing her ass all across town. I wanted her to go back with me. She took off in a huff. Her bike was found under a bridge out by the interstate. The

last thing she said to me was 'You always expect me to be perfect.
I wish I could live somewhere else,' and I said, 'By the time I get
home, you'd better be there.' "

"But she wasn't."

"No."

"You mean you haven't seen her since then?"

Judy shakes her head. She's looking at her hands, fingers inter-
locked and shaking. "Tess has stayed out all night three other times
this summer. When she comes home the next day, she refuses to
say where she's been. Last time she did this, Bill wanted her to
spend some time at the youth shelter, for a cooling-off period, but
I didn't want to admit we couldn't handle the situation. This time
I just figured she was testing us again."

"For *three nights*?"

"I know." She looks like she might cry. "Yesterday I kept reaching for the phone to call you, and then I'd convince myself I had
to keep the line free. You haven't come around much lately. I know
something's going on with you and Charlie, but I need you, too.
The vast majority of runaways return within forty-eight hours, on
their own. Did you know that?"

"I must have been the last person to see her—"

"So maybe she's not a runaway. Maybe someone did something
to her. Sunday morning Bill started talking to people, retracing her
steps. All I could manage was waiting by the phone. When she
wasn't home by last night, I went cold as ice at how passive I'd
been. Bill says I only care about what people think, but, of course,
he's as scared as I am. I'm just paralyzed, remembering her face as
she stormed out of here." Judy hugs herself, stroking her arms for
friction. " 'Cold as ice,' those are Bill's words. He doesn't mention
Luci's murder, but when I look at his eyes, I know that's what he's
afraid of. I kept thinking Tessie was about to show up, or call again.
I still think that. Don't you think she will? Say yes."

"More likely she'll walk through the door."

"She said something else. She said, 'I'm so tired of watching you every minute.' "

"What did she mean?"

"It can't be good." The front of Judy's white blouse strains apart in crescents. She pulls on a bust-level button nervously. "I'm afraid of her, Linda. She has something in her we didn't put there, some influence. She's the one who bears watching, not the other way around. Don't say you were the last person to see her. It sounds like you mean *ever*." She flinches as the bell signals the arrival of another customer.

It's the paper carrier, a tan-haired boy of about ten, with *The Linden Times*. She's reading from it as she walks back toward me. "I wanted to tell you before you saw this. We should have called the cops sooner. We just kept thinking she'd come home."

The fuzzy photo of Tess smiling with her lips held carefully together is from last year, when she wore braces on her teeth and still looked like a little girl. That was before her torso lengthened and she started wearing lipstick and short dresses, like in the five shots of her and Russell Weber scattered across my worktable. In one of them she is trying not to smile at him. It's not hard to imagine that Luci might have looked at Weber in that coy way. But Tess? "She's an innocent girl."

"That's the whole point, isn't it?" Judy sinks into a chair and covers her face.

"Let me help," I murmur as she takes a shuddering breath. "I'll enlarge one of the pictures I took of Tess Saturday, make copies." Cropped, of course. With Russell Weber cut away.

Maybe Luci was right when she accused me once of being too self-contained, minding my own business instead of getting involved to the point of friendship in the lives of people around me. If only I had put down my camera and walked across the parking lot, before Weber showed up, and said, "Hey, Tess. What's with the angry face? Who you mad at?" As I stroke Judy's hair, I realize how absorbed I've been in my own worries. "Has Tess ever talked about Russell Weber?"

Judy's lips part soundlessly, as if some terrible possibility is dawning for the first time. "Why?"

"Has she?"

"No."

As I tell her about the conversation I witnessed between her daughter and Weber on Saturday, I remember another picture I took, the one of John Bender, watching from the alley. I wasn't the last person to see Tess in the neighborhood. While I was taking *that* picture, Weber must have seen Tess get on her bicycle and ride away.

In the clearest photo Tess's face is turned to the left, in profile, talking to Weber without looking at him. He is looking at her feet, suggesting a furtive exchange that I entirely missed until now. Or maybe the camera is lying, in the same way the human eye can lie. I walk to the back window of the studio. Judy has locked up Little Read and gone home. The rain is over for now, leaving the sky a dark navy blue. I return to stare at the copper plate lying on the table, at that empty, unfinished sky over the house where Luci died.

I'm more certain than ever that Charlie was wrong when he said there is no one out there who could harm us. In a flash Tess is sprawled the way Luci lay, and I stand up abruptly, reminding myself Tess is just an angry kid, making her mother pay. When I showed her these photographs, Judy saw nothing at all stealthy in the way Weber looks at Tess. Such is the power of denial in the eye of the beholder.

According to Judy, Bill has organized an afternoon search of the wooded area adjacent to the abandoned railroad trestle where Tess's bicycle was found, so I drive out past the edge of town to where the blacktop turns to gravel. The long, multicolored gauze skirt I've got on is not really appropriate for tramping through underbrush, but I don't want to take the time to go home and change. If Tess is with someone who wishes her harm, finding her could be a race.

Three other cars are already parked off the road by the time I arrive to begin the walk along the muddy trail. The tracks that lay along this raised bed have been replaced by parallel paths worn by hikers. Branches of trees meet overhead, loaded with songbirds. After about ten minutes I can see a section of chain-link fence across the path in the distance. Behind me I think I hear a car door, but when I look back the way I've come, I see nothing but a star-shaped piece of sky at the end of the tunnel of trees. Up ahead the fence marks the place where the bridge once took off over the wide creek bed. It's there to save me from walking off the edge of the earth. A twig snaps behind me, but this time I don't look back.

When I get to the steep path around the right-hand edge of the fence, I slide down to to a level, dirt area beside the concrete footings for the ruined trestle. I can't see water through the brush, but I can hear it. Clouds of tiny black midges hang in the humid air. The timbers of the collapsed trestle lie carelessly strewn below, across the deep ravine, like Lincoln Logs. There's ample evidence kids meet here—beer cans and the charred remains of a campfire inside a circle of rocks. One of the two-foot-thick timbers is charred, and the stone-gray concrete bridge support is cool to my touch and covered with graffiti. Crouching, I grip a fistful of damp, black dirt and hold it until it warms in my hand. I wish I could believe that Tess herself stood on this very spot, and that if I concentrate hard enough on this fistful of dirt, I might imagine where she went from here. It's the sort of fanciful impulse I'd expect of Rosemary Lindstrom, Charlie's secretary, who is known for her uncanny way of revealing secrets by holding inanimate objects in her hands. I drop the fistful of dirt in a hurry.

Tess is so smart she skipped a grade. Last summer when she used to come over to my studio and watch me work, I'd give her paper and oil pastels and she'd draw happily for hours. She got her ears pierced the day she got her braces off, though her parents had forbidden it. This summer she's been too busy to come see me at work, busy with things I don't know about, apparently—like staying out all night. She's shy and quiet, a personality that masks her cleverness and maybe unhappier traits as well. It's not a lot to know about a person.

All of a sudden, with a violent updraft of sound, birds rise straight up in fright from the trees, wings beating the air. A painful drumming enters my chest. John Bender is sliding down the embankment, gripping the fence post to stop himself. He sees my expression. It takes all my breath to say, "What do you think happened to Tess?"

He's watching me closely. "I figure she met someone here, someone with a car. But none of her high-school friends saw her Saturday night." I look toward the closest of the two concrete supports, which is a good four feet wide and six feet tall. Tess's name appears there like magic—bold and prominent, though the surface is solid with color. The letters are layered over earlier graffiti and embellished with vines and flowers, like a book illumination, the S's curved as snakes. Under her name is a bright red heart, and under that another name, painted in the same elaborate style. I walk over to the wall and trace the serpentine S's, then the heart, with my fingertips. Bender is right beside me. I'm so panicked I feel as if breathing is an act of will.

We both stare at the snarl of spray paint and chalk, sentiments so weathered as to be illegible with a kind of chaotic and—because Tess is gone—sinister beauty. "I never would have picked that out," he says. "And here you see it right away. 'Tess loves Russ.' " He clears his throat. "Jesus." He studies the colorful surface up and down. Then he leans against the concrete. His favorite posture, it seems. His left shoulder bruises with color that rubs off the concrete onto his shirt, orange browning into blue.

"You know the other day when I was getting my hair cut in Le's?" I ask him. "When you followed me down there?"

"I wasn't following you."

"You weren't going down there to get your hair cut." He fingers what I know is the usual red rubber band at the nape of his neck. "You don't seem like someone who'd frequent such a place. Russell Weber was in the salon at the time. Maybe he's the one you were checking out. Maybe you thought there might be some other business going on down there besides hair." I stare at the TESS and RUSS, separated by the valentine stand-in for the word "love." "You think this could be Russell Weber?"

Before he can answer, we both turn our heads toward the sound of voices and the rustling of someone tramping through the underbrush. John moves uphill a bit, shading his eyes.

"If I had known about your interest in Weber," I say, "I'd have been across that parking lot like a shot when I saw Tess talking to him. Detective Hansen asked me what I thought they might have to talk about." I pause to swallow before I continue the lie. "Hansen has a pretty good idea."

"What did he tell you?"

"He told me why you've been watching Weber."

"I keep my eye out to help Hansen, but I've never seen Weber pass anything to anyone. Maybe he's clean. I can't go around starting rumors and blow Hansen's investigation."

I remember one of the photos: The Girl and The Cook, refusing to look at each other, all four hands out of sight for the moment my camera happened, by chance, to record. Suddenly the sounds around me rise to a level I can't ignore: the sweep of the stream below, the dreary buzz of insects, the distant throb of trucks on the interstate—sounds that surge up through my body as I brace myself. "The high-school auto-mech teacher is due back in a couple days from a family vacation," Bender says. "I'm going to find out what he remembers about Luci's car. You're not afraid of where this might lead me, are you?"

I falter, wiping the sweat off my upper lip with the back of my hand. A series of shouts off in the distance come closer, and I sink heavily, hugging my knees to my chest, hearing a roar. Crouching down in front of me, Bender gently lowers my hands from my ears, his face so close I avert my eyes and stare at the thin white line of scar on his suntanned right hand and the oval red stain on my fingertip, from the graffiti heart. Rubbing finger and thumb together makes the color spread, and onto the palm of my left hand when I try that. Even when I close my eyes tight, I see red.

"Don't try to talk."

I raise my head and glare at him.

He says my name gently, coaching me to lift my shoulders with his, exhaling when he does. "Yes," he prompts me. "Good." Gradually my heart slows. His face is still close to mine, until the moment embarrasses me and I stumble to my feet. He's kneeling on the hem of my long skirt, and I lurch sideways to pull free.

His hands grip my shoulders just long enough to steady me, and then I twist away to look longingly at the uphill path leading over the embankment above. "She has to be okay."

"We'll find her."

"Hansen didn't tell me Russell Weber is suspected of dealing drugs. I was bluffing," I manage to say at the very moment Bill appears out of the brush, his round face shiny with the heat and the band of his green baseball cap stained with sweat. I can't tell from his grim expression whether the news is good or bad.

"We didn't find anything," Bill says to Bender, who says, "Thank God." Bender proceeds to introduce me to the other two men, Alan Gunderson and Robert Reed. They nod, wiping their faces with handkerchiefs, silent with fatigue.

Bender falls into step with me as we walk to our cars. Ahead of us, Bill Allard smooths the back of his head with his left hand, replacing his green bill cap on his shiny, bald head and quickening his pace as if he could know he fits the description of the man Detective Hansen told me was seen emerging from the woods on the day Luci was killed. Bill knew Luci in college, long before I knew her in art school. For the first time I wonder if their friendship was as innocent as everyone thought.

As usual, Bender is pretending not to watch me. "Thanks for the breathing lessons," I tell him, "but don't get the idea that makes us a team."

I sit in my car for a few minutes while the others pull out and head for town. Bender is the last to go. He actually waves. Something dark and immense blocks the sun, and I lock my doors. It's only a cloud full of rain, which moves on, giving back the light, but not the heat. I put my car into gear. Driving on loose gravel will require unhurried acceleration, so as not to skid and slide and lose control. Being seen in a fit of hysteria by John Bender has turned my fear to anger. I open the window and taste the metallic, storm-laden air. Something tells me I've suffered my last panic attack.

As soon as I get to my studio, I call Ken Hansen to tell him about the snapshots I have of Tess Allard. "A recent photo might help," he says, "if this doesn't get resolved right away. The girl's been abusing alcohol, coming home in bad shape. Her dad thinks she's been experimenting with other substances as well." Hansen wants me to hang on to the photos for now, but when I describe Tess standing next to Weber, smoke rising from his mouth, right shoulder nearly touching the back of the girl's head, the detective says he'll come right over and get them.

I've fanned out the pictures in my hand. I ask Hansen if he's ever suspected Russell Weber of illegal activity, but he doesn't answer right away. I figure he can't tell me that kind of information. The photo of Bender alone in the alley is on the bottom of my hand, at the far right. I pull it out so I can see it better, as if it were a card I don't know how to play. Hansen is telling me he has already questioned Weber about Tess's disappearance because Bender remembered seeing them together on Saturday.

6 ◆ As soon as I get home, I try to call Judy. Her line is busy. From where I stand just inside the kitchen, I can see Charlie in his recliner in the living room, the newspaper folded and forgotten over his knees. I know I don't have to explain that my rush to the phone has to do with the front-page story about Tess. Usually when I open the back door, the sound brings him into the kitchen, to kiss me hello.

Finger still on the switch hook, I tell him about the place her bicycle was found, about Judy's denial of the danger Tess might be in, and about Bill and the other men searching along Onion Creek. I tell him the police have questioned Russell Weber, because she was seen talking with him behind the Grubstake right before she disappeared. "I'll bet Judy's talking to Tess right now. Or someone's found her. Otherwise they'd be keeping the line free."

Charlie comes to stand close enough for me to touch his arm. "If Bill was raising volunteers," he says, "I wonder why he didn't call me."

I never thought of that.

"I know the place you mean. I used to go out there when I was visiting my grandparents, to drink beer and sing dirty songs."

"And spray-paint your initials? Did you do that?"

"Considering what kids write on walls these days, those were innocent times." His expression alters, but he can't quite smile.

This time when I punch the tune of the Allards' number, the phone purrs three times, and Judy answers. "Bill was talking to someone about doing flyers with that picture you took. We have to keep this short. I made him go take a shower. He said he saw you this afternoon with a reporter. What was that all about?"

"I'll do anything I can to help. Charlie, too. I'll blow up the picture tonight and bring it over." She sniffs softly as I describe the graffiti, the bright colors and layers of lines, a record of generations of area teenagers who have survived adolescence to become fine adults, just as Tess will.

Charlie looks sadder than I've ever seen him, lines carved into his forehead and down from the sides of his nose. The thought that Peter Garvey, a local boy once, too, might have written his name there when he was a kid presents itself in my mind and is covered over immediately by the gestural S's of TESS and RUSS. "When she comes back," I say to Judy, "I should give her some real drawing lessons. I could tell she did those initials herself. She has a good mark." Judy sniffs again. "I know Tess knows Russell Weber. Does she know anyone else named Russ?"

"Yeah. He was her steady boyfriend."

"*Is.*"

"She broke up with Rusty a few weeks ago. She actually told us about it."

"Rusty?"

"Rusty Burkhalter. You know Mandy and Fred Burkhalter?"

"No."

"You're lucky."

It's such a relief to learn about this other Russ, a red-haired boy, a reasonable candidate for having his name chalked on the trestle pillar. "Whose idea was it to break up, hers or his?"

"Hers. Our all-too-obvious relief really set her off, though."

"So she wasn't surprised or hurt by the breakup." I wait a minute, until Judy's finished blowing her nose. "Not despondent or anything."

"Definitely not despondent. More like royally pissed. This is not it, Linda."

Judy asks to get off the phone, but when I hang up, it immediately rings again. It takes a beat or two for me to realize whose voice I'm hearing: "My mom isn't there, is she?"

"No, Tess. Where are you?"

Charlie stays where he is, relief rolling across his features like water over sand, removing the lines from his forehead and around his eyes. "Our line's been busy," Tess is saying. "Then I got so scared they'd answer this time, I called you instead."

"Tell me where you are."

She makes the jerky inhaling sound children make when they've been crying themselves to exhaustion. "I'm not really ready to talk to my mom yet anyway. Or Daddy either. Can you come get me?"

"If you'll tell me where you are." This time she does. She's in Creston, a town about sixty miles from here, calling from a minister's house, a Reverend Cooper. "He's really nice," she says sweetly, as if she's been away at camp. I'm sure he's standing right there.

"I'll call your folks for you as soon as we hang up."

"How about if just *you* come?"

"You've scared them to death. It's their place to come get you. Nothing's changed that, has it?"

"I guess not."

"You're all right?"

"Yes." Her voice is small and tired.

"I'm very glad you called here, Tess. So is Charlie."

"Yeah, well, I saw my face in *The Des Moines Register* this morning."

"It was in *The Linden Times*, too."

She groans. "Seeing that picture, I got really scared for the trouble I've caused. You took that snapshot of me on my birthday last year, remember? You came over and brought me some pearl earrings because Mom had told you I wanted to get my ears pierced, but Daddy hadn't given permission. So there was this big fight after you went home, you know, like one of those really stupid arguments they have over some little thing that's supposed to be about me and then ends up leaving me out. Seeing that picture scared me, but it made me feel good, too. My mom admires you. She talks about you all the time. I thought you'd be someone who maybe they'd listen to, if you know what I mean. I could always talk to you anyway."

"It's been a long time since we had a good conversation, Tess. I miss your coming over to talk while I work. I guess this summer hasn't been an easy one. But as for your folks, I think you have their attention."

"I just want to come home."

"We'll be there in an hour."

"I cut my hair," she says hopefully, as if she's not quite ready to end the conversation.

"Stay put, okay? We all love you."

The Reverend Cooper gets on the phone and assures me she's fine. I write down the address before I hang up, and Charlie calls out from the other room, wanting to know where she's been all this time. He's angry.

My throat contracts, and I'm mutely shaking my head no because we still don't know where she's been, and there could be something terrible in the answer to that question. When I recover myself, all I can say is "She cut her hair." I step into the doorway so I can see him while I press the buttons of Judy's number one more time. He's pacing the living room, fists at his sides.

When I hang up the phone, Charlie says, "You can count me out." With both hands he combs his hair back from his temples and forehead two, three times. "She's had half the town thinking she's been kidnapped, or raped. Or worse. Staying away this long is not a lark. If she were mine, I'd lock her up for a month."

"I think we should offer to drive Judy and Bill to get her, upset as they are. It would really help them. Anyway, Tess asked me to come. You'll be over your anger by the time we get there. She's safe, Charlie. I don't understand your reaction. She's coming home."

He walks to the front door, where he stands looking out across the gravel drive and the lawn and the road and the cornfield beyond. Judy and Bill are probably waiting at their front window, watching for us, resenting Tess for pulling us into her homecoming. Charlie's stillness hangs in the air like an unfinished conversation. When he turns around at last, he sits on the sofa and puts his face in his hands. I'm not sure touching him is the comfort he needs; I'm not sure what he's thinking. So I simply sit beside him, and he says, "You go. You don't need me. I think I'll move Luci's things out of the garage tonight. I wish to hell I hadn't hired Weber to help build that garage. Now every time I hear his name, I can't help wondering what Luci might have done with him behind my back. I need to get her out of my life for good. Lately everything reminds me of her."

"We can move her things another time, Charlie. Right now we can help Judy and Bill. I don't feel like going without you. I want you with me."

Charlie's look tells me that's just what he wanted to hear.

After his attempt at refusal in the living room, Charlie stood up and said, "Okay, I guess we'd better go, then," and proceeded to drive us all in his rattletrap, cavernous van to Creston. Tess has cut her hair short as a boy's—a spiky flattop with a tiny, braided tail at the nape of her neck. She's dressed like a boy, too, in faded jeans and a London Hard Rock Café T-shirt that looks as though it's been used to polish furniture.

Charlie hasn't stopped talking since Judy and Bill rushed down their driveway to get into the van, and now he's dominating the conversation on the ride home from Creston, too. Tess claimed the passenger seat up front with him, slipping past me as soon as I opened the door—despite the protests of both parents, who wanted her in the backseat with them. Now Charlie's trying to relieve the tension by telling one of his bee stories, the one about the Carmichaels, who live north of town and who do organic, no-till gardening and whose bees kept vanishing by the hundreds last summer.

"How would you solve this mystery?" Charlie has just asked Tess. "I made five trips out to the Carmichael place in a two-month period last summer, and every time I installed a new package of bees, I'd get a call in a few days that there were hardly any survivors left in the hives."

Judy, sitting between me and Bill, sighs every few minutes. "We shouldn't have let them do this," I hear Bill say, though his voice is low.

"You mean drive?" I bend forward to look past Judy. Bill is looking straight ahead. "We really wanted to help."

"Yeah," he says. "I'm sure it was a relief to her." Leaning forward, he reaches between the front seats toward Tess's shoulder.

She shrugs off her father's touch. "I don't know," she says flatly to Charlie. She's looking off to the right, where the sky has the same layered, silver sheen of another evening, another mackerel sky.

Bill freezes, his arm extended for long seconds, and when he sits back again, it's with a shrug of frustration. Judy's left hand goes onto his knee. "We'll be home soon," she whispers. The thin stripes of Bill's black-and-white shirt and his high, pale forehead render him more visible in the dim light of the van than is Judy, who in pink seems to fade away. "Count to ten. Empty your mind."

"Well, *think*," says Charlie to Tess. "You've got a lot of missing bees. What could the culprit be? You're the detective."

"Bee detective?" Tess says, a drone of sarcasm in her voice. "Yeah, right." In the brief sweep of light from an oncoming car, her profile turns toward him, her forehead and nose shiny, her haircut revealing the delicate stem of her neck.

"This is a serious matter," responds Charlie, meaning it. "They have an orchard, and alfalfa to sell for cash, and they'll lose most of their crops without pollination. They depend on bees."

Judy clears her throat, and I nudge her gently with my elbow. Silently I hope Tess cooperates with Charlie's attempt to make this seem like a normal outing. The van's tires tick over the lines of this often-mended section of road, and Bill coughs once. "Why does she want to look like that?" he asks. "And who gave her that shirt?"

With this, Judy stiffens, addressing her daughter for the first time since we all shut ourselves into the van together. "You know that picture Linda took of you out back on Saturday, Tess, just before you left? I've been imagining your face on the sides of milk cartons, all in a row at Hy-Vee. Your long, shiny hair. Looks like you were trying to make yourself look as different from that girl as possible."

"What picture?" Tess has risen up to look over the back of her seat, right at me. She's definitely not pleased.

"You were busy talking," I tell her. "Behind the restaurant. You didn't see me."

Her eyes narrow, lips parting. "Well, aren't you full of surprises," she says at last. Then she rises up even more in her seat, moving her gaze from me to Charlie, then to her father, then her mother, fixing each of us with a glare of accusation. Finally she settles down again so I can't see her face. "You never know when you can trust a person, do you?" she says, in a tone only Charlie is meant to hear.

"What about the bees?" he asks her.

"The bees have a disease."

Judy's laugh is manic. Against my left shoulder, I feel her tense. *"Leave it alone,"* I whisper. We'd all rather listen to Charlie talk about bees than witness an explosion of feelings here in this confined space. "Put your hand back on Bill's knee."

"This road is for shit," he's calling out to Charlie, over wind noise and rattles. "I don't know why you came this way." The van smells faintly of honey, though there's none on board.

"There are no bodies, so it can't be disease," Charlie is saying. "Guess again."

"Then I suppose it was a bee thief," says Tess wearily.

"Be serious," says Charlie. He glances over at Tess as she twists her body to face him again.

She pulls backward slightly, her face in profile. She's not too sure of this. "Be serious?" she echoes.

Charlie deepens his already deep voice. "There are no serious bee thieves around these parts, I assure you. Here's a hint. It has something to do with religion."

"Religion?"

"Religion."

Judy sighs.

"She's a bit beyond bee thieves, Charlie." This is Bill. "She's fifteen."

"You're the one who forgets she's not a child anymore," Judy says to him coldly.

"A cult got them," guesses Tess, turning to frown at her father, as if to say he's wrong to fault Charlie. For him she has a smile, and finally a playful tone: "They sacrificed the bees to the gods on tiny altars."

"Be serious," pipes up Judy beside me.

Tess leans over between the divided front seats to give her mother another long look. "Well?" she wants to know, turning back to Charlie. "Am I getting warm?"

"I'll give you another hint," he says. "It has to do with praying."

"Praying?" Tess pauses for thought. "Let me get this straight. The bees disappeared, right? And this really happened, right? You're not making it up?"

"I'm not making it up. You can ask Linda."

That she ignores. "Okay. The bees disappear because someone prays."

"Not exactly some*one*," admits Charlie. "Not even I would refer to an insect as some*one*."

"Yeah, because they don't have souls. So insects don't pray. So this is ridiculous. They're atheist bees," she adds, looking over at Charlie for approval.

"Say that again?"

"Atheists."

"No. Before that."

"Insects don't pray."

"Don't they?"

"Okay," says Tess. And then, "Oh. I get it. They prey, right?" As in eat each other?"

In the dim light of the car Charlie nods.

"But that's not fair."

"Fair has nothing to do with it," says Charlie. "The Carmichaels don't use insecticides, don't believe in them, and they had a bumper crop of pests, so they ordered a large shipment of—are you ready?"

"Yeah?" says Tess suspiciously.

"European mantis egg cases. Ordered them from a catalog." He looks away from the road to see Tess's reaction. "You know, praying mantis. *Mantis religiosa.*"

It's Judy's turn to groan.

"Jesus," says Bill.

"Those skinny, long-legged insects that look like twigs and that fold their bony hands and pray?" Tess makes a laughing sound like air leaking from a balloon. "I learned about those in school. They prayed the bees would die, I suppose."

"They ate them," says Charlie as the van clatters over a bump.

"They hated them?"

"They *ate* them. By the bucketful. The Carmichaels had read that mantises are biological control agents. But what they didn't know is that mantises don't discriminate. So they become pests themselves. And there were a lot of them. They preyed on the bees, get it?"

"Ohhh," moans Tess.

"A real sweet feast," says Charlie, slowing for the exit off the interstate.

"So how did you get rid of these pests?"

"That's the best part of the story." Charlie clears his throat importantly. "The female mantis," he begins, "usually devours the male during mating, so I lit candles and played soft music in the fields, and they romanced themselves to death."

Bill has been still for a while, but for some reason this makes him shift his body.

"Entomology is full of mysteries and passions," says Charlie darkly, hamming it up for Tess, who chuckles again. "Few people realize that." She's looking out the window to her right at her own tree-lined street, the lineup of houses on well-kept lawns, porch lights on. We're all silent for a moment, until she says, "But all the females would have been left. The lady mantises would have been just fine, and probably still hungry for bees. So I question that part of the story."

"Well, here's an interesting fact," he says, looking to the left, signaling for a turn. "Because mantises can move their heads freely, they're the only insects who can turn to see who's behind them." Pulling into the Allards' driveway, he shifts into park and cranks the emergency brake. "And they cock their heads to the side, like dogs."

Tess inclines her head his direction. "Like this?"

"Yes," he says, looking into the backseat, at each of us in turn, focusing on Bill longer than on anyone else. "Just like that. We're home."

Judy presses her body in my direction, anxious for me to open the side door and let them out. Tess hasn't made a move yet to open her door either. She bows her head and looks down to the right and then left in momentary confusion at undoing the seat belts in a vehicle she's not used to, and then she scoots to the front edge of her seat. "Thanks," she says to Charlie in a low voice, as though they've got something on the rest of us. Then she gives me a look so withering I'm sure that if she ever needs help again, I will be the last person on earth she will think to call.

When we pull into our driveway, Charlie stops short of the open garage door. He turns off the engine but doesn't make the moves that usually follow: opening the door and vaulting off the high seat onto the gravel drive. He's gazing through the windshield as if the trip's not over, hand still on the ignition. When I say his name, he pulls out the key and examines it as though it were suddenly very interesting. "I'm starving," I say, unbuckling my seat belt. "Let's go in."

"You took a picture of Tess when she didn't know you were doing it?"

"From the back of my studio."

"I see." He clears his throat. "I need to sit here a few minutes." As I reach to touch his arm, he signals my hand away with a forward shift of his body, circling his arms to lean against the steering wheel. "I'm not going anyplace, Linda. I'm asking for a few minutes alone, is all. I don't feel like explaining myself. Don't make an issue of it."

I go on in and start heating up the spaghetti sauce. When the van starts up, I go into the front room to watch out the window as he backs it around the front of the house, then pulls forward toward the road, finally backing into the long driveway. The rear doors of the van are only a couple of feet in front of the open garage. He's slid the van's side door open. The garage lights go on.

When he finally comes in a few minutes later, he says, "I'm getting rid of Luci's things. By myself. No discussion." I have the bottle of salad oil in my right hand, the vinegar in my left, and I lower them to the counter as he touches my shoulder, my hands still gripping like fists. "Can we please not discuss it?" he repeats with such firmness that I wonder if he means the opposite.

"Fine." I douse the salad with olive oil and red-wine vinegar. To my surprise, he fixes himself a plate of spaghetti and salad, pours himself a glass of ice water, and takes the food with him out the back door without a word. I step outside and watch him disappear into the garage. In a few seconds the lights go on in the room out there.

Twice while I'm moving food around my plate, trying to eat, he comes back into the house, once to get a roll of garbage bags out of the cabinet over the washing machine, then again for the broom we keep by the refrigerator. Last year, when I suggested we might clean out Luci's studio space so we could use it, he resisted. They weren't legally his things, he said then, because he and Luci weren't married. At the time I wasn't up to a debate over ownership, when to me, too, they were still *her things*, so I let it drop.

When I hear sounds of pounding and of wood breaking, and then the bounce and ring of something metal rolling across the concrete floor, I can't stay in the house any longer. "Don't get rid of her shoes, Charlie," I yell as I approach the door of the studio. "Save them, at least."

From the doorway I see he's got a length of splintered wood in his right hand. It's part of the loom, which lies at his feet, hinged together by the twisted folds of Luci's bright, beautiful tapestry. "Shoes?" he repeats, as if I've said something absurd.

"Yes, shoes. And I want to save that weaving."

"I'll roll it up." He begins jerking it free. "If you want it so much, I'll leave it. But I want to do this alone."

"So you said." I step back—and decide that I can't return to the house and listen to him so noisily destroy what little is left of Luci. I tell him I'm going to my studio for a while. Tired as I am, I'd rather get some work done of my own, something creative. "Something for you." He wipes his forearm across his sweaty forehead and refuses to ask me what I mean.

It's a natural enough impulse to think I can always escape into the comfort of work, but when I get to my studio, I realize I'm way too tired for this. As I get organized anyway, my heart sinks even more. The painting lacks even a single element to transcend the ordinary. It's a cheat, this sketch—okay for a real-estate ad maybe, but devoid of the strong, conflicting emotions I feel as I approach the actual place every day. That empty sky over the house says it all. *Empty.* Maybe this barren perspective is the real truth about what Charlie and I are coming to.

If I can't bring life into the composition, I'm going to have to start over. *Lower your brush,* I tell myself, given a push by memory. *Step up to the door full of sky, throw yourself onto the air.* Suddenly I feel, rather than see, that the lines of the composition have gathered around this empty space all along, like rays of light. *Lower your brush.*

I finish the plate in about an hour. When I get back home, completely worn out, Charlie is gone.

About ten miles west of our house there's a county landfill for non-garbage dumping—the Glory Hole, Charlie calls it—and I'm guessing he's taken Luci's things there, though I'd think the gate would be locked at this hour. He probably woke someone up to let him in. I take a quick shower and crawl into bed, but sleep is out of the question. I can't help thinking about the lanky blond man I saw leaving the house with a bandanna around his forehead and blood on his jeans.

When Charlie returns a while later, he comes into the bedroom and sits on his side of the bed, lowering himself slowly. "I'm awake," I tell him. He shifts his weight, dropping a shoe onto the floor with a thunk. The resinous smell of insect repellent has come into the room with him, and the salty sweetness of grit and perspiration. I lift myself up on one elbow. The hallway light is still on, and he looks at me over his shoulder.

"It upset me that you were rummaging through her things, Linda. I told you, there's no diary, if that's what you were looking for. I can't expect you to put it all behind you unless I am willing to do the same. Now we can use that room behind the garage for something else besides a shrine to Luci. Maybe now she'll leave us alone."

I sit up and reach out to touch him, my gesture falling short, I'm so unsure of what's happening. I've kept so many things from him—my trip to see Peter Garvey, the story he told me about a diary—to avoid his reaction. I've been wrong to do that.

"Try to sleep," he says gently. He's standing in the doorway, halfway out.

"I would have helped, you know, Charlie. Where did you take her things anyway?"

"The best way to help is to let me work this out in my own way. I don't want to hear her name for a while." He closes the door behind him.

Soon my thoughts drift to tomorrow, when I will work again on Charlie's print, when the ink will be dry enough for me to coat the copper plate, squeezing the viscous beeswax-asphaltum from a plastic bottle. In my imagination the dark stuff runs down to coat the entire plate until I can barely see the image underneath. To-morrow afternoon, after the dark beeswax has hardened on the copper plate, I'll run the hot water until steam rises, fill a water tray half full, and submerge the plate.

My heart always quickens at this point, when nothing matters but what's happening below the surface of the water. Cracks will appear on the dark skin as I watch the house begin to lift. I'm always tempted to stop short and preserve some of this unplanned texture. But gently tipping the tray to speed up the process, I know

I'll force myself to allow all of the painted image to separate from the plate this time—not stop early to work off the unexpected marks that delight me about printmaking. That's not the sort of surprise I'm going for this time. This one's for Charlie.

A couple of times, when the water's cooled, I'll have to drain the tray and fill it carefully with more hot water, until the image has lifted completely. Tonight when I lowered my brush to the empty sky above the roof, I finally saw what I'd saved the emptiness for—a fine, fat fish, long and light-bellied, ribbed with copper. Now I catch myself, jerking wide awake. So much depends on the way this turns out.

I've made it winter, for the sake of design, when branches cast shadows across the lawn like empty nets. The fish appears voluptuous over the house—quilted with overlapping scales that suggest the W shapes of flying birds—authentic down to its pointy dorsal fin and forked tail. I turn over onto my back. After what seems like an hour of concentrating on the emergence of *Mackerel Sky*, I'm no closer to sleep. I try to imagine Charlie receiving his gift and remembering the night he decided this was what he wanted—the last night we made love, I realize, counting backward through the days.

7 ◆ EXHAUSTED AS WE ARE, Charlie and I both work unusually long hours in the days that follow Tess's return. I place a call to a man named Robert Chapman, who is heading a marketing team for the Linden Grove Mall, which is being built on I-35 just east of town. After a trip to Des Moines to show him my portfolio, I secure an agreement to compete for the design job. I will bill him $60 per hour for visual-identity sketches—ideas for a logo that could be used on brochures, shopping bags, signage for each individual store and for a huge sign that could be seen from the highway. My drafting table is soon adrift with sketches of nearly round, heart-shaped leaves with toothed margins and of various configurations of linden trees with dense, oval crowns. The more sketches I produce, the more chance a good idea—combining original type with a defining image—will come to me.

Charlie calls the American linden by its more common name here in Iowa, basswood. He uses basswood for the frames of honeycombs because the wood is light and soft, easily worked, and imparts no taste or odor to food. His work is seasonal; in winter he prepares apiary supplies for the spring and does occasional cabinetmaking jobs for local people who know Charlie Carpenter as a man who lives up to his name.

The night Luci died, Detective Hansen got me a room at the Holiday Inn. He had suggested I see a doctor, maybe get something to help me relax, but I had declined. The motel bed was too soft. I was sick to my stomach, and freezing cold. My mind swarmed with details of what I had seen in that kitchen, and I heard unfamiliar sounds all night and couldn't sleep. By the time the sun came up the next morning, I was at my studio and had my coffeemaker plugged in at the desk. The neon sign for my front window, LINDA GARBO DESIGNS, had been delivered a couple of days earlier, and I turned it on for the comfort it gave me while the coffee perked. It was my place. It had my name on it.

I drank coffee until Ben Webb, the plumber, arrived at about nine with his helper. They were unloading supplies from their truck when Charlie showed up. He looked like he hadn't slept either. The skin under his pink-rimmed eyes was loose, and his lips looked chapped. I stood holding the back door open, watching him get out of his van, at a loss as to what I could say that would ease his mind. "What in the hell," he said slowly, "is *that*?"

Those words would lead to the best kind of comfort either of us could have wished for that day: work.

"Now, just wait a minute." Charlie's impatient tone stopped Ben Webb cold; he didn't move a muscle. Charlie was staring at the unsightly object Webb was pulling out of his truck—the kitchen cabinet I'd settled on so impulsively the morning before, when Luci was still very much alive and I had not wanted to spend another night under the same roof with her. The metal cabinet was so awful I'd been surprised that even Ben Webb, whose backroom proved he was a hopeless pack rat, had saved it.

"All I care about is that I have a home, as soon as possible," I said to Charlie. He didn't understand what I meant, of course. I had to explain about how the custom cabinets I'd ordered had been defective, and the replacements were on back order. And that only after the plumbing for the new kitchen area in the loft was inspected would I be granted a permit to live in my building. So this was temporary, this metal cabinet.

"You have coffee?" Charlie asked. I nodded. When I returned to the parking lot, Webb and his helper were in the backseat of Charlie's van, and Charlie opened the passenger-side door for me. He was taking charge, that was clear, but of *what* I couldn't be sure. I was too dazed from lack of sleep to question what was happening. I simply responded to his air of authority. "I don't know what to do with myself," Charlie said as we turned onto the main street and headed north. I never could drive with one hand and manage a cup of coffee with the other, the way Charlie can. He looked over at me. "At least we can save you from an ugly kitchen."

Charlie drove us to a row of storage buildings at the edge of town and raised the door on his collection of treasures from estate sales, flea markets, and salvage yards. With the help of the other two men, he moved a waist-high stack of flooring aside and dragged out a deep 1930s butler's sink set into a battered pine cabinet painted a warm, earthy red. "There's a countertop somewhere, too," he announced, heading back through a narrow aisle that led into the depths of the garagelike space. He was forgetting himself, excited to be producing something of use. In a few minutes he emerged towing a long slab of shiny, honey-colored wood. "It's teak," he said. "I found this under a layer of Formica, but I gave it lots of sanding and twelve coats of varnish. If you want it, it's yours."

I touched the smooth wood and accepted his offer. The three men and I spent the rest of the day creating a kitchen complete with glass-doored cabinets mounted above the counter. After the plumbing inspector stopped by just long enough to sign the permit for residential occupancy, around three-thirty, Charlie said, "One last thing, and then I'll go." He asked me to step up to the sink. "Notice anything unusual?"

The sink was a foot-deep rectangle, with straight sides and a ten-inch exterior lip across the front. The flawless, creamy porcelain felt smooth as a plate. "It's unique. That's even better than unusual."

"Pretend you're washing dishes. What's different?"

I let my hands drop into the sink, fingertips circling the drain. "There were moments, now and then," I said, "while we were getting this job done, that I wasn't thinking about what happened yesterday. Like when we were making this fit." My fingers followed the lip of the sink where we'd had to struggle to get the countertop to slide into place. I looked at him. "How are we going to live with what's happened, Charlie?" My eyes filled with tears, and all at once I leaned forward for support.

Side by side, we both had our hands in the sink. His shoulder was nearly touching mine, so close I could smell the damp, bitter scent of exertion on his skin. "This is six inches over standard," he said.

"Wide enough for two people to work in at once, is that what you mean?"

"Two *tall* people. Have you ever worked at a counter before where you didn't have to bend over? The countertop is six inches—"

"Higher than standard," I finished.

"It's right for you, Linda," he said.

As I stood there touching the bottom of that sink, I felt something shift, and it all hit me—the stress of pulling up roots and moving to Linden Grove, the horrific shock of discovering Luci's body three days later, the stupefying effects of sleep deprivation, the exhaustion from working alongside Charlie all day. Standing there, I knew that nothing about my life was going to feel familiar for a long time. Charlie was saying something about how tomorrow we could match that earthy red and repaint the cabinets, and then he stopped. I guess he realized what he was saying. In that moment I think we both saw how our common grief over Luci's death had disarmed us. We felt comfortable together, like old friends, but we barely knew each other.

Only one thing was certain. We were both hungry. That was something immediate, something we could do something about. My new kitchen had no food in it. "I know a place we can get a good pizza," he said.

The least I could do was buy his supper. I turned on the sink faucets, both hot and cold, to calm myself with the sound of running water. "Works good," said Charlie. He left then, so I could take a shower. An hour later we met at Mona's to share our first meal. And the next day we did paint the cabinets together after all.

It's been a week since John Bender waved good-bye to me out at the trestle. I haven't seen him since. I still look over my shoulder for him all day long; now it's his absence that makes me uneasy. As for Tess, Judy and Bill took her to Omaha a week ago for substance-abuse treatment, where they are joining her today for family therapy. Even Russell Weber is gone. When I stopped in the Grubstake on Friday for lunch, a plump, gray-haired woman in a flowered apron was in the kitchen. Angela just shrugged when I asked. "The register came up short a couple days in a row, and as soon as I noticed it, he stopped showing up," she said, counting out my change. "Just like that. No notice. I hadn't accused him. Just asked." She slammed the cash-register drawer harder than she needed to.

That sent me back to my studio to call Rosemary Lindstrom— The Fortune-teller, I call her. Charlie's secretary is something of a character to my mind, her powdered face made even paler by contrast to the crimson lipstick and tangled layers of necklaces I've rarely seen her without. I asked her to check on the exact date of Weber's work on the garage, the last day he would have been around Luci. I could hear those beads click as she came up with the answer: "Six days before she was killed." I heard a file drawer close. "I wish you wouldn't stir things up like this, Linda. Charlie's letting things slide here at work."

"Is that why you drove out to the house the other day?"

"I'm surprised he told you about that. I guess that explains why you're asking about Weber."

I remember her in the driveway, hands on hips. "You were pretty upset."

"We had a misunderstanding. I guess Charlie told you that, too."

At that she said good-bye and hung up while my mouth was still open. She wouldn't have ended the conversation so rudely unless she'd guessed he hadn't told me a thing.

As sunlight entered the bedroom this morning, while I was still squinting against the light and running my tongue over my teeth, Charlie murmured something about swarming bees. I closed my eyes again, drifting. He smelled like soap. The hair on his chest felt cool and damp to my fingertips. "It isn't as if I've wanted to keep things from you."

"Like what, Charlie?"

If he is ever going to answer that question, I guess it will have to be here, in an open pasture, away from the house. He's talked me into wearing one of his long-sleeved shirts tucked into long pants for protection from the bees. I feel like a giant bride, decked out in ankle and wrist clips, gloves, and a brimmed hat with a veil that filters the meadow into soft focus as I follow him uphill toward the row of white box hives at the edge of Carmichael's pasture. "I'll make sure nothing happens to you," he's saying. He knows bees scare me; he doesn't know how much. "You just need to know what you're doing. Honeybees are not aggressive."

Charlie ascends the rise to Carmichael's orchard faster than I do, his khaki coveralls a blur up ahead. I hate having my vision obscured. I know I lowered the veil too soon, but the two times I've been stung by bees in my life, the swelling was painful. The last time I ran a slight fever. I'm getting nervous. Carrying a small pack on his back and the new hive frames on his shoulder, Charlie is gesturing to the left, pointing out the honey plants for this late in the season: clusters of sweet clover and spikes of goldenrod; tall, scraggly aster plants—browned out and brittle, but bearing pink and lavender blooms; and wild pansies, or heartsease—so called, Charlie is shouting back to me over his shoulder, because they were once believed to cure the pains of love. He lets me catch up.

The grasses of the meadow are high and tangled with the stiff sienna and ocher remnants of last year's growth. The sky is a cloudless, faded blue. An early morning like this, when the weather is warm and forage is abundant and most of the insects are out of the hive, is ideal for multiplying colonies, Charlie is explaining as I reach his side. "Making increase," he calls it, a term that rings false, like bad Indian dialogue in old Western movies. Under my veil I smell coffee on my breath. I'm starting to sweat. At the edge of the orchard it's a bit cooler.

Hefting the new hive onto the ground beside the tallest stack in the lineup of eight at the edge of the apple orchard, Charlie swings his pack off and takes out a large piece of netting to cover his own head and a smoker that looks like a small oilcan with a bellows on its back. Lighting it, he runs puffs of smoke along the bottom of the hive and around the lid before he pries off the top of the old hive. He faces away from me, and I keep my distance.

"We've lost ground this summer, haven't we," Charlie says, "you and I? In our marriage, I mean." He glances at me.

It's the kind of question that contains its own answer. "Love has to go through changes. There are setbacks. Is that what you mean?"

"I'm not sure I see the point in talking about love," he says. "Saying the word doesn't make a person loyal." He observes the open top of the hive for long seconds before he says, "I just don't want to lose it."

"Feelings, you mean?"

"Your attention. My feelings for you are not going to change,

Linda. I don't want to lose your attention. You've been preoccupied. We haven't been speaking our minds. Either of us. I've been guilty of it, too."

I step closer. "You know why," I say softly. Despite the heat, I shiver as a bee bumps with an angry buzz against the gauze of my veil. His declaration the night he cleared out Luci's things, *I don't want to hear her name for a while,* turned out to be more than a request inspired by exhaustion. Whenever I've mentioned her since, he has held up his hand, palm forward, and stopped me with one word: *Please.*

As if we're of one mind, he says, "It was wrong of me to declare any subject off-limits." He removes the glove from his right hand, and I know Luci is about to become the subject of this conversation. But then he says, "I have to look for the queen."

I guess he'll let me know when he finds her. He can take his time. As I survey the pasture, locusts tune up to emit a louder and louder ratchet of noise that suddenly subsides for a couple of minutes before the cycle starts up again. I try to relax by taking a deep breath. Behind me, Charlie does his work.

When I asked him once, soon after Luci's murder, if he believed in life after death, he explained how bees survive the Iowa winter—not going dormant or dying in favor of a new generation waiting to hatch in the spring like other insects, but clustering into an engine of heat from the furious wing-beating of their thoracic muscles. Deep in snow, the hives keep humming away. "So what are you suggesting?" I wanted to know.

"We fight for life as long as we can, but then we die. Death isn't a next step, a phase in our growth. That's like saying divorce is a stage of marriage, or that a fatal heart attack is a stage of exercise. Death isn't a stage of life, it's the end of it. We'll never see her again, in another life. Death is not sentimental. Luci's gone." He paused to think. "Unless there's a next generation to continue. I suppose that's a kind of survival, too, the survival of the species, of the race."

Now here we stand, under the apple trees, replacing a queen while Charlie works up the nerve to tell me something he couldn't tell me at home. If he persists in being so mysterious, this time I'm going to ask.

Dangling from my right hand, in a small paper bag, is a lump of honeycomb that holds an unborn queen. He entrusted it to me back at The Honey Barn as if I were about to participate in an important transaction, and I accepted the role with the same patient eagerness with which I'd watched him point out that the queen cell was larger than the others and protruded from the comb like the end of a peanut shell. He cut her away in her tiny square of beeswax comb. "I won't be able to see much from behind this veil," I say now.

"Sure you will." He lifts the upper section of the hive and sets it on the ground, which increases the volume of the hum from inside. I rear back as he tilts the hive cover on its edge and uses it as a seat, proceeding to direct a few more puffs of smoke at the entrance to the hive and across the top before he pries off the inner lid. "See them scramble?" He leans over the hive and looks where he wants me to look. I turn my face away. "They're going for the honey cells to save what they can. Instinct tells them there's a fire."

I take his word for it, swallowing, fighting instincts of my own. My mouth is dry. I suppose this is where Charlie is most at ease these days. He selects a frame from the hive and takes it over to the new box and inserts it, trading it for an empty one. "Remember last fall?" he asks. "When I killed most of the bees?"

Charlie depends on the weather a lot in his business, and now he reminds me how last fall he studied the historical weather cycles and read about sunspots, concluding that the winter ahead would be long and harsh. He was right. It was a winter not so much of snow but of ice and dangerous wind-chill readings, with more days below zero than usual. In the evenings, because of the ice and the wind, branches of trees behind the house would break under the force of their own weight, snapping with loud reports, like gun-shots.

He pulls frame after frame from the hive as he talks. Even though he expected the harsh weather, and killed most of his bees during the fall to make the winter feed supply stretch, many that survived were killed by the cold, wet, windy weather of last spring, a spring so nasty that the half-starved bees couldn't start their nor-mal nectar-gathering chores. By April he'd lost most of the bees that had started the winter. So now, to build his colonies back up, he's dividing hives. And he's brought me with him today to talk about the discomforts of love.

The other night he started knocking out a wall between the two rooms upstairs, and since then he's been scraping cracked linoleum off the floorboards, starting right after supper—dismissing any of-fer of help I might make with "Call me when it's time for the news, if you think of it." From down below I listen to the sounds of demolition and rehearse what I should go upstairs and tell him, the accumulation of things I've kept from him lately. All week my heart has leapt every time I've heard a phone ringing, and I've tensed for the sound of Bender's voice in my ear, announcing some theory about Luci's car. He may be reaching for the phone right now, even as Charlie is displaying a comb for my benefit, pointing out brood, eggs, and honey.

I recognize the queen without his having to tell me what I'm looking for. She's larger and more wasplike than the other bees, with a long, slightly tapering abdomen and loosely attached thorax. The series of concentric circles in several combs in the center of the hive tell him this is a good brood nest, the sign of a good queen. He seems proud of her as he shakes frame after frame of bees gently around her. "Lately it's seemed beside the point, all this," he says.

I'm not sure what he's getting at. He takes the embryo queen I've been holding all this time and with four quick pokes of his knife cuts an opening for her in a comb from the old hive. With luck, the bees will tend this new cell, and soon there will be a new virgin queen for the hive.

"Linda," he says, "I want you to know why I've been so remote lately, so angry with you for talking about Luci's death." He watches his hands as he speaks. "A few months before she died, I accused her of something. Unfairly, as it turned out. She thought she had to explain herself, or lose me. At any rate, she told me something she hadn't planned to tell anyone, ever. It was extremely difficult for her. The ordeal took all night and all of the next morning. Afterward, she made me promise to keep her secret forever, because there were other people who could be hurt. So there's this once piece of knowledge about Luci I can't share with you." He pauses. "I know a man should be able to tell his wife anything, but the way she died has changed that, because when someone's murdered every bit of information assumes a kind of possible importance. This feels to me like an unfair barrier between us, but I can't help it."

I want to move closer to Charlie and his bees, but he says, "You're entitled to tell me if you're worried or afraid. I regret shutting you out. That's the point I'm trying to make."

He pauses to consider my features—indistinct to him, I suppose, in this disguise I'm wearing. Then he goes on. "The other night, when I hauled Luci's things away, a kind of pressure had been building up inside me for a while. I was afraid you were about to start raising a lot of new questions about her." Bees mumble through the thick air. "The truth is, if I had talked about her with you at all that night, I'd have ended up telling you too much. I made a sacred promise to her that has nothing to do with us, or with the way she died. But I promised you even more, being your husband, so this is bothering the hell out of me. I'm not sure what to do. You and I have been holding each other almost at the breaking point lately, and I need some relief. That's all I can say."

Lines of sweat run down the sides of my face. "Is this about the child she had?" His expression doesn't change at all. "Is that it?"

"Not exactly."

"Then *what*, exactly?" I reach up under my veil, admitting a cool breeze, to wipe the irritating perspiration from my face with a gloved hand. That's when I get it, a needle of pain below the eye, which instinctively I slap and press deeper into the flesh.

The bee sting swells my eye shut and makes me feverish. Each time I wake up during the night, Charlie turns on the lamp by the bed and presses warm cloths, then cool, over the injury. He gives me the tiny white tablets the doctor prescribed after giving me an injection of epinephrine, for venom shock. When dawn lights the window, we're both awake. "I know this isn't exactly what you had in mind when you took me back to nature, Charlie." I smile at him with my one good eye, and we finally hold each other the way we wanted to yesterday morning.

"I had hoped for something more like this." He touches me slowly, telling me not to fight the fever's stillness, but to let him do all the work. Straddling me carefully, he presses his kisses deep into the side of my neck, then moves on until after a while I come with the kind of relief I've been needing for days. A hundred and three degrees of fever is a surprising state for all this pleasure.

He seems to feel he's shared a secret with me by justifying his refusal to do so on the grounds he made a promise to a dead woman. But he's a good lover, even with a feverish, one-eyed partner. He'll tell me eventually, and I'll press him, but gently, until he does. "Beautiful," he murmurs against my skin.

Still, when John Bender does turn up again, what he has to say may make me remember this day for the tension between Charlie and me that caused him to take me to see the bees. For a moment there I nearly forgot I'm the one who's holding out, keeping secrets. My heart throbs under my eye. It really hurts. "What is it, Linda?" says Charlie softly. "I thought I was pleasing you. All of a sudden you went tense."

*   *   *

I doze throughout the morning, barely waking up when Charlie comes into the bedroom to check on me. Upstairs he is steaming sepia cabbage roses off the walls of the room he suddenly has begun referring to as "the kid's" room. Have I missed something? Charlie has the energy of someone who just received good news.

Nothing's more boring than a mild illness. At 3:21, according to the digital alarm clock, I rouse myself and pad to the living-room sofa, which is the color of peach jam and has a curved depression that fits my backside perfectly. I love this room. The large, many-paned window looks out across the gravel drive—where the van is parked now, blocking the view.

Opposite, the fireplace wall is lined with bookshelves. The pine floor is bare except for three worn Oriental rugs. Charlie's navy recliner, with its broad, pillowed back, arms worn shiny, squats close by with the insolence of a long-standing tenant who knows he'll never be put out of the house. I get to my feet and sink into its wide comfort, pulling on the lever to be cradled backward as Charlie's reassuring footsteps knock across the floor overhead. The ceiling, newly plastered and painted last fall, just before I moved in, is such a flawless expanse that I lose focus with my one good eye, the last thing I know until I wake up cold and the room is in shadows.

It takes me a minute to remember it's Sunday and why I feel so bad. "Charlie?" I say, as if some sound he made woke me up. When there's no answer, I reach for the recliner's lever. The chair springs to sitting position. I stand up, stiff and disoriented, and stagger toward the bookcase, my right hand out. The book I touch for balance is *Art on the Streets of SoHo*.

In the tiled bathroom the sound of my peeing is very loud, expanding the familiar room to a cavernous, almost public space around me. Something registers, something Luci said, and I head back to the bookshelf. A few of these art books were hers, but I left them here when I packed her things because I thought I might want them myself. I can't see much with my swollen right eye, but

I find the book I'm looking for, tilting it toward me—*Art on the Streets of SoHo: A Photographic Collection.* The cover photograph is of a mime perched on the edge of a trash barrel on a crowded street. Inside the dust jacket is a journal, the binding covered with gray fabric, repeat-patterned with dots, lines, and half-moons of muted green. Every page is crowded with Luci's handwriting and occasional sketches.

Suddenly I'm freezing. Clutching Luci's diary to my chest, I tremble with weakness. In the bedroom I find a big sweatshirt that smells like Charlie and pull it carefully over my face and down over my bathrobe. I cup my swollen cheek, still hot to the touch, with my hand. "Charlie?" I call out again, through the window screen. Where's he gone? At the back of the garage, I see a light.

I open the book. On the page is a sketch of Charlie's face, but beardless, with a weak chin. On the next page is another drawing of him, identical except for his actual chin, the one I recognize from old photographs. The third version has the strongest jawline of all. I close the book and open it again to a page about a third of the way through. My swollen eye waters as I squint to make out the difficult script. "The sublime and ornery"—Lifting the book to the light, I see the word is "ordinary," and I manage to read on:

The sublime and ordinary—meet in kitchens. So today Charlie and I made pesto—a whole vat of it!—and before we were done, we tasted of basil head to toe—I never knew how good pesto could be—before this. There'll be no end to it, I said to Charlie. Cooking up one pleasure—after another. What we consume in the kitchen—we burn down the hall.

The book snaps shut of its own accord, exhaling a sniff of dust, as I hurry into the living room, disguise the diary again as *Art on the Streets of SoHo*, slip it onto the shelf, and head back to the bedroom.

I sit on the edge of the bed and pull the covers around me to wait. The ring of the phone makes me jump. *Bender?* I only have to scoot along the bed a couple of feet and get my right arm untangled from the quilt to reach the phone by the second ring.

"Did I wake you up?" Judy sounds surprised.

"You're back. Good." I have imagined her and Bill and Tess sitting in a circle with other troubled teenagers and parents, shouting at each other, crying. "How was it?"

"It was incredible. Are you sick?"

"I sound bad, don't I?"

"Disappointed, I thought at first. I did wake you up. I'm sorry."

"You can't imagine how glad I am you called." I turn on the lamp by the bed. The light hurts my eye. "Charlie's outside. I'm feeling deserted."

I ask about Tess and Bill, but Judy evades my questions with questions of her own, and I'm prattling on about the bee sting and the fever. Looking out the window across the dark yard toward the light from Luci's studio, I take courage from Charlie's presence out there and from the sound of Judy's voice. "Charlie's really been struggling with his feelings about Luci, after all this time," I hear myself say. "He vacillates between refusing to talk about her and—" I stop before I can say *holding out tantalizing secrets.* "I'm beginning to think his relationship with her was more complicated than I realized. I don't know how to help him."

"Just take care of yourself." Judy talks for a few more minutes. The phone is heavy in my hand. When I hang up, I turn on the overhead lights in the bedroom and hallway, bathroom and front room, and even the amber bug light outside the kitchen door, banishing the darkness.

Outside, the air is chilly, the first cool night all month. I have to concentrate to lift my feet, not to shuffle but to move flat-footed toward the garage. I feel every rock distinctly through my heavy socks. My feet barely make a sound in the gravel.

Instead of entering the garage, I circle to the left of the building. From here I can see the side window of the studio. What could he be doing there, in that empty space? His shadow moves around inside. He plans to turn the space into a woodshop; maybe he's doing some measuring. In my terry-cloth robe, sweatshirt, and socks, I must look like a madwoman—swollen and one-eyed, sodden with sweat, panting. The ground lists, and I steady myself. I should have stayed put. Even this slight exertion has made my heart race. My face is throbbing, and I feel too weak to shout, but at least I'm impatient, no longer afraid. However he tries to explain himself, he's still shutting me out.

Inside the dimly lit garage, a dark oil spot marks the center of the floor, and I walk around it. "Charlie, what are you doing back there?" I can hear the irritation in my voice, and it's about time. Patience is no virtue when someone you love is going through terrible grief. He needs to talk. I need to insist. In front of the studio doorway I hesitate, my left foot lagging behind, as the light in the studio goes out.

In the dark someone bumps against me hard enough to push me aside, and footsteps fall away behind me across the concrete of the garage floor. With both hands I cover my mouth, where my heart beats. I'm struck by the bright headlights that blaze into the driveway.

Though the light hurts, I stare into it until the rumble of the engine shuts off and the headlights go out and the van's familiar bulk replaces the tunnels of light. I'm hugging myself so that my right hand covers the spot on my shoulder where the intruder pushed against me. I'm operating blind, but the stale smell of tobacco stays with me, and something about the rhythm of his stride convinces me John Bender has made another appearance.

8 ◆ WHILE CHARLIE WALKS the perimeter of the backyard, I sit in the kitchen, sickened by the garlic and sesame smells of the Chinese food in front of me on the table. He startles me as he bangs through the back door. "Whoever it was, he's gone," he announces, pausing to glance at the flashlight stuck to the side of the refrigerator. It's like the one in his hand, chrome with a chunky magnet on its side. "This was on the table in the back room out there." I notice he doesn't refer to the place as Luci's studio. "Everything's locked up tight now." The awkward way he holds the flashlight with his fingertips as he upends it on the table negates his comforting tone. He's treating it like evidence.

He withdraws a square white carton from the paper bag and unfolds the lid to let out a starchy whiff of steam. It's the rice. "You going to call the police?"

He shakes his head. "Nothing seems to be missing, and neither of us got a good look at him."

Too exhausted to argue, I watch Charlie remove the cartons of food from the bag bearing the droopy, pagoda-like logo I designed for The China Palace: Orange Beef, Garlic Chicken, Shrimp with

Black Bean Sauce. He dishes food onto plates. "I hope this looks good to you. I got all your favorites."

Though I haven't eaten much all day, I shake my head at the egg roll he lifts over my plate. He uses chopsticks with Chinese food, and when I wave my hand in refusal, he keeps the small egg roll moving full circle and bites into it. Why am I the only one who's upset over what's just happened? As if he reads my mind, he leans over to touch my forehead with his mouth, a testing kiss. "Your fever's broken." He lifts my chin to rotate my face, examining the still-swollen eye. "I had no idea I was exposing you to so much harm."

He's right about the fever. The chills and light-headedness have passed, leaving me limp. I guess I'm cured. "I'm sure it was just a transient," he says. "My fault, for leaving the garage door up all the time. I'll be more careful from now on."

"Weren't you thinking we could give the cops the flashlight?"

He nods. "But on second thought, I don't think it matters. Let's eat."

The next morning, for the second day in a week, Charlie is out of the house before I wake up. As I prepare to leave for work, I take Luci's journal from the bookshelf and slip it into my shoulder bag. The flashlight still sits on the kitchen table. If whoever was in the garage last night was looking for something to steal, he must have been disappointed. Charlie could be right, and it was someone seeking shelter. Without certainty, without proof, I don't want to admit I think it might have been Bender.

Before I leave for town, I unlock the studio and study the clean-swept floor, the empty worktable, the shelves—bare also, except for a row of five shoe boxes. A cardboard box Charlie must have missed the other night is on the floor, its contents jumbled: a road map of Iowa, a pair of winter gloves, a camera, a brown extension cord, and three picture postcards, which I read quickly. One of them's from me, an announcement of a show in Santa Fe with a quick message scrawled on the back: "I got a series of five small prints into this one." That was five years ago. I sent those cards to everyone I knew. Now, after cranking open a window to admit a bracing, early-day breeze from the damp trees outside, I hoist myself up to sit on the worktable and pull Luci's diary out of my shoulder bag, finding a page headed by a lineup of shoes. Luci's handwriting is small and cramped:

Of course he would leave me to imagine who they might suit— what strides might be taken by elegant, large women—while my poor feet wander lost as the rest of me. To burn them would be to give up the only way he tried to please me. They follow me everywhere—these Unsuitable Shoes.

I read the paragraph again, the oddness of the phrases leaving me with a sense of dread. The words—puzzling enough that they might be profound, or they might be nonsense—*sound* like Luci. Nothing preceding those words identifies the *he* in the passage about the shoes. Turning back to very beginning of the diary, I skim the pages. At first I find nothing but more unattached pronouns—*he this* and *he that*, with no reference. Finally I find a name: *Bill came up out of the woods behind the house along the old path behind the garage and saw someone hammering away on the siding and singing at the top of his lungs.* On the next page I learn that the *someone* hammering on the siding was Russell Weber. And that she and Bill met again, and did a lot of kissing. Thumbing through the pages, I find Bill's name over and over. I drop the book into my bag and get in my car to head for Ken Hansen's office.

The halls of the police station are deserted this time of day. Hansen's got puffy, early-morning eyes and a shiny, just-shaved smoothness along the jaw. His pale-blue shirt is still starchy and unwrinkled at the armpits. He gives off the leathery smell of cologne. I stand the flashlight, bulb end down, on his desk in front of him. "An intruder left this at our place last night."

His hand is halfway to the flashlight before he stops, narrowing his eyes. "What happened to you?"

The focus of his stare reminds me that the discoloration around my eye has left me looking like a victim of abuse. I tell him about the bee sting. "I'm here about this flashlight. I want you to check for prints."

"Could this have anything to do with Bender?"

"Why? Have you two been talking about me?" He nods solemnly. Neither of us has smiled yet. I sit in the oak chair facing him, my back straight, leaning forward slightly. "Bender's guessing, you know. Exactly what did he tell you, and when?"

Hansen leans back, stifling a grin. His chair squeaks. Maybe I am coming on a little strong. His amusement tells me he means to slow things down a bit, and that whatever Bender told him, he's not taking it too seriously. If he wants to buy some time so he can figure out how to handle me, fine. I'll wait. On his feet now, the detective offers me coffee. "Cream?"

"Black." Let him go. Let him collect himself.

When he returns, he brings coffee mugs and grimly tries to smile again. I don't thank him for the coffee, though I have to stop myself from the reflex of good manners. "I know Bender's a friend of yours. I'm wondering how that might affect your objectivity." My voice is formal, flat. If Hansen registers my insult, he doesn't let it show. The coffee is better than the police-station coffee I remember, maybe because it's fresh at this hour of the morning. "I think I have a right to know what he has said to you."

"John's been out of town most of the week," says Hansen, as if that were the information I was looking for.

"I think he's back."

"No, he won't be back for a few more days. His father's ill, in Racine, Wisconsin." We're both staring at the flashlight standing up on the desk between us like a primitive object. "Where did this come from again?"

He knows very well I haven't gotten that far. I tell him about the intruder, what time it happened. "If there are any fingerprints on this, I want to know if they match any of the unidentified prints found in the kitchen when Luci died."

His eyes meet my gaze and lock there for a moment. Then, sighing with exasperation, Hansen does something very uncharacteristic. He looks away in disgust, fed up and not caring if I know it. "Come on, Linda," he says, shaking his head. "What you're asking is not appropriate, not even rational."

"I thought John told you—"

"He told me you're still so upset about Luci's death you're second-guessing yourself enough to exhibit paranoid suspicions about him."

"Will you check this for prints?"

"Tell me who you think was in your garage last night."

"I can't be sure. Someone tall, about my height."

"So we have nothing concrete to go on."

"We have this." I point at the flashlight. "Charlie brought it into the house, so his prints will be there."

"You're proposing that we might find a second person's prints and that they might match untagged prints from the scene of a crime solved a long time ago? Is that where you're going with this?" It's not a question that requires an answer. He walks to the window, rubbing the small of his back just above the belt with the knuckles of his fist.

When he turns to face me again, he clears his throat and then speaks slowly. "John has looked at your original statement. He thinks I may have led you with my questions." He's silent for a moment, thinking. "He can be a bit of a loose cannon, Bender. He seems to think you're suffering under the moral weight of believing you convicted Garvey all by yourself, that you're vulnerable to suggestion, doubting yourself in some way that might surprise us. I can't help wondering if he hasn't hit on something, the way the case is still eating at you. Why don't you tell me about it?"

"Check the flashlight," I say firmly.

To my surprise Hansen slides a pencil through the triangular handle on the top of the flashlight and carries it to the doorway, where he pauses. "Tell you what. I'll give this to Dennis Johnson. I saw him come in a few minutes ago."

"Who's Dennis Johnson?"

"He's one of our guys, in training to match prints. He's not certified as an expert witness at this point, but if I send these to the lab with all the lift cards from the Garvey case, the way you want me to, it would likely be three or four months before we hear back anyway. I think Dennis could get an answer in a few days. But I need a clear reason to ask him to do that." Hansen steps out of sight into the hallway, then reappears to deliver one parting comment: "I have to remind you, Linda, that one of the most damaging pieces of evidence against Peter Garvey was that his prints were on the knife blade."

And on Luci's forearm. I know he's thinking that, too. If not for the way she died, I would never have learned that the smooth skin of a breast, or the inside of the wrist, or the inside of the upper arm can hold a latent fingerprint for many hours, especially from a hand as oily and soiled as Peter Garvey's was that day.

I finish my coffee and wait for Hansen to return. After what seems like forever, he comes back with a file card bearing a crude sketch of the flashlight, a rash of X's showing where prints were found. The date, hour, and location of the trespass are neatly printed on the card, along with the initials D.J., for Dennis Johnson. Four other cards bear smaller sketches, each also bearing a single, lettered X and white space awaiting the photographs of the prints when they've been developed. The camera they use makes negatives the same size as the original fingerprint. I remember seeing some at the trial. Hansen straightens up and walks around his desk.

"I don't think I can justify spending any more of Dennis's time on this, Linda."

"Then why did you bother lifting these?" I touch the top fingerprint card and turn it around to face me on the desktop.

"Even if we did get a match, we wouldn't know whose prints they were. All we'd learn would be that last night's intruder had been in your house before."

"That's what I'm afraid of," I say, meeting his eyes. "I'm asking you to prove to me that I'm wrong."

"You want me to relieve your anxiety."

"Will you do it?"

"It'll get bottom priority," he says. "If you think of anything that would move it up on the list, you let me know."

By the time I get to the sidewalk outside, I realize I've left without so much as a good-bye.

For a couple of hours I work in my studio, finishing up a logo for Jennifer Lilligren, a local dentist who wants to emphasize the word "family" in advertising her dental practice. By placing dots above the l's in the "illi" part of her name, I've managed to create a strong visual suggestion of a nuclear family, using typography alone. She'll be pleased with the results. Late in the morning I walk across the parking lot to the bookshop. "You're smoking again" is the first thing I say to Judy as I step through the back door of The Little Read.

She pulls the cigarette out of her mouth with a breathy *pfft* and a tossing gesture. "No kidding," she says, letting go with a pissed-off exhale that has enough force behind it to fill a sail. "What else is different about me?"

Though she usually wears makeup, today her ginger-colored eyebrows and eyelashes are barely there, her eyes pink at the corners. "Why do you do this, Judy?" I smile, hoping to ease her mood. "Don't make me work so hard. You still act like a second-grade teacher sometimes, running the class with guessing games."

She's up to her elbows in books she's unpacking from a cardboard carton on her worktable. "You'd guess wrong anyway."

She's angry all right. "How about if I go out and come in again?"

"Can we just talk about other things first, not about my week-end?"

"Who said anything about your weekend?" I grasp the carton she's shoved my way and stack it on top of another empty box on the floor by the door.

"Did I miss much the last couple days?" Judy pulls another cig-arette out of the package and strikes a match.

"Russell Weber no longer works next door. The new cook doesn't know how to make Angela's Special. She substitutes cole-slaw for tabbouleh."

"I hear Weber was stealing from the till."

"So you knew he was gone."

"It's probably not true, though. The customer who told me couldn't even remember Weber's name. Called him 'that guy with the weird hair.'" Judy gives me a sharp look. "Your detective ques-tioned Tess about being seen with Weber out back the day she took off. Hansen wanted to know what they were talking about, if Weber has ever given her grass, or any other drugs. Tess insists he was telling her about some piece of music he was working on, impressing her with his plan to make a demo tape at a studio in Des Moines. If you ask me, Weber's guilty of nothing more than *looking* suspicious, living up to some stereotype of the wacked-out musician, drifter."

"So you think he has nothing to do with Tess's running away?"

"Right. Turns out she made up with that boyfriend of hers, Rusty Burkhalter, and they got into some Saturday-night partying with kids from the community college. One of the college guys took the party on the road. He was from Creston, and drove a carload to his parents' house. Parents who were gone for a few days, of course. So Tess found herself in a strange town, with peo-ple she didn't know, who were drinking way too much, then sleep-ing it off, then starting all over again. She got scared when one of the guys got too aggressive with her, and took off walking toward the only landmark that made sense to her—a church steeple. Hence the call from the minister. This is the short version of her adventure—" She pauses. Her confidence falters, but she sniffs and straightens her shoulders. "Russell Weber had nothing to do with it."

"What about Rusty Burkhalter?"

"He was home by ten that Saturday night."

"Why didn't he come forward when she was missing?"

"The Burkhalters left for a family reunion in Nebraska on Sunday and continued on to Colorado for a vacation. They didn't get back until after Tess was safely home, so Rusty didn't know anything about her disappearance until it was too late to help us find her." Judy inflates herself with another lungful of smoke.

I cough. "Why'd you give up on the nicotine patch?"

"Would you believe that in the middle of the night last night I got up and put one on each arm, to see what kind of pickup it would give me? Three in the morning and I'm abusing nicotine patches. *God*." She looks at the cigarette in her hand, then takes another dramatic drag from it, leaning her head back and exhaling upward.

"You remind me of Bette Davis in some old movie."

She lowers her eyelids and does a suggestive side-to-side thing with her shoulders. "Right now," she says, smoke drifting from her lips, "this is the only way I have to get my heart racing." Despite her put-on, Judy looks anything but vampy, her face so pale the freckles stand out like grains of sand on a white sheet of paper. She's tries so hard to hide her misery, but she's no actress. She's blue under the eyes.

"You can quit later, when you're not so worried."

"Quit?"

"Smoking. What did you think I meant?"

"I thought maybe you thought I was into denial or something."

"That is what I think. I wouldn't dismiss Weber as a threat to Tess. If he has been providing drugs to high-school kids, are you sure she would say so?" I hope my tone is both firm and gentle. "You don't think you know exactly where Tess was all that time, do you? Or what she was doing every minute? She was gone for *three days*, Judy."

That does it. She turns her face away. "Bill and I are dealing with her the best way we can. I'm not dumb. There was most likely something sexual going on, and we don't know who these people were she was with." Judy takes a shaky breath. "What other neighborhood gossip do you have?"

"Well, I found some postcards among Luci's things. One of them is a card I sent her years ago, a brag about an art show I'd gotten into. The fact she saved it tells me she attached some value to it. When I decided to move down here from Minneapolis, I imagined she and I might get to know each other a lot better than we ever had before. She really worked at persuading me to make the move. It took some convincing; this is such a small town. What I discovered in the few hours I spent with her right before she died was that she was more conflicted, more emotionally fragile than I knew."

"Why were you looking through Luci's things?"

I ignore her question. "I know Bill and Luci knew each other when they were college freshmen. After she came here to teach at the community college, she told me about running into him again. She read a lot into the coincidence, as if his presence had drawn her here in some mystical way. Did he ever talk to you about what she was like when he first knew her?"

"Sure." Judy seems calmer now, so maybe getting her off the subject of Tess for a few minutes is a good idea. "He said Luci was very intense, very bright. They had been in the same freshman humanities class, I think it was, at Carleton. I guess they had a few meaningful conversations about Greek plays, and then she hadn't come back after Thanksgiving break. She lived here awhile before he heard from her. She wanted to befriend him again. He almost seemed a little afraid of her, I thought, at first. He would complain she was calling him, wanting to have coffee and talk, that sort of thing. She didn't make friends easily. Later she met Charlie, and the four of us did things together sometimes, and she was fine then. I really enjoyed her, but Bill thinks Luci was kind of a case, that Charlie put up with a lot, that Luci tended to hide behind being overly dramatic. I never heard her say much about her background, did you?"

I shake my head. "When her dad died during the time we knew each other in art school, she didn't go to the funeral, which I found more than odd. All she would say about him was that he was very charming and handsome, and that he had worked for a company that manufactured shoes, somewhere in Missouri. Her parents—her mom was a teacher—had been separated since she was little. Back in school, if I'd ask Luci questions about her family, the facts would change, like it was a game to continually reinvent herself."

"So she was a liar."

"Or like a child who tells tales because she's afraid no one will accept her for who she really is."

"Like Tess." The name slips out like a sigh. I hope that means Judy will finally talk about her daughter without being so brittle and defensive. For long seconds Judy is motionless with thought. Then she shrugs herself to attention. "I'm not so sure our family problems are about Tess at all. Getting her back to where she's safe is going to cost us a lot, me and Bill. I never bargained on that."

"Cost you how?"

"I'm not talking about money."

"I didn't think you were, Judy. What happened?"

"I'm not really sure. Tess seems to feel there needs to be some deep revelation about our household to make this family-therapy thing really fly, like there's got to be something we're not owning up to."

"I don't know what you mean."

"I don't know what *she* means." Judy ticks the pages of a new book against her thumbnail, pausing to stare at the words. "But I think Bill knows. I always thought the three of us were a reasonably good family unit." She spits out the word "unit" with disdain, as if it's a body part not commonly mentioned in polite conversation. "I've got all week to stew. We can't see Tess again until Friday night." She goes silent again, and when I startle her by clearing my throat, she says, "Bill, of course, has decided the therapist doesn't know her ass from her ego."

"Is that what you think?"

"I think he knows what Tess is talking about. That pretty well defines the mystery, doesn't it?"

"Back up. You've lost me."

"I'd really rather not talk about this."

"I know this is difficult. But don't clam up like you did when she disappeared. I'm not going to let you get away with it this time. It was a mistake, you have to admit, that you wanted to keep quiet about her running away when talking about it was your best chance of finding her. Now it's important that you understand what happened to her, so she won't take off again."

Judy crushes out her cigarette in the ashtray, and with every stab and grind of the butt she sniffs dryly. Her teeth are clenched, and the narrow glitter in her eyes means she's having a hard time holding herself together. She turns her back on me, jerking open a file drawer.

She rifles through folders for a few minutes, and when she turns around again, a sheaf of papers in her hand, her smile is actually pretty convincing. "What else have you been up to?" She rubs her nose with the back of her hand and sniffs again. "Besides being attacked by killer bees."

"Only one bee, and I was the aggressor. I forgot the rules and trapped it inside my veil."

"I thought artists made up their own rules."

"Tell that to the bees. Anyway, that's a damning, romantic myth, that free-spirit artist stuff. What made you say that?"

"Tess mentioned you over the weekend. She thinks you're brave and talented. She wants to be like you."

"She's over being mad at me?"

"I was jealous." She pauses. "I don't think she's over anything." Judy is cutting open another box, drawing her X-acto knife toward her, and I take the knife from her and show her how to hold it close to the body and push the blade away with the heel of the hand. Anybody who's ever gone to art school has seen more than one accident resulting from a careless slip while cutting a mat board. A sea of red flashes in my brain.

Judy has no comment as I retract the blade and place the knife carefully on the table. My fingers are shaking. Taking the top book out of the carton, she opens the cover and reads the dust flaps. " 'The smoky chiaroscuro of familial love recalled through time,' " she reads. "Yeah, sure." At least her sarcasm is cheering her up. "That's a clever way to recall something, all right. Through time."

"Come on. Tell me more about Tess. It might help you put things into perspective."

Judy settles into her swivel desk chair, and I face her across a chin-high stack of books, shifting a few of them to another pile so my view of her will not be obstructed. "It was like the end of the first act of a little Greek tragedy," she begins. I'm about to get the long version.

"Picture this." She gives me a few broad strokes—a dim conference room, a circle of chairs. I add a wash of gray carpet, a steely glow from closed metal blinds on the high windows, bluish overhead lights turned low. "Anyway, it's the last session of the weekend, which Bill and I have been thinking is pretty calm and helpful, dealing with our expectations about substances, with us telling Tess how we feel when she comes home drunk, when the therapist, Susan Ginger-Banning, starts pushing Tess really hard to talk about something she had apparently alluded to privately as 'this underlying tension at our house.' " Judy stops for thought, and in my mind's eye Susan Ginger-Banning sprouts long red fingernails, good for pointing at Tess, whose eyes are round. Her mouth, too, is round.

Judy starts again, but slower: "There's been plenty of tension—and not all that underlying either—since Tess started coming home this summer with beer on her breath and throwing up. I spoke up, of course, and Susan asked Tess if she thought I was accurate in attributing the tension between us to the drinking, or did she think her drinking could be an effect, and not simply a cause, of another problem. Tess looked down at her hands, glancing off to the side now and then, refusing to look at any of us, and then finally she said, 'Well, if there is something, why does it have to be me who brings it up?'

"No one was talking. So that's when it happened. I just gradually began noticing, in all that silence—with Tess and the therapist and me not moving a muscle—that Bill kept scratching, clearing his throat, switching positions in his chair. All three of us noticed.

"At first he didn't catch on. He started looking from Tess to me to Susan, back and forth, and then it dawned on him. He settled on Tess and said her name in a tone of voice he used to use with her when she was little, a warning pitch that would get her to stop whatever naughty thing she was doing.

"But this time she repeated herself just to him: 'I don't think it's fair that I should have to be the one to tell.' Right on cue Susan Ginger-Banning stood up and walked over to the light switch by the door and turned the overhead lights up to high."

My lips part, but I wait for the finish.

"It was like stage lights going up. I swear she planned it that way, to leave us hanging. She should be a goddamn theater director."

"That was it?"

"She's a grandmotherly type. Family therapist. It didn't sink in until Bill and I were in the car, starting for home, that she'd given us an assignment to complete before next weekend. I got the idea

she suspected Bill knew something about Tess's troubles that I
didn't, and that maybe if *I* figured that, I'd get it out of him."

"That seems awfully manipulative. Surely she would come out
and say what she thought."

"That's exactly what Bill said, before we were even out of the
parking lot. He thinks that with therapy these days there always
has to be someone to blame. And that Tess has apparently latched
on to the idea that the pressure will be off of her if there's some
malfunction in our family to pin her problems on."

"I think it's *dysfunction*."

"Whatever. If there's some buried *treasure* in our family, she'll be
off the hook with this drinking thing. He thinks this therapist is using
tactics with Tess that are very suggestive, and that he and I are going
to be expected to defend ourselves as soon as the guessing starts. I
pointed out how he'd given himself away by twitching around back
there in that room when the three of us were so calm, and he demanded to know why *I* hadn't been more uncomfortable. Was it because I wasn't smart enough to see what was happening? It was awful.
I cried. Then he wanted to go back and get her. We stopped at a rest
area and seriously considered it." She sighs. "It was hot, but the rest
area is on a hill above the highway. You know the one?"

I nod.

"There was a nice breeze, and we could see for miles, both east
and west. I wasn't getting back into the car until we were agreed
about what direction to go—home or back to Tess. I said, 'You've
got to stop this, Bill. She needs this help. You can't play games
with what they're asking us to do.' He got tears in his eyes."

I've stopped at that rest area along I-80 and remember the steep
rise of turf-grass hillside and the molded-concrete picnic tables,
each under its own triangular roof of shade. I can almost see Bill's
high, rounded forehead grow shiny in the heat. The bell on the
front door signals a customer, a young woman with a ponytail and
blue shorts, and Judy hurries away from me.

By the cash register, Judy looks toward me, her features obscured by the faded afternoon light in the plate-glass window behind her. She takes a book from the customer and examines the blurb on the back, gesturing as she speaks. I can't make out the words from this far away, but the inflection of her voice, without the earlier sarcasm, suggests "the smoky chiaroscuro of familial love." Is that really what she's saying? As the ponytailed customer reclaims the book and returns to the shelves to browse, I stand, intending to walk to the front of the store. But Judy stops me by shaking her head with such vigor that I know she needs to hold herself together until Miss Ponytail decides to go.

Tess was only thirteen when Luci was murdered—a woman she knew, a friend of her parents. Charlie stayed with the Allards for a couple of nights after it happened. None of us has wondered if Tess, too, may still be frightened by that horrible event and may not even know what is bothering her. Who was it who said a crime like that has many victims? The effects will be with us all our lives.

They follow me everywhere—these Unsuitable Shoes.

We're as healthy or as sick as the secrets we keep. Though I've yet to read it carefully, line by line, it's clear from Luci's diary that she was a lot closer to Bill than Judy knew. From her safe position at the front of the store, she watches her customer browse. She has no idea what I am about to do to her.

9 ◆ WHILE WAITING FOR JUDY to come back from helping her customer, I pick up *The Intelligent Investor* off the nearest pile of books and open it to a page that might as well read "Today we made pesto," for all the jealousy I've felt since seeing Charlie's name in Luci's journal.

A diary is a controlled version of a life, not a reliable record. We all tell stories, trying to master the events of our lives, entertaining ourselves in the process. Isn't that what Judy did just now, setting the scene of her conversation with Bill at the highway rest stop, so I'd relive the drama, feel her confusion about what's happening to her family? I know one thing Bill didn't tell her during that conversation—that one day during the last months of Luci's life *he came up out of the woods along the old path behind the garage,* according to Luci's diary, *and saw someone hammering away on the siding.* I'll look again tonight, soon as I get home, but I'm sure there's no way to get onto our property from the back. The ravine is too steep for a path. It drops at least fifteen feet at every point, and the ridge runs for a mile on either side of us.

If Luci's diary is part fiction, how can I believe any of it?

Bill's gotten smaller around the middle since he's taken to running this past year. His shoulders seem narrower, too. Though his hair's thinning on top, he's let it grow into a smooth curl over his collar. In his early forties, he has a pleasant, broad-cheeked face and a classroom manner when he speaks, his grammar-perfect delivery explanatory and reserved. Except for times like the other night in the van, when he was upset, he has a gentle way of trying to redirect others' opinions without being wishy-washy. He's a quiet but no-bull, straight-from-the-shoulder kind of guy, probably why his students like him so much. I like him, too, though sometimes I wish he'd loosen up.

If it's true that Bill's relationship with Luci was sexual, I wonder if his straight-arrow demeanor masks other behavior he'd be unwilling to share with Judy. Has Tess discovered something about her father her mother doesn't know? I try placing him in Big Earl's, a topless juice bar at the edge of town, but it doesn't quite work. I try watching him inhale lines of coke off a cracked rearview mirror in the backroom at Carney's, the local auto-parts store where he works every summer, but that's ridiculous, too. I try putting him into something strange but not truly bad, like Judy's underwear. Maybe he hides spiky high heels and Victoria's Secret panties in the back of the storage closet in the high-school chem lab, and one day poor Tess was looking for a box of pipettes—

"Hey, Linda." The book snaps shut in my hand as I turn toward Bill's voice to confront the hollow above the top button of his shirt where a fuzz of graying hair curls proudly. "What happened to your face?"

My hand rises to touch the memory of pain. "A bee stung me." My laugh's a nervous reflex at what he's caught me thinking.

He looks puzzled. "What's so funny?" He pokes upward at the bill of his green seed-corn cap, moving the embroidered flying ear of corn back slightly on his head. Then he lifts the open book in my hand so he can see the cover. "Ah, yes, Benjamin Graham. That's a funny one all right." He's teasing me. Two skeptical lines crease his forehead. "I had no idea you were interested in the stock market, Linda."

"We all have our little secrets."

"I guess you've been talking to Judy."

"Until we got interrupted." He hesitates, and the silence makes me uneasy. "Did Luci know you lived here," I say quickly, "when she took the job at the community college?"

He straightens his back, turns, and is out the door, just like that.

Stunned by his sudden departure, I watch him through the screen door and then decide to follow, reaching his car just as he puts it into reverse, his attention focused behind him. When he turns his head and sees me, he shifts into park. He speaks before I have a chance to. "Judy's upset enough without your putting ideas in her head," he says.

"I haven't done that."

"You will, if you keep asking about Luci."

"Looks like *you're* the one upset by that."

He puts the car in reverse again, his foot on the brake, letting me know this will be a short conversation. "To answer your question, Luci did not know I lived here when she took that job and moved to town. It was the kind of coincidence a weak-minded person might see as fate, our ending up in the same place for the second time in our lives. I'm afraid seeing me again stirred up something in her. We weren't particularly close in college. For one thing, she was only there for the first half of fall semester. She was shy and intense, very serious. Most girls back then tried to get me to talk about myself. She wanted to talk about *The Birds*, a play we'd had to read for Humanities." To my surprise he smiles, remembering, then sobers. "She wasn't the same agitated woman who showed up here years later. Charlie calmed her down, though." He pauses to think. "She couldn't make it work."

"Make what work?"

"The idea that her running into me again was a sign there was some kind of extrasensory bond between us." His chuckle is dismissive. "It turned out she'd said something about me all those years ago, something untrue, and had always felt guilty about it. Once she got that off her chest, I was able to persuade her that taking a job in a town where I just happened to live didn't mean anything in particular. Except that we felt closer, as it turned out."

"Had you dated her, back in college?"

"No, it wasn't like that. We were friends, until the end." He squints up at me into the bright sunlight. "Why bring this up now?"

"I always knew she had some real contradictions in her personality. Now that she's gone, I wish I'd asked her more questions."

He nods, but with deliberation, as if my explanation doesn't satisfy him. "Linda, I was just by your place, looking for you. I was hoping you could give Judy some moral support. Tess ran out of the final therapy session in Omaha and went back to her room without saying good-bye to us. Did Judy tell you that?"

"Not exactly."

"The doctor tried to explain that Tess's resentment is part of her recovery, but Judy was too hurt to hear that, I guess. All Judy's defenses have gone up, and I can't seem to get through to her at all. Maybe you could talk some sense into her."

"A minute ago you accused me of putting ideas in her head."

"Tess is the one who's doing that. Sorry I'm so jumpy, but Judy's reaction is really throwing me." He gives me a sad look. "I don't think I'm a bad father. Just talk to her, okay? I don't seem to be very good at it these days." He looks at his rearview mirror and backs away.

Inside, Judy wants to know why Bill didn't wait for her. "Why did he take off that way?"

"That was my fault. I asked him if Luci knew he was here when she moved to Linden Grove. He didn't like that."

Judy sinks into the nearest chair, silent for a minute or so. I suppose she's thinking about Luci, but then she says, "Bill thinks the family therapy is deflecting attention away from the real issues of alcoholism, suffering consequences, setting limits." I pull a chair over and sit beside her. "He figures that if *I* think Tess was accusing him of something during the session, the therapist probably thinks so, too. He's pissed that Ginger-Banning allowed the session to end the way it did. He thinks she should have tried to keep us all in the room until Tess explained herself."

"Couldn't you have gone on talking with the lights on high?"

"Sure, but Tess got up and left. Running away again, according to Bill. He doesn't remember it at all the way I do. He thinks the therapist raised the lights *after* Tess left the room, that it was Tess who brought things to a halt. The only thing I'm sure of is that Bill and I were sent off to fight it out; I'm just not sure by whom." She moves her hand across her face, smearing tears. "I do love him, Linda, but sometimes I hate him just for being a man, just for the possibilities. What if the awful secret Bill's supposed to have from me is that he's cheating, and somehow Tess found out about it? He denies it, of course. I asked. My dad ran around on my mother, and I always had to protect her from the obvious. Once she found a pair of black underpants under the car seat, and Dad told her he kept it there for when he checked the oil, to wipe off the dipstick."

"She must have known."

"Yeah, but I didn't think so. It was awful."

"If Tess knew about such a thing, like you with your mom, she'd be staying close to home, not running away, and certainly not bringing it out in the open, knowing you'd be hurt. That would be the last thing she'd want."

"Unless—" she begins. Behind her, two middle-school boys with baseball caps on backward come into the store to read magazines. Judy keeps her back to them. "A mother's supposed to protect her daughter, not be gullible, not be blind. There's something she wants me to know. Why can't she just tell me? What's she trying to do?"

"Make trouble between you and Bill. Divide and conquer. Take the heat off herself. Maybe he's right."

"That's not like her."

"Hasn't she done other things lately that aren't like her?"

Judy bites on her lower lip. "Linda, I asked him last night if he'd ever done anything to Tess, touched her in a sexual way. He's acting as though my asking that question was a breach of trust."

"I take it the answer was no."

"Of course the answer was no. And now that I think about it, if Tess had told Susan Ginger-Banning she'd been sexually abused, even so much as *suggested* it, the therapist would have confronted Bill herself. So I should have known it wasn't that."

"If the question was in your mind, you had to ask it, Judy."

"Right," she says. "I had to ask."

"And you accept the answer?"

"I'll have to ask Tess, too, but I've never had any reason to suspect such a thing. Never." She looks at me, shaking her head. "I know, Linda, you think I'm a champion of denial, but not this time. A mother's supposed to protect her child."

What about a child protecting a parent? Doesn't it work that way, too? I wonder, even as I look for a way to bring closure to the conversation before I have to go back to my work and let Judy get back to hers. Maybe I can talk to Tess myself when she's back from Omaha. "I have a chance for the design account for the new Linden Grove Mall," I say, "but I'm having trouble coming up with ideas for a visual-identity system, and the deadline is in just a few days. Maybe I could bring over some of my sketches, get your opinion."

Judy frowns. "I heard there's going to be a Lemstone Books in that mall. One of those stores with religious books and wise-saying coffee mugs and angel figurines."

"That won't hurt your business, Judy."

"Of course it will. I do have a religion section, Linda. Malls *kill* a small town's shopping areas."

"I don't have the job yet, Judy." I think of the scatter of linden-leaf drawings on my desk, as alike as if they all fell from the same tree. Lack of variety in thumbnail sketches is a sure sign a good solution will be hard to get to. "Maybe I'll give up the idea."

"Don't do it on my account."

I do want the job. But at this point the last thing I want to be called in Linden Grove is an outsider.

As I step out the back door of The Little Read Book Shop, a handful of sparrows flies up to the power lines, where they wait in rows, chirping with complaint. I wish I could move my loft to a town where no one knows me and where if anyone has trouble, I'm not aware of it. By habit I listen for the distant drone of the interstate, the way people near the ocean must pause sometimes to listen for the surf, and for the same reasons: a reminder the world is vast, beyond this speck of a place, and there's a way out.

From the back door of the Grubstake, Angela flings another handful of crumbs, and the birds gather on the pavement again. I inquire after Russell Weber fondly, as one who loved the dishes he cooked for me. "I just let everyone know the register was short," she says. "I didn't accuse him. But he's gone, so he must be guilty, right?"

I shrug, feigning unconcern about what the guilty might do. "If he figured you weren't going to believe him . . ." My voice trails off. I'd be gone in a flash, too, if someone implied I'd put my hand in the till. Halfway to my door, I turn. Angela's still there, sunning her broad, shiny face. "So you think he has a temper?" I call out.

"Not about this. Got a call about him this morning, checking references for another kitchen job. Don't you think that's strange?"

"A place here in town?"

"Yes."

"Did you tell them he was a thief?"

"I recommended him highly. So maybe he knew I'd figure out I was wrong. The thing is . . ." She leaves the frame of her doorway and walks out to me at the edge of the parking lot so she doesn't have to talk so loudly. "I've come up short since he's been gone, too. I've started counting out the change again, the way I used to. And the new cook's slow. This morning I had to do some of the prep work myself."

"You could offer him his job back."

She considers that. "After this, he wouldn't trust *me* anymore, so why would he want to come back? I discovered when I asked him for references, when I hired him, that he never stuck with any job for long. It was something for him to stick with me for as long as he did. And then I went and did this."

She returns to her kitchen door. Her hair is the color of ashes under the control of her hair net, which she removes now, fingers spread to lift it in a mime of penitence. "*I* wouldn't come back," she calls out to me, turning away. The rest of her words are lost. She's a heavy woman. Moves slowly. Especially now, with what she's thinking.

Pretending fondness for Weber just now was not so difficult, I realize. I'm becoming a good liar. The door to my studio doesn't yield at first, so I twist the key again, and it opens easily. Alert, I hesitate just inside the door. The desk chair squeaks at the far end of the room, and John Bender's head and shoulders appear beyond the etching press, his dark eyes wide, as if I've caught him at something.

With his hair pulled back and his high cheekbones, his expression looks carved, aloof. For a long moment we consider each other across the space of the studio. I'm afraid to move closer to him, yet angry enough to cover half the distance before I speak. "How did you get in here?"

He turns his head to where I'm pointing—at the sign hanging by a cord in the front-door window. OPEN it says, on this side.

When he looks at me again, it strikes me that he looks tired. His mouth is nearly a straight line. "The door was open back there," he says, "so I figured you weren't far away. I've been waiting." He stands, palms open as if to appease me. He *must* be tired. "I was leaving you a note."

"The door was open?"

"Well, unlocked."

With a single, sweeping glance, I take in the studio between us: the drafting table and print files to my left, the counter along the wall to my right with its sink and acid bath, the work surface under the skylight, where the plate for Charlie's print lies faceup on last week's newspaper, the image bitten and ready for ink. No sooner do I think his name than Charlie's face appears behind the OPEN sign. We make eye contact. He raises his hand.

"I don't appreciate your talking to Hansen," I'm saying to Bender as I walk around the end of the worktable toward Charlie's face, framed by the window in the front door. "And don't let on to Charlie that I've been to see Garvey."

Bender's already on the far side of the worktable, headed for the back door. He stops. "You've been to see Garvey?"

I twist the deadbolt lock to admit Charlie, flipping the sign automatically, CLOSED side in. Smiling, he kisses me on the mouth. "I tried calling, but I had to pick something up at Ace Hardware anyway." He looks toward the sound of the back door snapping shut. With a touch to my chin, he tilts my face to examine it. "I didn't want to wake you this morning. You feeling okay?"

"Like new."

"Who was that?" He lowers himself into the desk chair, which is no doubt still warm from Bender's body.

When I don't answer, Charlie looks up, eyes still asking the question. "He looks familiar." He's rotating my sketch pad to look at six variations on a group of trees surrounding the words LINDEN GROVE MALL.

I move papers around on the desk, covering Bender's note. "The leaf of the linden is not symmetrical," I point out. "The base is unequal; one bulge of the heart is bigger than the other. I thought I might use that heart shape. Every idea I came up with this morning was as trite as that. So I took a break and went over to see Judy." I sit opposite Charlie, in the chair reserved for customers. "Tess is in good hands, I think. The place is called Three Oaks. It's a complicated business, treatment for alcohol abuse. Especially with kids. I'm afraid Judy and Bill are resisting how much the whole family's affected."

"I'll bet. Wasn't that the reporter? Bender?"

"Yeah, it was."

"I do remember him." Charlie's leaning back in the chair, splay-legged, broad hands resting on the arms of the chair. "You haven't mentioned him for a while. What was he doing here? He's not still bothering you?"

"He might like to. I won't let him."

"I don't like the sound of that. He left in an awful hurry."

"He came by to see if I was still upset with him. I gave him a lot of grief when I thought I'd caught him harassing me. I was over at Judy's when you called earlier, like I said." I clear my throat. "I don't know why he left so suddenly."

Charlie surveys the studio. He looks back toward the iron stairs that rise along the left wall up to the loft. Up there, obscured from view by a blue-and-white coverlet I threw over the railing for privacy, are a queen-size bed and a chest of drawers, an overstuffed chair and reading lamp, all draped in old sheets. I haven't gone up there much since last September, when Charlie and I got married. His gaze scans the work surfaces, lingers on the etching press, returns to my face. "He's not very friendly, is he? At least when I come on the scene. Maybe he's got his eye on you in a different way than you thought."

I shake my head. "I doubt that, Charlie. Detective Hansen says Bender's a nice guy. You made me check him out, remember? And now you have to go, too. Your etching's in plain sight, and I want to run it this afternoon." Charlie's eyes wander the room again, but I turn him toward the front door. His van's parked right there, at the curb. Outside, the air smells fresh. There's a nice breeze. Charlie's in no hurry to leave. "Judy hates the mall," I say. "She seems to think I should refuse to help promote it out of loyalty to her and other small-business owners in town."

"It will have a big impact, I'm afraid," says Charlie, "but at this point the mall's a done deal. It would be a good account for you."

"I'd make a lot of money, and it would lead to other work; but maybe I should consider seeing things from Judy's point of view. What if I were to work with the merchants who feel threatened by the mall, help them develop a marketing strategy to cope with the change—an identity for Linden Grove Old Town shopping? A logo, street banners, brochures. Judy is so upset about Tess, and she and Bill are having problems. If she and I could start a project together it would do her good."

"She's getting to be a pretty good friend for you, isn't she?"

"She's hard to get close to. But then so am I, I suppose."

"Not for me." He kisses me carefully, under the eye, where the bee sting is still tender.

"Do I still have a mark there?"

"Almost gone. Just a little bruise."

I tell him that since the therapy session over the weekend, Judy and Bill are barely speaking. Charlie has always thought they were an odd match—Judy's so flighty, Bill's so solid. "Something the therapist said made Judy ask him if he has abused Tess sexually, but he denies it."

Charlie's face darkens, and he looks at the ground. Then he opens the van door. "Did Tess accuse him of that?"

"I don't think so. I don't know what Tess is up to."

Charlie shakes his head. "Tell that reporter to get lost," he says, forgetting our usual kiss good-bye. "I'll see you at supper."

Back inside my studio, I cross to the desk and uncover Bender's note:

I've been out of town, and the one time I called, I got your machine. I wanted to explain myself in person. I know you're mad I talked to Hansen about you, but I had to check out his attitude toward Luci's case. That one got him his promotion, so he has a lot invested in believing he handled it right. It's your safety I'm most worried about. I've hit a dead end with Luci's car.

I stare at his confident scrawl for a moment, then head for the worktable to give a final polish to *Mackerel Sky*. Who does Bender think he's kidding, *my* safety? Why *did* he take off like that when Charlie showed up? Bending over the table, my breath stops in my throat. Across the copper plate, diagonal and deep, run two deep slashes.

A terrible X. In disbelief, I trace the jagged line, then stare at the hairline of red the torn metal has left across my fingertip. Finger to tongue, I taste the salt of my own blood, backing instinctively toward the front door to keep the whole room in sight, especially the coverlet that blocks my view of the loft.

10 ◆ MY MIND FLASHES through redoing the plate and printing it in time for Charlie's birthday on Friday, but I'm frozen where I stand. Whoever X'ed out the house had to know how personal this violation would be.

The police dispatcher promises to send someone right over. As I hang up the phone, my gaze settles on the quilt hanging over the loft railing, a pattern called Log Cabin, worked in a watery progression of blues, scraps of old clothes. It was part of Luci's collection of folk quilts, and she gave it to me the day I took possession of the building. That was a couple of months before she died. I had come to town for the closing, and because the building was already empty, I had arranged for plumbers and electricians and carpenters to start renovation work right away. I'd drawn up the plans myself. When I finally moved in, the day after the murder, I was grateful that the quilt not only added color to the space but blocked the view of my sleeping area from down here at a time when I didn't have blinds in the front window.

Now I strain to remember leaving for Judy's shop earlier, but the act of locking the back door is lost along with other automatic moments since the day began. The back door latch is a big, square mechanism. It's hard to believe it wouldn't hold. Bill said he had come by looking for me, to make sure I realized Judy needed a friend. Maybe he saw something.

Maybe he came into the studio himself.

Ken Hansen arrives in a few minutes and precedes me up the stairs to the loft. When I snap the sheet off the overstuffed reading chair, I disturb enough dust to make both of us sneeze. He hunkers down to sweep the space under the bed with his flashlight and then goes into the small bath. I hear the shower curtain jerked aside as I hitch the cord controlling the shade for the skylight over the bed, allowing sunlight to illuminate the loft. From the bathroom doorway Hansen surveys the space approvingly, as if I'm a realtor and he might want to buy the place.

Back downstairs he inspects the damaged plate while I remind him Bill Allard was around earlier and John Bender was *right here*. Hansen lifts what he says is a thumbprint, then flips open the cover of his notebook and refuses to look at me as he says, "What dollar amount would you attach to this?"

"I can't duplicate it exactly. So I can assign it a standard amount, but as a loss, it's priceless."

"I can't write down 'priceless.' "

"*Mackerel Sky* was to be a gift for Charlie."

The detective writes something in his notebook. Then his eyes meet mine as the phone starts to ring. "Any reason you can think of that anyone would want to frighten you like this?" We count three rings, four, until the answering machine clicks on and my own voice says, "Garbo Designs. After the tone, please leave a message."

The caller speaks: "I got another letter just now from Garvey, about your visit." Hansen picks up the phone. "Bender?" His voice reverberates through the machine, an auditory version of reflections in a room walled with mirrors. It's an old machine, with a tape; I should replace it with better technology. I intercept

Hansen's hand before he can touch the "off" button. "John? It's Ken."

The recorder hums with silence for a second before Bender says, "What's happened? Is Linda there?"

While the detective tells him about the vandalism, I leave the machine on so I can hear both their voices. "We've got one scared woman here," Hansen says evenly, "and she tells me you've been paying too much attention to her lately. You had opportunity. Stop down later and let me take your fingerprints. And you can explain to me what you're up to, that business about hearing from Garvey."

My skin goes cold. "Let me talk to him."

Hansen holds out the phone. I press the button as I say hello.

"The machine's off?" John Bender's voice is private, low.

"Yes."

"I shouldn't have taken off like that when Charlie showed up."

"Then why did you?" I ask. Silence brings no response. "What's in Garvey's letter? I want to *see* it."

Hansen's gray eyes narrow at the mention of Peter's name. A muscle works in his jaw. He takes off his glasses. In my ear Bender is saying, "Garvey says he told you he remembered Luci Cole wrote in a notebook sometimes. He says no one will believe he suddenly remembered such a thing unless it's found, and now he figures if you find it you'll destroy it. He always insisted you lied about him to protect someone."

"He couldn't get out on bail if his trial was reexamined, could he?" I watch the effect of my words on Hansen.

"What are you two talking about?" he says. "The guy was convicted of murder one."

I back up a couple of steps and trace the jagged X, rough as a bread knife, in the copper plate while Bender repeats in my ear that no one was around my studio earlier, when he got there. He saw no one. "From now on, Linda," he says, "whenever you go out, don't forget to lock the door."

*   *   *

Detective Hansen has a tape recorder with him. He places it on my desk, by the phone, and clicks it on. He pronounces the date, the time, the place. Then he asks me to say my name, to declare that I have asked to make this statement about my testimony in Peter Garvey's trial, and then to explain why.

"There's one thing I should have circled on the statement I signed after Luci Cole was murdered," I say carefully. "The description of what I saw outside her house that day. I should have deleted the part where I say Peter Garvey slid himself out from underneath the car and stood up. The part where I described the grime on his face, how sweaty he was. The part where I said we exchanged a few words. What I'm saying now is that it's possible he stayed under the car the whole time that day, it's possible he didn't speak a word to me, it's possible I didn't see his face at all. I may have confused those details with what happened the day before, and the day before that, when I came walking up to the house and he was working on Luci Cole's car. Three days in a row I walked past him and went into the house, except that the third day—" My mouth goes dry, and I swallow. "I discovered Luci's body."

"Did you see Peter Garvey outside Luci Cole's house that day?"

"Yes, but I'm afraid the only time I could have seen his face was from up on the road. At that distance a man is known by the color and shape of his body, and his hair, and by the way he moves. It's not possible to recognize more than that from such a distance."

"So is it possible it was someone else you saw?"

"It's not likely. But it's possible."

I look at Hansen. He waits. He doesn't want to lead me with his questions this time. "When did you first realize your earlier statement might have been misleading?" he wants to know.

"The day I signed it. But even then, *even then* I went back and forth in my mind about whether he had stood up and talked to me at the house that afternoon. I had no doubt it was Peter under that car. What I doubted was that I'd be *believed*, if it turned out I hadn't seen him face to face. I thought my admitting to mental confusion might allow him to get away with killing her. I overcame my uncertainty by repressing it." I turn to look over at the vandalized etching plate. "More recently I have realized that what I did was tell a kind of lie."

After a few more questions and answers, Hansen turns off the tape recorder. Neither of us speaks for a few minutes. Then he stands up to put the tiny machine in his pocket and says, "I'll get this transcribed and over to the county attorney's office, Linda. If you want my opinion, this won't change anything, considering the other evidence in the Garvey case." He touches the point on the etching plate where the two lines intersect, and I wonder what he thinks it means.

I have to admit that talking with Detective Hansen about the doubts that have been on my mind all summer was the biggest letdown of my life. Instead of the strong reaction I expected from him, he made it sound as though my great confession is not likely to make any difference. Now what do I do to protect myself?

As soon as Hansen leaves, I call Wayne's Lock and Key. Wayne turns out to be a slight man in his sixties with a wide forehead that swoops up over the top of his head, giving him a gnomelike appearance. "Most gals changing locks are fighting with their husbands." He waits, as if he's used to his customers telling their life stories at the drop of a dead bolt.

"Charlie and I get along fine."

"Glad to hear it."

He's all business as he gets down to work. The back of his sunburned neck is mapped with pink lines. "This latch is loose, but there's nothing wrong with the lock. It's a classic old beauty, a Yale from the twenties. Sure you want to replace it?"

I'm sure. The front-door lock, too, and I want them keyed the same. While he's working, I settle down to rethink *Mackerel Sky* and prepare a clean copper plate. As soon as he leaves, I lock the door behind him and call directory assistance for Russell Weber. There's no listing for that name. I want to find out if he's still in town.

Next I find the pictures I took of Tess the day she ran away, selecting a shot that includes Weber. Seeing it brings back the way he pulled the bandanna off his head to scratch his scalp, revealing the brassy color of his ropy hair.

In less than a minute I've hurried down the alley and descended the narrow steps to Le's Salon, where both Doug and Sylvie are busy with customers. Sylvie's finishing up a little girl of about ten with the curling iron. Seeing me, Doug raises his eyebrows in question.

Sylvie removes the vinyl cape from the girl's shoulders and smiles at me, then returns to the child's reflection in the mirror. "What do you think, Janie?" Sylvie's dark hair is pulled back tightly, her dark eyes outlined as usual with black and her generous mouth a bright, purply color. Janie tilts her serious face to study her helmet of dark brown hair, smooth and round as a buckeye.

"I need to ask you something," I say to Sylvie as soon as the girl and her mother are gone.

"Shoot."

"You know where I could find Russell Weber? The cook upstairs? I know he comes here—"

"Yeah, he lives over at one of his uncle's rental places, over on Railroad Street, twelve-twelve. My boyfriend stays there sometimes, too." Well, that was easy. "Russ quit upstairs, you know."

"I heard he was fired."

"Maybe." She seems disgusted. "Russ is okay, you know? He just never can bring himself to finish anything."

"Did he have something to finish at the Grubstake?"

"He promised me and my boyfriend he'd hold a job steady till we had enough money to go somewhere they could work on their music again. My boyfriend could get transferred easy, and I—" she gives Doug a quick glance, lowering her voice. "I can't see myself working in this town for the rest of my life."

"He's a musician?"

"They have big plans to send a demo tape to Nashville."

"He's that good, is he?"

"I suppose he could be, if he'd ever finish a song."

Railroad Street turns out to be an unpaved road at the edge of town near the lumberyard. By the ruined sofas in the front yards, I would guess most of these are rentals inhabited by kids attending the local branch of Des Moines Area Community College. Twelve-twelve is a white clapboard with black foundation, a box of a house, trim painted a clean gray. The basement lights are on. The grass is mowed, and the place is well kept, unlike the houses on either side. I've stopped my car across the street, and as I linger, a dirty white Dodge turns into the drive. The young man who gets out is dark and thick-waisted like Sylvie, wearing the brown shirt and matching, belted shorts that UPS drivers wear. He pauses to collect the mail at the front door. He returns something to the mailbox and heads back to his car.

After shopping for frozen shrimp and some tart apples for the curry I've decided to make for supper, I drive by The Honey Barn. Charlie's van is not there, so I stop to see Rosemary. She's typing on the computer, her head tilted back in order to see the screen with her bifocals. Her dress is bright yellow, her Gypsy beads red and orange and hot pink. She smiles her hello. "Ah, Linda. What brings you by?"

"Charlie head home already?"

"He's around here somewhere." Rosemary examines a crimson fingernail and opens her desk drawer to pull out an emery board and smooth the nail with a soft scraping sound. "He's cleaning one of the extractors. Come to think of it, he did mention he had to go after some gizmo or other. He's been in and out all day." She could manage this part of the business single-handedly if she had to. A widow, she lives just two doors away. She's worked for Charlie for years.

She pulls two tea bags from a burgundy box marked LAPSANG SOUCHONG and places them into flowered cups. I didn't plan to stay long enough for tea, but the phone interrupts my protest. She raises her chin a notch as she answers it. "You'll need to set them aside for us to examine. No, I'll have it picked up within a week." She listens. "Well, of course, but not until we've seen the product." She's pouring hot water into our cups as she speaks.

"Someone found a fly in a jar of honey," she huffs when she's off the phone. "I'll believe it when I see it. Charlie gives every jar a personal look-see." She lifts the tea bags out of the cups. "Though lately his mind's somewhere else half the time."

"You hung up before I was finished talking the other day, Rosemary. I was asking about the disagreement you and Charlie had over Russell Weber." I try sipping my tea, which smells like stale wood smoke and menthol. She's ignoring me. "Rosemary?"

"You've been good for Charlie," she says simply. "It's no secret I didn't think much of that other one. The more she hurt him, the more he wanted to marry her, as if that might change things. It wouldn't have."

"It was humiliating for him to find out about her and Peter after she died. For me, having to tell him about that was one of the most difficult parts of the whole ordeal."

"He already suspected about Peter and Luci. I heard gossip about Peter visiting with Luci a lot while Charlie was at work, and I thought he should know what kind of things were said about the woman he wanted to marry. He was angry with me for days, but at least I warned him."

I'll never be able to drink a whole cup of this tea. It's awful. Boiled oak leaves would taste like this. Rosemary's wrong. I told Charlie about Peter and Luci as gently as I could. I remember his face as his feelings evolved from disbelief into hurt, then to anger. I can't believe he had suspected that Luci and Peter had been intimately involved. Rosemary's recollection is no doubt colored by her dislike of Luci.

"He called me late that night and told me to be sure and tell the police he was here all afternoon," she says. "He thought it was important for me to be definite about that." She tastes her tea with an apologetic wince, teeth held tight together.

"He *was* here all afternoon, wasn't he?"

"Of course he was."

"Most days he's in and out?"

"That day wasn't like most days." She stares at me steadily.

"Remember when you saw my car on the road above the house the other day, Rosemary?" She stops blinking. "I was walking along the edge of the field. From up there I could see you standing in the driveway, talking to Charlie. It was clear from your body language you were mad about something. I think you were upset because he'd given Russell Weber money."

"Why don't you ask, so you won't have to guess?"

"Okay, I'm asking."

"Charlie's been neglecting the business. He's convinced you're sorry you married him, and that just kills me. After what he's been through, he deserves better." She starts to sip her tea but lowers her cup into its saucer with a knock. "Sorry about this. It was on sale. It tastes like a cure for something."

"A cure?" It's Charlie, in the doorway. "You telling fortunes again?"

"Linda's fortune is a good one." Rosemary reaches for the switch to turn her computer off, retrieves her purse from the bottom drawer of her desk, and hoists herself up out of her chair, adjusting the belt of her shirtwaist dress. "I see good things ahead for both of you."

Charlie's hand rests on the small of my back. He says he's hungry, and I mutter something about shrimp thawing in the front seat of my car. Rosemary dumps out the teacups, drops the box of Lapsang Souchong into the wastebasket, and turns out the light.

*   *   *

Wednesday is my regular day off. I spend it cleaning house, working in the garden, doing laundry. When I go back to work on Thursday, I miss being at home. My studio no longer feels safe, since the vandalism. All morning I struggle with ideas for the Linden Grove Mall and finally decide that the reason I'm not making progress with my sketches is I'm too ambivalent. My mind keeps turning to ideas for promoting Linden Old Town. Before I can change my mind, I call Robert Chapman and tell him I appreciate the opportunity to try for the mall job, but that I have decided not to submit sketches. I won't be billing him for my time.

I devote the rest of the day to redoing *Mackerel Sky*. I've gained something by having to start over. This time the fish above the house is not pasted onto the sky like an afterthought but woven into the lapping clouds. By the time I've gotten the plate bitten in the acid tank and cleaned, ready for inking, I'm almost glad I had to start over.

Thursday night I call Judy, asking her to drop by in the morning to watch me pull the artist's proof. She and Bill will drive to Omaha in the afternoon for their second weekend with Tess, and she plans to close her shop for the whole day. "I've given up the idea of doing the design work for the new mall," I tell her. "I've called around, and nobody seems to be thinking about how the town might benefit from the inevitable changes."

"Like how?"

"Once people get off the interstate to shop, we could entice them to drive three miles further and check out what we have to offer here in town. I'm thinking about some new signage, defining the unique products we might be selling here. We could do a long-term plan for storefront restoration, maybe even find a grant to apply for."

"Develop a concept, you mean?" She's teasing me.

"And there's something else I want to talk with you about. I found a diary Luci kept the final months of her life."

"Have you read it?"

"I've skimmed it, only reading full paragraphs when I've come to a proper name. Her handwriting is difficult. If we'd had this diary during her murder investigation, some of the people mentioned would have been interviewed by the police. They might have seen something unusual at the house around the time she died, but they had personal reasons for not coming forward."

"Like what?"

"Let's just say Garvey wasn't the only man who came around when Charlie wasn't home. I want you to read a couple of passages and tell me what you think. Bring bagels."

Friday morning Judy arrives just minutes after I fitted my key into the solid new lock in the back door and entered, relieved to find the plate—a coppery rectangle in the skylight's pale, early light—in the condition I left it yesterday. I check out the place as I do every morning now, climbing up to the loft, looking for signs of disturbance. Judy's at my elbow, the paper Bagel Works bag crackling in her fist.

After making coffee, I assemble my materials while Judy hitches herself up onto the counter near the press so she can watch me work—coffee in her right hand, Luci's journal in her left, violet half-moons under her hazel eyes. She hasn't put on her makeup yet, so her eyebrows and lashes are nearly invisible, giving her a faded, watercolor look. She holds the white mug near her tight, chewing mouth, waiting until she swallows so she can sip her coffee, put the mug down, open the book.

I make a mental note of the time, another fallout habit from Luci's murder, as I slip my canvas apron over my head. Over and over, every day, I register the time, as if someone might ask. *Exactly what time was it that you stopped along the road to look down at the house?* It's 8:52 when Judy opens the book and I roll the bed of the press out to its full length toward her. Just seeing Judy with that book in her hand gives me a nervous rush. Even as I tell her to read every word, I am wondering if I will bring myself to show her the first appearance of Bill's name. "From the beginning. You need to see the state of her mind, the way she describes men."

"Where else would I start but the beginning?"

"Just stay away from the middle of the book for now." My hands are flat on the printing blanket, on the press bed. "How are you and Bill getting along?"

"He wanders the house all night. This morning he seemed like he was at the end of his rope. I said, 'I suppose you aren't going to admit to knowing what Tess was hinting at, are you?' and he said, 'Not unless it's absolutely necessary,' like it was a joke. He's accused me of inventing things out of whole cloth because I'm convinced he's holding out on me. He says what I'm doing's as bad as anything I might suspect him of."

"Maybe he has a point." I unfold the second felt blanket and smooth it flat, the friction of the wool warming my hands.

I take her silence to signify she's angry, but when she speaks again, her tone is unchanged. "The two people I love most in the world are in this power struggle, and I'm the focus of their attention. We should be concentrating on Tess."

"You will be, in a few hours." I turn the handle until the overlapping ends of the blankets are caught, then smooth the free ends up and over the large roller to clear the bed for the plate and the paper. With my back to Judy, I step to the worktable to lift the plate with my fingernails, angling it to catch the light for a final inspection. For a few long moments neither of us speaks.

Then she says, "Listen. I want to make him see what we've done—what chances we're taking." She sounds like she's talking around a bite full of bagel. "I'm so scared of driving—" She pauses, probably to swallow. I still have my back to her. "Driving him further away."

"You should have seen Bill tramping the creek bed that day, looking for Tess." I lift the plate off the worktable and carry it to the press. "He was frantic. Tess means the world to him. Your suspicions about him are based on fear, not evidence. You've both been worried to the breaking point since Tess took off that day. This is no time—"

"Linda, look at me." I glance at her. "That was Luci talking." Two-handed, Judy has raised the journal to chest level, like a choir singer, and I realize, of course, she was reading to me. I've skimmed the book for passages that have to do with Charlie, Bill, and Russell Weber, but I have not gone over each line, each page. "Doesn't this sound just like Luci?" Judy looks down and reads it again: " 'I'm so scared of driving him further away.' " When our eyes meet again, mine unblinking, Judy is alert, amused—maybe even vindicated—by my confusion. "Okay, I'll start again." Her pronunciation is as deliberate as a reading teacher's, which is what she used to be. " 'I want to make him see what we've done—what chances we're taking.' "

"Back to the beginning. Who is 'he'?"

"This *is* the beginning." Judy picks up her mug of coffee and manages a hurried, noisy sip. "Well, that's just like Luci, isn't it? Turning up here out of the blue, moving in with Charlie. Slipping into his perfectly calm life, starting her story in the middle like this."

"*She* knew who she meant."

"Making us guess who she's talking about."

"She didn't write it for us."

Judy ignores that, and proceeds to read:

MARCH 12, 1995.

I want to make him see what we've done—what chances we're taking—without blowing the whole thing. But I'm so scared of driving him away. I need him in some perverse way—to help me get out of here. I don't have the nerve to tell him I'm leaving. He has to see he's better off without me. Anyway, I can't stand it sometimes—thinking I'll be here forever. He wants everything about my life to be decided. How do people stand that?

Peter is not complicated. Mostly I love his body—the lean muscles in his arms that thicken when he moves, the pulsebeat in the hollow of his throat—the whiteness of his skin where the sun never strikes it, swirl of light brown hair around his nipples and down around his belly button, narrowing to a thin dark line—drawn all the way to the brushy stubble of his privates.

"Privates," Judy scoffs. "The way she's getting warmed up you'd think she'd come right out and say 'dick,' or 'cock.' Or wait." Her eyes move across the page. "There's tons of description here." She turns a page. "Listen to this. Lists of words, organized by senses. Under 'SMELL' she has 'motor oil, new-turned garden soil, loamy.' " She reads on silently, apparently looking for items worth reporting: " 'starchy after sex,' " she says, " 'like laundry soap.' " She looks at me.

My face feels stiff as a mask.

"I'd like to know her brand of detergent." Judy reads silently again. "Oh, how about this one: 'When he comes in from work— his skin smells sour and ready, like wet grass rotting in the sun.' " She draws her shoulders together in a fast shudder and in one continuous motion snaps the journal shut and slams it flat onto the countertop with a sound that's louder than she expected, judging by the way she flinches. My own reaction is one of relief. What was I thinking, placing that book in Judy's hands?

She picks up her coffee cup and glares. She takes a very long, deep breath, then shivers. "Remember Peter in court? In his suit and blue tie to match his eyes, fair hair all trimmed, clean as a priest? Imagine reducing a man to what he smells like. Why write such stuff anyway? Luci wasn't like this. Are you sure this is her handwriting?"

I'm sure. I dampen a thick blotter, then wipe it down with a sponge. I'm seeing the perfect circles of Luci's gold earrings, seeing her eyes narrow as she concentrates. On a later page will she cat- alog *Bill's* smells? I toss the sponge toward the sink and miss. Bending to retrieve it from the floor, I say, "If she hadn't turned into such a bitch, she'd still be alive."

"God, Linda. I can't believe you said that."

"Well, isn't that how she got herself killed? Trying to escape Charlie by sleeping around? Isn't that how that sounds?" Still hunkered down, I point in the general direction of the journal. In my hand the sponge smells sour.

"She didn't *get* herself killed, Linda." Judy slides off the counter and adjusts her slacks down around her thighs. "Luci may have complained real life wasn't exciting enough, and God knows what she was trying to prove with *this*, but that doesn't mean she—"

"Oh, I know that." I manage to push myself upright, sluggish with size and the impossible, dead-weight-burden of Luci's body in my mind. "You know I didn't mean it."

"Maybe you did," says Judy quietly. "You're still plenty mad at her. We both know Luci was a lot more complex," she says, lifting the journal in her hand, "than this." We shouldn't fault her for not writing great thoughts in her diary. After all, she never dreamed this would be all that would be left of her."

"I've just told Detective Hansen I think the man I saw that afternoon might have been someone who just looked like Peter. I'm pretty sure he stayed under the car that day. I didn't see his face. Hansen doesn't think a change in my testimony will change the conviction, but it's not up to him. It's up to the lawyers. If the case *were* to be reopened, anything in this book that reveals what Luci was up to before she died might be investigated." *No matter who it hurts.* I should take it from Judy's hand right now, protect her from Luci's ghostly gossip.

As if Judy reads my mind, she says, "Reading this is like walking in on someone at a very bad moment. Let's stop."

"Judy—"

"Wouldn't there have to be new evidence for the murder case to be reopened? This diary just makes her relationship with Peter even more clear."

My mouth is dry. "I think I'm in danger. It isn't just that vandalism on Monday. Someone was prowling around our garage Sunday night."

"But, Linda—"

"I know you think this is survivor's guilt, or delayed terror—"

"Everyone thinks that. You've acted so strange, for weeks."

"Like who?"

"Oh, Rosemary Lindstrom. And you have to admit you were
ignoring me there for a while, until Tess ran away and you knew
I needed you. Angela says you jump out of your skin when she
approaches your table to take your lunch order."

"She startled me once—*once*, when I was daydreaming."

"Even Russ Weber brought it up."

"You're kidding."

"And Tess, of course, flat out envies your grief."

"Weber barely knows who I am."

"When he was working at the Grubstake, he'd come in for his
paper every day and we'd chat, the way people do, small talk. I
admit I have my doubts about him now, after Tess's trouble, but
I always saw him as a hometown boy who couldn't cut loose, who
keeps coming back to regroup."

"He's hardly a boy, Judy. He's at least my age."

"He talked about other people in the neighborhood all the time.
It would take him half an hour to buy his paper. His theory about
you was that Charlie shouldn't expect you to live in the same house
where you found Luci's body, that that's what's keeping you scared.
I think Russ found you attractive. I know you go into the Grubstake every day for lunch, but I wonder if he noticed all the customers as much as he noticed you. He mentioned to me that you'd
lost weight. I hadn't even noticed that."

I glance down past the familiar terrain of my body, flexing the
fanned-out sinews of my right foot in its sandal, studying the knobs
of my ankle. "Exactly what did you tell him?"

"I told him you act like Luci's murder case isn't settled."

"I wish you hadn't done that."

"Gossip can be very caring. It's not like I said you're stupid, or crazy. You're deeply affected, that's all." She pauses, realizing how that sounded. "I mean, not affected as in weird, but distressed, upset. People around here care about you." Judy's face inclines toward mine with concern. "If it will make you feel better, I'll take the journal with me to Omaha and give you a full report when I get back."

Pulling the thin volume gently from her hand, I manage only a shake of the head to convey my displeasure. She follows the journal with a look of longing as it disappears into the middle of three pockets in my canvas apron. It's a tight fit, and hangs heavy. As I turn back to the press, my hands shake.

I center the damp blotter over the etching plate and smooth the three blankets, one by one, on top of the paper, trying to calm myself. So I've been discussed around the neighborhood, have I? Poor Linda, addled for life by what she saw. "Why don't you just go to Omaha and straighten out your own life? You're right, I don't consider Luci's murder *settled*, as you call it, but I never dreamed, of all people, you'd speculate about my fears with Russell Weber—"

"Is that what you're so mad about?"

"Who else did you discuss this with?"

She's gathering her things, dropping a half-eaten bagel back into the bag, crushing it shut with a vengeance. "No one," she says calmly. "Well, Bill, of course. I do talk to my husband. At least I *try*."

"Luci mentions Bill in her diary," I say, tapping my pocket.

"I'm sure she had plenty to say about all of us. I'll see you when I get back from Omaha."

When she tells Bill about this diary, maybe he'll come clean with her about how close he and Luci were, and I won't have to be the one to give her the bad news. I feel a twinge of guilt. After all, Judy's in trouble of her own, and I've upset her further. And we didn't even talk about Linden Old Town. Cranking the press slowly and evenly, my hands—warm now, and steady—tighten to overcome a slight resistance as the roller mounts the plate.

11 ◆ AFTER JUDY LEAVES, I keep working until an edition of twelve prints of *Mackerel Sky* is stacked on the counter, layered with newsprint and blotters. John Bender, calling my name through the screen door, snaps me out of my trancelike concentration. I left a message at his office earlier. If he was the one who came here and X'ed out the original image for this print, I want him to see it takes a lot more than that to make me give up a project, especially if the project has to do with finding out the truth.

He rattles the door to remind me I locked it. As I approach him, I wipe my right wrist across my forehead and roll my shoulders, stiff and tight from the long hours of work. My fingers hesitate on the lock. "You brought Garvey's letter?"

"Yes."

"Your note said you hit a dead end with Luci's car."

"Neither of us is going to figure this out alone."

Bender follows me over to *Mackerel Sky*. As he steps close enough to inspect the print, I resist the impulse to back away from the fish's staring eye. "Ummm," he says thoughtfully. "Fish and bird. This makes me think of those metamorphosis prints where

black birds become negative spaces around white fish." His pointing finger hovers above the fish's scalloped scales, woven with sug-
gestions of clouds and birds in flight. "I'm not explaining it well."

"Probably Escher." Bender doesn't react. "My work is based on
gestural drawing, not repeat-pattern design." This could be the
start of a conversation I'm in no mood for right now. "My idea
came from Charlie's metaphor for the way the sky looked one
night. Maybe it's more personal than original."

"It wasn't a criticism." Seeing my dismissive shrug for what it
is, a signal to change the subject, Bender pulls a long envelope
from his pocket. His name and address run across the face of it in
large, sprawling script. Peter's letter is a lot shorter than I had
imagined and ends with a direct order: "You scared her enough to
get her here. Watch what she does next."

"Watching me is an assignment you're well qualified for."

"Garvey really gave you an earful, didn't he? That business
about a book Luci wrote in."

It's clear to me Bender sees this letter as confirmation he and I
are in this together. My right hand moves protectively against the
hard surface of Luci's journal in the tight pocket of my apron. I've
been reading it word for word, in bits and pieces all day: *Gradually
I can feel myself already transferring to you some of my great need to
depend. I love your self-sufficiency, crave it for myself.* I need another
mind to grapple with to understand what happened to her, but it's
not going to be Bender's. My fixation with him could easily become a dangerous game. "Luci knew she was risking everything
with Peter, but she couldn't seem to help herself. It's almost as if
her toying with him was part of a self-destructive plan."

"What did he tell you?"

"He remembered something about birds roosting in the woods
behind the house, something about horses bolting." I pause, imagining the raucous crows, their long, jointed wings flapping against
the sky—like those rising across the belly of the fish in my print.
"Hansen says your father's been ill."

"I was back and forth for a few days. It's a four-hour drive. The funeral was yesterday."

"He didn't tell me that. I'm sorry."

"He didn't know yet, when you took him the flashlight. Dad had time to get used to the idea of dying. We talked a lot at the end. He told me being an old man was the most interesting part of an interesting life. His mind was flooded with memories of things he hadn't thought about for years." He hesitates. "This makes it harder for you to be mad at me, doesn't it?"

I return my attention to *Mackerel Sky*.

"This is Charlie's house, isn't it?"

"Not just his." Turning my back on Bender, I walk over to the print cabinet to retrieve the vandalized plate. "I guess you know I've given Hansen a new statement about what I saw the day Luci died." I lick my lips as I place the plate with its wild X on the surface of the worktable.

"Yes, he told me." Bender gauges the scratches on the copper plate with his thumbnail. "This has to be the act of someone who knows your work but not your character."

We look at each other. "I'm still very much an outsider in this town," I say. "The only way I can imagine speaking frankly, with someone I could trust, would be to find a professional counselor. For a while this summer Charlie was encouraging me to do just that, until he gave up. It wasn't a suggestion I took kindly to. I understand from Detective Hansen that you think I'm a bit paranoid, too, but counseling won't undo this."

"Unless you did the damage yourself."

My back stiffens.

"I don't think you did, but you should know that Hansen has his doubts about you." He leans a hip against the thick edge of the worktable. "This is a telling kind of vandalism. It has to be someone who knows you well enough to know what kind of artwork you do but not well enough to know this wouldn't scare you off."

"That's not something you could have known about me until now."

"You're forgetting I observed you closely during the trial. You appeared self-possessed and prudent, exactly the traits I see in you at this moment." He traces a diagonal scratch that bisects the image of the house. "I didn't do this, Linda. I'm more than a little worried about who did. I stopped by Hansen's office Tuesday so he could take my fingerprints. All I can do is ask you to believe me until the thumbprint he lifted here Monday rules me out. In the meantime you have something to gain by making a leap of trust."

"That's hardly necessary." I tell him that up until the week before Luci died, Russell Weber had been helping Charlie build the garage. I never laid eyes on Weber until this summer, when he became the cook at the Grubstake, so I couldn't have been aware at the time of Luci's murder that he was tall and blond like Peter Garvey. Now I wonder if it could have been Weber lying under her car that day. It's a preposterous suggestion, and the only way I can think of to recruit Bender without trusting him the way he wants me to. He places a finger on the X that crosses out the house. Within a minute, he's out the door.

Charlie insists on celebrating his birthday quietly—no surprises, no cakes, no big deal. I take home one of the proofs of his print, and after dinner of chicken and roasting ears fixed on the grill and strawberry shortcake, I give him his gift. His kiss is the kind of double-peck bestowed with public awards. He tells me I'm brilliant. "I might not understand what the fish means," he admits. "Maybe I'm too literal-minded."

"It's about seeing, and imagination, *your* imagination, Charlie." He props *Mackerel Sky* on the mantel, moving a pair of blue-patterned Polish candlesticks in front of it to keep it from buckling and sliding down. We're side by side, looking at the mackerel sky the way we looked at the real thing in the parking lot outside

Mona's Pizza. But that silence was comfortable, and close. This silence makes me uneasy. "Don't worry about being literal-minded," I tell him. "I'm more interested in how you feel."

The pressure of his arm against mine diminishes. "Are you going to leave me?"

"Of course not." My lips stay open with surprise as he backs up and sits on the edge of the sofa, open hands braced on his knees as if he might push up onto his feet at any moment. "Why would you say that?"

"I ran into Ken Hansen having lunch at Mona's. He assumed I knew you'd asked him to check that flashlight against prints from Luci's murder investigation." Charlie stands, unbuttoning his shirt. He jerks his shirttails free of his belt, wide gestures to get him out of the room into the hallway.

"Then he must have told you he didn't want to do it, that my request was inappropriate. I'm sorry if I neglected to tell you how foolish I felt." My loud voice doesn't bring Charlie back. I hate it when he leaves the room angry. Water's running in the bathroom. His face is wet, half covered with his dripping hands, when I step into the doorway. "I wanted tonight to feel like a celebration."

"It's fine," he says, toweling his hair back from his face. "Really. I love your present."

"I did that plate for you *twice*, Charlie."

A sigh deflates him and he looks as dumbfounded as when I first told him about the vandalism. He sits on the edge of the tub, a blue towel draped across his knees. His upper body is muscular across the shoulders but rounded below the ribcage, a slackness that makes him appear old, weary. As if he knows what I'm thinking, he fingers his belly, giving it a dismissive slap. "I do love you, Linda," he says then, as if it were the logical next thought, the gesture and the words so incongruous I'm afraid I'm going to laugh.

Instead, tears blur my vision. "I know that, Charlie."

"But I want our life to be uncomplicated. If it's not too late for that." He's wiping the towel across his forehead again, and then he sits motionless. "You start. This is too hard for me."

"I'm not trying to start anything."

"You want something from me you're not getting. You want me showing you how I feel." He looks at me, combing his wet hair back with his fingers. A vein stands out along the inside of his forearm. "And if you don't get enough from me, you'll go else-where. Talk to Hansen behind my back. I thought we decided there was no point in reporting that intruder to the police. What connection could you possibly make between that event and Luci's death? And why haven't you been talking to me about these things?"

"Because you think I'm being irrationally fearful."

"Don't you think I have good reason? If I seem to have lost confidence in you, maybe it's that I've lost confidence in everything else. After Luci—"

"Don't project Luci onto me."

"Then don't give me a reason to."

For a moment we're both silent. Then I say, "Luci's death has called all kinds of things into question for me, too, doubts about my own character. I was too eager to blame Garvey. It was such an ugly death, and it caught Luci at such a bad moment."

He starts to smile but catches himself. "She doesn't deserve your kindness."

The matter-of-fact coldness of his voice returns my attention to the bright chrome faucets and the glint of mirror above the sink. "I was sure it was Peter I saw that day, but I shouldn't have sworn to it."

"Hansen told me you're second-guessing yourself. I have to learn my wife's weightiest thoughts from a police detective. Now, *why would that be?*" Charlie backs me out of the room and braces his arms on the doorframe. He is exactly my height with his shoes off. His face darkens even before he starts to speak again, pronouncing his words in a measured, aggressive whisper. "Garvey took her *life*, Linda. You can't let him get away with ruining ours, too. I know what you found that day. I saw the pictures. You seem to forget that. If you can't put Luci's death behind you, maybe you *had* better leave, until you get help to deal with it."

Shaken, I'm against the wall of the dim hallway. "Charlie, we can't have things simple and uncomplicated right now, the way we want. But that doesn't mean we have to give up on each other. I need your comfort, and your reassurance. I should have told you I took the flashlight to Hansen. I don't know why I didn't."

For a moment his concentration falters, but then his eyes narrow and his nostrils grow larger. He's breathing hard. The light from the bathroom doorway behind him outlines his hair in a jagged red line. "You certainly don't think *I'm* going to leave, do you?"

"Nobody's leaving."

"It's my house," he says simply, dropping his arms to his sides and backing away, "not yours."

Later I can hardly remember packing a few things, driving to the studio, climbing to the loft, and falling asleep under the dust sheet, too tired even to make up the bed properly. I wake in full darkness, trying to recall locking the door.

It's cold in the loft. I leave the bed just long enough to pull Luci's blue coverlet off the railing. Wrapped in the quilt, my view unobstructed now, I can see across the studio to the front window below, where the blinds filter slits of light from the street onto my desk. Luci's journal is visible even at this distance. The skylight admits a gloss of moonlight, and I shiver, wide awake. I turn on the lamp by the bed to look at my watch. Three fifty-three.

Eyes closed, I fumble around in the duffel bag on the bed with me, pull on the pair of socks I find there, and pad over to the kitchenette to fill the coffeemaker and lug it over to the small lamp table within easy reach of the warm covers. I have to make another trip downstairs to get my favorite cup and Luci's journal, closing the front blinds while I'm at it. Once I'm back upstairs, the smell of the coffee revives me. "Charlie," I whisper against the rim of the cup, missing him. I pull the quilt close around me. I lift the coffee, actually taking a sip this time, swallowing fast because of an impending sneeze, which echoes in the cavernous space. I shiver at the smallness of the sound and scan the first entry, which Judy read to me yesterday, and continue to read:

MARCH 17, 1995.

This house has become my prison. But how could I have accused Charlie last night of wanting to keep me away from life—as if this frozen state I'm in were his fault? He reminds me how our life together was to give me more energy to create, not less— more time and space for my art. So why isn't it working out that way? he wants to know. His protective, generous love terrifies me—he doesn't suspect how unworthy I am.

Every day I betray his love in ways I don't mean to—deeper and deeper entrapping myself in my own secrecy—until now there seems to be but one way to stop—the obvious one—to let him discover I am not what I seem. Lately the Old Darkness has come over me again—giving me a warped talent for drama, with him one of the unsuspecting players—and me a woman who sets things in motion, but who rarely appears to start anything her- self.

I let the quilt slip off my shoulders as I shiver again, but not with the cold. Years ago, back in school, Luci used to suffer what she called the Dark Blues. Could that be what she means here by the "Old Darkness"? At those times she'd mutter about the myth that the artist has to be out of control, baffled by convention, and in near-constant torment. She'd try to make light, in her ironic way, of what I could tell were terrible times for her. She'd get behind on projects, mope about, sleep too much, wake up with a blazing headache and a bad case of guilt over her lack of control, punishing herself for being "stuck."

Sometimes she wouldn't get out of bed for two or three days, but she was gifted enough she could get away with it. Suffering really did appear to fuel her creative energies; at last she'd get up and take a shower and begin to work in a white heat. The whole show did little to support my view that agony, far from being the source of her creative ideas, just delayed their arrival. She refused to talk about those blue times, once they'd passed. Moving the lamp closer to the edge of the bed so I can see the page better, I back up and reread, then move on to the next entry, where I find a proper name I missed in my earlier, hurried scanning: Gustavson.

MARCH 18, 1995.

Reverend Gustavson's features are large, rather thick, but his mouth is so sensual—full-lipped and unguarded. I can make him shift in his chair simply by looking at him obliquely. The first time I went to Reverend G—— in the church office, all I did was cry. I couldn't speak at all, I cried so hard. I was embarrassed—too suspicious and upset to tell him what was wrong.

But the second time we met, I told him I was trying to break off a relationship with a man in his congregation—and that I'd sought out G—— to give me courage. I knew he was a trained psychologist. By the time I left him that morning, G—— had suggested my depression might be situational, not clinical, and assured me he makes "pastoral calls"—I must have seemed seriously distraught!—and suggested I try writing down what troubled me—what I do, how I feel, day by day—so we could discuss my dilemma like a text—objectively. Look for patterns and remedies. Analyze my motives. Tell myself the truth for a change, he might have said.

So I watch Reverend G——'s eyes while he reads the pages I've written for him. When he looks up at me over his glasses, I find myself stroking my neck with slow hands—licking my lips, turning away from him only to glance back, sidelong—tilting my face to meet his gaze. I observe these movements as if I am no longer in myself, but watching another Luci repeat an old pantomime. I see the signs of his responding, but I'm so careful—I go slow. He cares about me. He says so.

Lying beside Charlie at night, I dream of G——'s eyes caressing the words I've written for him—see them draw him in despite his will. Because he struggles not to move or react the way he wants to, being a professional, a man of God—but wants passion nonetheless, I can tell—he's oblivious to what he's inevitably bringing about. And because it all seems so familiar, and I am so ashamed, confiding in him is now impossible.

When I come home, I shake, cold, disgusted with myself for all my sexual failures. At least he hasn't caught on yet. But today I went too far. He wouldn't give back the pages I'd written, describing the way he'll look at me just as we're finally about to touch. He told me he had destroyed them—afraid of his own desires—not mine. So much for the two of us facing my problems objectively together! He's torn them up. Turned me down. Denied his own preoccupation. My face burned with remorse. I deserve this shame, for testing him. He's seen the last of me.

So I'm going to write this for myself—or for someone who isn't so easily frightened, someone who won't be ashamed of what's in my mind. If I'm going to get myself under control, I'm going to have to name the shocking, vulgar things that are back there, recover from this sexual paralysis. Or I'll lose Charlie. I can't keep on failing him the way I do. Sometimes I come so close to telling him everything, but I just can't.

What follows are the exercises in physical description Judy read to me yesterday, unorganized phrases and lists of details describing Peter Garvey, as if Luci were trying to shock herself. By the dates I see she abandoned her journal in March, then picked it up again in May. I take another sip of coffee, remove the sleep-sand from the inner corners of my eyes.

And out of all the details I recall about her when we knew each other in school—at first, I suppose, because we were older than many of the other students, then because neither of us was as social as most of our classmates—a few begin to surface to contradict the Luci in the journal. She, even more than I, was a loner—the one who never had a steady boyfriend, the one who dropped Life Drawing the day they brought in a male model because she couldn't stand to stare at a naked man. She said it made her ill. She told me at one point, with some pride, I thought, that she often skipped her period— because she was too thin, according to the doctor at Student Health. Still, she starved herself. She gossiped about men she found attractive—but made a point of insisting she saved her passion for her work. Years later, when she called to tell me about Charlie, laughing about how she'd met an entomologist at a flea market—he was shopping for old hinges and doorknobs to use in renovating his house— she was so giddy, talking in the same breath about how well her work was going *and* how wonderful it was loving Charlie, I figured she'd found a good balance, a healthy happiness.

Reverend Gustavson is the minister of the church I did the centennial etching for last year. I'll pay him a visit as soon as I can arrange it. Wide awake, I return to the page, skipping over sketches of horses and lizards and rabbits with Peter's head and shoulders. And read on:

MAY 5, 1995.

Peter's eyelids are heavy, puffy. I see him growing old over there, puttering in his workshop, his brain dim from too much late-night drinking—but now, at thirty-three, those fleshy lids give him a sleepy look—Peter of Languor, I call him—out by the fence with the horses, he slowly blinks, turning my way so I can gaze into his eyes that reveal intelligence, but a remarkable lack of ambition.

I rest one foot on the lowest cross-pole of the fence—shading my eyes as we talk—allowing each encounter with Peter to last a few minutes longer than the last—patiently teaching myself that I can safely love the lean muscles that thicken when he moves—love even more the pulsebeat in the hollow of his throat—the freckles on those lazy lids when his eyes are downcast, so uncertain when he sees me approaching the fence—then meets me halfway. By now I am lost, thinking about him all the time—and he about me, I am sure of it!

I long to throw myself away on nobody. Why? To prove I can give myself? To succeed at last in staying away from B——, and forget all he makes me remember? It was no accident, my moving to his town. Some force must have pulled me to where he was—so I'd be reminded of what happened all those years ago. So that I'd have him to talk to as I remembered how I had wronged him then—and make things right between us.

Could it be true that keeping B—— close and seeing him so often is a hedge against the fear of giving myself to Charlie? I'm still closed up with Charlie, so afraid, so unable to feel that desire for him, the one I want to want so much. I fantasize about B——. I have shocking dreams after he and I talk, where the moment he penetrates me, I have won, and he can no longer deny me anything. I know how much he fears putting so much at risk for me—a wife, a reputation. So I must be worth something.

But Peter has nothing to lose. So what am I doing with him?

I've grown colder, but I have to leave the warm bed for the bathroom, returning in a hurry to skip ahead a bit, starting with a paragraph that catches my eye because of the words "Peter" and "knife."

MAY 15, 1995.

Yesterday Peter took me into his workshop and showed me a curved knife he uses for cutting leather—for harnesses and saddles—and sliced a narrow strip for me, tying it around my wrist—the pungent smell of the leather heavy as musk. Later he backed me into his bedroom—and I was horrified that I could submit unfeelingly to a man whose hungers are so base—so uncomplicated. It was as if a powerful ghost had risen up and rendered me passive as wood. Peter didn't even notice there was something wrong.

Worse, I crossed the yard just as Charlie was driving in—forcing me to spin a lie out of my confusion, my dampish smell—pretending I was coming down with the flu—running past him, moaning in the bathroom—and Charlie so concerned and tender with me that I was even more convincing, chilled and shaken by self-loathing and the most terrible guilt—as he cared for me. He placed a cool cloth across my forehead while the smell of the leather thong on my wrist made me physically ill.

My finger falls on the words "and I was horrified" and moves over to the margin, where she's added, "Are *you* horrified by my telling you this?" I lower the book for a moment. Who's this note for? I think how gentle Charlie must have been with her that day, how unsuspecting. The dates of these entries remind me that during the same period of time she was writing this, she was talking to me on the phone about how Charlie's business was expanding, about their plans for finishing the house renovation, about juried shows she was planning to enter. And about which flowers were starting to bloom in the yard.

MAY 16, 1995.

Today I took apples as far as the fence for the horses and waited
for Charlie to come home—so he would believe that's what I
was returning from yesterday—simply feeding the horses, over
the fence, when suddenly beset by illness. I'm so afraid of discovery. As soon as Charlie left for work, Peter came to the
kitchen. He was wearing a clean shirt. His fingernails were clean.
He sat down—played the part of the guest—only more familiar,
calmer, as if something had been decided. And I was the old Luci
again—the good wife, holding her breath.

MAY 17, 1995.

In my college sketchbooks I used imagination to turn what I saw
each day into visual, waking dreams. Now it's a struggle to make
myself record the ways I hide my actions from people around
me. I have to hide even more, now that I've done this terrible
thing behind Charlie's back. Outwardly I am loved, admired,
devoted. No one knows how devious I can be. Or how I long to
be free of pretense. I'm the Good Luci on the outside—at war
with a freak no one knows.

The sublime and ordinary—meet in kitchens. So today Charlie and I made pesto—a whole vat of it!—

I lean to pour myself another cup of coffee before facing the vat
of pesto. Above the skylight, darkness has given way to a rosy glow.
In the tree behind the building a bird has started to sing.

Conventional wisdom says that loving on the rebound is foolish.
The last lover is still too much in the mind. Loving the new person
may be more a reaction to loss than an embracing of another,
unique human being. Charlie and I talked about that in the beginning. Even conversations about the chance we were taking to marry
so soon brought us closer.

Luci was small, vibrant, erratic, and in a rage. She worked in
color. I was the steady one, overgrown, awkward, protective. The

Girl Scout. The one who worked in black and white. The one who needed to be needed.

I envied her. I wanted to *be* her. Charlie loved me because I was not. Now she's telling me what their life was like, her version. No use putting it off any longer.

12 ◆ "She said writing in her diary was like talking to you," Peter Garvey told me in prison. "It was you she wanted to be with." Since the moment I pulled this book from the bookcase and recognized it for what it was, I have tried to imagine she meant me to read it one day. I raise the book slightly, rushing past the familiar words: "the sublime and ordinary—"

meet in kitchens. So today Charlie and I made pesto—a whole vat of it!—and before we were done, we tasted of basil head to toe. I never knew how good pesto could be—before this. There'll be no end to it, I said to Charlie. Cooking up one pleasure—after another. What we consume in the kitchen—we burn down the hall.

But my mood rang false. Licking a touch of pesto off his lower lip—I guess I embarrassed him. I don't like it when you're like this, he said, it doesn't turn me on.

Charlie <u>knows.</u> Peter comes to the back door with strawberries from his yard and I catch Charlie looking at me with distrust, on the verge of hating what he sees. Only in his arms do I feel secure, small, delicate, and good. He is big and caring, protective, telling me what is best. It could all be so extremely simple without the sex. But he moves over me like darkness, and I can't breathe. I just want it to be over. I want to be the one who's bigger, taking charge. He <u>knows</u> he's not the only one. He just hasn't decided what to do about it yet.

He presses me to marry him—tells me the plans he's got for rebuilding the garage—a studio for me—a skylight and lots of space to work. He wants me all set, installed. If he admitted that I've been untrue to him, by confronting me—he'd take other actions! I <u>have</u> to settle into this life and be an artist again! I <u>have</u> to let him give me space to work—the skylight, the privacy, marriage. But living with him, I'm helpless to work, to have any independence. I can't control the darkness.

I have no talent for being happy.

Am I too much the weaver?—knowing what can go behind and under?—unwind, then twist together?—testing how many chances I can take before pulling back, just in the nick of time— before he figures out the pattern, and pushes me away? Is that what I <u>want</u>?

Can I let him discover my secret without actually telling him?

In the bathroom I run cold water and splash my face and neck and the insides of my arms. The coffee's made me wide awake but fuzzy-minded, as if my brain is overloading, confused by what Luci's trying to say.

The journal waits for me back in bed, turned onto its pages, and the coffeepot is still half full. I wish I had something to eat. But I'm hooked by the possibility that Luci's secret life will make sense any minute now. I skim over some art notes on adjacent colors and their reflections. Another page beyond that, Russell Weber arrives on the scene.

JUNE 11, 1995.

Russ is working alone today, bracing the interior wall of the garage. He comes to the kitchen for iced tea. The fingernails on his right hand are long for playing the guitar. He strums the air, singing to me, taking a long break while Charlie is paying him by the hour. Don't give me away, Russell sings, grinning, making me a conspirator against The Boss, he calls him—as if he senses I will not object. My complicity gives him permission. His eyes linger on my face after our conversation has stopped. We just look at each other. He doesn't know I started it, this lingering— to see how long he would stay. He thinks it's his idea. You have to go back to work, I tell him, and I take the glass away. He resists letting it go, our hands touching.

When I try to picture Russell Weber's face, what comes to mind is the photograph I took of him, stretching lazily in the sun, not the man himself. For a number of pages Luci reflects on her artistic goals. Russell Weber has vanished as abruptly as he arrived. I expect him back.

JUNE 12, 1995.

These are the reasons I lie: to conceal unflattering behavior and because I'm afraid of hurting others—Charlie, my mother, Susanna. Because I believe in being loyal, kind, honest—and I am not any of these things.

How much work am I willing to do to understand myself? According to the checklists in the books and magazine articles, I have all the symptoms: insomnia, hypochondria, fear of darkness, compulsive desire for thinness, perfectionism in my work, fixation on detail, inability to remember long stretches of childhood, desire to be invisible, and on and on—fifteen out of twenty. There are eighteen books in The Little Read that hold the theory that moments from childhood can tick in the mind like a time bomb. But there's no story like mine in those books.

I've got to focus on my work—to actually complete something—the way Russ cannot. I see him out there working on the garage one minute—the next he's vanished—and I find him sitting behind the foundation, facing the ravine, smoking and lazing his head against the wall. Seeing his inability to concentrate has made me recognize my own tendency to abort every good idea halfway to completion.

He talks openly to me—as if we are conspirators—but I prod him—because Charlie trusts him to work steadily while he's counting his time. Still, my body swells, and my heart races, like with Peter that disastrous, shameful afternoon—wanting to run my hand along Russ's arm, wrist to elbow, over his shoulder to the tender spot behind his ear. Why do I have such thoughts? He has a degree in agronomy, he told me today—but can't get a job in his field, and I laughed—causing a fury to come over him until I calmed him down. I was surprised, that's all, and thought he might be making it up—a bad joke on himself. But I was sorry for my insensitive laughter.

I lose jobs, he says, I misplace them. He laughs a lazy laugh. Like a good salesman, he waits for the fertile moment when I want to make it up to him for laughing at him—and shows me a bag of brownish powder. Telling? he asks. I shake my head. How did he know I wouldn't tell? Then, standing up inside the garage's framed-in, phantom walls—he pulls me to him, kisses me, where anyone driving by could see. Where Peter, beyond his horses, could see.

Later, back out of sight, I do a single hit—the flush outlining each single leaf with orange light. Half the rush comes from daring, after so long, and half from wanting to go down in flames. Russell takes none for himself. He's the one laughing this time.

Tomorrow is Saturday. Charlie and Russ will work side by side all day—and I'll drive a few nails myself. Perhaps Peter— running the horses—will hear the many blows of the hammers and look over to see who's working with such industry. And I will have set things in motion to be thrust out of my life with Charlie. I wonder that I ever thought I could be what Charlie

wants. I'm so ashamed, I'm starting to enjoy seeing things go
wrong—to let catastrophes and misunderstandings accumulate,
explode. Soon it will all be out of my hands. And I can pay the
price at last.

JUNE 23, 1995.

God, Linda, I loved having you visit! You're just what I need!
Your nervous excitement over the closing on the building and
lining up contractors was terrific. The way we stayed up talking
half the night was like old times! I <u>like</u> the way <u>you</u> take
chances—deciding in a moment to invest in that funky old wreck
of a building (God help the plumbing!) in this narrow place
where I'm the only person you know. I'm scared, I can tell you,
since it was my idea, and if things don't work out it will be on
my head. Don't be unnerved—with your talent and background
you'll make a go of it—and you'll have time for your wonderful
prints, too—no one can draw like that!—but I'll have to get back
to work, or you'll put me to shame. <u>And your visit gave me this</u>
<u>idea. If I tell you all I've been up to—if I give this to you, and</u>
<u>you read it—it will be real.</u>

I read the June 23 entry again. Suddenly the tone of the earlier
entries—stilted and oddly formal, has shifted, as if she's pulled up
a chair, leaned close. Now she's talking to *me*. The next entry is
one I've already read. I read it more slowly this time:

JUNE 24, 1995.

You'll be happy to know that since I decided to break off with
Peter, I <u>do</u> have a greater feeling of confidence. But Bill Allard
is still a problem. With you arriving for good in a month, I have
a new reason to take action <u>now</u>. In Hy-Vee today, B—— got
right behind me with his cart and talked to me with canned goods
in his hands. Our friendship doesn't have to be over, he said,

staring at a label. <u>What would he say if he knew I'd put his name in the public record?</u>

Let's at least have one more good, long conversation, he said, putting the cans back on the shelf, stacking them with meticulous care (he's so like that!). One good-bye leads to another, I told him, but we kissed in canned fruits, and I could feel what might happen if we were really alone. The store was nearly empty that early in the day. The feeling of excitement lasted until I reached the frozen-food aisle and felt the chill.

Outside the store I pretended not to see Rosemary Lindstrom going in. She'd love to think I'm about to break up a family—the worst way for me to expose myself, especially in a town this small. B—— admits he's been driving by the house. He claims that yesterday he came up out of the woods along the old path behind the garage and saw someone hammering away on the siding and singing at the top of his lungs.

If there's one thing that will make me ashamed enough to give him up, it's that I've made friends with his wife since moving on from my curiosity about romance novels (I bought six, read one!) to the DEPENDENCY/RECOVERY section. The irony that I'm trying to avoid loving her husband compounds the guilt, so I have to buy an extra book for <u>penance</u>! She'd never dream I've deprived her of B——'s love, my only atonement that I can prevent him from telling her. By ending things with him, I'll stop him from wanting to marry me. Marry me! She has no idea I save <u>her</u> marriage every day.

I'm reading more quickly now that I'm familiar with Luci's handwriting. I jump over passages dwelling on plans for her artwork, plans she didn't have time to carry out. When I come to my own name, I slow down again, rereading sentence after sentence, startled by her point of view.

JUNE 26, 1995.

Gradually, even before you get here, I can feel myself transferring to you some of my great need to depend. I love the drawings
for the loft. And I love your self-sufficiency—and crave it for
myself. I remember your ways: to choose a few close friends and
talk things over with them. Cross you, though, and you clam up
tight. (Don't deny it!) You either tell the truth or say nothing,
another kind of lie.

But there are lies we <u>have</u> to tell, lies that deform our char-
acters but which create a necessary illusion when we don't live
up to our own ideals. Maybe that's the worst kind of deceit, but
the most human. How do you deal with that? Telling you what
I have done will make it real. I swear I will make you my con-
fessor, Linda, if it's the last thing I do.

The irony of this book's falling into my hands now is almost
too much to bear. Underneath the glib brightness I remember that
during the last three days she was alive, she was ashamed, desperate
for me to hear her. I blink away the tears so the words will come
back into focus:

Sometimes I wonder if I'm still writing this for Reverend
G——. But I'm not. I'm too angry. He was glad enough to see
me again, but unfortunately he suggested it was something in my
childhood that started this <u>love of flirtation</u>. So I told him that
I remember nothing before the age of sixteen. I think he believed
me. I like it better when he talks about leaps of faith.

You were always such a paradox to me, Linda—big, broad-
shouldered, blond, striking—missing chances because you didn't
notice the way men looked at you. I wanted to be like that! You
thought you had to wait for them to come to you, not realizing
they were daunted by your very presence!

I got the idea for a journal before I went to talk to Rev.
G——. I have very little income of my own, and I didn't want

Charlie to pay for a therapist, or to guess why I needed one! So I started reading every self-help book I could get my hands on. One, a workbook, suggested writing exercises as a way to deal with past events. First you have to DECIDE TO HEAL, the book said. So I decided to give it a try. I was afraid I was going to lose Charlie. And lose my self-respect besides.

I had already read so many books, ticked off so many check-lists. Events from childhood, the books agreed, can cause symptoms of shame. One afternoon I tried the writing exercise in the middle of the book. You are a child of six, and you are all alone. Focus on the first person who comes along. The instructions asked for details: smells, sounds—like the sound the door made when it went shut. Whatever comes into your mind. Don't stop writing until the time is up.

I started with a day when I stayed in from recess because I had a cold, thinking of my first-grade teacher, the red birthmark on the back of her neck, the enlarged knuckle on her right hand, the smell of chalk. I even remembered the dress she was wearing that day.

Next my uncle Marty came to mind, hiking with me along the lane to Grandma's farmhouse—his limping walk, the way he bent down and pulled on his left ear because he couldn't hear so well. And I wrote more pages. And then I thought of my father. I set the timer for fifteen minutes and began to write.

By the time the timer rang, they had all done unspeakable things to me. I wrote until my hand cramped.

What I'd written was all lies. I took the pages out by the garden and burned them—burned the book, too, with its tricky predictions:

You may resist believing your memories.

You may wish to think it never happened.

You may be afraid to tell.

I went to bed for three days. The voice in that workbook had peopled my darkness with monsters and ordered me to go in there and drag them out with a version of the worst that could have happened! <u>It was right after that I went to Reverend Gus the first time,</u> desperate to tell him it wasn't some perverted childhood abuse that was haunting me but something I'd been a willing party to. <u>And he asked me to write, too!</u> This time I had my guard up and wrote about the present, not the past. I can't go back to him, Linda, but I can't go on the way I am either.

The truth lies in the past like a beast in the shadows, ready to leap and strike. After years of keeping to myself, I felt like a virgin again when I met Charlie. Even now, you're the only one I could face with what really happened years ago. I'm not even sure I can tell you. But I'm working up to it. I'm going to try.

JUNE 30, 1995.

Today B—— called and apologized for the grocery-store business. Said he knew I was right, it had to be over between us. Said, What if someone had seen us kissing? Everything could have been lost. I sat in the kitchen and cried for an hour. I don't know why.

JULY 2, 1995.

I'm a prisoner here. I pace, hating this house. Some days that's all I do.

JULY 3, 1995.

This morning I saw B——. Late this afternoon—my mouth still tender from B——'s kisses, I went to see Reverend G—— to tell him that his counseling has worked and I've given up my married lover—a sordid, outrageous lie! I wanted to please him, but at the same time I wanted him to see through me. I could tell at once that G—— was encouraged by my unexpected visit and, caught off guard, far more open to me than before—believing he'd done me some good, saved me from a dangerous situation. How easily he swallowed the credit I offered him like bait! It's surprising that someone trained in psychology can be so easily fooled. G—— has told me all along that I won't be able to get away with concealing my lies about B—— from Charlie much longer, yet I deceive him so easily.

JULY 7, 1995.

Linda, you're my only hope, a true friend.

All that's left to finish the garage is exterior work, so last night Charlie and I moved my loom out there—and I've finally started the tapestry I've been planning all these months. It has a checkerboard border of tiny indigo and violet squares—with a central pattern of gold, yellow, and ivory—a complicated, technically challenging piece.

She's describing the weaving she finished the day I arrived in Linden Grove for good, when my building was almost ready for me to move in. This was the tapestry that was on her loom when she died. The one I asked Charlie to save for me the night he got rid of her things.

I'll work day and night to get enough of it done to show you I have been a serious artist all this time!

Today I went to Reverend G—— to say good-bye, but secretly to mock him, by thanking him for his help. Finally, after all the days and hours of subtle moves that turned him on more than he dared admit, he gave up all pretense and kissed me passionately—moving his large hands over my breasts and down between my legs. He was panting, hurried by all the weeks of talk that had brought us to this—undoing his belt, pressing my hand against him.

I stopped him. I told him to wait—kneeling by the ugly, pea-green sofa in his office—until I returned from the bathroom— and when I did, he hadn't moved a muscle—elbows on the sofa—trousers down around knees still pressed into the carpet.

His passivity disgusted me. Don't move, I had whispered into his ear. He had taken me literally! He looked so foolish, all desire left me—though I had moved toward the moment for so long. He drew me to him again, terribly excited. It was fast, without pleasure for me. He mistook my shudder as a sign of satisfaction. It was one of those times I wasn't fully present, but outside myself.

And to think I went to this man for help—I swear it! He was remorseful—the final insult!—showing a terror of what he had done, saying that for someone in his vocation, such behavior was unforgivable, unnatural! Unnatural. A door closed in my mind.

You see, Linda, how it is? I came home determined to face this page and write this: If we had not had a child together, we would never have been ashamed. Why did I have to be to blame? My bones are like metal, I am so cold. I make myself sick. You see?

JULY 8, 1995.

What can be immoral about my infidelities if the harm I've done myself is unknown to others? How much will I dare tell Linda about Susanna?

I'm getting cold feet.

JULY 10, 1995.

I seek weak men—or do I make them weak by toying with them? Can I be an artist trapped like this in ordinary life? Today my wool came UPS, and I meant to work all afternoon on the tapestry, but Peter was here. I spent the afternoon with him next door—and could hardly pull myself away.

He didn't know it was the last time.

JULY 14, 1995.

I told Russ I'd sell him the Chevy if he's serious. He's decided to sell his Peugeot for cash to pay a debt, but he still might want to trade for the Nova. I'm not interested in what he has to offer. I want no more of that. Angry, he did no more work. He left. It was only ten-thirty. I should have stopped him weeks ago from hiding stuff under that board. But I went out to check, and it's gone. I don't believe he'll sell his Peugeot. He loves that car! But he doesn't seem to stay with anything for long.

JULY 15, 1995.

Now that your arrival is approaching, it's amazing how good I am to Charlie, and I think there might be hope for me. He took me with him Saturday to check some hives—and we stopped at a junk shop where I found an antique doll in a crocheted dress, missing its head. The woman went to the back to rummage around, looking for it, because of course she couldn't believe I'd want a doll without a head. She marked it down to one dollar instead of four, when what was missing was what made the doll speak to me! Charlie laughed like crazy when we got back to the van. She's not used to the ways you look at things, he said, baffled by his love for me.

Home, I told him I was sorry I've been so depressed this summer, so cold to him sometimes, and that he shouldn't blame himself. And I showed him the snapshot of my mother, afterward spending the afternoon and half the night working up the courage to tell him everything at last. He listened quietly, and I was so grateful to him for holding me when it was over. I fell immediately into a deep, deep sleep—the sun was coming up already—so content and happy it seemed everything would be all right.

On the opposite page is a sketch of the headless doll with a wide, old-fashioned, lacy dress, arms curved forward at its sides, and penned underneath, "The Woman Whose Voice Was in Her Fingers." Below it is taped a two-by-four-inch, black-and-white snapshot of Luci and a dark-haired woman she strongly resembles. In the picture Luci looks like she's six or seven years old.

JULY 18, 1995.

This afternoon when I walked out for the mail, I found a packet of sugar with its edge folded over, Russ's name signed there in black ink, fastened with a paper clip onto the mailbox's red flag. For four days he doesn't show up for work, and now what am I supposed to make of this? I licked a few bitter grains off a wet finger, then dumped the rest onto the gravel driveway. I don't know when he put it there. Last night? Early this morning?

What if Charlie had found it first? I can hear what Russell would say: Charlie wouldn't know what it was. It's unbelievably expensive, this stuff—left like a message, for the first person on the scene. Russ is playing my game of daring, in plain sight.

JULY 28, 1995.

This morning Russ showed up, wanting to test-drive my car— asking me if I got the first payment. I warned him how the Nova hesitates before accelerating from a full stop—a lot like him, but he didn't find that funny. He dropped me off at Hy-Vee for a half hour so I could shop for your visit, but he didn't come back, so I had to beg a ride home.

When he finally did show up here, he was mad, blaming me for some kind of noisy vibration when he went over twenty-five—a shaking, he said, like going over speed bumps, or a washboard road. He had some money and demanded I give him the title to the car—a hundred something, nowhere near what I'd asked for. He said my price was out of line. But the car never did that before, and I thought he was trying to put something over on me. He pulled out two more sugar packets—his last offer. I'm tired of him. I told him to go, and he did, walking toward the woods, promising to be back with the rest of the money before the afternoon was over.

But he didn't come back. Why doesn't that surprise me?

JULY 29, 1995.

I'm trying so hard, Linda. I explained to Peter that I want to spare him from my need to win men, then push them away— and protect Charlie from the pain of having a rival. But when I tell the truth, Peter doesn't believe me. You're not like that, he said. You need a lot of loving. You wouldn't punish anyone. You're too kind, he said. And I felt so guilty! He's so sure I won't be able to give him up. Later, when I wouldn't let him back into the house, he looked at me long and steady through the screen of the door. He wants to fix the car. He says it's the universal joints. It's all that's left between us. Guilty, I gave him the key. That's all he'll get from me.

It was hot today, and humid. I wore a sundress and sandals and slipped down the path through the woods to where B—— was waiting on the road for another one of our good-byes. But this time I'll mean it. You see? I've settled things with each of them, Linda. And Charlie's gone silent and patient with knowl- edge, and still loves me. I can talk to him so freely now—nothing shocks him. My sordid secret, in fact, makes him draw me close, to feel forgiven. Tell me again, he'll say. Tell me Tell me Tell me. When he touches me like that, I feel I've died and gone to heaven.

And tomorrow—you arrive!

Full sun yellows the skylight. Lying back on the bed at last, I close my eyes, my mind swarming with questions. Who is Susanna? Where have I heard Reverend Gus's phrase "leap of faith" re- cently? What am I to make of the path Luci took through the backwoods to meet Bill, the path he will have no trouble denying because it isn't there? Among all these questions, one thing is certain: The so-called recovered memory Peter Garvey told me about when I visited him in prison was a lie. There is no entry in Luci's diary for the day she died.

The shrill ring of the phone erases the questions and sets my heart thumping. The cadence of my own voice on the answering machine at the far end of the studio issues its invitation, and then I hear a higher-pitched, more energetic voice, familiar in its rhythms even at this great distance, as Judy begins to speak.

13 ◆ JUDY'S UNINTELLIGIBLE VOICE rises from the answering machine down below. I look at my watch. Surely at this hour she would expect me to be home in bed with Charlie. Maybe she called there first and woke him up and found out—what? that we're separated? My stomach lifts and growls, unsettled by all the coffee. I could hurry down there and pick up the phone, but I don't feel like talking to Judy with Luci's journal still in my hand, heavy with bad news.

At last the message ends, and I drop the book onto the bed behind me, realizing by the way my shoulder muscles relax that I've been straining toward my friend's voice. I hurry downstairs to bring it back.

Her words come fast, probably because she feared running out of tape before she got it all said: "Things are going pretty well here in Omaha after all. Bill's in the shower, then we're going for an early breakfast, a pecan waffle in my case, to celebrate. Things are okay between us now, maybe better than ever after last night, and again this morning. Tess was pretty calm when we saw her, her little game more innocent than I thought. We see her again at ten. Tell you more when I get back.

"But look. I knew if I called you at home I'd wake you up, so I decided to leave this message for when you get to work. Bill and I talked about it on the way over here in the car yesterday, and I think I was wrong—well, to not take you seriously. I was dismissing your fears when there's obviously some kind of responsibility you still feel for Luci. I shouldn't have said anything to Weber. I won't gossip about you anymore. I promise.

"It's awful to think of you mad at me, especially since you've been holding my hand so much lately. I wanted to see your fish roll off the press, but maybe it's more fitting for Charlie to be the first to see it. Say happy birthday to him for us. I'll call you Monday morning."

I hit the "save" button on the machine. The studio is completely silent. Outside on the street a car slows. *The Linden Times* swishes against the front-door screen like a broom. I open the blinds that cover the plate-glass window and switch on LINDA GARBO DE-SIGNS. The oval loops of lime and lavender neon buzz like gnats—barely audible, frenetic sounds. Before my mind has a chance to counter the impulse, I pick up the phone. After eight rings, Charlie answers. "I woke you up," I say gently.

"Um-hmm." There's a pause. "What time's it?" He's getting his bearings, not only in time but in space, too, I'm guessing, with me on this end and not under his hand that automatically reaches for me in the bed when he wakes up.

"Twenty to seven. You slept, it sounds like. I wasn't so lucky."

"Ohhh," he says, a drawn-out indication that he's remembering last night, and why I'm not there. "Linda?" he begins apologeti-cally, but it leads to nothing more than muffled sounds of discom-posure and sliding covers, suggesting a struggle to sit and maybe the wipe of a broad hand over his features. "What's wrong?"

"Everything."

"Yeah." He sighs thickly.

With clarity, I see how Luci tempted fate with her own words. How was it? I try to remember: *What can be immoral about my infidelities if the harm I've done myself is unknown to others?* Who knows how many people I'm about to hurt, how many lives I'll disrupt? If only I could snuggle up to Charlie's rumpled body, keep her selfish secrets. "I miss you. But it isn't your house, it's ours, our home. I shouldn't have let you get away with saying that, by leaving."

"I don't think I slept either, though I must have, just now." He clears his throat. "I thought my life was over, too, when she died, but you changed that. I never thought you'd walk out on me."

"I think you did, but I shouldn't have. That's what I just said."

"You shot out that door like you were waiting for an excuse."

"It was plain you meant it, about the house. I didn't know you felt that way."

"Neither did I."

"We need to talk about it. You want me to come back?"

"I have an idea you won't rest until you've stirred up questions about Garvey's trial. All you'll succeed in doing is letting what he did to Luci become an obsession that will take over your life. I can't live with that."

I'm too tired to argue. Is this what's meant by the world ending not with a bang but a whimper? "I guess I'll stay where I am for a few days."

"Maybe you'd better."

"We'll get through this, Charlie. I love you. Get some sleep."

I hang up the phone and step outside the front door, where the morning air is clammy and still. The rolled-up *Times* lies bound by a red rubber band, and I recognize the source of the bands Bender uses to hold his ponytail. From beyond the two-story, boxy building where he lives in the next block, a garbage truck rumbles its way around the corner and two men in navy-blue coveralls dismount, noisily dragging their huge plastic containers along the concrete. Without even trying, I can hear traffic moan on the interstate a couple of miles away, a sound masked during the day by more immediate sounds in the neighborhood. In my hands, the

newspaper rolls apart, revealing the headline: DRUG DEALER DE-
TAILS HOW RING IN DES MOINES UNRAVELED. I close it back up
and replace the rubber band.

There's been no food stocked in the small kitchen upstairs since
I moved in with Charlie, and right now all I can think about is
breakfast. So before I head for the loft to shower, I call Bender
and ask him to meet me at Perkins.

"Perkins?"

"For breakfast. I crave a waffle. Maybe a pecan waffle."

"Waffle?" Surely he's heard of waffles. "Christ, Linda, what time
is it?" He yawns extravagantly.

"I have something to show you. It makes a connection between
Russell Weber and Luci's car."

His breath huffs across the phone. I have his full attention. "I'm
out on a story all morning, but I can be in my office by the middle
of the afternoon. Let's say two-thirty." The series of clatters before
he hangs up suggests he missed the cradle the first time and has
to pick up and aim again.

I did an etching of The United Church of Christ a few months
ago for their centennial celebration. The cornerstone—salvaged
from the congregation's first permanent building, which burned in
the twenties—bears the date 1917. Inside, the minister's study is
an odd-shaped space no doubt carved out of a floor plan that didn't
originally call for an office. Three stained-glass windows grace the
brick wall to my left, bottom panels swung out on hinges to admit
a breeze. The room is comfortable, even with the humidity, because of the thick walls. Rev. Jonathan Gustavson is using the computer on his desk, but as I step through the doorway, he rises to
shake my hand. He's expecting me because I called him from Perkins. "I'm Linda Garbo," I said then.

"Yes. I know who you are." After all, he knew Luci, didn't he?
Quite well. And no doubt followed the trial, in which I was an
important player. "You're the artist."

"The engraving of the church building, yes."

"How can I help?"

"It's about Tess Allard," I told him, a half-truth. "The Allards are friends of mine. I know they're in your congregation. I'm worried about Tess."

"Of course. We all are." He told me I could come right over, his voice gentle, almost conspiratorial, bordering on patronizing, which allowed me to envision someone small-chested and overly solicitous, not this robust man who greets me now with a firm handshake, saying, "Call me Gus."

He moves to an oxblood leather wing chair, gesturing me to the sofa, a sectional without arms that I recognize from Luci's description as the site of their sexual encounter. I flush slightly as I feel the thin carpet under my feet where his bare knees pressed. As I sit, my own knees nearly touching the coffee table, an ornate iron openwork surface about three feet square, I stare for long moments at the date, 1923, worked in iron. I wonder what possessed me to come here this fuzzy from lack of sleep and without a clear strategy for questioning him.

"The table's made from an old heat-register grate we found when we remodeled."

"Was that recently?"

He nods. "We believe in recycling." He pauses, perhaps noticing the oddness of my question.

"I share that belief." I return his smile, and the conversation stalls.

"Well, then . . ." Barrel-chested, he appears to be in his mid-forties, probably a golfer or tennis player by the bronze color of his face and forehead, which recedes slightly into the thatch of short, steel-gray hair. It wouldn't occur to me to call his features thick or his lower lip sensual, as Luci did. I'm drawing a blank, confused by my upsurge of embarrassment over what she wrote happened here. His hands are splayed on his sturdy thighs. I sit straighter, which relaxes me a little. After all, just because I'm the one with all the power doesn't mean I have to use it.

On the bookcase behind his chair is a photograph of the minister with a plump blond woman and two little girls with large hair bows. The daughters look to be about ten or twelve. He sees me looking and turns to smile at his family. "Twins. I suppose you could guess that." He pauses, turning to face me again. "Family life can be difficult," he continues by way of transition.

"Yes."

"You wanted to talk about Tess."

"That's not the real reason I'm here." Reverend Gus's face tilts almost imperceptibly to the side. "I've been feeling panicky," I admit, "and some of my friends, including Judy—and especially my husband—have been urging me to talk to a professional." The minister listens earnestly, apparently waiting to discover what this is about before committing himself to a reaction.

"I know you have credentials for counseling," I continue, relieved to have covered my excuse for being here so convincingly I almost believe it myself. "I'm not a practicing Christian anymore, in any formal sense, though I was raised in this denomination and I still hold values like loving-kindness, my favorite word from the Bible, and honesty—though these have turned out to be more complicated values than I ever dreamed." He is nodding encouragement. I wonder if he thinks I've come here to renew my faith.

"I used to pray," I rush on, as if he'd asked, "but I gave that up in my late teens, when I stopped asking 'Who is God?' and began asking '*What* is God?' It made no sense to talk to him—and that was a problem, too, the *him*. So now, as a practical matter, I guess, I test a belief by questioning what effect it would have on my actions. Talking to God became talking to myself, which is worth doing, but hardly constitutes religious practice."

"Oh, I don't know."

"When it comes to God, I neither believe nor disbelieve."

"That's perfectly all right, Linda." His serious, dark eyes narrow into a merry squint as he smiles. "That's not an admission requirement for talking to me. But you know, you don't want to let—"

"I seem defensive, don't I?"

"We can talk about anything you like. Is it something personal?"

"I interrupted you. Something about what I don't want to do . . . ?"

He hesitates, probably trying to recover his place from a moment ago. "Oh, yes," he says, "sometimes an agnostic position shuts off a lot of questions."

"Such as what?"

"Are there no consequences, ultimately, of our behavior? Other than the ones social scientists describe? It's just a question."

"Ultimately? You mean eternal punishments and rewards?"

"Not necessarily eternal. But okay, start with that."

"The afterlife question is a bit beyond me. For an ethical person, aren't the rewards of good works right at hand?"

"I don't think belief in an afterlife is ethically very important either, Linda, although I think the lack of it tempts some people to a kind of nihilism, the belief that there's no purpose—"

My body stiffens. "I know what nihilism is." It's clear my abruptness has startled him. The train of our conversation spins away from me.

"Sorry, Linda. I didn't mean to suggest—"

"A kind of moral forgetfulness."

He looks confused.

"You were warning me about the dangers of not believing."

"Then maybe we'd better start over." He smiles. "Unless you're ready to take a leap of faith."

"I'm not here to talk about God."

"I didn't think so." He leans back again, waiting.

"I want to talk about Luci Cole."

His hand covers his mouth, top finger against the base of his nose—as if he's suppressing a sneeze. He gets to his feet.

"Charlie Carpenter is my husband, has been since last September. I suppose you might know that, since you knew who I was when I called."

"I did know that." He crosses the room, where he sits on his large mahogany desk, hands gripping the edge of it, legs straight and crossed at the ankles. As a casual stance, it's unconvincing. His shoulders are up around his ears. "So this is about Luci."

"Charlie's just now working through his anger over losing her, and it's hurting our marriage. I thought that talking with me back then helped him work things through, but I'm beginning to suspect that being with me so soon after losing her delayed the grieving process." Gus takes a deep breath as I continue. "Recently he's been disposing of her possessions but missing her terribly in the process, as if he suddenly realizes he still loves her in a way that precludes his loving me at the same time. At least that's what I'm afraid of."

Gus's shoulders have lowered a bit. He seems relieved. "I doubt it was just being with you that blocked the stages of grief, if that's what's happened." The formal tone he used on the phone is back, but this time I welcome it. "Luci didn't die in an ordinary way, after all. Finding out about her sexual relationship with Peter Garvey in such a public forum must have been very painful for Charlie."

I nod. "I think that made it harder for him to remember the happy times. He's told me she needed something he didn't have to offer. He still worries about that, with me."

"Sometimes," says Gus, "people who grieve most terribly over losing a spouse are those who have suffered the most unhappiness. What they grieve over is the lost possibility. The person dies at a point when there's still hope that what's going to happen any day now, with just a few changes in behavior, will be love."

I nod again.

"And sometimes they feel the need to pretend, even to themselves, that the relationship was happier than it was, and not real and knotty, the way marriages are at times. That denial, that pretense, blocks the anger which is necessary in dealing with loss. With a violent death, at the hands of a newly discovered rival, the matter would be even more complicated, don't you think?"

"They weren't married."

"I don't think that changes the dynamics of what I'm talking about. Do you?"

"Maybe not. But you used the word 'spouse.' "

"Forgive me," he says, smiling easily. "Sooner or later, they probably would have—" He stops, appearing to reconsider what he was about to say.

Which was what? *Come into the fold?* "What I haven't told you," I say softly, "is that my own need to discuss Luci's death all over again is what has precipitated Charlie's working through his feelings for her. And now, because he thinks *I* haven't come to terms with her death, he's sometimes very cold to me. So I really need someone to talk with. I hear you're an effective counselor." I gesture toward the framed credentials on the wall above his smiling family. He shifts his weight to uncross his legs, resting one foot casually behind the other, a more relaxed posture than before. "Luci told me all about you." *Your sensual lips, your large hands on her breasts.* "That's the real reason I'm here. I know you're bound by rules of confidentiality not to reveal what passed between the two of you." My words fall slow and careful as I watch his face for their effect. "But Luci was bound by no such rules."

He walks around the desk, where he pauses for a moment with his back to me before turning to look my way again. "What exactly did she tell you?"

"I don't think anyone knew about your connection with Luci. There's a chance the case will be reopened, so there will be questions. Do you remember where you were the afternoon she was killed?"

"Right here, writing a sermon."

"Alone?"

"Alone." He sits in the desk chair, as if to demonstrate. "Barb and the girls had gone to Osceola to meet her parents at the train station. Amtrak from the west is almost always late. They didn't get home until nearly nine. I stayed here until she called to say they were back. What do you mean . . . ?"

"You didn't eat supper?"

"Not until late. I was upset."

My mouth is dry. "What were you upset about?"

"Luci had planned to meet with me that afternoon, but she didn't show up."

We stare at each other, unblinking.

"At the moment she was murdered," he goes on, "I was sitting here, waiting for her. I'd counseled her for a while, but then she'd ended the relationship. But I expect you know that." In the silence that tells him I'm not going to make this any easier, I'm aware, in a way one hardly ever notices another person's breathing, that his chest is expanding and contracting to greater and greater extremes. He gets himself under control. "I didn't hear about her death until the evening news."

"What did she want to talk to you about?"

"I thought I had helped her. I may have underestimated how troubled she was."

I walk over to the wide desk, leaning forward on my hands to look down at his face, an arm's length from mine across the cluttered surface. "What would you say if I told you it wasn't Peter Garvey who killed her? That I lied when I said he got out from under Luci's car when I reached the yard, and spoke to me."

"You lied?"

I straighten up and return to the couch.

For a moment we're both silent. Then he says, "I should tell you, Linda, before you go further, that I won't honor confidentiality beyond this point. Maybe you'd better not say any more."

"I was confused at the time, but I pretended to be certain. So I consider it a lie. I hold myself responsible no matter what it's called."

Gus returns to the leather chair again, looking watchful but tired. "How much did she tell you?"

"She kept a journal."

"And you read it just recently?"

"That's right."

"Which is why you're here now." I nod. "In the end," he says softly, "her hostility toward me was immense. I had hoped to use that to help her break through to what was really making her angry."

"By having sex with her, right here on this very sofa?"

His eyes meet mine. "We call it transference, what you're talking about. She liked to write things *down*, Linda," he says, his voice growing angry, "as a way of creating her own reality. Sometimes to get a certain kind of reaction from me. Like the reaction you're getting right now."

"I'm surprised you'd talk about this."

"I'm only defending myself. It's plain you're prepared to believe the worst. That I might have—"

"She said you were a bad lover."

His mouth opens with surprise, but he catches himself and struggles to inhibit a grin. Eyes averted, he shakes his head to relax his face again. Hardly the reaction of a man who feels threatened.

Then his expression turns grave. He looks embarrassed. "A journal, you should remember, is imaginative, and not subject to the same ethics as recounting events face to face."

"She addressed the last half of the journal to me, so I can't help feeling she wanted to tell me something."

"I daresay she never expected you would read it. Be careful. You don't know what kind of truth you're dealing with."

On the way out, I pause at the door and allow my gaze to focus on the unfortunate, pea-green sofa across the room. "This conversation is far from over."

"If there's any harm to be done me now," he says sadly, "it won't be your doing. I've brought it on myself. *Of course* we need to talk again."

We make an appointment for my return.

Halfway down the steps I'm struck by the tiring effects of a sleepless night. The sensation of falling forward reminds me of Bender's invitation to a "leap of trust," a phrase similar to one the minister used a few minutes ago. I stop and go back up. "One more thing. You must be the person John Bender talks to about leaps of faith."

The minister smiles. "Bender's a good example of the skeptic who insists that God is dead, but whose every return to the argument proves the matter is not settled."

14 ◆ LATER, MIDAFTERNOON, I find Bender in his cluttered office at *The Linden Times*. "I just talked with Jim Howard again. The auto-mech teacher," he reminds me. "After what you said about Weber being under Luci's car, I had a brainstorm. What did you want to show me?"

When I move closer to look over his shoulder at the computer screen, he twists in his chair to face me squarely. "Sorry. I'm on top of a syndication deadline." He moves to sweep a pile of books off the only other chair in the space.

"I can't stay anyway."

"You'll change your mind."

I sit.

He runs his long fingers over the top of his head, through the long brown hair, giving his scalp a quick rub, like he's been concentrating too hard on something. "You remember Ben Petersen, that high-school kid who died last year?"

"The boy who had a heart attack brought on by a drug overdose?"

"Right. He was with a buddy when it happened. The cops interviewed all the teachers the boys had that term, but came up with nothing to trace the source of the drugs. I got to wondering if Howard was one of those teachers. Turns out he was. Both kids were taking auto mechanics that semester. Howard is still broken up about it."

"What does this have to do with Luci's car, or Weber? You think this teacher had something to do with two untimely deaths?"

"I don't know what the connection is. Maybe there isn't any." Bender gives me a long, distracted look, until I hand him the page I photocopied from Luci's journal: *I told Russ I'd sell him the Chevy if he's serious.* I tell Bender I searched through her things again recently, but I found nothing with any reference to her car—like repair bills or gas receipts—except for *this*, something she wrote to me once. "That car was a junker," I remind him, "faded red with a long, rusty dent along the driver's door. The red-and-black upholstery leaked curds of dried-out foam rubber. Above twenty-five it would shimmy like when you're going over those rough speed-strips by dangerous intersections. Why would someone like Weber want to buy it?"

"Maybe he was strapped for cash." Without asking a single question, Bender folds up the page, puts it in his pocket, and offers to walk me to the front door. "You headed for home now?" He looks at the clock tower on the Brenton Bank across the street, always five minutes slow.

I tell him yes. Where my home *is* now, he doesn't need to know.

Monday morning I wake up early, worrying about the path Luci mentioned in her diary. I decide to drive out to the road that runs along the north side of our property so I can tramp the mosquito-infested woods at the bottom of the ravine behind our garage. The closest thing I can find to a path is a line of erosion that leads up into tangled brush. The incline is so steep only a mountain goat could scale it. When I get back to my studio, I decide it's time to call Hilda Clark, the county attorney. She says she can spare about twenty minutes this afternoon, around four.

About three-thirty I leave my studio and drive to Winterset, the Madison County seat. Hilda is an attractive, dark-haired, sinewy woman in her mid-fifties. She seems glad to see me as she ushers me into her cluttered office, but because I know she doesn't have a lot of time, I ask her immediately if she's received my new statement from Detective Hansen. She hasn't, but they have talked about it.

"What will you do when you get it?"

"I'll share it with Clifford Nichols." She pauses. "The defense attorney?" I nod, remembering the gleam of his scalp through shiny, blue-black hair. "As a principle of newly discovered evidence, any that's exculpatory—which might contribute to a legal defense—must be shared with him, of course. So when I receive your new statement from Ken, I'll study it alongside the old and reread the trial transcript, then offer the new material to Nichols. He may decide he has basis for a motion."

"And there could be a new trial?"

"Within three years of final appeal a postconviction relief hearing is a possibility. It's not a simple matter to think through what implications this difference in testimony might have had to the trial's outcome, or for our strategies as attorneys." She stops, tilting her face to consider mine, her eyes narrowing as if something's occurring to her. "We are clear, aren't we, that it's your confusion *then*, not your confusion *now*, that is at issue."

"Yes, we're clear on that."

She leans forward slightly. "Panic attacks are serious. You look thinner, Linda, and tired."

"No one wants this all behind me as much as I do. I keep thinking how the trial would have gone differently. I mean, if the defense attorney hadn't introduced those spots—"

"Be careful, Linda." She smiles, raising her hand to stop me.

"It's the blood that's the problem."

"Yes," she says. She's remembering, as I am, that the case turned on the issue of missing evidence. Based on my eyewitness identification at the murder scene, the police got a search warrant right away and found Peter Garvey passed out in his house next door, wearing nothing but his underwear. His blood-alcohol level was .453, more than four times the legal definition of intoxication in Iowa, a level that might have killed an inexperienced drinker.

My testimony had to fill in for the fact that Peter's blood-stained clothing was never found. Clifford Nichols called me as his first witness, questioning me about what I had told the police the afternoon of the murder, testimony that placed his client at the scene of the crime. His first challenge came when I said, "I saw Peter Garvey come out the front door of the house."

"You were in your car, at the top of the hill, looking down at the house, is that right?"

"Yes."

"Let's back up a little bit. Focus on what you remember about the front door of the house. Tell me exactly what you saw."

I hesitated, concentrating. "There's a small roof over the front door, over the steps. I saw Peter Garvey come out the front door and walk to the car."

"The outer door to that house is a screen door, is that right?"

"Yes."

"Describe it."

"It's made of aluminum. It opens out. Hinges are on the right."

"And what did you observe about that door, at the moment you first saw Peter Garvey?"

I glanced at the judge, a blur of black robes and white hair, then back at Clifford Nichols. "I'm not sure I understand the question."

"Was the door open or closed?"

"It wasn't the door that caught my attention."

"So you didn't notice if it was open or closed?"

"No."

"But something drew your attention to the front door, even though you don't remember it opening. What was that?"

"I saw Peter Garvey emerge and walk toward the car. He got under the car, on his back, to work on it."

"You saw Peter Garvey *emerge*?"

"I saw him walk away from the front door."

"Then he didn't exactly *emerge*, did he?"

"He emerged from the shadows."

"Oh, there were *shadows*."

"As I said, there's a roof over the front door."

"So maybe that's why you didn't see the door open?"

Hilda's objection on the grounds of speculation was sustained.

Nichols walked to the defense table, where he stood looking down at his notes for a few moments. Then he asked me to describe to the court what I had observed that day about the condition of the accused's clothing as he lay under the car. I repeated word for word what I had said in the police statement, that I had seen dark "drops of something" on the legs of Peter's jeans as he lay working on the car.

"According to what you told the police the day of the murder, what did you think those spots were when you first saw them?"

"I thought they were oil."

"And why did you make that assumption?"

"Because he was working on a car."

"Because he was working on a car," Nichols repeated thoughtfully. He paused to check the jury for attention. Hilda Clark hadn't expected Nichols to introduce the issue of the stains on Peter's clothing, when it would seem to have been in his client's best interests to leave it out. Nichols walked over and spread his arms to touch the jury rail with his fingertips, looking at their faces, not mine, as he said, "In your police statement, Ms. Garbo, when you said, 'at the time, I thought it was oil,' that implied, did it not, that at the time you *made* the statement, the day of the murder, you had already made a different interpretation, away from the idea it was oil. What was that second thought you had?"

My stomach tightened. "After I found Luci, I looked out that front door where Peter lay so close by. I remembered the spots, and I thought they must have been blood."

"I see. But when you had first seen those stains, a few minutes earlier, you hadn't become alarmed, had you?"

"No."

"You hadn't thought, 'Oh, he has blood on his clothes'?"

"No."

"Because the spots on his jeans were not red, were they?" He turned toward the jury. "*The spots on his jeans were not red, were they, Ms. Garbo?*"

"No."

"The spots were not red, they were merely dark, correct?"

"That's correct."

He didn't challenge any other details of my testimony.

Hilda Clark had anticipated the possibility that Nichols might question me about the color of those blood spots. She had submitted my Kansas City Art Institute transcripts, along with catalog descriptions of my courses in color theory and transparent dyes, to the court, and I had been qualified as an expert witness. She explained that to the jury and then picked up on the color issue in her redirect: "Ms. Garbo, it's been established that right after you found Luci Cole's body, you changed your interpretation of what you had seen, those drops of 'something dark.' Defense counsel seems to believe that fresh blood on a pair of blue jeans would appear red, definitely red. What was it in *your* experience that made it so easy for you to believe that what you had seen could have been blood?"

I took a sip of water from the glass that had been placed to my right, on the rail of the witness box. "When I was a student at the Art Institute in Kansas City, there was an accident one day in one of the painting studios. A classmate was using a utility knife, and it slipped. She sliced into her left hand, through the fleshy, webbed part between her thumb and first finger. There was a lot of blood. I was the closest person at hand, to help her. She had on a man's white shirt, as a smock to protect her clothes. I had her take that off so I could use it to make a pressure bandage. She was wearing cutoff jeans and a bright yellow T-shirt." I paused, swallowing. "Afterward, I found I remembered the bright red soaked into the white fabric; the orange spatter across the front of her yellow T-shirt; the dull, mahogany stains on her denim shorts. It's an experience I have always remembered in vivid color."

"You were observing the way one color absorbed into another becomes a third color. You have studied the various ways colors mix and change, haven't you?"

"Yes."

"Mr. Nichols has established that in the late afternoon the house where Luci Cole died casts a shadow over the front drive. Were Peter Garvey's legs sticking out of the side of the car that was toward the road or toward the house?"

"Toward the road."

"So he was in the shadow of the car, which was in the shadow of the house, is that right?"

"Yes."

"How would those conditions affect color perception?"

"The gray-green light in shadows like that would dull color even more."

"So it would come as no surprise to you that fresh blood on blue jeans would look dark, not red."

"That's right."

"What if the jeans had been especially worn and faded?"

"The effect wouldn't be much different, especially in that kind of light. The color on the lighter threads of the fabric's weave would look redder at very close range. But I was standing over him, and anyway a brighter red woven through dark magenta would be mixed by the eye to a duller color, the way colors in a weaving are blended by the eye."

"Is there any way that drops of fresh blood on denim blue jeans, under the conditions we've described, could possibly be red?"

"No possibility at all."

In the end, during his final argument, Clifford Nichols attempted to persuade the jury that I had not seen his client emerge from the house, through that front door, but *from the shadows in front of the door*. Peter Garvey, Nichols insisted, had not been coming from inside the house at all. And as for the blood, "Linda Garbo did not merely see what was literally before her. She *participated* in the art of seeing and added much on her own. Her reinterpretation of those dark stains, that they were actually drops of Luci Cole's blood, does not amount to evidence. She was eager to believe her own speculation, just as she was eager to believe that Peter Garvey had just killed Luci Cole and then emerged from the house and immediately gone to work repairing the victim's car. Don't be as gullible as she," he admonished the jury.

He nearly had me convinced. I was worried. The moment he finished addressing the jury might have been the moment my self-doubts began. But Hilda Clark's appeal to common sense, along with the fingerprint evidence and the presence of motive, reassured me. Peter had admitted being in the kitchen earlier in the day, she reminded the jury, so fibers didn't matter, or hair. It was blood the case needed, to link Peter with the crime scene. The testimony that I'd seen blood there, on the legs of jeans that were never found, had to overcome the lack of actual forensic evidence. Hilda's final words were these: "Linda is an artist. She knows how colors interact. She had no trouble recognizing that the 'something dark' she had seen on his jeans was blood."

Apparently the jury didn't have any trouble believing it either.

"If those weren't Peter Garvey's legs, his jeans," I say now, "then your 'something dark' argument might have proved an innocent man guilty."

Hilda closes her eyes for a moment, then meets my gaze again. "Hansen's told me you have some other concerns, about a couple of break-ins. I'll tell him to send me what he has right away. I just wish the case wasn't so long ago, the trails so cold." She looks at me steadily. "You were a very convincing witness."

That's because I knew he was guilty is what I can't bring myself to say.

I was right that day at the trestle when it dawned on me that anger was the best antidote for my anxiety. I haven't suffered a panic attack since. Instead, there's a nervous tremble in my stomach, and I've lost my appetite. At night, when I stand naked before the mirror in the loft, I can count my ribs as I run my hands over my flat abdomen, my narrowing thighs. When I call Charlie, I no longer detect anger in his tone but indifference, the opposite of love. I need to talk to Rosemary again—in person and alone this time, so we can't be interrupted before I've gotten answers. I invite her to supper. "I'm lonesome, and I want to be with someone who sees Charlie every day."

"I'll be there." Her voice is oddly melodic, with intimations of pity.

"I have to confess, I want something from you."

"How about a couple pieces of Baker's Square pie?"

I laugh. "I could use the fattening up. But that's not what I meant. When Charlie gave Russell Weber money recently, he must have paid him by check from the business account. I want you to bring me the canceled check. Put it in an envelope, or a plastic Baggie. Touch it by the edges, okay?"

"Linda—"

"You can do that, can't you?" I say, interrupting her before she can start singing with pity again.

"I'd rather not."

"That and a couple pieces of pie."

"Nothing good will come of this, Linda. I know what you're thinking."

She doesn't. "Chocolate French Silk's my favorite," I say.

*   *   *

Since her treatment in Omaha, Tess seems unnaturally subdued. All Judy has said is that Tess didn't mean anything by her vague accusation of some deep, terrible family secret. The suggestion that her dad knew something her mother didn't was a misunderstanding. I don't buy that, especially now that I've read Luci's journal. Today I'm going to find out.

Tess's flattop haircut has grown an inch and fallen limp. I liked the punk look on her. Now she's at my back door, her mouth drooping, almost triangular, like a small child's in its musculature. She looks hot and bored. Her assignment for today's drawing lesson was to bring items that have personal meaning to her and will fit into a standard grocery bag.

She's taken this last limitation literally, I see, as she places the bag on the worktable, shifting it to line up the edge of the bag parallel to the edge of the table. She's become obsessively obedient. "Doesn't that make her an ideal student?" Judy asked, after Tess's first lesson, when I expressed concern about her docile behavior.

"Just the opposite. It's hard to teach drawing to someone who's afraid to be spontaneous, and Tess won't be taking any risks if she's this determined to please me."

"I thought this was what you wanted," Tess is saying now. She's pulled a teddy bear from the bag. I must be frowning.

I'm wearing a cotton gauze dress, and so is Tess. Hers is sky blue with short sleeves and a high yoke. "There are no wrong answers in an exercise like this," I say, though that's not what I'm thinking. "Let's see what else you've got."

I had made only one other stipulation for this assignment: nothing with hearts on it. I guess I set myself up for this bear. It's certainly no well-loved artifact. The red ribbon around its neck is sharp at the edges and wrinkle-free. Next out of the bag come cosmetics, a school yearbook, a dried corsage. Any of her classmates could have come up with this collection. I asked for objects that would define her character.

I guess I've forgotten what it was like to be her age. What did I expect, a Trick or Treat for UNICEF bag and one of the Great Books? I can't very well take exception to the way she sees herself. She is, after all, wearing gold circle hoops in her ears, just like mine.

"You just wanted ordinary stuff, to draw, right? So what's the problem?" Tess pulls a white price tag off one of the bear's brassy paws. The sticker's on the tip of her pointing finger, which she holds away from her body as if the spot of white were something disgusting. A hardness tightens her eyes as she rolls the price tag in her fingertips, prolonging the tiny gesture as she considers me.

Her shift in mood has firmed the soft droop of her mouth, to which she begins applying bright orange lipstick, pouting into the mirror of an onyx compact. I know she'll wipe off the orange before she arrives back home, engaging in the kind of dual personality teenage girls resort to when out of favor with their parents. She's inviting me to conspire with her.

The UPS delivery at the back door is a welcome interruption. As I sign for the box of heavy inks, I hear the sound of paper tearing behind me. With a, "Thanks, Max," I hand the computerized clipboard back to the driver. "Would you rather just talk than draw today?" She has her back to me.

Tess has the gangly, all-limbs look of a young girl whose bones are still growing. Under the thin gauze of her dress, her shoulder blades jut like budding wings. Her right hand rests on the tabletop, elbow elevated awkwardly, head slightly bowed, as if she's been told to stand there for punishment. Her confidence appears shot. This is not the posture of that pissy girl with the orange mouth.

"My folks don't care if I learn how to draw. They just want to know where I am. I still don't appreciate your spying on me, and I know you and my mom tell each other everything." I wait. "Some things you can't."

"I can't what, Tess?"

"Tell her." She pulls the boxy grocery bag toward her and folds it flat.

For a clue, I look at the table, at what she's arranged for her drawing.

She's looking at the bear, too. "At first I thought about what I'm supposed to be like, my personality. But then I was starting to see things, like they really are, you know? In some ways I'm not like my friends."

"Tess, turn around."

She does. She's trying not to cry. Her face looks stretched. And we both take a deep breath, like I'm leading her, like John Bender coached me under the railroad trestle, helping me calm myself, breathing in deeply, breathing out. She's angry and tense enough to run out the door.

"I think it's time I showed you the picture I took of you and Russ Weber the day you ran off." At this she freezes, turns away. "No, Tess. Stay and hear this." I move quickly to the desk at the front of the room and return with one of the snapshots. "There can be only one reason you haven't brought this up again, after being so mad that night in the van, mad that I would take a picture you didn't know about."

"And what is that?"

"You didn't want to risk my asking what the picture might reveal."

"We were just talking."

"He wasn't passing something to you?"

"That detective already asked me all these questions." She looks at the snapshot again. "We were exchanging a few words." She hands it back to me. "That cop wanted me to say it was drugs."

"I thought you might tell me something you wouldn't tell him."

"You never have a right to know everything going on inside a person. I bet you have your secrets, too."

"Maybe I'd be willing to share one with you."

"I wish you and Charlie weren't separated." Shuddering, she lets me close the distance between us and hold her, lets me take her thin arms and move them around me like a belt, lets me caress her shoulders. When the tears are over, it takes her a while to relax. I get her a drink of water.

On the table the teddy bear sits atop the flat, open high-school yearbook, the bright red ribbon retied around its mouth like a gag. Pinned to its right foot is a picture of Bill, torn from a page of teachers. As a composition, this arrangement shows an unsophisticated teenager's penchant for cliché and melodrama. Something closer to art makes that beside the point.

Though Tess isn't in a mood to draw, I crank up the height of one of the stools, adjust a tabletop easel for her drawing paper, and put a stick of vine charcoal into her hand. To know the world she must construct it for herself, but she's wrong about why Judy and Bill arranged this. Tess has talent, and I'm going to make her try some contour drawings, today's lesson, even if she doesn't want to right now, help her walk a line around this bear—a line that separates the object from everything around it, "a line that wraps around the visible form, suggesting even the part of the bear you can't see but know is there." As she gives it a try, the drag of charcoal against the rough tooth of the newsprint is the only sound.

Tess's dried prom corsage is pinned to the bear's chest with a long pin that looks to be piercing its very heart. Subtlety would not have forced the issue of whatever she has on her mind. She wants me to ask.

Next I have her try a blind contour. Keeping her eye on the bear, she lowers the charcoal and slowly defines, with one continuous line, the bear she sees, not looking at what she's drawn until she's lifted her hand. The second attempt—a line hopelessly sprung apart—makes her laugh, and again she turns the page. Without looking up from the bear, with her hand moving more quickly this time, she says, "Mrs. Lindstrom—you know, who works for Charlie?—came to our speech class last year and talked about superstition and sensitivity. We all had to bring a favorite object to class. But she only wanted one small thing. Mine was a whistle my grandpa made for me out of a willow twig—and she could tell us things about ourselves. Sort of like fortune-telling. It was neat."

"How did your teacher tie that in to giving speeches?"

"You think it was a waste of time?"

"No, I just—"

"When a willow twig is green, the bark slides right off in a tube, it's so slippery inside. And then Grandpa carved into the wood and slid the bark back on. You'd move the bark back and forth when you played it, like a tiny trombone. Grandpa made them for all the kids." Lines of charcoal uncoil onto the page as she speaks. "The one who lives in Illinois."

"Rosemary could tell all that by holding your whistle in her hand?"

Tess pauses in her work to give me a dark look.

Artists are notorious collectors. Picasso, I tell her, felt he had to possess the objects that inspired his art. It wasn't enough to draw tiny pre-Columbian figures, he had to handle them, to receive something magical from them. When he was finished, he reburied them, in a way, with other junk, in the back of a cupboard. "We're all collectors. Some people believe that our magic rubs off on things we wear or love or make ourselves." I think of Luci's possessions, carried off into the night. "I don't think much has rubbed off on this bear. It doesn't look like you've had it long."

"Mrs. Lindstrom told us how she does it," she says seriously. "She learned a lot about me from that whistle. It starts out like a trick, but it's really just skillful interpersonal communication."

"And not just another example of showbiz masquerading as education?"

She actually smiles. "My dad's one of the best teachers at the high school. Everyone says so."

"Everyone's right about that."

Tess has stopped drawing and is studying my face. "Charlie stayed with us the night Luci was killed."

"I remember."

She puts the charcoal on the table. "That night, when he came over, my mom told me someone had killed Luci and that Charlie didn't want to stay in his own house because he was so upset. I tried for a long time to go to sleep, but I couldn't. I just lay in bed wondering if my mother died if I'd have to sleep somewhere else. I didn't know that Luci was murdered in their own kitchen. I kept getting up and walking into the hallway to listen to them talking. Once my dad called my name up the stairway and told me to go to sleep. But I was too scared." She turns back to her drawing. "If I showed this to someone, they wouldn't know what it was."

"The point isn't for it to look like the bear, not yet." She raises her eyebrows. "A contour line suggests what it conceals, if you think about it. The point is to communicate some aspect of the object back to the viewer."

"Aspect of bear," she pronounces. "Who'd ever guess?"

"It takes time. You have a good eye. And a scary sense of metaphor." She tries not to look pleased. "I won't tell your mom anything that you want kept private. I expect the same from you."

"What makes you think I have something to tell you?"

I unpin the small, torn picture of Bill from the paw of the bear. "This isn't exactly subtle."

She picks up the charcoal again, rolling it in her fingers, even drawing it across her palm to see the mark it makes. "Finally," she begins slowly, "that night, you know?" I nod. "Everybody went to bed. Once I heard the phone ring. After that I almost went to sleep, but I heard Daddy walk down the hall and go back downstairs."

Her feet dangle a good four inches from the floor. She's hooked one sandaled foot on the top rung of the stool, tucking the other behind it, and she swivels back and forth a couple of times. "Charlie was sleeping down there, in the den, and I went out onto the stairs. My dad was in the kitchen, and then Charlie came out, and they sat in the living room where I could see them. I walked down the hall to my folks' room, but the door was shut, and I didn't think I should wake my mom up. When I got back to the landing, Charlie was crying. I don't think my dad knew what to do. He just sat there and cried, too. It was awful."

She turns another page and begins another contour. "I'm going to look at what I'm doing this time," she announces, as if the rules must be stated. Her concentration precludes any more talk for a few moments. "You guys are a neat couple."

"You think so?"

She shrugs, picking up the yearbook picture of Bill I've left on the table near her easel. "They had a terrible fight. Charlie was mad at my dad." She swallows. "Charlie kept saying, 'You did that to her, you did that to her,' over and over, calling my dad a son of a bitch. They were standing up, circling each other. My dad kept saying, 'Keep your voice down.' And then Charlie got real loud, yelling, in fact, and then he said, 'I know it was you.' I remember the exact words. 'Why don't you just admit it?' My dad hit him, right in the face, but Charlie is so much bigger it hardly fazed him, and they grabbed each other and kind of rocked back and forth together, standing up. Then they just pushed each other away. And I hurried back to my room."

Tess was barely thirteen then.

"I knew my dad had killed her."

I hold my breath.

"I should have known he could never do such a thing. When that Peter Garvey person was arrested, I was so ashamed of what I'd been thinking, I couldn't tell anyone. I never did."

I start to breathe again.

"My mom and dad had lots of arguments after that, but they were careful. I could never quite hear. I figured she must have found out what Daddy had done to Luci to make Charlie that mad. I started watching them very closely, all the time. That Susan Ginger-Banning person, in Omaha, kept asking me, 'Does your father touch you in inappropriate ways?' I hated her for that, and I hated them for sending me there. I didn't care if we all finally had to talk about what Luci and my dad did, but the minute I started it, I was sorry. I could have ruined everything. Now I know for sure Mom doesn't know about Luci. She almost made me blow it, that Ginger-Banning woman. People shouldn't meddle in other people's lives."

"You were there because of the drinking, Tess, and maybe drugs, too. You needed help."

"You can't say anything about this. But if I didn't tell someone, I was going to take off again. I could feel it. Next time I might not be able to keep my mouth shut. And anyway—" She pauses. "I don't have anyplace to go."

I hand her a Kleenex. "You think you're the one who keeps your family together, by protecting your dad?"

"They started arguing about what to do with me, blaming each other for the way I was turning out. *I* was what made them mad at each other."

"So you ran away."

"I think Luci and my dad were having sex. Sometimes I wish my mom knew. Then I wouldn't have to worry every time he goes somewhere at night or is late coming home. I just want to finish high school and leave. When I go off to college, then they'll have to take care of themselves. And one more thing. Please don't keep asking about Russ Weber. I'm not about to get him in trouble. I'm not that kind of a person."

She stuffs the yearbook, the bear, and the torn picture back into the grocery bag. Then, the object of her attention out of sight, she returns to her drawing. Her hand moves quickly, the way I instructed her, drawing a circuitous line, a remarkably good version of the bear she remembers, spiky with cheap plush, potbellied, heavy of limb—a contour line suggestive of jagged energy and unmistakable anger. She's left off the ribbon that was tied around its mouth. She's unburdened herself, and I'm proud of her. *Aspect of bear.* "Maybe I'll major in art," she says.

15 ◆ WHILE WE FINISH our chocolate pie, Rosemary and I sip our decaf in silence. She enjoyed the salad, garlic bread, and simple pasta dish—fresh Roma tomatoes, ripe olives, and mushrooms, sautéed in olive oil with onion and garlic. Now her frown as she lowers her fork fills me with an uneasy feeling of expectancy. Since the day I saw her gesturing angrily in the driveway out at the house, I've asked her twice what she and Charlie were talking about. She's been as evasive as he, so I'm going to have to play it just right in the next few minutes if I'm going to get a straight answer this time. Weber's canceled check lies on the far edge of the table.

It's Rosemary who breaks the silence, asking me for the spare key to this building so she can give it to Charlie. The request surprises me, but without a word I walk the few steps to my dresser and find the key, on a key chain that features a red, Iowa-shaped plastic ad for Wayne's Locks, in a box in the top drawer. I place the key beside her plate. "You sure you want him to have this?" she asks.

"Of course."

Behind her the railing divides the light around the table from the murky shadows of the studio below. Her complexion is sallow except for strokes of mauve under the eyes. Devoid of her usual bright makeup and bosomy layers of beads, she seems small. "He doesn't need the grief you'll cause if Peter Garvey gets away with murder." She sets down her cup so fast it clatters against the saucer. "Charlie doesn't deserve to be pushed around." Her shift in mood suggests she's the one with the agenda.

"Who's pushing Charlie around?"

"Luci certainly had him by the balls, pardon my French." Rosemary's face deepens to the next shade of pink. Maybe I shouldn't have offered that second glass of wine. "She did have something, though, a kind of spirit that could light up a room. She misused her attractiveness, if you ask me."

"You mean by being unfaithful to Charlie?"

"By charming him, then withholding her affection."

"He told you that?"

"I deduced it."

"You deduced it from what?"

"I don't remember, exactly. His changeable moods, I suppose. He's gotten to be that way again in recent weeks."

"You think I'm a bad wife? That I'm letting him down?"

"I'm sure it's not my place to think that."

"That's not exactly a denial."

To my surprise she looks sorry. I drain the final drop from my wineglass, open my eyes wider to stare at Rosemary's immaculate hairline, her smooth forehead. "Something had you so upset the other day that you closed up the office and went looking for Charlie at home. That's very much out of character for you, Rosemary."

Her unconvincing smile is tight at the center. "Not so much as you might think."

I reach for the Ziploc bag containing the canceled check. "You don't think Charlie should have given this to Weber, do you?"

"If you already know, why ask?"

"I don't know. I'm trying to find out. Charlie says you were

DISCOVERING THE BODY   213

angry he's been out of the shop too much, not taking care of business. That you end up taking the heat when customers are kept waiting. But I think you've disagreed about other things lately, too. I get the feeling he's protecting me from something."

At the edge of my vision a spot of red disappears as Rosemary covers the key chain with her hand. "Weber had a nerve showing up for back pay, after so much time, after walking off with no notice." She sips her coffee, licks her lips elaborately to slow down the conversation. "This is nice, Linda. Such a good meal."

"Here," I say quietly, turning her hand over to press the key lightly into her palm. It's time to engage her in the game she's known for. "Tell me something about myself." Her eyelids lower, and she strokes the key. "I understand you have a gift for interpersonal communication, dressed up with some fancy finger work."

Her thumb stops its circle of movement. "Ummm, a skeptic." She sounds relieved the confrontation is over. "The key tells me you changed the locks to this place."

"Well, you do have a gift," I tease her. "But I want something mystical here, some convincing clairvoyance. Some view of the future."

"To keep someone out."

"What?"

"The locks. You changed them to keep someone out."

I look at her with skepticism. "I hope this gets better, Rosemary."

She smiles at that. "You were still living at home with Charlie when you had the locks here replaced."

"Yes."

"You were afraid whoever damaged your artwork would come back."

"Of course."

"Charlie still had his key. He hadn't lost it or anything?"

"It was in his pocket that day, like always."

"You asked him?"

"I asked him."

"From the time you took possession of the building, you and Charlie have been the only two people who've had keys."

"And your point is . . . ?"

"What do you suppose he thought, when you changed the locks?"

"I know what he thought. We discussed it. Locking the door is something I do automatically. I was sure I had locked it that morning because I always do. But I couldn't remember doing it."

Her eyes are still closed. "You let Charlie know, by keeping both keys, that you mistrusted him."

"That's ridiculous."

The Iowa shape on the key ring is made of flexible quarter-inch plastic, transparent as Jell-o and slippery-smooth. She's curved it around her middle finger and is rubbing it. Her expression is trancelike, embarrassing. I have to look away. "I suggested to Charlie you could have scratched that etching plate yourself, Linda," she says, "and that you made up the story about someone breaking in here to convince him someone was after you. He said you were too honest to do that, and then it struck him that maybe you thought *he* could have committed the vandalism, and that's why you changed the locks, to keep *him* out."

"If he thought that, he would have said so."

"And then he said, 'Women are inscrutable.' "

Two realizations crowd my consciousness in rapid succession: that Charlie would never use the word inscrutable and that Rosemary is lying. The key clinks against the edge of her plate as I pull it from her hand and slip it back into my pocket. I'm on my feet, gathering up wineglasses in one hand, silverware and dessert plates with the other. The sink is three short steps from the table, and I turn on water to rinse the dishes, letting it run until it's hot.

"*I* could never doubt Charlie, not for a moment," she says, raising her voice over the noise I'm making. Shaking a fistful of silverware in the rushing water, I hear her say something else, but I can't understand the words. I escalate the sound by increasing the faucet's blast, which brings her to my side. She touches my arm. "Linda, turn that off for a second. Just listen."

I dry my hands as she retreats to her place at the table, facing me calmly. For a moment there's no sound except for the last gargle of the drain. "Don't you see how I might have thought you'd turned against him? He didn't ask for a key. It was my idea to ask for it. I was afraid you wouldn't give it to me."

"Rosemary, what are you talking about?"

"When I saw you the other day in the office, I had no idea there was the chance of a new trial. Now he tells me that's what you want. I'm afraid you may have gotten the idea I wasn't positive he was there all the time, that terrible afternoon."

"You made yourself very clear, Rosemary."

"After he came back from lunch that day, he didn't leave again until late afternoon." She pauses, looking down at the key chain. "I had to find out what you think he's capable of."

"Certainly not murder. It would make as much sense to accuse *me* of killing her."

"When Charlie told me you'd changed the locks here, I asked him if you'd thought to give him a key. It didn't seem to bother him that you hadn't, but it's been bothering me."

At the door, purse over her arm, she hesitates as I turn on the outside light. "Don't be too quick to dismiss my act as a parlor trick," she says. "It's a simple matter of using a token object as a way of disarming people. It always surprises me what people are eager to tell me about themselves." She looks tired.

Now that I've seen how inscrutable, even devious, she can be, I see Rosemary Lindstrom in a new light. I may have gotten her to confirm my hunch that her argument with Charlie was about giving this check to Weber, but she got her answer, too, without even asking the question. She has indeed revealed something to me about myself: I probably *didn't* want Charlie to have this key, or I would have remembered to give it to him. Reaching into my pocket, I realize how glad I am to have it back. But if I don't send it to him now, she'll tell him I refused, and I'll drive him further away. "You weren't sorry to see Luci go, were you?"

The question shocks me as I ask it, but Rosemary doesn't even blink. "Her death was an awful business, but I didn't shed any tears. There's a name for what she was: a C-O-C-K tease."

I might have known she'd be a speller. I pull the key out of my pocket and hand it over.

When I go downstairs to start working the next morning, I discover a message on my machine from Ken Hansen, asking me to come to his office as soon as I can. I try calling to see what's on his mind, but he's on another line. Then I call directory assistance for Darlington, Missouri, Luci's hometown, and find there is no listing for anyone named Cole. And next I phone the Gentry County Recorder to request a search of birth records for someone named Cole, possible first name Susanna. The clerk tells me she is not allowed by law to do a search for me, that I'll have to come to Missouri myself and look through the records.

The small town of Darlington has only one law officer, who answers the phone himself. He listens to my request as if he'd been hoping for something to do besides issue traffic citations. I talk him into going to the courthouse to look for proof that Luci had a child when she was very young. He remembers Luci's mother, a local teacher. He thinks she moved to California a few years back.

The moment I arrive in Ken Hansen's office, he picks up the phone and presses a single button. "Dennis," he says cryptically, "can you bring that now?" Dennis Johnson is the young police officer in training for fingerprint certification. He turns out to be in his mid-twenties, balding already, very tan. Hansen introduces me to him as the eyewitness in the Luci Cole case. I offer my hand to Dennis, and he stares for a couple of beats before shaking it, revealing a shy, too-earnest wariness he'll have to get over if he's going to make a career of police work. He has a file folder in his left hand. I know that the fingerprints on the metal plate vandalized in my studio have been sent to a lab, but I'll bet anything Dennis practiced on them first.

Dennis hands the folder to Hansen, and we all sit down. Hansen opens the file, studies the top page.

"Okay," he says. "Let's see what we've got." He places a finger on the page. "Flashlight. We used the prints collected for elimination purposes during the Cole murder case: Charlie Carpenter's, Bill Allard's, Judy Allard's. Yours." He glances at me. "We also checked against John Bender's."

"Bender's?"

"Just bear with me." He clears his throat. "We found Charlie's prints on the flashlight, just as we expected. There were two other readable prints, but no other match."

"There were clear prints on the flashlight besides Charlie's, but you couldn't identify them?"

"That's what I just said."

"And you checked for John Bender's."

"I'll explain. After the break-in in your garage, and then the vandalism at your workplace the very next day, I decided to check the prints at both scenes against the entire list I just gave you. In light of your admission of doubt about your testimony, I was hoping we'd rule out any connection between these two recent, disturbing events and the murder scene." Hansen clears his throat and turns to the next page of the report. "Now for the etching plate. We were surprised your prints weren't on that."

"A fastidious cleaning is part of the process," I tell him. "I thought you found a thumbprint on it?"

"I did. A clear thumbprint, and we got a match on that one. Bill Allard."

I stare at him. "How long have you known this?"

"Dennis here called me first thing this morning." Hansen gives me a long look. "I'll be talking to Bill Allard right away. He and Bender were the only two people seen close to your workplace that morning. Oh, and Charlie, of course. I decided that because there might be a pattern of harassment forming, I'd rethink the seriousness of your request to check prints on that flashlight, and I threw Bender in for good measure on that one. I know there was a time you thought even he was against you."

"I was beginning to see a threat behind every face I saw, but I wasn't entirely wrong, was I?" I pause. "Bill Allard," I say, picturing the crude X slashed across my picture of the house. "It's hard to imagine him doing something like that."

"Random violence, or vandalism, doesn't have to make sense," says Hansen. "But the damage to your artwork does seem to me to be a very personal kind of surrogate violence. In order to imagine why Bill Allard would do such a thing, we have to wonder what he was trying to achieve by this action. To instill fear, that's the only motive I can come up with. Do you have any other ideas?"

We talk for a while longer, but "to instill fear" is the best we can do.

I drive straight home from the police station and park by my back door. For a minute I just sit there, trying to reconcile the idea of Bill's indirect violence against me with what I know about his character. I shiver even as I stand up in the warm sunlight and stare at the locked door of the studio for long seconds before letting myself in.

Inside, I listen to the two messages on my machine. One is a customer. The second is John Bender: "Call me as soon as you get in." I enter his number, and he answers on the second ring. "I'm tied up here for the rest of the afternoon," he says, "so I thought, if you could come over to my place about six. . . . I've got a pile of research to show you. The thing is, I set something up for tomorrow. Remember Ben Petersen?"

"The one who was in Jim Howard's auto-mech class."

"Right. I couldn't remember the name of the second kid involved in that, so I looked it up. Name's Michael Lassell. The two boys got their hands on some crank, and Petersen died. The autopsy revealed a congenital heart condition. When the methamphetamine got into his system, it elevated his blood pressure, and his heart virtually exploded."

"Yeah, I remember reading about it at the time."

"This Michael Lassell was the one who called the emergency room. They were best friends. It happened at Lassell's house one night when his parents were out. These were kids who'd never gotten into trouble, good grades. Since then we've seen more and more crank in the county. We never did find out where these kids got it. Anyway, Lassell's a sophomore at Iowa State now, and he's on campus already for the fall semester. He's agreed to meet us there tomorrow morning."

"Us?"

"He doesn't remember what I look like. I guess you know from personal experience how forgettable I am." He pauses, in case I missed the sarcasm. "For identification purposes, I told him I'd be with a tall, great-looking woman with long blond hair wearing a short orange dress. He'll be looking for you."

"What if I can't make it?"

"This won't work unless we do it together. I had to do some fast talking just to get him to agree to this. I promised him it would be off the record. Keeping drugs away from this town is a kind of crusade of mine. Just now I told him we were working on cracking a drug ring here in town and that we needed his help. His friend's death really devastated him. I could tell it still hurt when I brought it up. I want you there to help convince him he has to talk to us, that he owes it to Ben. I have an idea, but I need you to make it work."

"Why my orange dress?"

"You were wearing it that day we had lunch at the Grubstake. He'll notice you right off."

"You remember what I was wearing?"

"I'm a reporter, remember? I'm trained to notice things."

In a heartbeat of silence I realize I can ease off on the suspicions I've harbored against Bender for so long—that he could have been the one who brushed against me in the garage that night and who made that awful X on the etching plate. Detective Hansen has ruled him out of both incidents. "Why would Michael Lassell talk now, if he wouldn't a year ago?"

"He's older, more mature. I got his number from his mom. She remembered me. At first Michael refused to discuss a meeting, so I told him we've figured out where he and Ben got the drugs. The fact that he agreed right away makes it a sure thing he didn't tell the truth before. He'll meet us at the fountain by the student union at four o'clock."

"You didn't think I'd go along with this, did you, unless you set it up so Michael would be looking for me? What connection could he have with Luci?"

"Since you showed me that note she wrote about selling her car to Weber, I've been doing some archival work at the paper. If we forge this a link at a time, we may be able to connect Weber to your friend's death."

"I talked to Hansen this morning."

"What?" he asks. The one-word question tells me my very tone of voice has communicated the seriousness of what I'm about to say.

"He ran a check of your prints against the thumbprint on the copper plate. He also checked that thumbprint against all the elimination prints from Luci's murder case. That time he turned up a match. Bill Allard apparently came in here that day and left his mark on that etching plate."

Bender is silent. "Well," he says. "Has Hansen talked to him yet?"

"He may be talking to him right now. Hansen just got the report this morning."

Right after I hang up, I lock the doors before going upstairs, where I pull the orange dress out of the closet and hold it in front of my body. It's an inexpensive cotton knit, but I've worn it only twice. The color's still bright. Because of my height, it's shorter than it would be on most women, a good hand-span above my knees. Too short, according to Charlie. Maybe that explains why it was one of the garments I brought from the house; the dress pleases me, but it doesn't please Charlie. Now, pulling off my loose, gauzy dress, I drop the orange fabric over my head and smooth it over my breasts, belly, and thighs. In my jewelry box I find earrings the same color, bursts of tiny beads strung on wires, like fireworks. Judy gave them to me for my birthday last year, but I've never worn them. I remember opening the gift, wishing I were the type.

Absentmindedly brushing one of the earrings against the palm of my left hand, I feel a dozen touches sending a tactile message to my brain, and I begin to undress, tossing bra and panties onto the bed. In the floor-length mirror my hands pass down over corrugated ribs, barely visible beneath the smooth flesh, cup my full breasts briefly, then move down past the heavy-lidded eye of my navel to the sudden sharpness of pelvic bones. Feelings stir that haven't arisen since Charlie's last touch—a touch I've stopped yearning for when I lie down at night, I realize. Maybe that explains my not wanting him to have a key to this place. I've withdrawn from him.

I find my hand mirror in the top drawer of the dresser. I turn my back on the full-length reflection to hold the small mirror high, reaching upward with my left hand and stretching to alter the serpentine alignment of shoulders, torso, and buttocks—the classic female nude, almost beautiful. It's a good body when caught by surprise like this, mercifully free of scale, the indirect light carving shallows, gilding the curves. I'm smiling. Where did this nervy agitation come from? Last time I felt like this, I was getting ready for a date.

I don't look half bad. Am I usually blind to my own body, afraid of where it wants to take me? Maybe I should be. *I'm a reporter. I'm trained to notice.*

No matter how confused I feel, I could never betray Charlie, the way Luci did. I stare at the crumple of orange on the bed.

Dinner turns out to be pizza delivered from Mona's and a six-pack of Michelob. After we eat, Bender disposes of the cardboard pizza box and brings two more beers poured into fresh mugs from his freezer. His apartment is actually rather classy: hardwood floors, old oak furniture, two huge paintings—swirls of bright colors, gestural as Kandinsky's—Bender's own efforts from when he minored in art. Not bad for being so derivative. Books line two walls of the living room and are stacked everywhere, even on the fireplace mantel and on the hearth.

He scoops up a bulky file folder from the cluttered desk at the far side of the room. "I keep thinking about the way the house was slashed on the intaglio plate, how the act echoes the way Luci died." He pulls a newspaper clipping from the folder. Some are microfiche copies, some originals. All I can think about is Bill, with a sharp object in his hand. I shudder, but Bender doesn't notice. I lean back against the corner of the couch and take a sip of beer.

"I want to go over some things with you, Linda," he says, sitting beside me, "and while I do, keep in mind the question that led me to this research: What could possibly explain why anyone other than Garvey would have been lying under Luci's car that day?"

"If it was someone else," I say, "he had to look enough like Garvey that I could have made the mistake." We look at each other. "Someone tall and blond, who ties bandannas around his head. Like Russell Weber."

"Right. And this is what I've come up with: About three years ago there was a fatality out on the interstate involving a Des Moines man bringing drugs from the south, from Kansas City." Bender hands me a wire photo of an auto crash. "The guy was involved in a high-speed chase with the police south of here out on I-Thirty-five and was killed when he rolled his car. The cops used a drug dog. In the frame they found tubes of pure cocaine, with a street value of seventy thousand dollars. The guy probably thought he'd be safe, crossing the state line with it stashed below board like that." Bender points to the grainy photo of a car lying wheels up against a tree. "In his pocket was an address book, with encoded records. Russell Weber's name was in it. That's what brought him to my attention, but I've never caught him in anything illegal."

I hand the clipping back to Bender, and he slips it to the bottom of the pile on his knee. "Let's say Weber was offered a chance for a good drug deal if he'd go after the stuff himself, and he borrowed the idea of stashing it in the frame of a car. If he could come up with the money, Weber would take this kind of risk. He really hates to work."

"How much money?"

"Usually guys are pulled into dealing with a promise they can double or even triple their money, but they have to come up with a round sum, say ten thousand—"

"Where would he have gotten that kind of cash?"

"Luci was your friend. What do you think? It was her car. Maybe it was her money."

"She didn't have money, and if there were drugs under her car, she didn't know about it." I struggle to remember: *This morning Russell showed up, wanting to test-drive my car—asking me if I got the first payment.* "He once gave her a packet of a bitter, brownish powder," I say quietly, "but that only made her angry." *When he finally did show up here, he was mad, blaming me for some kind of noisy vibration when he went over twenty-five—a shaking, he said, like going over speed bumps, or a washboard road.* "He borrowed her car. There was something wrong with the universal joint."

"How do you know he offered her drugs, or borrowed her car?"

Bender gazes at me without interrupting while I tell him about finding Luci's diary. I report on every entry I can remember that had to do with Russell Weber, or with the Nova. "Luci doesn't say how long he was gone the day he borrowed her car. He could have covered a lot of miles, to Missouri and back, or even Nebraska, between midmorning and late afternoon. Let's say something between them gave him a motive to kill her. Afterward he dived under the car to retrieve the drugs he'd stashed there, just as I came along. I tapped his boot and said, 'Hi, Peter.' Weber had to get out of there before I came back out of the house and saw that he wasn't Garvey. So he took off before he'd gotten the goods, and Peter Garvey got the blame. And then this summer, Weber came back to look for the car, thinking the stuff would still be under there. He could have been the one in my garage that night."

Bender nods. "Thinking Charlie still had the car. He couldn't have known that after the murder the car ended up at the high-school auto lab. I'm hoping Michael Lassell will tell us tomorrow that he found the methamphetamine in the frame of that car."

For long moments we sit in silence. Finally I say, "At best, all we're doing is constructing a theory, with no evidence to back it up. Even if we manage to connect Weber to drugs, drugs to Luci's car, we still don't know what his motive would have been to kill her."

"If my speculation holds together tomorrow, we'll give it to the police, Linda. It's their job to get concrete evidence."

"What makes you think your friend Hansen will be any more concerned about doing that now than he was a couple of years ago?" I'm on my feet, picking up empty Michelob bottles by their necks, heading for the kitchen. "It gives me a real boost, though," I call out toward the living room, "to know there could be a rational explanation for someone other than Peter Garvey being under her car. Until tonight even I thought I might be crazy."

In the silence that follows, I'm aware of Bender's presence behind me in the doorway, and I turn around. I'm not about to cry; I just need to hide my confusion behind my hands. He offers his handkerchief, a wrinkled ball. "It's clean," he says. "I just don't fold."

When I return his handkerchief I observe his face as he considers the damp cloth in his hand. This is the first time I've noticed the scatter of freckles across his lowered lids, the laugh lines traced in white at the tanned outer edge of each eye, the unconscious way he covers his high forehead with one long-fingered hand whenever he's concentrating on thought, like now. He catches me looking at him intently and his breathing deepens, as if shoving his handkerchief into his back pocket were an act of extreme exertion. "I think I should go," I say quickly. "I'm really exhausted."

I rush into the living room and gather up the notes and clippings on the couch and the floor, stacking them on the coffee table, avoiding Bender's gaze again the way I used to, just a few short weeks ago, when I'd sense him staring at me on the street, or in line at the automatic teller machine, or in Ace Hardware. "I'll walk with you to the corner," he says, "and watch till you're inside. After you've checked things out, I want you to flash your neon sign to let me know everything's okay."

"I'm not the kind of woman who needs protection."

"Being a woman has nothing to do with it."

"Yes, well . . ." I lose my train of thought as I pause before stepping past him into the kitchen. After I've rinsed forks while he's stuffed the pizza box into a trash can in the corner of the kitchen, we turn to face each other, and quickly turn away.

I've remembered the Ziploc bag in my purse, and I show him the canceled check Charlie made out a few weeks ago for the work on our garage, endorsed by Weber. "On paper, a fingerprint can last forever. On paper, someone's touch—" I pause, remembering that during the days following Luci's death Hansen told me about how the fingerprints of Egyptian scribes can be detected on ancient papyrus by a modern chemical test.

"Only unglazed paper can hold a print like that, and anyway, a canceled check has been handled by lots of people." Bender sounds distracted. I'm staring at Charlie's signature, at the C, big as a nickel, the other letters trailing off, not his usual confident signature. When Bender's silence makes me look up, it's plain he's no longer thinking of fingerprints.

"You're staring at me again," I say with a smile.

He shrugs. "I guess I never could keep my eyes off you," he says.

It's a pitch-dark night—new moon—and the breeze out on the street is chilly. We walk fast. At the corner Bender touches my arm. "I'll come to your back door at two tomorrow afternoon. I figure it's about an hour and a half to Ames. Lassell's meeting us at four, but I want to be early. I'm nervous he won't show, or see us and lose his nerve. We'll have to be careful how we handle him. We can discuss that on the drive up." Under the streetlight Bender's forehead is high and pale in contrast to the dark wash of whiskers down his jawline and across his chin this late in the day.

I left the green-shaded desk lamp in my studio on, so I wouldn't have to come home to complete darkness. Stepping inside, I see I left the light on by the bed upstairs, too, the one I'd used while I was trying on my orange dress earlier. The answering machine is blinking. I'll listen to the messages tomorrow. Now I'm too sleepy, and starting up the stairs to the loft, my body's heavy, like I'm hauling myself up out of a swimming pool. Pausing, left hand on the iron banister, I hear something from above, a tight composition of sounds I can't identify.

Holding my breath, I sag against the wall, mouth open with an instinct to hear better that way. Adrenaline thickens my heartbeat. I'm unwilling to move until I hear the intrusive sounds again.

Then I remember: I promised to flash the neon sign to let Bender know everything's okay. Looking down toward the front window, I gain courage from the mirror-written silhouette of script against the light from the streetlamp. He's out there, looking this way.

Heart slowed to almost normal, I move up onto the next riser, then the next, pausing again only when my line of vision comes up to floor level. From this odd perspective, furniture legs—the table in the foreground with its graceful, turned supports; the curve-legged bentwood chairs; the unmade bed, its Hollywood frame on casters off to my right—touch down onto the plane of dimly lit polished floor. The bathroom door is ajar, and the light's on in there, too. My mouth opens with the effort of standing my ground, and suddenly the dryness closes my throat, making me swallow. I knead my tongue against itself to wring forth what little saliva I can.

The moment the phone rings downstairs behind me, the sound shooting a dart of pain clear through me, I duck down below floor level again. The second ring is worse. With the third ring my eyes are glued to the line where the top step meets the floor above me. I'm afraid to blink as I feel my face rising slightly, drawn by curiosity and anger. The fourth time, before the answering machine clicks on, the caller gives up mid-ring. Slowly I begin to ease myself back down, keeping my face tilted up into the pale shadows above, every muscle straining backward to step once again onto a level surface.

And then the toilet flushes up there, and I hear footsteps and my own groan of surprise.

"Linda?"

It's Charlie. "It's me," he says, and then goes on saying something I don't quite get. From this sharp angle and in this light, his impressive stature is foreshortened to bulges of thigh, stomach, and chin. My hand lets go of the banister as he pulls the chain hanging from the ceiling fixture so that the loft is flooded with light. "Where the hell have you been?" he wants to know.

"You scared me to death." My mouth is open. I'm breathing hard, as in a moment he's down the stairs, embracing me. He takes my head in his hands, pulls back to study my face as my heart slows. "You're coming home with me. We can't let this happen. I should never have let you leave."

Behind me there's one loud rap at the front door, and in an instant I open it and Bender steps inside.

"Linda won't be needing your help anymore," Charlie says. "I want you to stay away from her."

The two men stare at each other, and then Bender looks at me. "You want me to go now?"

Yes. I tell him to go.

There's something about being rigid with fear, then feeling the adrenaline subside, that leaves the body limp. Charlie and I go upstairs. The quilt on the bed is rumpled, where he lay all evening, waiting for me. I begin to tremble, and he smooths my hair with his hands, pulls me against him, so warm. "What were the two of you doing all night?"

"Eating pizza. Talking about the methamphetamine problem in rural Iowa."

"Like a date."

"No. Not like a date."

Thankfully, he doesn't need to hear more. My mind gives up on everything but the slow lines his fingers trace on my body. He told me once he has the strongest orgasms after touching like this for a while. He's like a woman, he said, liking to hold back for a long time so that when he comes he nearly passes out. Now he kisses me long and deep and enters me at last. Ending the kiss by speaking against my lips, he slows his rhythm and says, "You wanted to kiss him tonight, didn't you? *Say yes.*" I admit to nothing of the kind. We make love until we sink into a stupor of exhaustion.

No, my mind tells me once, as I jerk awake. I must have spoken out loud, because Charlie presses against me again.

16 ◆ I WAKE UP the next morning to the smell of bacon frying. When I prop myself up on an elbow, I can see Charlie standing at the stove. "I went home to shower and change," he says, "and brought back some food." He sits on the edge of the bed, smoothing hair out of my eyes. His hand moves under the sheet to caress my stomach. "Your little kitchen isn't very well stocked." I open my legs so he can cup the rise of pelvic bone with his broad hand.

I close my eyes again. "I didn't hear you leave."

"You were dead to the world." He touches a nipple with his mouth, so fast I murmur with complaint when he stops. "I guess we've gotten Bender out of your system," he says, smoothing the sheet back over me, up to my chin. "He's a menace." Charlie bends down again and kisses the backs of my hands. One, then the other. "I'll cook your eggs just the way you like them."

In a few minutes he has breakfast ready, and I've taken a shower and put my nightgown back on. Joining him at the table, I pick up a strip of bacon. Jealousy, I'm thinking, is what drove Charlie's prolonged passion last night, while mine arose from relief, maybe even gratitude that I hadn't ruined everything.

"Try to eat." He cuts into the yolk of his over-easy egg.

He wants me to come home. His staying here last night was a concession to my reluctance, his lovemaking an act of persuasion, I suppose. "Give me one more day, Charlie. I'm scheduled to go to Ames this afternoon, on business. I won't be back till late." I lick my lips. "I'm just not able to deal with so much all at once. I can't face the house right now."

I stand up and walk around to hug him from behind, pressing my lips into his neck just below the beard. He stands into my embrace. "Bender's a freak," he says, "using your fears to get close."

Charlie's jealousy is so confusing, I'm not sure what's happening, why I'm yielding to him as if I have no power to refuse, why I can't simply say, *You're the only one who holds me close.* I know he'd believe me, because it's true. By the time we tangle on the bed, I'm outside myself, observing how much my panting sounds like exhausted pleasure. The same shudder of release. For the first time with Charlie, I'm a fake. "I need more time," I tell him again. "I can't go home just yet."

As soon as Charlie leaves for work, I call Bender, all business: "You said Michael Lassell won't talk to anyone but us, right? If we put him off, we'll lose him. If we lose him, we lose Weber."

"We're still on for today?"

"*Yes*, John." I pause for a deep breath. "They store bodies at just above freezing in the morgue, did you know that? The cold rises up off the table. They let me see Luci while they were setting up for the autopsy. I wanted to see if I remembered how she looked, what he had done to her, and I had. *Objects* I have no trouble recalling. It's *people* who keep changing shape the more I try and know them. A body with no life in it is nobody's friend. I was remarkably unmoved."

"Don't do this, Linda."

"The circles of blood on the kitchen floor were twisted, as if someone had used a sponge, or a mop, to obliterate footprints. The only shoe prints in Luci's case were mine."

"Linda . . . ?"

"I walked out of my sandals, left them in the house. When I talked to you that afternoon, my feet were bare. I remembered that, even if I didn't remember you."

"You don't have to go with me."

"Why would Charlie say you're a freak?"

"You had a bad time after I left last night, didn't you?"

"Some women cry," I say firmly, remembering Luci, her damp face against me, my fingers on the small of her back, "so someone will come to the rescue. I'm not a crier. I have broad shoulders. I'll go with you, just like we planned. Charlie's jealous, so I didn't tell him about our plans. I should have."

"Ken has made it clear this is his case from now on, but Michael Lassell would never open up to anyone but me—or maybe you, I'm thinking. For one afternoon you and I will have to be unaccounted for. Your being an artist, not a detective, will be useful with Michael."

I'm not sure what Bender means by that, but I'll ask him when I see him. We make plans to have lunch in Des Moines on the way. I figure by then I'll be hungry. While I'm getting dressed, I remember the one-o'clock appointment I made the other day, allegedly to discuss my irrational fears, and I call Reverend Gustavson to cancel. We set a time for tomorrow.

By four o'clock in the afternoon, I'm sitting on a cement bench by the Four Seasons fountain on the Iowa State Campus. The four statues of Native American women have their backs to each other at the center of a round basin catching plumes of water. Whenever the breeze shifts, I feel a faint, cooling mist on my face and arms. Spring faces me, head bowed, holding an infant on her broad thighs. She cradles the baby in hands larger than her own face.

The artist added volume to every aspect of the limestone figures so that from a distance, or covered with autumn leaves or driven snow, detail would not be lost. From this close, the woman appears bloated, too substantial to be admired. I know how that feels.

But right now I am enjoying the knowledge that someone nearby, a young man in a red golf shirt and white shorts—handsome, with close-cropped blond hair, broad shoulders, narrow waist—is eyeing me with favor, me and my orange dress, which slides up my thigh another inch as I cross my legs. Dressing sexy for this college boy seemed vulgar this morning, given the way my day began, but I managed. Another triumph of sheer will. And here I am, the decoy Bender wanted me to be.

The weather is lovely. Bender is off in the distance, out on the grassy, parklike sweep of central campus, near the campanile. He decided Michael Lassell would be less likely to get cold feet if he spotted me here alone. I turn my face toward the guy in the red shirt and smile, stand, walk over the flagstones toward him. "Michael?"

He returns my smile uncertainly. "Sorry. Wish I were." For a split second he doesn't move, until a friend hails him. He looks back as he walks toward a break in the evergreen shrubs that ring the plaza, and his gaze drops down the line of my body. He looks eighteen. Half my age.

It's after four. Maybe Michael Lassell's not coming. Off in the distance Bender has started walking this way, and I tip back my chin in acknowledgment, not wanting to wave. When I turn around to reclaim my place on the bench, there's no mistake about who's standing there waiting, because he says, "Are you Mr. Bender's friend?"

He's not as good-looking as the first one: lanky, narrow-shouldered, eyes shifting restlessly in deep sockets. Still, his short brown hair is cut well, feathered over forehead and ears. His smooth skin is clear. His teeth are even and very white. His handshake, an unexpected formality from a college kid, is firm. "I thought so, by the dress," he says, ears pinkening. His eyes are bloodshot.

I glance down at myself. "I'm glad you found me."

"I'm kind of in a hurry. I have to go see my adviser. What's this about?"

Propping my large purse on the bench, I pull out Luci's journal, the gray-and-aqua patterned cover bent at one corner. I brought it as a prop, to help me carry this off. Bluffing isn't my forte. "I found this." I lift it between us.

"What is it?"

"It contains the name of a drug dealer."

Michael stares at the book, then looks past me, over my shoulder, then glances around the fountain area, an oval flagstone terrace ringed with low evergreens. The fountain whispers and flings another cooling net of mist our way.

"In reading this," I say softly, "I figured out where you and your friend Ben got the drugs that killed him."

Michael's casual demeanor changes. He fills his mouth with air, exhales with exasperation. "I don't think so." He continues to stare at the journal. He swallows. "What is that anyway? Where'd you get it?"

I wish Bender would hurry up. "It's my friend's diary. Luci Cole."

"The lady back home who was murdered?"

I nod. Another nervous drift of Michael's glance over my shoulder gives me a hint that Bender's approaching, so I turn, but he's still thirty feet away. "She tells about a friend of hers who was in on a drug deal. He thought he'd make himself a pile of money, without a lot of trouble."

"Good for him," says Michael. "I don't think I need to hear this." And he walks around me, right toward Bender.

As they approach each other, I see Bender do a sidestep to block Michael's way, put his arm out to grip his shoulder, shake hands,

reintroduce himself. And then it's the three of us standing in sunlight blown with mist from the fountain. "Linda tell you what she
has?" he asks Michael.

"I'm not interested." He turns a dark look on me and makes
another move to walk away.

But Bender has a hold of his upper arm, blocking his way again.
"You won't be in any trouble if you talk to us off the record,"
Bender says, voice deliberately slow and quiet. "If you don't, I can't
promise anything. Keeping evidence from the police the way you
did, that's a serious matter."

"I don't see what this has to do with me." The kid's both scared
and curious, that's clear. In the car on the way up here, Bender
and I decided the only reason Michael would show up would be
to find out what Bender knew, if anything. Apparently we've
hooked him, because now he walks with us into the Memorial
Union, passing through the revolving door into a hushed, darkened, stained-glass-windowed memorial to the dead of American
wars, their names listed in perfect letters on the limestone walls.
Beyond this cool passageway we go downstairs, through a crowded
hallway into the brightly lit, noisy Commons, a huge, low-ceilinged
room full of square oak tables, crowded with students and faculty.

The room's a hash of aromas made up of the smells of tacos,
french fries, and meat-and-potato dishes served in the cafeteria
line. Bender goes after Cokes while Michael and I wait at the table,
my nervous fingertips tracing initials carved on the surface. This
was part of our plan: that Michael's conversation with me would
not include Bender at this point. "Luci was my best friend." I place
the journal in the center of the table, moving salt and pepper shak-
ers aside. "I could have prevented her being killed."

Michael avoids looking at the journal, or at me, but raises his
hand to wave toward the far wall. A dark-haired young woman
waves back, and Michael sits up straighter.

"Wouldn't you like to know how?"

"How what?" He seems annoyed, or embarrassed.

"How I could have prevented her being killed?"

"I still don't see what this has to do with me."

"Ben Petersen was your friend for years, the way Luci was mine. We have something in common."

He shifts his body in the straight-backed chair. Before my nerve can fail me, I reach out and put my hand gently over his on the tabletop, only to feel his fingers tense under mine as he braces himself forward to rise from his chair. The touch was too much, a mistake. "We can solve the mysteries around why they died," I say, and to my surprise he simply leans back in his chair again. "But only if we help each other. That's all we have left. If we trust each other, it will help us both. And lots of other people who were affected by their deaths."

Michael's eyes roll with disgust as he looks away. "You want to get to the point?"

I lean toward him as though I have a confidence to share. "I know you wouldn't tell where you got the stuff because you didn't want the cops to find out there was lots more of it, and you didn't want to have to turn it over to them," I say as John approaches. I straighten my back.

Now it's Bender's turn. "So," he says, placing tall red paper cups in front of us. He sits across from Michael. "Let's get started." He leans forward so what he says, too, in a lowered voice, will be taken as a confidence: "You and Ben Petersen had a class together the semester he died."

Michael stares at his Coke.

"Remember?"

"I might." He refuses to look up.

"What was it?"

"This a quiz?"

"The class. What was it?"

He sighs. "Auto-mech lab."

"Right. Do you remember the car you were working on?"

Michael looks at Bender, his forehead furrowed. "Car?"

"It was an auto lab. You remember what you did to that car?"

"We rebuilt the engine, tore down the carburetor, lots of things." He chuckles. "There wasn't much left of that car when we finished with it. But then it wasn't much when we started either."

"What do you mean?"

"People don't give valuable cars to schools for students to practice on," he says, crunching ice. He swallows. "It was a 'seventy-seven Chevy Nova. Rusted out. Red plaid interior. A real toad."

"Where did you get the drugs?"

"In a Copenhagen can in the parking lot," says Michael, not missing a beat. "Like I said before." He sniffs. "When Ben died."

"I remember what you said. I didn't believe you. I knew that Ben was your buddy, that you were pretty upset." They look away from each other, then back. "More than upset, Michael. I know that your folks were worried about your blaming yourself."

Michael swallows a sip of Coke, eyes narrowing. "You think someone was selling to us, don't you? Well, you won't hear it from me. It had nothing to do with Ben. It was an accident, with him."

"You're still using, aren't you?"

"Yeah, sure. Right in front of your eyes."

"And dealing. I called the registrar's office," says Bender. "Your mom thinks you're registered for the fall semester, but it turns out you're not. Still, here you are, looking for all the world like a student. I'm guessing you're no great shakes in that department, but what better place to deal crank than here where thousands of people, most of them under twenty-five, live in one place, a lot of them stressed out, money in their accounts." Michael glares at him. I glance around, but no one nearby seems to be noticing this little drama. "By now I'll bet you're close to the big money, right?"

Michael looks at me. "Is he about done?"

"Just about," says Bender. "I think you know what the penalties are. I can guess how many eight balls you got out of what you and

Ben found. And I can guess how much you're pulling down these days. The name Cooper Van Meter mean anything to you?"

Michael looks bored.

"Convicted last month of conspiracy and drug trafficking. Life in prison without parole. Gary Luloff?"

Michael bites his lower lip.

"Probably'll get the same sentence. Harris Simon? Fifteen years. Jim Sullivan, ten to forty. Brian Cooper got fifteen to eighteen. Tony Williams got seventeen. Names familiar to dozens of small-town dealers. Methamphetamine's exploding in Iowa, isn't it, Michael? It's everywhere. I bet you have a hit in your shoe right now. Or in your jock."

Michael tries to laugh, but it comes out on his face like pain. He shifts in his seat. "This is making no sense to me."

"You're just an errand boy, but I'm here to tell you, you are *known*. You come clean about Ben, I'll help you out of this."

"I don't know any of those guys."

"But you know about Ben, and the car in the auto-mech class."

Michael's on his feet. Now it's up to me. Halfway across the Commons, I catch up to him. "Look, Michael," I say, falling into step beside him, "there's no way you can get hurt by this, honestly. You guys had Luci's car up on the rack, right?"

"Luci's car?" He stops so fast I bump into him. We're surrounded, in a crowd. Time approaches for the ten-minute break between classes, which explains the sudden upsurge in activity. Moving a couple of steps to the wall, we get out of everyone's way.

"The Chevy you and Ben worked on in high school was Luci Cole's car. After she was murdered, the car was donated to the high school. I think the murderer had hidden drugs in the frame of that car. He was under the car, trying to retrieve the drugs, right after he killed Luci. But then I came along and walked right by the car, and as soon as I was out of sight, he ran off. He was afraid I'd see him and he'd be convicted of killing her. He left town. If I'm right, you found those drugs when you had the car up on the rack, to work on the underside, months later. You or someone you know."

Michael looks with envy at the stream of students, but he's stuck against the wall. I'm in his way. He's probably trying to make the connection between what I want from him and what Bender wants, confused by Bender's antagonistic, confrontational attitude and my pleading tone.

I'm taller than he is, and he has to tilt his head back slightly to look at me. "It was her car?" he wonders. "But then what . . . ?" Half spoken, his thought dies in confusion as we resume walking into the wide hallway. He moves forward slowly, preceding me up the hollow-worn steps that lead back up to the War Memorial Hall. There, where a dim, bluish light comes from the high stained-glass windows, and where the air is cooler, I manage to bring him to a full stop by saying, "If you did find the drugs in the car, then it will help me prove that the man who really killed Luci Cole was not Peter Garvey, who was convicted, but someone else."

He stares at me, his expression transient with thought. "He's wrong about me."

"Bender?"

"Yeah. The worst thing I've done lately is flunk out of school."

"Either you didn't find drugs in the car or you're not willing to tell me because Bender's got you scared. Which is it? Can't you at least tell me that?"

"Huh." He laughs. "You really don't know the answer, do you? You and Bender both let on you knew something for sure, but you don't."

So much for our well-planned interrogation.

"You tell him for me that I'll try real hard to remember if I found anything on that car that wasn't standard equipment. But if he tells my mom I'm not in school, then he can kiss off any idea of my remembering anything. You keep my folks out of this."

"We need you."

"Well, I sure as hell don't need you." He heads for the revolving glass doors that lead outside.

Defeated, I consider the wall of names, the long dead from World War I: Edgar Grant Collins, Robert William Chapman, Hortense Elizabeth Wind, James Rupert Ellis. There's just enough light in here to read the three-inch letters. I lower myself to sit on one of the benches lining the hall and lean back, allowing the stone cold to penetrate my shoulders. I shiver as nausea makes me swallow two, three times in rapid succession. People pass in front of me, only shapes, movement. I blew it, said the wrong thing to Michael Lassell, let him get away without telling me what I need so desperately to know.

When he reappears, sitting beside me, I hardly react. "Just listen," he says, though I haven't said a word. "It wasn't just Ben and me at my house that night. The two other guys left when Ben got sick. They took the stuff with them, all of it, one of the guys did. When I called an ambulance, this guy said the stuff shouldn't be there or we'd go to jail, so I gave it to him.

"He was the one who'd known what it was right off. I'd never seen crank, only heard about it. I'd smoked pot before, but mixed together like that it was really something. In a few minutes I found out what the big deal was."

He licks his lips, wipes his mouth with the back of his right hand. "I told Benny to take his turn. After a while we tried some from the one bag that wasn't as brown as the others. The powder was more of a yellowish color, not as lumpy. Maybe purer stuff." He looks at me sidelong. "This guy, I guess he knew. We mixed it with grass and put it in the pipe and passed it to Ben. It gave him a heart attack."

Michael stops for breath. When he goes on, his voice is hoarse. "These guys, the ones who got out of there right away and took the stuff with them, never even intended to give it back. A few days later this one guy said he'd give me a hundred bucks if I promised not to tell anyone about it, ever. He already knew I hadn't told, but when I took the money, it was like I could never change my mind. I was in on something. At the end of the summer he bragged he'd already made over ten thousand dollars off it and had half of it left, and I started to see what I'd done. He was selling it an eighth of an ounce at a time, like Bender said. He'd made a real ass out of me. It was bad enough that I had to be wrong. I had to be stupid, too."

Michael leans forward, resting his arms on his knees, head down. Off to the right, Bender appears in the archway by the stairs. But when he sees us, he turns and leaves the way he came, guessing that his timing is bad. Michael didn't see him.

He straightens up, then leans back against the wall, matching his posture to mine. We've been sharing confidences in this solemn near-darkness as if it's a confessional. "What made you come back just now?" I ask.

"It ruined my life, seeing Benny die like that. If it wasn't for me he would still be alive. For a long time I told myself it was his weak heart that killed him, but I knew I was lying to myself. He didn't want to do it. He was afraid of drugs. Bender didn't scare me. You were the one who scared me."

"I scared you?"

"It was like you knew, not what happened, exactly, but how I had something to feel guilty about. I walked outside just now, and I couldn't stand not telling someone at last, right now, before I lost my nerve. Bender's got me all wrong. I wouldn't use now, not after what happened. I've done enough damage, by what happened to Benny. Maybe that's why I keep messing up everything I do."

"What you've told me will help set things right. Sometimes that's the only way to forgive yourself."

"I'll never be able to do that," he says, sitting up straight. "I told Benny it felt great, awesome, and he'd be a fool to miss it. Pretty soon he was strutting around like crazy, jumping up on the furniture. We were best friends since first grade. He was down in the dumps a lot, a really serious person. When he took that last hit, it got to him fast. I'd never seen him so happy, like he'd just gotten the best news in the world."

For a few moments of silence it seems like we're honoring the dead. Then I have to ask the question I feel sure he will answer at last. "Michael, you didn't find that big a stash in a Copenhagen can in a parking lot. Tell me where you got the drugs."

"Like you thought. It was stashed in the frame of that old Chevy Nova. I didn't know exactly what it was at first, but of course I knew it was some kind of drugs. I showed it to Ben, and then to the other guys." He licks his lips. "They were big Ziploc bags, rolled up and tied like sausages. There were six of them."

Heading for home, Bender pulls the Bronco into the automatic car wash at Arnie's Petro Palace near campus, possibly a delayed response to my earlier comment that his car was so dirty I had to be careful not to brush against it. Now my orange dress is the last thing on my mind. We've said little since our conversation by the fountain when he hurried up behind me, shoes crunching the loose stones on the flagstone terrace, greeting me with a cautious "Well?" Our eyes were on Michael, across the street already, headed across the grass. "What happened?"

"He denied everything. Then he came back and told me the whole story."

Now, watching the dripping, fringed roller of the car wash drag down the windshield, I raise my voice over the roar. "When Michael first met me this afternoon, he said he had to see his adviser. Why would he say that if he's not enrolled?"

"To convince you his brush with drugs was a onetime thing." I frown. "Okay, think what you like. He could hardly sit still, he was so wired. His student persona is part of a sales pitch. The adviser line was part of that. He's not dumb."

Pulling out of the car wash with the wipers on, we drive to I-35 and head south toward home. Neither of us says anything for a while. On the way up to Ames we talked nonstop, planning our strategy. Now all I can think about is what I'm going to tell Charlie when I get back, and why I'm so immobilized by his jealousy I couldn't even tell him how wrong he was.

Finally I bring my mind back to something Bender said back on campus. "Michael told me he'd never do drugs again after seeing his friend die."

"He's thin as a rail, jumpy. His nose runs. His eyes—the conjunctiva—were red. His breath's like rotting fruit." We're in rush-hour commuter traffic now, approaching Des Moines, and Bender doesn't take his eyes off the road.

"You made *me* jumpy, naming all those drug dealers. Anyway, it's hay-fever season. I turn in the seat to face straight ahead as Bender switches lanes to pass. I'm still feeling pumped that it was my strategy of empathy and guilt that turned Michael around, not Bender's tough approach. His hands, on the steering wheel, are long-fingered, ropy. A man's hands, large, like mine, but with a white line running from pinkie knuckle to wrist. Without thinking, I reach over and trace the thin scar, like a cord running just under the skin.

"I take it Charlie's been asking around about me."

I withdraw my touch. "Why do you say that?"

"You said he called me a freak."

"He feels threatened by you."

"His using the word 'freak' tells me he's been asking someone about me. Ever hear of polydactyly?" I shake my head. "Means extra fingers. A sixth digit on each hand. You can imagine how the other kids teased me. I can still be kind of solitary because of it, I suppose."

"When did you have surgery?"

"When I was ten."

"That's late."

"It's usually done at birth. I don't know why they waited. Operations cost money, I guess. Changed my life, though. I hated being monstrous."

"You weren't monstrous."

"You didn't know me then. I'm nicer with only ten digits. Trust me." He smiles. "If we despise ourselves, Linda, we're lost."

I've noticed he doesn't use the side mirrors. He stretches to eyeball the right lane before moving over. I'm silent for a few minutes, and then I say, "You think Michael's dealing drugs. What if you're wrong?"

"There's too much at stake for me to worry about offending him. The cops raided a meth lab in a motel room right here in Des Moines just last week. Crank is the drug of choice with Iowa kids. People in sleepy little towns like ours are in denial."

"Those names you used with Michael, to scare him about their long prison sentences, they were real?"

"Very real. Meth addicts make up ninety percent of all mental-health commitments in this county. Even doctors can't always tell the difference between a mether and a paranoid schizophrenic. And Ben Petersen isn't the only kid who's died of it. So no, I'm not afraid of accusing Michael wrongly. If he's clean, my suspicions won't hurt him, believe me." As traffic slows for the I-80 exit up ahead, Bender moves to the left to go on through the city. "If he's not dealing, I bet he knows more than one person who is. I could kick myself for not following up on this sooner."

"So what do we do now? Before Luci died, Weber had the opportunity to stash the crank under her car, and we figure he left town immediately after the murder because he was so afraid I would realize that was him I saw outside the house that day, and he'd be accused of killing her. Then Charlie gave the car to the high school, and Michael and Ben found the drugs under the car in auto-mech class. It all fits, but we can't prove that Weber had anything to do with all this. So what have we gained?"

"We know we're a good team," says Bender. He pulls out to

pass a faded red pickup loaded with furniture, an upended rocker tied onto the top of the heap. A cigarette hangs from the driver's mouth. He returns my stare, eyes slitty from the smoke.

As we pull ahead, I watch the battered pickup grow smaller in the side mirror. "I'm glad you quit smoking."

"I bought a pack last night, after leaving your place," he says.

For twenty minutes or so there's no more talk, until Bender signals for our exit. My mind wanders back to last night, to Charlie, and then I realize Bender's talking again—about flying too high, of all things. "A kind of euphoria," he says. "Above it all. They have to be trained to avoid the seduction so they don't get too far out, away from gravity's pull."

"Sorry, I wasn't listening. What are you talking about?"

"Test pilots. I had some heady fantasies last night, trying to sleep. About what we might be able to make happen with Weber. That he might be so blown away by our cleverness he'll confess everything."

"I think he'd be most likely to confess to me. I had such luck with Michael." I smile. "But we can't count on Weber to have a conscience. I've had the same fantasies of confession."

We need proof. Off to the left lies a field of soybeans, green singed with gold and rust. Before long these plants will be brown, mature pods rattling on the breeze. Harvest isn't many weeks away. We're silent until we pull up to the back door of my studio. "Well, we got what we went after," he says, "but I'm not—" He stops midsentence. "Well . . ." It's an awkward moment, both of us staring at the windshield.

Inside, I'm drawn to the front desk by the blinking red light of the answering machine. I simply sit, staring at it. I pull Luci's journal out of my purse, and it falls open to the picture of Luci and her mother. Idly I peel fragments of tape from the corners of the snapshot and lift it from the page. I read a few words, turn the page, then another, more discouraged than ever. Bill, who came in here and vandalized my work to scare me off, may turn out to have had more reason to hate Luci than Weber did. So may Reverend Gus, whose marriage and career she might have jeopardized by accusing him of sexual harassment. The man lying under her car that day might not have come from inside the house at all. Maybe Luci never let him through the front door, and I saw him give up trying. Or maybe Peter Garvey was the last person to see Luci alive in that kitchen after all. The only evidence connected to any of this is that Bill's prints match those on the etching plate.

I reach for the machine. The first message is from Craig Murdock, deputy sheriff, Darlington, Missouri: "Susanna Cole was born to Lucinda Marie Cole twenty years ago." His message includes the date of birth and the name of the father: William Scott Allard. If I'll return his call, he'll tell me how to order a copy of the birth certificate.

The second message is from Charlie. "I stopped by and saw your car. I guess you didn't go to Ames, or wherever you went, by yourself. I wonder who you could be with. I guess that's why you wanted to wait till tomorrow to come home." His voice is heavy with sarcasm. "Call me when you get back."

I call, but he doesn't answer. I let it ring for a long time.

17 ◆ I CALL THE HOUSE many times during the evening, but Charlie's not home. About nine-thirty I call the Allards. Bill answers. He tells me he'll have Judy call me in the morning. Now isn't a good time. She's gone to bed already. "You're the one I want to talk to," I tell him.

"About what?"

"Your act of vandalism, for starters." He's silent. "A vicious act, and hardly the way to make me stop asking questions, if that's what you were trying to do. I thought you were smarter than that. I don't know you at all."

"Yes you do," he says calmly.

"I wonder." My tone is bitter. "One thumbprint and you become a man of some mystery. And then there's the baby Luci Cole had the year you were both freshmen at Carleton."

The sound of the dial tone brings me to my feet.

In ten minutes I'm in the Allards' driveway. The upstairs of the white colonial house is dark. Before I can ring the bell, the front-hallway light goes on, and Bill opens the door without a smile. "Judy's asleep. I don't want her disturbed."

"Tess is here?"

"She's at her grandmother's."

I look at my watch. Bill stands just inside the door, but I step forward anyway. He follows me past the stairway and through the dim living room into the family room at the back, where the television flickers. He's put a video on pause. The Moo-Vies rental box is open on the floor.

He remains standing while I sit on the red sofa. The room is overdecorated, ruffled skirts on sofa and chairs, ruffled lampshades, lots of red plaid and tulip prints. He needs a shave. Brushstrokes of darker yellow curve up from the armpits of his yellow shirt, suggesting he's been exerting himself, though the house is air-conditioned. "Tess seems to think it's my fault you and Charlie are having trouble," he says, eager to start the conversation on his terms.

"Kids jump to conclusions whenever a couple argues. She likes Charlie. You can tell her I'm moving back home tomorrow."

"We can't have this affecting Tess."

"We can't have *what* affecting Tess?"

He moves a hand over his broad forehead. "What have you been telling her?"

"I'm not the one who's done her harm."

He hunkers down to eject the tape from the VCR. The *snap-snap* as he squeezes the plastic movie box shut startles me, and I stand. Still crouched in front of the TV, he looks up as if I've cornered him. I could so easily knock him off balance, step on ankle and leg bones. I've never had such thoughts before. He shows me the palms of his hands, a passive gesture that only increases my urge to hurt him. "It's just that Tessie came home late," he says, "this morning, actually, nearly three. She smelled strongly of booze." He pauses to swallow. "Judy wants her to go back to Omaha, and Tess was screaming about how Luci Cole poisoned our family."

"The night Charlie stayed here, Tess heard you and Charlie arguing, in this very room."

He glances at the ceiling. "She was asleep."

"Like Judy's asleep right now?" I lower my voice. "Your daughter heard Charlie accuse you of killing Luci."

"That's not what he was accusing me of."

"Tess figured that out, after Peter Garvey was arrested. She knows you slept with Luci."

Bill touches the carpet to push himself to his feet. He's at least four inches shorter than I am. I take a step closer. "That's what Charlie thought, too. But no, I didn't." He shakes his head. "Those last months it had been harder to refuse her when she wanted to see me. Every time I tried to pull away, she would up the ante."

"What do you mean?"

"As long as no one knew we were such close friends, there was always the chance I might give in. Maybe that's why I always felt so guilty, even though we never did anything wrong."

"She had a baby girl when she was eighteen. Your child. Your name's on the official record of birth."

A shrill, distant *chirp* pierces the silence. Startled, we look at each other, but the sound doesn't repeat itself. "We had a class together freshman year," he goes on. "Before I got up the nerve to ask her out, she would start telling me about some guy or other, like I was her buddy." He walks around the sofa to place both hands on its pillowed back. He waits until I sit. "She was very pretty," he goes on, looking down at me. "I was trying to figure how to get her to see me as something other than the brother she'd always wanted, and then one day she blurted out that she was pregnant and was going to leave school as soon as she could figure out where to go." Bill's looking across the room now, eyes unfocused, remembering. Or maybe repeating a story he's been saving until he needed it. He makes the mistake of the guilty, giving me the long version.

"It turned out Humanities was the only class she was still attending. She'd been working up the nerve to confide in me, all the while studying those Greek plays with a vengeance, even though she was about to take off. She figured she'd lost her chance for college, and I didn't have the sense to disagree with her. Even after she told me about the pregnancy, we'd sit under a tree and discuss *Medea* instead of what was really wrong. I thought it would be bad manners to ask her who the father was, or why he wasn't helping her. I even thought about marrying her myself.

"Then one night she showed up at my dorm. Her father had come to see her, and he had told her she'd get no help from him. He was furious with her. We lay on my bed, and I held her. When it came right down to it, I couldn't offer her any more than that.

"When we ran into each other here in Linden Grove years later, she told me I was there when she had most needed a friend. We met for coffee a few times. It was summer, so I wasn't teaching. But when I wanted her to meet Judy—" His gaze moves to the ceiling. "By the end of the summer I realized that secrecy was an essential element of Luci's attachment to me. That should have been a red flag. I told her I was uncomfortable meeting her where no one would see us. When I finally told her I wouldn't see her again under those conditions, she broke down and told me she had used me unfairly all those years before, back in college. She had to see me one more time, to apologize."

"That's what you meant by upping the ante?"

"Only if I forgave her would she let go, leave me alone."

"What did she need forgiveness for?"

"She had convinced herself that ending up in the same town with me was some preordained kind of payback, not just a coincidence. All those times we had talked back in college, she made sure she found out my middle name, my birth date, where I was born, so she could name me as father on the birth certificate. Telling me about it at last seemed to drive her off the deep end, make her face the loss of that child for the first time. The baby was half grown, a teenager, by that time, and Luci imagined that the girl might turn up on my doorstep and announce she was mine. She looks just like Luci."

"You've seen her?"

"No, of course not. She'd left the baby with her mother to raise. She told me that years after the child was born she had some kind of breakdown and convinced herself she was pregnant again. That was when you knew her so well, in art school, right?"

"Not so well."

"She went home to see her mother, for the first time in a decade, and to see the girl."

"And she took a picture of the two of them?"

He nods.

"Susanna."

He nods again. "I tried to convince Luci it wasn't too late to go back, make amends, that she'd given up too much, that she didn't need to be ashamed. She said she was seeing a psychologist."

Another penetrating *chirp* interrupts him, and this time we both look upward. "Must be a cricket," he says, "against one of the screens upstairs." He clears his throat and looks me full in the face. "By the time Luci died, Charlie had seen the birth certificate. So what Tess overheard that night was Charlie accusing me of being the father of her child, and of being her lover again when she moved here, and right up to the end. He was in shock. It took a while to calm him down. I owe him a lot for protecting me and my family. He and I have never spoken of it since.

"I want you to know, Linda, that when Luci tried one final time to insist she had one more thing to tell me, another final secret, I told her she should be talking to Charlie. Sharing her confidences with me was leading to such—"

"Intimacy?"

"I was going to say temptation."

I remember what Luci wrote in her diary, that he kissed her in the grocery store.

"I told her to tell *Charlie* her stories, not me, not anymore. It was our last conversation. Be careful what you say to Tess. She's unstable, like her mother. You must see what a tenuous grip Judy has on reality at times, trying to blame me for Tess's problems.

Luci was even more unreliable. I can see my daughter headed toward more trouble than all of you."

"All of us?"

"She's too emotional, too excitable. Her moods swing too widely for anyone to be sure what she'll do next. Spending time with you gets her even more agitated."

"I left my door unlocked that day, didn't I?"

"Yes, you did. If you had just left town after the trial, we would all have gotten back to normal. Ruining a piece of artwork is nothing compared to the harm you're doing to the rest of us."

The cricket tweets brightly overhead. Bill turns on the stairway light. "There's no need for you to come up," he insists, but I'm not letting him out of my sight. Someone who would do the violence he did to that piece of copper might do as much to me, despite his apparent meekness, if he could get his hands on something sharp and gain the element of surprise. On the top riser he stops. The sound is much louder up here. He stands completely still, mouth open. "The smoke alarm."

The high-pitched signal is coming from the ceiling at the end of the hall, near the door to the master bedroom, which is closed. He stretches up to reach the alarm before it sounds again but falls a few inches short. I'm the one who can reach it easily and twist off the cover. I pull the battery free and turn to hand it to him.

But he's gone back downstairs. I consider the bedroom door. Judy wouldn't have slept through that shrill, penetrating sound, a sound meant to be impossible to ignore. My skin goes cold.

Bill and I are alone in the house. I get to the bottom of the stairs before I say his name. He doesn't answer. For a second I just wait, but then the light in the family room goes off, and I hear his footfalls, hear a scraping sound, like a drawer opening. *Too emotional? Unreliable? Headed for more trouble than all of you?* Who knew he had such opinions? I wait for the next sound.

Bill's a mild man with the kind of anger that never raises its voice, a meek man whose anger stays hidden until it strikes. He wants to protect Tess from me. How does he plan to do that? I step into the hallway. There's a light on under the kitchen door.

When it opens, a loud gasp escapes me. My heart hammers. This close, Bill smells of stale perspiration and beer. He's got something in his hand. "Where is Judy?" I manage to say.

"She hasn't been sleeping well. The doctor gave her something to knock her out." He hands me a new battery. "What did you think, that I'd done away with her?"

I'm glad for the excuse to go back upstairs, where I turn the doorknob silently and open the door to the master bedroom. I stand there for a few moments, listening to Judy's slow breathing, mechanical as a cat's, then close the door again and replace the battery in the smoke alarm. When I go back down to the front hall, Bill is out of sight. I leave quickly, without saying good-bye.

Back in my loft, about midnight, I decide I should try to sleep. I bring the upstairs phone into bed with me. The pillow and sheets still bear Charlie's scent, or so I imagine as I curl up, remembering how we held each other last night. I try calling him one more time. I let it ring. The purring in my ear goes on and on, until finally the repetition dulls the senses and lets me drift.

In the morning a pulsating two-note warning drags me from a deep sleep. After a moment of confusion, I realize I've knocked the receiver off the hook, and I slap at the tangled sheets to find the phone and end the sound. The faint light in the room tells me it's early, so I lie still to let my heart slow. I sleep till nine and wake up to the memory of Charlie's angry, sarcastic message. *I wonder who you could be with.* After showering and hauling a few clothes and toiletries out to my car, I head for home, my mood an edgy mix of anticipation and dread. He has every right to be jealous; I've been so evasive.

Approaching the house, I see with relief that Charlie's van is in the drive. Bees are buzzing among the fringed blossoms of coral zinnias by the back steps as I rap on the door, which is locked. It's so quiet here, except for the tick of insects and chattering of birds from the woods behind the house. Tomato plants at the edge of the garden are heavy with fruit. I pinch off a leaf and inhale the pungent tomato smell. Twenty feet back from the garden the woods begin, and I walk the width of the lot, searching for a way down to the bottom of the steep ravine. Behind the garage, where Luci wrote that there was a path, it's so shady there's no grass, just gravel and sparse, low plants. Behind one of the posts supporting the studio above, I find a tangle of brush. By the dead leaves among the green, it's plain Charlie has been using this as a place to toss pruned tree limbs, weeds from the garden, and grass clipped from the lawn. This must be the top end of the eroded crevice I found the other day, from below, when I was searching for a path. As I step closer to the top of the incline, my foot slides, so I reach out instinctively for balance. Looking up, I see something in the branches above. A rope. It appears to be knotted every foot or so. It's frayed, weathered gray, too high to reach.

At the front door of the house I knock again, but not too loudly. Key in hand, I hesitate before I let myself in. Inside the living room, the blinds are down. The ceiling fan stirs the air. Newspapers clutter the floor around the recliner, and *Mackerel Sky* leans against the wall over the mantel. "Charlie?"

I hear his answer, and then he appears, a white towel slung around his middle. His hair and beard are curly from the shower, chest and belly hair scribbled against his skin. He watches me watch him, no sign of anger.

"When you go to the woods to collect honey from the hives down there, you drive around to the back road, right?"

"Right."

"Didn't there used to be a path behind the garage?"

"It wasn't exactly a path. We called it The Chute."

"We?"

"You know how kids like secret passages. We thought we were clever. One person could go, but no one else could make it down until the one at the bottom had come back up."

"With the rope for balance?"

He looks at me steadily. "It was supposed to be a one-way, one-person-at-a-time arrangement. A few of us had a pact, when we were kids. A long time ago. I started filling it with brush after the night we saw someone in the garage. He ran around to the back, as if he knew the way. I was afraid someone would break his neck." He chuckles. "I was afraid it would be me. I'm a little old to rappel down an embankment."

"Bill Allard knew about the way up from the woods."

Charlie's smile fades.

"Luci must have told him about it. Weber would have seen the path, too, when he was working on the garage. I was at the Allards' last night, talking to Bill. I kept calling you, till nearly one."

"I wasn't answering the phone."

"To punish me?"

He frowns, securing the towel around his midsection with a single abrupt tuck. "To let you know how it feels."

"John Bender and I went to Ames together yesterday, to talk with someone who might connect Russell Weber with Luci's death. Is that what you want to hear?"

"What I want to hear is why you didn't tell me that in the first place." He heads for the kitchen. Standing by the sink, coffee mug in hand, he raises his shoulders as if they're hurting. "Don't forget. Bender's the man you were so afraid of for so many weeks, since way last spring. All I heard about was 'that man who's staring at me.' " Charlie turns his head to check my response. "Now you're thick as thieves."

"Not exactly."

"Then what, exactly?"

"If I'd told you what we were planning to do yesterday, you'd have tried to talk me out of it."

"Well, I didn't talk you out of it. So tell me more." He sips his coffee.

"I'm not sure it was Peter Garvey I saw here that day. I think it could have been Russell Weber."

"Rosemary told me you wanted his canceled check. Bender put you up to that?"

"No. That was my idea. I'm going to explain it all to you, if you'll listen."

"You don't think it's strange that a guy who's been skulking around for months without saying a word to you suddenly wants to be your best friend? But then fear is what turns you on, isn't it?" He inhales deeply. "I didn't think you'd do this to me. You said you'd come back."

"I am back."

"Not the way I mean. I think a lot more happened after I went to work yesterday morning than you're likely to tell me." He starts to sip his coffee again, then changes his mind, thunking the heavy mug on the table.

I sit across from him, my hands flat on the table. For long minutes neither of us moves or speaks. Finally I start. "That night you cleared out Luci's studio, I assumed you took her things to the county landfill. She was just starting to work again those last weeks of her life. The tapestry was beautiful." I remember him bent over in the gloom of Luci's studio that night, banging away at the splintering wood. "You didn't save it for me, the way you said you would."

Returning to the window over the sink and its view of the yard, he raises his hand to protect his eyes from the glare of sunlight.

"When I saw you breaking the loom," I say softly, "I should have stopped you, but I thought you were grieving, that you needed to be left alone, since that's what you wanted. Did you really trash all her things, the way I thought?"

"I put a few of the boxes in that storage shed I rent. You know. You've been there. Where we found your kitchen sink." He looks at me with such sadness that I take a step toward him. "I wanted her things where I didn't have to look at them, but I couldn't bring myself to destroy everything. I loved her once, you know." He looks away again. "I did go to the dump that night, but I couldn't let go of some things."

"Was the tapestry one of them? I asked you to save it for me that night, leave it in the garage. But it's not there."

"What tapestry?"

"The weaving. The work that was on her loom."

He clears his throat. "I can't say I remember it, but if you asked me to save it for you, I'm sure I left it in the garage."

"If you did, that means whoever broke into the garage that night took it. Give me the key to the storage shed, so I can see if the weaving is there." He straightens his shoulders. A curly path of dark hair swirls down from his broad chest to his deep navel, then crosses his tan line to disappear under the white towel. I look away. "The tapestry is a treasure, Charlie. Think of what people remember her for, cheating on you and getting killed for it. Is that what you want?"

"What I want never had anything to do with it." He leaves the room, and I hear window shades slap open in the bedroom. Dresser drawers slam open, shut.

When I step into the bedroom, he turns to face me, and he seems caught off guard, his expression open, expectant, which moves me to feel affection for him, sorry for all the difficult moments he's been through in this house. "I found Luci's diary," I tell him. "It won't be easy for you to read. You'll see a version of Luci I daresay even you never saw." He simply stares at me. Finally he blinks, and looks away. "I'll bring it home tonight, the diary. We'll talk. I'm sorry I've been secretive. I had the idea I was protecting you from worry until I'd satisfied myself I was right about seeing Peter that day after all. But it hasn't turned out that way. I think I made a terrible mistake."

He's visibly shaken, and I tell him I'm going out to my car for my things while he gets dressed and collects his thoughts. I'll be right back. Outside the front door I pause to study the break in the bushes along the road where I stopped three years ago to look down at this very spot.

If this were that moment, and I were Russell Weber, and I had just killed her, I'd be scrambling to get those six sausage-long bags out from under Luci's Chevy and running for my life before someone discovered her body behind me in the kitchen. And if I were Russell Weber *now*, I'd be figuring out how to get my hands on that car because I'd believe the stuff was still under there, and I'd be sure that when I found it, I'd be a rich man.

Despite the fact that the temperature is in the high seventies, I shiver. Whatever Weber is doing to find that car, Bender and I need to be right behind him. The simplicity of that knowledge propels me onto the narrow strip of grass between the steps and the gravel of the circular drive. I reach out my hand, as I did that day. I step forward, as I did then, to place my hand on the warm fender of the car. I say his name, "Peter." I had no doubt *then* whose boots had left those two crescent-shaped marks in the dust. Unnerved, I see the flash of movement and feel the stumbling touch on my forehead and hear the buzz.

Panting, I make it back inside the screen door—pointing, speechless, at the honeysuckle bush just outside. "Bees," I say stupidly.

Charlie brushes past me wearing only a pair of the loose boxer shorts he wears in the summer, white with a thin blue stripe, flapping above strong thigh muscles. Quickly he steps outside, the wood-framed screen door closing behind him with a gentle slap—then returns to open his fist slowly, touching my shoulder to keep me close. "It's a flower fly. Perfectly harmless. See?" The amber-and-black insect drags itself across his palm. "A look-alike to the honeybee." He nods as I bravely pinch the creature up in finger and thumb. Gently rotating my hand, he points at the thinly striped abdomen for my inspection. "Not a stinger in sight. It's not a bee at all." He speaks with the the calm tone he used the night he told Tess the praying-mantis story. It's all I can do to keep my fingers closed. My skin crawls as the fake bee struggles to escape.

Charlie opens the screen door a slit so I can reach through and let the insect go. The chill leaves my skin. "I know I can't tell you what to do," he says, "but I wish you'd stay away from Bender." Charlie's skin smells like soap. His voice is husky. My hand finds the small of his back, where his skin is still damp to the touch.

18 ◆ ON THE WAY to my studio I overshoot the center of town and drive to the east side, to where Russ Weber lives, on Railroad Street. I'm relieved to see his car in the driveway. I'm worried he'll leave town again. The strip of lawn this side of the sidewalk is browned out, but the yard is lush, as if it's been watered. I pull onto the shoulder of the unpaved street and look at my watch. I have a few minutes before Tess's drawing lesson. Two basement windows in the house's front foundation are curtained in red-and-white fabric, backlit and vividly floral.

The basement lights were on the last time I drove by here here, too. The trunk of Weber's dusty green car is open, revealing a fringe of fanned-out wire coat hangers. By the time I'm halfway up the front walk, I'm as winded as if I've been running. What will I say if he appears? Maybe he's watching me from behind the blinds that line the windows like notebook paper. I back up two steps, then hurry back to the car. All I can think is, *If he takes off, where does that leave us?*

I reach my studio at five to eleven and turn on the LINDA GARBO DESIGNS sign. The first answering-machine message is a callback from Detective Hansen, agreeing to meet me at four-thirty. After a tone, another voice says, "Weber was booked during the night for trespassing and possession of burglary tools." Bender's diction is slow, deliberate. "Jim Howard is meeting me in a few minutes to check the records on where Luci's car went when the high school was done with it. My hunch is it's at Carney's Salvage Yard, which is where Weber was arrested. He's seeing a judge this morning. I think we should think about getting you some kind of protection. From now on, if you have to go anywhere after work hours, leave your sign on till you get home."

My gaze fixed on the loft as soon as I heard the word "protection," and I continue to stare upward for long seconds after the message ends. There's no sound in the building, none at all. I sit quietly and let time pass until it's clear Tess is not going to show up for her lesson. No surprise, given that Bill said she was staying with her grandmother last night. I call the Allards, but there's no answer. There's no answer at Bill's mother's farmhouse west of town either. I call a few of Judy's friends, but none of them has heard from her in the past couple of days.

I hurry across the parking lot to the back door of The Little Read. It's locked, so I run through the alley and around to the street entrance. Taped to the front door is a card bearing the words CLOSED UNTIL FURTHER NOTICE. The neat, teacherly penmanship is Bill's.

Ever since I told Charlie this morning that I'd bring Luci's diary home at the end of the afternoon, I've been worried about how her words will hurt him. Now, driving toward the church to meet Reverend Gustavson, I remember his warning that Luci's journal is a record of thoughts, impressions, and wishes, not reality. *You don't know what kind of truth you're dealing with.* When he hears me knock on the frame of his open door, the minister looks up from his desk and waves me in. He looks awful. The skin under his eyes is loose, eyelids pink along the lashes. He works his mouth as if he's dehydrated, but I don't ask what's bothering him. I tell him I can't reach Judy, or Tess. "If she's drinking again," he says, "Judy's probably taken her back to Omaha."

Maybe he's right, but I can't help remembering Judy's slow breathing and the piercing *chirp*, penetrating enough to rouse someone from a deep sleep. Right now I need to concentrate on what I wanted to find out when I made this appointment. Gus resigns his shoulders backward against the maroon leather of his chair as I describe Luci's collection of shoes, each toe stuffed tight with tissue paper, size eights and nines—except for the gold ones, which are twelves, my size. "Luci wore a seven," I say, as if this were the punch line.

Gus looks puzzled.

"I didn't know what to make of the shoes, unless they were irregulars from her father's company, or styles that didn't sell." Opening my wallet, I slip out the picture of the child I had assumed until last night was Luci, with her mother. I want the shoes to mean something, but what?

"You're hoping I can tell you something about Luci's background?"

I tap the image of the little girl in the snapshot, Susanna. "Have you seen this before?" He shakes his head, and I decide not to press. "Luci angered a number of people during her last months," I say, "mostly men."

"Yes." Gus closes his eyes. His lips twitch, and I realize he's trying to appear relaxed. He unclenches his fists. "You mentioned something last time you were here," he says, "about what she said about me—" He pauses for so long I think he's about to admit having sex with Luci, or deny it more elaborately than before. "She told you I believe in the powers of the intellect to correct defects in character," he goes on. " 'Defects in character' would have been her words, not mine. She had an overwhelming sense of being defective. She insisted she had forgotten long stretches of time when she was a child."

"Didn't that make you suspect that something terrible had happened to her?"

"I wanted to help her identify consequences of her behavior, rather than causes. I thought childhood stories would surface naturally as she gained control over her life."

"You concentrated on her most urgent problem."

"She was able to remove herself from a destructive relationship."

"With a married man."

He doesn't respond, and I place the snapshot on the coffee table. Silently, I remember Luci's version from her journal: *I went to see Reverend G—— to tell him that his counseling has worked and I've given up my married lover—a sordid, outrageous lie! I could tell at once that G—— was caught off guard, far more open to me than before, believing he'd done me some good, saved me from a dangerous situation. How easily he takes the credit I offer him like bait!*

"The Luci I remember from school was good at putting painful events behind her," I say, "as if they had never happened. One semester she told me she was pregnant. She had a miscarriage and then never mentioned that whole experience again. In her journal she makes it clear there was something she longed to tell someone but couldn't, something that had left a mark on her."

He smiles sadly. "If she were here, she'd accuse you of going for the 'sick story.' " He rises to his feet. "She hated the idea that if there's pain in the present, there has to have been a childhood event that caused it. Luci was relieved to discover I had no interest in pressuring her to dig up key memories. She mistrusted the subconscious mind. She was leery of stimulating her imagination by projecting feelings about herself back into the past."

He's becoming agitated, his voice rising, words coming more quickly. "In the beginning I thought I was someone she could work with. I don't subscribe either to the theory that it is our life's work to locate a particular harm that's shaped us. I find that premise Calvinistic, destructive, and all too often a self-fulfilling prophecy."

Abruptly he stops pacing and faces one of the stained-glass windows, staring as if he could see through the opaque glass.

Finally he walks over to shove some papers out of the way and sit on the edge of his cluttered desk, body braced by his hands that grip the wood so hard his knuckles tense in a white row. "Don't be unfair to me," he says. "Luci was very bright."

"I know that."

"And very destructive. She seemed happier after the first few talks we had. She applied to the Iowa Arts Council for a grant to do a project in the schools. She had me convinced she was calmer, less self-absorbed."

"She praised your emphasis on the will and the intellect."

He nods. "She refused to believe that all her achievements and mistakes were unfolding according to a predetermined pattern that she'd never be able to stop."

"She was obsessed with that possibility even as she rejected it?"

He ignores my question. "I wanted her to believe she was a child of God, and worthy of loving-kindness, to use your word."

"Then she stopped coming here. There was a breaking-off."

He bites his lower lip.

"At a certain point in the journal," I tell him, "her tone changed, and she began addressing me by name, revealing things she had never told me in person. I don't understand what she was trying to say." I pause. "There is a significant difference between the sexual encounter she says she had with you and those she describes with other men. You told me her feelings for you were a matter of transference, that those feelings were really for someone else. If that's true, and she made up the incident involving the two of you on this sofa, she must have provided me with that story for a reason. What could it be?"

"She wanted to hurt me, which is exactly what making that journal public knowledge will achieve." His gaze intensifies. "Instead of helping her, I had become part of the problem." He averts his eyes, looks at his fingernails. "The root of moral inconsistency is shame, Linda. A woman can have sex with many men without feeling she shares love, or loyalty, with any of them." He runs his tongue over his teeth. "She thought the world of you, but your moving to town provided conditions for an upheaval in her personality."

"So had reuniting with Bill Allard here, after so many years. You knew it was Bill? Her married friend?"

Gus's fleeting glance tells me he hadn't figured that out. "I wanted to suggest she talk to someone else, but I knew she'd take that as abandonment on my part, and we'd lose what progress we'd made."

"Luci and Bill may have had a child together, years ago. *This* child." I point to the little girl in the photograph.

Gus studies the image. His face is ashen. "Luci told you that?"

"I no longer believe it was Peter Garvey who killed her. You told me she was supposed to meet with you here that afternoon but didn't show up. It seems to me that under those circumstances you wouldn't just sit here and wait for her. I think you'd have been concerned enough to call, or even go looking for her. I'm guessing that you did call her the afternoon she died, but got no answer. So you went to see her. Am I right?"

The phone rings, and Gus crosses to his desk to take the call, swiveling back and forth in his desk chair as he talks. I tilt the shiny photograph to avoid the glare and stare at the tiny face of Luci's daughter. When he hangs up the phone, I hand him the snapshot. "Luci wrote about showing a picture to Charlie one night and telling him something that drew them very close. I think this might be the one. I'm going to ask him about it tonight, when I give him the journal."

Gus's eyes jerk to mine with alarm.

"He insists on reading it, even though I've warned him it will be painful."

Gus hands the photo back to me. "What are you really looking for, Linda? With all these questions?"

"I'm trying to find out who killed her."

"Yes, but it seems to be more than that. You feel you let her down, a failure you can't get out of your mind. My guess is you have great difficulty resisting people who need you. Let her go, or you'll be haunted by an unanswerable question forever."

"At the end of her journal she talked about ending things with Peter, breaking off with Bill. Making things right, tying things up. She finished her final weaving the day I arrived. It seems she was putting things in order the way a suicide takes care of business and gives away favorite possessions before committing the final act." I pause to swallow. "I moved here thinking she was happily settled into a good life, but the minute I got here, she let me know she was in trouble." I hesitate before trying one last time to get the information I came for. "She provided me with that seduction story about you for a reason, and that reason had to do with the difference between you and Bill, or Peter." *Or Russell Weber*, I'm thinking. "She had to be more clever, more powerful, to get *you* to touch her, and when she succeeded, *she* could be the victim."

"I didn't touch her."

"She knew I'd see your giving in as *your* fault, because you were a minister, a licensed psychologist. A strong sense of professional ethics should have restrained you."

"My strong sense of ethics *did* restrain me."

"She was supposed to meet you here the afternoon she died. You were waiting for her. You hadn't seen her for weeks. She was both a temptation and a threat, so when she didn't show up, you found it impossible to simply sit here and wait. She knew that would be the case. I think *she* was waiting for *you.*"

"What are you suggesting?"

"You were at the house that afternoon."

The minister takes a deep breath. "I did drive out there, but I didn't see her. I was behind you. When you turned in at her drive-way, I went on by and turned around in the drive next door. I saw you walk around Luci's car and go in the front door, and I saw Garvey get up and run around the side of the house. Murder didn't occur to me. Why would it? I kept on going, came back here."

"He ran around the side of the house?"

"Yes."

"Toward the horses or along the driveway, toward the garage?"

"Toward the house next door. I don't remember any horses."

I feel myself grow very still. "You're sure it was Peter Garvey you saw?"

"At the time I had never seen you before, or him either. He stood up the minute the front door closed behind you. He was plenty angry."

"How could you tell?"

"I suppose it was his body language. I don't think I saw his face."

"So you realized it was Garvey later, after I identified him?"

"After his picture was in the paper." He nods. "It was the same man. I knew who you were, that you were staying there. Luci had told me you were unusually tall, a striking blonde. He got out from under the car and stood with his fists on his hips. He had his back to me, facing the door you'd just walked through."

"You had followed me from town?"

"Not all the way from town. I caught up with you. As I ap-proached the top of the hill, I saw you parked there. I thought maybe there was something wrong with your car, but when you started moving, I wondered what you'd been waiting for. I still wonder that. I followed you down but kept my distance. I knew it was you, from the Minnesota plates. When you turned in at Luci's, I was sure."

"You're positive it was Peter Garvey you saw?"

"I'd swear to it."

*   *   *

Before going to meet Hansen, I take Luci's diary across the street to Kinko's and stand at a machine to copy every page. It takes longer than I expect. I return to my studio to lock the photocopy in one of my print cabinets. About five I arrive at the Grubstake, where I find Detective Hansen sitting with John Bender at a back table. I didn't expect Bender to be here.

The last thing my nervous stomach wants is coffee. As I slide the menu across the slick oilcloth—patterned with palm trees and tropical flowers—Hansen, who is sitting across from me, tells me Weber is out on bail. Bender slips a packet of sugar from the basket in the center of the table and inspects it, turning it over in his long fingers.

Hansen's gray eyes meet my own steady gaze. "Now that we have Weber's prints, we'll check for a match with the Luci Cole case and with the flashlight you brought in." The detective rubs the tiny, reddened dents on either side of the bridge of his nose, raising the glasses to check for smudges before replacing them on his face.

I asked him to meet me so I could offer information, to convince him to pursue the case with urgency, and now he's opened the conversation on his own terms. "We made mistakes," I remind him. "An artist's first lesson is that the mind confounds the eye. We see what we expect to see. Knowing that should have made me a smarter witness."

"Let's hear what you've got on Bill Allard. Then I want you to leave the investigation to us."

Is this is what he and Bender were discussing before I arrived? Bender is still fiddling with that flimsy pack of sugar. He has told me more than once that cops and reporters are natural adversaries who in some matters have no one else to talk with, and that I was wrong in assuming that because he and Hansen share information, they are buddies. Now Bender's silence implies he, too, thinks I should turn over what I have and get out of their way. "There was another eyewitness who saw Peter Garvey in front of the house that afternoon," I tell them. "He's even more unreliable than I was, and he may be lying to protect himself." I turn to John. "The man you debate the existence of God with."

"Gus?"

"Isn't the Bible full of murderers who believe in God? Isn't the whole point—"

"Tell us what you're talking about," the detective says.

I explain my suspicions about Reverend Gustavson, reporting on our two conversations. I give them the snapshot of the little girl who looks so much like Luci. I tell them about my visit with Bill last night, and about the birth records in Missouri that name him as the father of Susanna. Bender continues fiddling with the sugar as I talk, and I finally take it away from him to still his hand. Right away I regret the gesture for its implication of intimacy. "You're practically dancing, you're so wired," I tell him. He hasn't looked at me once since I got here.

"I need a cigarette." He pauses. "You need to listen to us."

"From what John tells me about Luci's journal," Hansen says, "we should expect a match of Weber's prints to the murder scene. Apparently he was in her kitchen around the time of the murder the same as you were, the same as Charlie, the same as—"

"Garvey," I say.

Hansen sips his coffee, then replaces the white mug onto the bright tablecloth, adjusting it dead center in the middle of a purple hibiscus. "It was my job to be suspicious of anyone who could have had opportunity and motive, and that still includes Garvey. Bender and I have two concerns. First, you are placing yourself in danger by being so emotionally involved. You have certain blind spots. You were part of whatever happened in that house up to the moment your friend died."

My lips part, but he holds up a hand so I'll let him finish. "If we find Luci's car at Carney's Salvage Yard, we can make the case that Russell was after the stash when he broke in there last night. But even if the drugs were still under the car, the way Weber might think, there would be no proof he put the stuff there, or that he killed anyone. With the trail cold and the evidence in dispute, there's no case against him. So the rule of the investigation is not to let him know what we suspect, not yet. Don't play hero. Luci Cole didn't die from a bump on the head, you know." Hansen's slate-blue irises are magnified by the shiny lenses of his glasses. "We can't make the same mistake twice and fix our attention on one suspect to the exclusion of others. I'll have another talk with Bill Allard tonight," he says, "and I'll see the minister, too."

The detective leaves the table to go after a refill on his coffee, and Bender clears his throat. "What would happen to methamphetamine," I wonder, "sealed in plastic in the frame of a car, out in the elements for a couple of Iowa winters and summers? Twenty, thirty below in the winter, over a hundred in the summer, to say nothing of—"

"Rats."

"Dampness."

"Imagine dozens of rats buzzed up on crank," says Bender.

"Wouldn't the stuff deteriorate? Smell? Lose its potency?"

"I'd say doubting the power of plastic to preserve any substance is un-American." He smiles, but he still won't look at me.

I pluck a packet of sugar from the basket in the middle of the table. The paper's the same brown color as a grocery bag. SUGAR IN THE RAW. Tearing off an edge and flexing it open, I peer inside at the blond granules, shaking it back and forth for its sandy sound. "How could we find out?"

Bender leans back in his chair, straightening his long legs, his right leg brushing against mine in the process—a touch from which, by reflex, he withdraws. "You heard what Ken said."

"I suppose there are things you've told Hansen that you haven't told me?"

"Nothing concrete. Only theories. This business with Weber has convinced him we're onto something, and with what you've just told him, he'll be hard at work on this case until it's solved,

Linda. He's going to ask you for Luci's diary. He'll redeem himself whether he strengthens the case against Garvey or frees an innocent man and finds the real killer. He's got even more at stake this time than he did before, when proving a murder case got him a promotion. He had a very convincing eyewitness." Bender looks at me gravely. "We all believed you."

Moving my chair back, I turn slightly away from him so I can look over my right shoulder, my attention drawn by the ring of the tiny bell that signals the arrival of Sylvie, Doug Le's assistant, through the front door. Her black-and-white dress, slit up the left thigh, is patterned in stripes that follow the curves of her body. Heads turn. Walking toward the counter, she orders, "The usual."

Bender has gone on talking. "Even if it occurred to Weber to worry about the chemistry of crank deteriorating—"

I turn back to him, not remembering what we were talking about.

"—who's he going to ask?"

I rise and walk over to Sylvie. "Your hair looks great." She smiles, her dark eyes haloed by almond-shaped black lines. Her own shiny black hair is cut in a chin-length bob, a comma of curl angling along each jaw. "Stop down soon. You're about due for a cut, aren't you?" She turns to pay Angela and to manage lifting a Styrofoam cup in each hand with a straight-fingered grip. Her long nails are painted mahogany, a dot of vermilion at each tip. She sees me looking, sets one of the cups back down on the high counter, extends a flexed hand for my inspection. "You like?"

"It's a wicked look." She regains her grip on the cup. "Have you seen Russ Weber in the last couple days?" I ask her.

Her answer is to turn her eyes toward the table I came from, where the detective has rejoined Bender. Her eyes meet mine again.

"I have something that's his," I say. Momentarily the whites of her eyes expand, then quickly shrink within their sooty borders— a reaction that jolts me as if I've just caught a glimpse of my own surprise in a mirror. "Something I need to give him before he leaves."

"Well, I'm sure it's not my business." Her gaze falters, lifts again to mine. "He's leaving?"

"His car is in his driveway, loaded with clothes."

For a moment she doesn't blink. Then, catching herself, she lowers her tarnished lids. "I have to get back," she says quickly.

After she's gone, her sharp citrus perfume stays with me all the way back to the table. Bender looks up at me as I pull out my chair to sit. "Doesn't she work for Doug Le, downstairs?"

I nod.

"She looks like a raccoon."

"I'm impressed it's her eyes you noticed."

He shrugs. "I'm trained—"

"To be observant. Right."

Hoisting his thick body out of his chair, Detective Hansen gives his navy plaid shirt an unnecessary all-around tuck into his jeans. He places a few coins on the table. Then, apparently as an after-thought, he sits again, leaning against the edge of the table and speaking low. "Don't get me wrong. I appreciate all you two have done." He glances at Bender, then back at me. "I'm going with you right now to get that book, Linda, so I can look it over and put it in a safe place."

I pull the diary from my shoulder bag and place it on the table. The detective opens it about in the middle, fans a few pages with a ticking sound. "We have to be cautious about anything Luci Cole wrote," he says. "From what Bender here tells me, you two have given her the upper hand as far as this journal is concerned."

"What do you mean?"

"A diary isn't sworn testimony."

All three of us stare at the closed book

Then Hansen says, "I'll get a statement from the Lassell kid. And as soon as the report shows up on Weber's prints, I'll talk to

Hilda. When Garvey's defense attorney gets wind of this, things will move fast. Until then, don't do anything foolish."

I've ripped open a brown sugar packet, licked my right index finger, and suddenly I'm remembering Michael Lassell, sitting with me in a darkened hallway, telling me about the first time he tried crank. Sticking my finger in my mouth, I let the sweetness dissolve across my tongue. On the back of the packet I'm reading that the natural molasses remains in the first pressing of raw cane, giving Sugar in the Raw its golden color. *In a few minutes*, he said, *I knew what the big deal was.*

19 ◆ Before I head home to Charlie, the photocopy of Luci's journal in hand, I look for certain sentences and reread them two or three times:

> This afternoon when I walked out for the mail, I found a packet of sugar with its edge folded over, Russ's name signed there in black ink, fastened with a paper clip onto the mailbox's red flag. . . . What if Charlie had found it first? I can hear what Russell would say: Charlie wouldn't know what it *was*. It's unbelievably expensive, this stuff—left like a message, for the first person on the scene. Russ is playing my game of daring, in plain sight.

Fingering the three small envelopes of sugar in my pocket, I hurry upstairs to get Weber's canceled check, then bolt for the door. All day I've been running late, and Charlie will wonder what happened to me.

I find him in the backyard, happily setting fire to a pyramid of charcoal briquettes. He shows me the potato salad and baked beans in the refrigerator, and the chocolate pie. "Not a single homemade item on the menu," he says, grinning. "A cholesterol pig-out." He kisses me and sends me off to the bedroom to change into shorts.

After we eat, I explain that I have turned the journal over to the police, but I have made him a copy and I want him to read it tonight so he won't be hearing certain things secondhand. "I have to tell you that even now she can hurt you," I say to him. He appears shaken by my warning. After I've cleaned up the dishes, I stand in the kitchen doorway and observe him as he turns a page, the tightness of his features showing how hurtful her words are. I'm going to the studio to give him time to read it all. When I get back, we can talk. I'm much too nervous to hang around the house, suffering his reactions. He doesn't look up, even to say good-bye.

On my way back into town, I decide to drive out to Perkins, by the interstate, and sit in a front booth for a while, drinking decaffeinated coffee and watching the American flag unfurl over the parking lot in immense slow motion. Finally I get back into my car and head for Railroad Street, but halfway there I double back toward the north side of town, where Judy and Bill live. The lights by the front door are on, though it won't be dark for another hour. But no one answers the bell. I don't want to go home yet, on the chance that Charlie's in the midst of his reading, so I decide to drive past Weber's house after all.

To my relief, his car is still in the driveway. The trunk lid's down now, but otherwise the car appears not to have moved, and I park behind it. The house is dark, except for the basement window adjacent to the cracked, concrete drive. This window, like those on the front of the house, is curtained, glowing faintly from the inside.

For a few minutes I sit in the car. Every natural impulse is to leave before anyone sees me. The street behind me is deserted. The house to the right of the driveway is dark. Nothing says Weber can't go somewhere without his car. Maybe something's wrong with this one, too, given his bad luck with automobiles.

Finally I get out and walk around to the front door and knock, heart thudding as the wooden screen-door frame rattles from my timid effort. If someone comes, I'll say I'm looking for Sylvie. When I open the screen to rap on the gray inside door, today's paper slides out of the space between the doors onto the top of my sandal-clad feet. I nudge it out of the way.

Around the left side of the house, away from the streetlight, it's cooler and darker, and I can feel the dampness of the grass on my bare toes. The basement window is curtained with a flat piece of cloth, but the hem is hitched up a bit, and I kneel in the long, itchy grass. All I can see is the top of a washing machine, lid up. Thank God I'm in shadow here, with my butt in the air and my head in the window well, fingers gripping the curved, corrugated metal surrounding it.

The possibility of Weber's leaving town has affected me more as the evening has worn on, like the onset of flu: light-headedness, bone aches, a growing dread that he could take with him all hope of our knowing for sure who killed Luci. For the first time in a long time I think of how easily Brad Tripplehorn stepped off ahead of me through the airplane hatch into the open air over Minnesota for another death-defying thrill—while I shrank back in panic behind him, in deadly fear that if I parachuted out of that plane I'd be risking the loss of an important part of my character. Perhaps it took another kind of courage to watch him fall away from me and not follow. Backing away was the right instinct.

But this is different. This is no sporting risk. It's only the attraction and repulsion of fear that feels the same. And Detective Hansen has forbidden me to do anything about it.

Lifting my long hair away from the nape of my neck, I admit a slight breeze against my damp skin. It's a warm evening. Rounding the back corner of the house, I stop. An egg-yolk-yellow bug light suspended from the miniature peaked roof sheltering the cement stoop—three steps up, no railing—casts a pool of turquoise onto the thick, new-mown grass. Someone has simply turned off the electric mower and walked away, leaving the grass beyond the business end taller by half than the grass on this side. An orange cord snakes its way to an outlet near my right ankle. This sign of such an ordinary task interrupted gives me an odd kind of courage, and I step up the three steps, open the back screen door, and rap my knuckles against the single pane of uncurtained glass that covers the top half of the inside door, moving my face through the negative exposure of my own reflection until the outlines of a refrigerator and stove come into focus in the pale sepia interior. Knocking again, I grip the doorknob, turn it, and feel the door yield inward.

Stepping through the door is the hard part. My heart's in my mouth. "Russ?" I call out. Then louder, "Hey? Anybody home?" The air-conditioning is colder than I like. I barely breathe as the door closes behind me, a defiant hip-thrust finishing the job of pushing it into the frame until the latch clicks. Hearing the sound, I twist the doorknob and pull hard to open the door again, trying the knob from the outside. Locked. I close it again, pushing until I hear the click. I can feel my heart beat. The room smells of bacon grease. There's a cardboard carton on the table, heaped with pots and pans.

The sun will drop below the horizon any moment, so I seek the only light I'm sure of, opening the door by the stove. I see I've guessed right by the lavender glow down there. "Hey, anybody here?" I call out again before I close the basement door behind me and begin my slow, careful way down the gray-painted steps. "Am I alone here? Anyone?" Oddly, it's warmer as I descend. Halfway down I sit, surveying the scene, my mouth opening into a foolish smile.

The loamy smell of damp soil drifts up from rows of long wooden containers of high, leafy plants. Fluorescent grow-lights are suspended from the ceiling, and arrayed across the floor at the base of the stairs are plastic gallon jugs of Windex-blue liquid, which I recognize from my own gardening as Miracle-Gro. I'm still grinning, as if what I survey is a garden of earthly delights.

My coming here without a plan might have been impulsive and foolish, but what I'm looking at will give me the upper hand if Weber shows up.

There's no mistaking the long, toothy leaves and the tough stems. The stuff's so easy to grow that even Weber, known for never finishing what he starts, is managing a fine crop. A few of the plants do look a bit bedraggled, and before I know it I'm lifting a jugful of the sky-blue fertilizer, unscrewing the cap, and giving the row of smaller plants a good soaking. There are hundreds of plants, some of them staked two feet high in round drums, some growing in flats on a long table, just tiny seedlings. All he needed was seed, soil, light, and heat. Passing under bundles of the weed hanging from the rafters into the room with the washing machine, I find eight bricks of marijuana, each wrapped in Saran Wrap and brown paper, next to the Surf and the Stain Out. Each brick feels like it weighs a couple of pounds. The street value I can only guess, but this is worth a fortune.

The sudden click and hum of an electric heater suspended against the far wall of the larger room don't keep me from hearing the scrape of a door and footfalls overhead. That I manage to reach the darkness under the stairs without making much sound of my own, crouching there with a cool jug of Miracle-Gro pressed between my knees, is pure luck. For long moments I expect the owner of the footsteps to come looking for me. My car, after all, is in the driveway. Gradually my heart slows, and I realize that whoever's up there came home to a locked, dark house. I place my hand over my face, pressing against the base of my nose to stop a sneeze. Where there's a basement, there's dust. And spiders. And after all that decaf, my bladder is painfully full.

I shudder as the door overhead opens and the basement light goes on, bands of pale yellow light falling between the open steps so that, looking down, I can see the high points of my body reflected: breasts, knees, toenails of light in my open sandals. The bare, masculine ankles on the open risers of the stairs a few inches from my face are no doubt attached to someone who's coming to water the plants and is about to find out someone's beaten him to it.

"There's no one down here," he shouts upward, stepping into full view. Weber is wearing the ubiquitous red bandanna around his head. "You sure it's Garbo's car?" Overhead there's another knock against the kitchen floor, another creak of the door.

"Maybe she took a walk till you came back," I hear a woman's voice say from the top of the stairs. It's Sylvie. "She told me she had something to give you."

"Like what?"

"She didn't say. But she knew you were leaving. And there was a cop at the table with her."

"I should have parked in the street." He sounds mad. "Now her car's got me blocked in. Go outside. See if you can find her."

"You might as well take care of things while you're down there. You're not leaving me with a bunch of dead plants." I think I hear enough footfalls overhead to account for someone else besides Sylvie, and another female voice—muffled, but vaguely familiar— mingling with hers.

"The best grass *is* dead," Weber is saying, his chuckle receding up the stairs as he goes. "The only good grass is up in—"

"Smoke," I hiss, risking the sound. The door has clattered shut above my head, taking his final word away. Hunkered down, the cement floor cold where I sit, I settle myself for a long, long wait.

Physical distress makes me bigger, more ungainly. The knobby bones of my ankles press painfully against the floor as I sit cross-legged and watch the glow from the windows fade, leaving me in gray, undependable darkness. I've outsmarted myself, and little wonder. I've always been better at minding my own business than at insinuating myself into others' confidence. My judgments are more often visceral than logical. A desperate leap of intuition has landed me here, in the dark. I was probably right the first time after all. Gus saw him: Peter Garvey, running off as soon as I disappeared into the house, where I would discover what he had done to Luci. Reverend Gustavson, who lacked the courage to come forward, convinced himself his testimony wasn't needed, because mine was so compelling.

I close my eyes and notice the sounds of birds in the trees behind the house, and I begin to envision, with my mind's eye, what Bender saw the day he looked at *Mackerel Sky*. Metamorphosis, fish to bird. Left to right, bottom to top, white to black, patterns of white fish-shapes recede as birds emerge in the negative spaces. I shift my stiff legs and grow even larger with discomfort.

Artists see ideas. One of my teachers told me once that the validity of an idea is tested each time it takes physical shape, and as long as new shapes form, the idea has not yet reached fulfillment. Outside the house the birds are settling down now, their calls infrequent, and I open my eyes and mouth wide, the kind of reflex that comes with revelation.

Peter made up his story about standing outside the front door at noon, talking with Luci, who would not come outside because she hated the hoarse cries of the crows. The raucous birds, big as chickens, arrived at the end of every afternoon that summer, thickening the trees with pointy silhouettes of wings, beaks, claws, their cries raspy as kazoos. Embedded in his story was an inadvertent truth. Peter may well have heard a commotion that day, *but not at noon*.

A loud, unexpected noise can send birds up like fire, a conflagration of wings and scattering cries. Hundreds of crows went up with a *whoosh*. Wheeling and cawing, they darkened the sky over the woods, settling back down as I pounded on the hood of Luci's car. When we talked at the prison, Peter remembered the horses bolting. It was the birds that spooked them. Someone crashing down the ravine behind the house had startled the birds.

A creaking of the floor overhead makes me move my legs and lean forward as the door at the top of the stairs opens. The overhead light goes on. Footsteps descend, and I watch Weber open a jug and water a row of buckets containing some of the largest plants on the far side of the room.

He is thinner than I remember, but then I've never seen him without a shirt. His arm and shoulder muscles are braided, muscular, his movements quick, jerky. Because it's the jutting bones of his pelvis that hold up his jeans, there's a gap between the beltless waistband and the pale flesh of his torso. Water slaps onto the cement floor, and when he tosses aside the empty jug, I flinch with every bounce of the plastic container. One by one he turns off the four long fluorescent lights.

My back and knees are stiff from sitting in the same position for so long, and all the water sounds have made me really have to pee, but Weber has other chores down here, so I press my thighs together and keep still. He approaches the wooden cupboard against the far wall, a green-painted freestanding cupboard about eight feet tall with two doors that open from the center when not held shut by a primitive tab of wood that he turns on a single screw. After some noisy rearranging of things, he pulls a duffel bag off a low shelf. Turning this way for the light, he's unzipping it, plunging his hand into the bag, shaking the cloth to make the opening gape more widely. His face jerks up suddenly, eyes alert to the stairs, as if he's heard something up there, clutching the bag protectively against his chest. Then he zips it back up and takes it with him upstairs. He turns off the basement light and closes the door.

Leaving me in the dark, afraid of him again.

My eyes are wide open, straining to see, finding only curly red scribbles of heater filaments, tiny with distance across the room. With my right hand I grip the edge of the stairway and step out from under at last. Working my shoulders to ease the stiffness, I can make out no sound but the heater's tick until a torrent of water drops through a soil pipe nearby as a toilet is flushed overhead. A few steps, guided by my outstretched hands, take me into the laundry room, where I pull down my shorts and crouch over the drain to relieve myself.

Weber can't use his car because mine is parked behind his. I've lost all sense of time, but surely by now Charlie, with Luci's voice ringing in his ears, is wondering why I'm not home yet. I don't remember turning off the neon sign when I left the studio in such a hurry. If it's on, maybe Bender will notice. Placing my right foot on the far edge of the first riser, I shift my weight carefully onto the lowest step, so it won't creak under my weight. With each step up toward the line of light under the door at the top, I pause to listen, hands touching walls for balance. I hear running water on the other side of the door, and the clatter of dishes. The phone rings a couple of rings, and footsteps come close, Weber's low voice muffled by the door. And then water runs again.

Finally there's silence. For long minutes, I consider the possibility that he's left the kitchen, and I even grip the doorknob with my right hand, but then I hear the rubbery slap of the refrigerator door going shut, and chair legs scraping on the floor, and the snap of a can's pop-top. I struggle to remember something Gus suggested the other day, that if Luci had been able to name the thing most missing from her life, she'd have had the key to gaining control of her sense of shame. What could Weber need so badly he'd kill for it? In the darkness below, the air-conditioner blower goes on with a *thunk*. In the quiet kitchen, Weber sneezes.

Like an echo, I sneeze, too.

20 ◆ THE SNEEZE BRINGS my hand to my face. I don't breathe until the basement door opens to a blinding brightness.

"What the hell."

I squint up at Weber. His narrow body looms, right hand out of sight, left hand gripping the doorframe. He's put on a faded green shirt. I see his mind working, brows drawn forward over deeply shadowed eyes. He looks past me into the darkness. Just when I think I'll faint from the suspense, there's a pounding on the back door, Weber closes the basement door on me, and I'm in the dark again.

Pushing the door ajar a couple of inches, I hear him say, "No she's not. Do you think you could move her car?" The rest is muffled.

"I'd like to see for myself." It's Charlie's voice, loud and clear. In a moment I'm up and into the room, where Weber can look from one of us to the other, my mind swimming with all Charlie has spent the evening reading: *wanting to run my hand along Russ's arm, wrist to elbow, over his shoulder to the tender spot behind his ear.* "You all right?" Charlie wants to know.

"Yes," I tell him. "Now I am."

Weber's skin reflects the green of his shirt. "You guys want to tell me what you're doing here?"

"Her car's behind yours," Charlie says. "Mine's behind hers. You're not going anyplace until we're ready."

"You were right about the marijuana, Charlie," I say quickly, watching his reaction, nodding to praise his lack of surprise. "He's got a huge crop downstairs."

Charlie's lips tighten at the corners, playing along as if he expected this. It's Weber who looks confused, turning away into the living room to check out the driveway through a side window. "We don't have to prove anything else tonight," I say to Charlie, quietly as I can. "If we report what's down there, he won't be leaving town for a while." I shove my hand into my pocket just as Weber comes back from the living room. My car key is warm against my fingers.

"Maybe you guys want in on this," he says.

"What have you got in mind?" asks Charlie.

"Hundreds of plants," I say quickly. "Grow-lights, heaters, fertilizer. I saw processed bricks, too. Quite an operation." I look at Weber. "But we're a bit put off by your poor success rate in business ventures and your lack of reliability in general, aren't we, Charlie?" Beneath the swath of a red bandanna, Weber's features are modeled by the strong ceiling light, the slope of his nose and the line of his jaw white as milk in contrast to the contours of his face. He stares at what I'm offering in my open palm. "You remember this?" I lift it toward him. "Here. Take it."

It's Sugar in the Raw. He picks up the packet, turns it over, examining his own signature in black ink, the signature I copied off the canceled check at Perkins, with the idea of turning Hansen's warning—*Don't play hero*—into a dare. Weber fingers the paper clip holding the torn edge shut. "What's this supposed to be?"

"*You* recognize it, don't you, Charlie?" Taking the small envelope back from Weber, I hand it to Charlie, whose dull stare, first at the object, then at me, makes my hand tremble. It isn't going to work. No one speaks.

Then Charlie says, "Yes. I can tell you what this is." His sly glance in Weber's direction gives me hope that Charlie read Luci's journal carefully, all the way to the end, and that every word of it is still fresh in his mind. He pauses for another long moment. "It was stuck to the flag of our mailbox." His eyes meet mine, and with a singular look that promises the spontaneity we'll need to keep on improvising like this, we're in sync, better than ever. My heart swells.

"You left it for Luci," I say to Weber, "to remind her of what you had to offer. To hint at the success you were about to make of yourself, now that she'd taught you a few things about taking chances. She should have known not to trifle with you. I think she meant more to you than just a good deal on a used car." Weber swallows, his Adam's apple struggling inside the tendons of his slender neck. "You liked her. She gave you nerve."

"I got to the mailbox first that day," says Charlie. "You didn't think I'd recognize what this was worth, or even what it *was*."

"This is making no sense to me." Weber crosses the room to lean against the counter by the sink, beside a red drainer rack full of dishes. "You're going to have to tell me what you want."

"It has your signature on it." Charlie hands the sugar back to Weber.

"Yeah, well, I don't know anything about this." He gives it one final glance before putting his hand in his pocket. With a chill, I wonder if Luci made up the whole sugar episode: *No one dreams how good a liar I am.* He rests a hand on the duffel bag next to the carton full of pots and pans on the table as he says, "My only concern right now is keeping your wife from telling anyone else what she saw downstairs."

"I'm right here, Russell. Don't talk about me like I'm not here."

"I'm not flattered," says Charlie to Weber, "that you thought I wouldn't know what was up that day. I mean, it *says* sugar, and why wouldn't you leave sugar on our fucking mailbox flag?" Charlie's gripping the back of a chair with both fists. "I knew right away that if you signed it, it must be a message. And that Luci would know what it meant."

Weber looks bored, but a rising flush reddens his neck, his ears.

"Someone offered you a deal," I say, "a chance to double your money."

"You took good care of that Peugeot of yours," says Charlie, without missing a beat. "A sharp car like that is like money in the bank, which is something you didn't have, right?"

I can guess by the falter in Weber's confidence and his quick blink to recover that we have finally struck a nerve. I stare at Charlie's profile. *Of course. Weber sold his own car.* How else could he have raised the thousands of dollars he needed to invest in a stash of methamphetamine? It figures. I step closer to Weber, so close I can smell the bitter, stale smell of cigarette smoke. "For once you had a chance to be a success, finish something you started, get into something really big. Luci's car was the sort no one would notice on the road, unless it started shimmying from bad U-joints. I guess you thought she should have warned you about that."

Weber shifts his gaze from my face to the basement door behind me. He's blinking a lot, the ridge of his nose and the bowl of his forehead shiny with sweat.

"I'm the one who discovered her body. You know that, don't you?"

He swallows.

"Did you think I lied, told them I was positive it was Peter under the car, to protect *him*?" I gesture toward Charlie.

A flicker of confusion affects Weber's eyes. "You mean you knew it wasn't Garvey?"

"I wasn't as sure as you seem to be." Leaning closer, I lower my voice. "You must have been there."

I rear back and raise my hand against the blur of Weber's arm to deflect a blow, but I've misread his sudden move to pull the red bandanna off his head to wipe his face, and my mouth opens with a gasping laugh. Stunned by the whiteness of his scalp, paler than his face, with only a drift of ash-colored stubble over the top of his head, my impulse for laughter is stopped by the way his eyes glint and his nostrils flare. In one continuous motion Weber steps to the table and lifts up a utility knife from behind the cardboard box full of pots and pans, extending the slanted blade to its full length with his thumb and twisting me around with my back against him so he can press the blade against my throat.

Charlie's hands rise slowly, as if he's under arrest, assuming a defensive stance: legs firmly apart, hands shoulder high, palms forward. Weber's fist clenches under my chin, where I feel more pressure than pain. Specks of light drift across my vision. His breathing is all I hear.

He speaks softly: "She let Garvey rack up the fucking car, when all I wanted was to take it and leave, get out of her sight. And now all I want is to get out of yours." He presses the flat of the blade against my throat. "I don't know what you guys are trying to do to me. I'm the one who really got screwed. Now, give Charlie your keys."

As carefully as I can without moving my head, I reach into my pocket while Weber instructs Charlie to get both our cars out of the driveway. "Don't attract any attention and she'll be okay. I'll be out of here, and this will be over."

With Charlie gone, my consciousness shrinks to contain only Russell Weber and me, his agitation establishing the rhythm for both our bodies, pressed together as we are, a proximity that repels me to the point of inertia. From outside I can hear the familiar roar of Charlie's van starting up, going into gear. Weber's right forearm relaxes a little, easing the pressure of the blade against my throat as I listen hard for the energetic whir of my own little car's engine.

Gently, he's backing me against the wall by the door, the tip of the sharp X-acto knife blade poking my midsection. The blue duffel hangs from his shoulder now, slung around onto his back. I raise my right hand to my throat, which stings as I touch it, and examine the single thread of blood on my fingers.

"Sorry," he says. "It's just a scratch."

"I didn't mean to laugh." I try not to glance at his shaven head.

"I don't like being laughed at."

"I see that." I remember Luci's words: *He has a degree in agronomy, he told me today—but can't get a job in his field, and I laughed— causing a fury to come over him until I calmed him down.* Weber is stretching his neck to gaze out the window of the back door, then flinches away from the glass, hitting the light switch to throw the room into darkness, turning me toward the light of the living room, managing to hold the knife against the hollow of my throat as he drives me forward with jerky steps because of the awkward embrace. The room has a couch facing the big window, a scarred coffee table, a drum set shoved against the wall to the right, an upright piano piled high with what I assume is sheet music. A single floor lamp, turned low. A scatter of folding chairs.

Parting a slit in the blinds with his fingers, he looks out, then lets the blinds snap shut. He glares at me. "The cops are out there," he says. "When were you planning to tell me that?" Suddenly his arm swings, and the gray blur of the knife flies off to the side to cause a crashing of cymbals, followed by a two-strike and rattle of snare drum. My heart is thumping wildly as the brassy sounds die on the air. Where is Charlie? He should be back by now.

Weber's face is shiny in the low light. "She knew I cared about what she did," he says, in a voice so low I'm unsure of what I'm hearing, "the weaving, and all." I wonder if he means her *last* weaving, and if Charlie left it in Luci's studio by mistake, and if Weber found it there and took it when he was in the garage that night. He's sweating profusely now, darker green staining his shirt under his arms. "Just tell me what you were doing in my basement. Tell me what that sugar business was all about. What was Charlie trying to prove?"

I take a shallow, shaky breath. "It was you I saw coming out of the house that day, the day she was killed." Now I've done it, what Hansen warned me against, tipped our hand. Oddly, declaring myself gives me courage. "Luci had told you to leave, a few days before that. Told you not to come back without the money for the car. She wouldn't even let you drive it again, until you'd paid for it. It was you I saw under the car, not Peter Garvey. We have the proof. From under the car."

Weber licks his lips.

"She didn't know what you'd stashed under there, did she?"

"When did you plan to tell me the cops are outside?"

I stare at the shut blinds. There's not a sound from out on the street. I look at Weber, at the terrible, cornered look on his face. Now he's in a trap, with a basement full of evidence and nowhere to go. So maybe if I really push him, he'll be desperate enough to break down, admit what he did to Luci. My hand goes into my pocket, and my fingers close around the canceled check for a thousand dollars, an amount that didn't register until tonight, at Perkins. A lot of money. I wonder if he still thinks it was worth facing Charlie to collect it.

Before I can think of what to say next, Weber says, "You're right. I was at the house that day. I saw your car coming around the ridge on the other side of the cornfield."

I can feel adrenaline pump into my bloodstream, feel my heart beat. A car door goes shut outside on the street. "I was standing at the front door," he says. "He told me Luci was expecting me, but when I tried to pull the door open, it was locked, and he kept me standing outside, talking through the screen."

"Who, Russell? Who are you talking about?"

"Charlie, of course. He kept me talking until I figure he saw your car up on the road, then told me to get lost, leave her alone. He must have known you'd be coming along about that time. He wanted you to see me." Weber wipes beads of sweat from his upper lip. "He couldn't have known I'd get under the car. He couldn't

have foreseen that, or that you'd say it was Pete Garvey you saw."
He pauses to get himself back under control. "It's you I can't figure."

I don't believe a word he's telling me. We stare at each other.

"Charlie knew I wanted the title to the car," Weber goes on.
"He kept me outside the door, making me think he was about to
let me in. He was fucking me over in the worst kind of way, by
making me part of it. The thing that should have tipped me off,
when he walked up to the door he was wearing paper bags over
his feet, for Chrissakes." Weber's shoulders rise up and draw together as he swallows tightly again.

Behind me I hear the back door open. Before I know it, Charlie
is standing beside me. He steps close to Weber. "The cops were
out there when I went out, and that reporter"—he glances at me,
then back at Weber—"but I told them you'd pulled a knife and
taken Linda away in a black pickup. Even gave them part of a
license number, to buy you some time. I suggest you take off while
you have the chance. There's enough stuff downstairs to put you
away for fifty years."

Weber leaves by the back door, and Charlie and I gaze at each
other silently as we hear the car start in the driveway and the slide
of gravel as Weber takes off down Railroad Street. "Why a black
pickup?" I ask.

"Seeing that knife against your throat, I had to get rid of him
in a hurry," says Charlie. "To do that, I had to get the cops to
leave." Now we have to call someone right away, so they can go
after Weber, arrest him for what he's got downstairs, but Charlie
puts his warm fingers on the sides of my face, a touch so familiar
I'm ashamed of my confusion. "Let's give him a head start," he
says.

For a moment I'm so disoriented that when I make a move to
head for the kitchen phone, I allow Charlie to hold me back. It's
as if time will wait while I try to understand what's happening. "I
can imagine what he told you," he says, "while I was outside. It's

not what you deserve to hear." His hands move up to cover my ears. "The guy's a complete loser, the kind she liked." His voice is low. "Luci," he says, "was not like you."

He puts his arms around me and holds me close, and in a flash I see her blood on the floor. The memory colors everything, and I know that the only way I can find out if there's any truth to what Weber said about Charlie is to stay this close and make him believe I'm with him no matter what happened to Luci, no matter how bad it is. Make him think it never once occurred to me my suspicions could bring me to this. "She told you, didn't she?" I say softly, as if these were words of love. "About the child she had. About Susanna."

"To protect Bill. Yes, she told me." He pulls back to study my face. "I guess you figured out Luci had a thing with him. Her diary makes that pretty clear."

"It doesn't tell the whole truth."

His lips part, waiting for me to explain.

"She told you Bill wasn't her baby's father, right? She must have said more than that."

"You don't want to know," he says, shaking his head. "You mean everything to me, you know. You're the one who gave me a chance to start over. Our stories fit like two parts of a shell around what happened, perfectly, a perfect pairing. It's still like that."

"Our stories?"

"It was Garvey under that car. He left his fingerprints on her body. Weber's not coming back. It's still the two of us, you and me."

My smile tells him *Yes, I never want that to change.* With such a smile there's a chance I can keep him close enough to tell me everything I want to know. But my gaze into his eyes is so traitorous I need to make myself grow detached in order to carry this off, this intimate interrogation. "Don't you think she really wanted to die?"

"Yes, it was a relief to her, believe me. She was in torment."

My breathing slows. "And so you—"

"Accused her of sleeping with Bill; that's how it started. She paced around the house. She cried. Finally, when she'd exhausted herself, she wanted me to believe it was *her own father* who'd gotten her pregnant, when she was eighteen."

My eyes stop blinking.

"Yes," he says. "It seems he would visit her when she was in high school, buy her expensive clothes and shoes to make up for not being around when she was little. He made up for it all right." Charlie's mouth clamps shut, and he swallows with a frown, as if his words have left a taste in his mouth. "She really found it a turn-on, telling me all the details. Who would believe such a thing?"

My mind resists. *Her own father.* But it fits, explains her terrible shame, her erotic anger. But would she find it a turn-on? Not the Luci I've come to know from her journal. *Never.* "You're the one who found it exciting," I say quietly. "The way you found it exciting to ask me if I'd been kissing John Bender. Remember how it turned you on, believing that?" I almost falter. Almost give myself away.

Charlie studies my mouth as I lick my dry lips.

"Luci wanted to stop talking about it, didn't she?" I tell him. "She told you the one thing she'd never been able to tell anyone. She had always believed saying it out loud would put an end to it. But you wanted to hear it again. The details. And then again. Until finally you might be able to believe her. Is that what you told her?" The way he's looking at me, I know that even this accusation stirs him, and he wants me to go on, say it all. "Finally she'd had enough. She couldn't say the words anymore. But you kept insisting, asking for details. You went on tormenting her. You killed her."

"Yes."

"Rosemary knew that Weber came around asking for money more than once. That's why you and she argued. It wasn't back pay he was asking for, was it?"

"No."

"It was blackmail. He was the only one who knew it was you."
I pull back from Charlie's embrace.

"He won't be bothering us anymore," he says quickly. In the
same moment car doors slam outside, and an amplified voice, metallic, emphatic, shouts unintelligible words.

It's Bender's voice I hear clearly, calling my name. Bender, who
never trusted Charlie for a moment. He's right beside me, relieved,
telling me that Weber is out in the squad car. Hansen was waiting
for him at the end of Railroad Street, after another car went chas-
ing the black pickup that turned out to be a lie. "We were never
far away, Linda, on the chance you were still in here, with *him*."

For all of that, Charlie is calm, the set of his shoulders high as
ever. He turns to me as Detective Hansen and the other officers
gather around us. "I thought you said Weber took Linda away at
knifepoint," someone says. "Be careful what you say, Linda," says
Charlie, his tone still hushed. "No one could ever love you the way
I do. Don't throw it away. Are you still with me?"

He sees my hesitation, no doubt pins his hopes on it. For the
frailest of moments I could say yes. They must all see it, how I
watch with such fascination as he curves his hands and places them
together like two halves of a shell. A perfect pairing.

"He killed her," I say, just loud enough for everyone to hear.

My sandals lie at the edge of the driveway, where I must have
stepped out of them so I could feel the wet grass on the soles of
my feet and feel anchored, I suppose, to solid ground. Two huge
oaks overreach Weber's front yard, their branches brightly under-
lit, leaves whispering as the evening air cools. Charlie is taller than
the two cops who flank him. He's looking around, but he can't find
me over here in the neighbor's yard, far enough away to be in the
dark but close enough to stare at him until finally he ducks his
head and gets into one of the cars.

Even now, knowing what he has done, I haven't stopped loving him, or I wouldn't feel so utterly forsaken as the car leaves, the first of three police cars parked along the street, and he's gone. I'm going to miss him. The very idea folds me up a little.

Ken Hansen sees me shudder as he crosses the driveway and stops to stand six feet off to my left. Weber's duffel bag, containing three fat rolls of bills and the tapestry he stole that night in the garage, is slung over the detective's shoulder. With concern, Hansen glances at John Bender, who is standing off to my right, close enough for me to talk to, if I ever decide to speak again. My last words to him were that Charlie trusted me after all, enough to tell me everything. And that I *used* his love for me, to disarm him.

Overhead a small plane passes—unseen, but I can hear its engine throb. "I had a friend who wanted me to learn skydiving," I say, tilting my face upward, smelling the air. "I was going to jump, but he put his hands on my shoulders, and it felt like a push. So I refused, and I ended up here. A single moment can change a person's whole life."

Bender has heard this story before, a story that used to be about a test I once failed. "I'm just going to stand here," he says to me now. He actually shows me the palms of both hands and takes a step back, away from the look I give him.

"Well, maybe 'push' is too strong a word," I admit. "He tried to *urge* me, a little too enthusiastically." I manage an unconvincing laugh.

"Friends do that sometimes," Bender says. "An open airplane's probably not the best place to do it."

I wonder if later we'll talk about how he and I solved a difficult puzzle without either of us ever seeing all the pieces until they were all in place. At this moment I can't think that clearly. Right now it's enough that he's willing to listen to me speculate about turning points when I've just learned that my husband has killed someone. While Bender stands his ground, I begin to realize how fortunate I am that he and Hansen got here in time. It's sinking in, what Bender said a few moments ago: "Charlie wouldn't have told you anything if he'd expected you to survive."

The two men move toward each other, a little closer to me. I wonder if they see how they're closing ranks between me and the stage of activity where Weber is being escorted to the second car. The way we've been talking, Hansen probably thinks John and I are friends.

"You ready?" someone shouts. A car starts.

"We're in no hurry now," Hansen says, to no one in particular. He exchanges another look with Bender, one that I recognize as proprietary and protective, and which I see in this moment as the most desirable thing in the world.